"*Nathan Parks is at it again with another intriguing tale from the world of the Nephelium. Parks takes you even further into the world of Angels and Demons in a light that you probably never thought to see them in before . . . a fantastic read to continue an amazing story.*"

— Joshua Dietrich

The Eternals

Book Two:

The Vapor

by Nathan Parks

Dedicated to

Stubby

You showed strength until the end, fought your demons,

forgave when forgiveness was needed,

and remained loyal to family and your brotherhood.

Table of Contents

Prologue

"Will you leave?"

"You don't deserve me! We are more than you can control."

"Then you control me--ALL of you--control me?"

"You are weak! We are strong, and we don't have time to waste on weak human flesh."

A figure scratched at the dirt that surrounded him and made up the walls of the small cave in which he found himself. He hissed and howled like an angry cat. His body was hunched in a "c" shape with his extremities gnarled and covered in open sores and gashes. What hair he did have covered his head in patches, and his eyes were clouded.

"You don't have time to waste! YOU!" He howled and hissed and bit at himself. "You made me this way!"

"No," a voice stated, oozing in sarcasm, "we did not. Your creator gave you a weak body; I just attempted to use it."

The man began to thrash wildly around, slamming his body against jagged stones that jutted out of the wall and, using human bone fragments on which he had gnawed before, stabbing at his legs and arms. "Get out!"

Laughter! It drowned everything out.

He ran himself hard into a rock formation. He was hoping to beat the voice out—rather, the *voices* out.

"I was a well-respected citizen!"

"I respect you! WE respect you." More laughter!

"LEAVE ME!"

He ran from the entrance of the tomb, scattering bones and holding his arms up in front of him to block the sun from burning his eyes. Its heat upon his naked skin was almost too much to bear.

"Kill yourself; then you won't have to deal with me. Go to the tomb of the warrior and impale your ragged, wretched body upon the spears there. We will help you."

"LEAVE ME!" His mouth opened, and bile and saliva spewed out, leaving a trail in the dirt and grime upon his face and down his chest.

"I am the Destroyer, and you are my pet. *Nomen mihi Legio est, quia multi sumus!* (Translation; My name is Legion, for we are many!)"

The voices taunted him from all directions. He swung wildly, his wrist shattering against a rock as there was nothing else to hit. Pain cleared his mind for a moment; he fell to his knees, grasping at his broken and limp appendage. He lay down in the dirt and cried like an infant.

At one time the creature was headed up the ladder of power and strength within his city; but now . . . now, no one even knew his name. His family had been stoned due to beliefs and rumors that they all had dealt in the worship of the Darkness. His little daughter, Jarasha, had knelt with tears streaming down her face as they prepared to kill her. She never hated him. She looked at him and whispered, "Daddy, I love you."

She had said something else; but the voices in his head began to torment him at that moment, and the supernatural strength had sent his body into convulsions. Breaking free that day, he had run down into the "Valley of the Dead," the tombs outside the city. He had run, leaving her there. He heard a scream that had stopped him in his tracks . . . and that was it.

Why? For what? A soothsayer had promised him a seat of power if only he would give his body over to a god, a being that needed a haven in which to hide. It would cost him nothing; that was what he had been told.

He cried. These moments of sanity now were brief. He didn't know if they were worth the pain of the memories that came with them, but at least he knew they were real. It was hard to distinguish reality from madness.

His tormentor was back. His body flung madly into convulsions, but this time there was something different: was that fear he heard?

"Get back! Now! I demand you to get back!"

"Get back where?" he screamed. "Back to the tomb?"

"Not you, Idiot!" There were thousands of screams blasting the walls of his brain and wrapping around the fibers of his thoughts.

"Get back! We have nothing against you! Leave us! How did you find me?"

The man was confused. "You have been here! You found *me*. I don't want you any . . ."

He watched his limp and shattered wrist be pulled back and then twisted in an inhuman position. His sentence was cut short with his screaming from the pain.

"You will be quiet, Fool."

He didn't understand it at first. What was this creature inside of him talking about? Had the madness within the madman gone insane? That would be irony. Would that equal it all out?

All stood still. It was a voice—a voice that brought everything to a quiet standstill. It was a voice that made every sinew in this man's body tighten in strength—tighten such as when a worn warrior hears the confidence of his commander saying that everything will be alright.

The sun continued to beat down hot upon his naked form. The pain from his shattered body was almost more than he could bear, but that voice created an atmosphere that made it seem that none of that mattered.

"Who are you?" the voice stated.

The heap of a man pulled his head up from the dirt as he looked up. There was a man—or more like a soldier without armor—standing near him. He had a small entourage of more men standing at different intervals around him. He had thick, black, wavy hair that provided a great accent to his strong facial structure. His eyes seemed to be emblazoned with the strength of a seasoned veteran, yet still had a shine to them as if to say, "I have seen death, but does anyone know a great joke?"

Even though he seemed to have the strong build of a warrior, he was dressed as a wanderer, his muscular frame draped in light and loose-fitting cloth.

"Who are you?"

"My name is . . ."

The man on the ground could not speak, the control of his muscles stripped from him. As his consciousness was being driven inward, the ripping of leathery membranes rushed forward, and the creature was manifested.

"You know who I am, Grigori. Leave me! Our Clan owns this man."

The wanderer allowed a smile to break across his well-defined face. "By what rights? I don't see Adramelech's insignia upon him or your mother's insignia."

"What do you want from me?" Legion spat. "I am not doing any harm to you or any of your puppets," he continued, motioning to the other men. "This man is mine. He chose to accept me."

One of the other men, a shorter individual, pulled a dagger from his side. "Let me have him. I'll show him who the puppet is."

The wanderer crossed his arms and just shook his head. They all had seen Possessors take over the body of a mortal before, and seeing the manifestation distorting this man's body was nothing new.

"No, Simon, I think this 'Mighty Warrior' knows that this isn't really going in his favor right now," the wanderer stated sarcastically. "Am I right, Legion?"

Legion was in full reaction mode. He wasn't just any Clan's member! He was the Hero of the House of Adramelech, the son of Hecate, the one personally being mentored to inherit the throne of the Morning Star, the ultimate seat of power within the Families!

He also knew that he was in one of his most weakened states. He had been sent here to hide until called up again by the Leaders of the Clans. He had grown somewhat lazy. There was not enough strength.

"Let me be, and you will have my promise, Eternal One, to not interfere within this province."

This drew not just a grin but a laugh. "A promise? A promise from the very protégé of the Liar of all Liars? Your master has taught you well, Legion."

The body of the man he inhabited began to tremble as Legion prepared for a battle that he knew he would not win, but at least it would not be said that the Hero of the Fallen just surrendered.

With as much strength as he could muster, Legion shredded the insides of the mortal. He pulled in anything that he could use as energy and drained the soul—or what was left of one—from him. He broke into the light with inch-long fangs bared and two curved swords wielding back and forth. The mortal's body lay trashed and lifeless, and standing beside it stood a man or a creature or even an evil metamorphosis of the two.

The group of men all stepped back, except for the wanderer. He stood unfazed by the antics of this being. He felt a surge of strength and power begin deep within His core as his arms went down to his side, and his hands began to curl as if holding invisible objects. The wanderer's head was slightly bowed yet tilted enough to detect any movement from his "would be" assailant.

The rush of energy and power began to travel up the paths of his body, and his muscles pumped with adrenaline. He looked up with not just a grin but also with flashes of what looked like fire in his eyes.

"You dare stand against me, Legion? The Grigori and Watchers are strong, and yet you will stand against me?"
Legion began to shudder as the inner workings of the creature which he really was fought to stay together. He was Legion; they were Legion, the only Fallen that was able to divide himself into multitudes of entities but all doing the will of the collective.

"You are the one who will not let me go. So, you are the one defying the prophecies that are yet to be written in mortal tongue, Grigori!"

Silver balls of energy crackled within the hands of the wanderer, energy unseen by the group of mortals that stood behind the wanderer. He was the last of the Grigori and the founder of the new Brotherhood, the Brotherhood of Watchers.

"Then be gone. You are to leave this province and territory."

Legion kept lunging forward, keeping his eyes upon the wanderer's hands, trying to get him to attack first. His mouth was watering for a fight; his fangs were longing to drink the blood that would truly give him power beyond anything within the realms.

"Where do you suppose me to go?"

"To Malebolge I bind you now!"

Legion swore. He knew he had no choice right now but to stand down. His time would come—prophecy stated it would. At least he was going home to Malebolge, the inner circle of the Abyss.

"I will go now, but our time will come, Eternal, and do not think that battle will be won with mere parlor tricks of water into spirits, food multiplying, or energy from the hands . . . many will suffer greatly! The blood of mortals will be mine, and I will be stronger than any who have come before either of us!"

The group of men gritted their teeth in pain as a thousand screams blew through them. If one could imagine the sorrow and pain of the dying on a battlefield all wrapped together in one soul: that did not come close. They collapsed! Legion shattered himself into a dark mist and swept over the men.

Not too far away, a young boy sat with his herd of pigs, unaware. The pigs screamed as if at the slaughterhouse and ran madly into a nearby pond. Legion would return.

"They had human faces; their hair was long . . .
and teeth were like lion teeth . . .
then there was war.
A shadow will be released . . .
some will call him Apollyon, or Legion."

~From the Revelations of a Watcher

Correspondence of the Watcher Brotherhood

A letter from Josephus, a Watcher, to John during John's exile on the island of Patmos. This letter was a response to John's earlier letter and was discovered in a broken jar in unearthed catacombs in the ruins of ancient Rome. It is not certain if there were any more letters after this one, but this letter clearly revealed that the Watchers were still in possession of the vial of blood.

Greetings in the Faith, Brotherhood,

I believe that I have discovered something that time has thought lost! I believe that humanity's arrogance of devising what they thought to be a "true collection" of writings and expelling that which they did not understand or feared has left us vulnerable to the coming darkness.

I fear that my research is revealing that we have had only part of the picture; and because of that, we have chosen a path that has led us only closer to our own prideful destruction.

The rise of the Dracon has been our focus, and yet when combined with historical documents that once may have been considered authoritative, the picture changes. I believe that the time of darkness is here. The gods of the shadows are at odds, but they will be united by the one. Do not be so naive to believe that we will be able to hold this back. I fear there is no overcoming our fatal mistakes and arrogance.

My notes are not fully compiled yet. I will notify you upon their completion or if I discover a way that we may be able to reconcile this before all is lost.

There is one key that seems to come through all of this: the vial . . . but I do not understand its meaning in this . . .

Only a fragment of the letter was found. It was removed from the site and stored with artifacts from the archeology site by the Watcher and Gatekeeper of the church in Heiligenblut.

Eve's Journal

I hate the saying that time heals all wounds. Those who say that have no idea what real wounds are. They are the papercuts within the gore of a Viking mauling; you may not feel them all the time; nonetheless, they are still with you.

I have no idea what heals wounds, but I know that I wrap mine in the dressings of revenge. Yes, it may not heal, but it sure brings on a nice, thick scab.

Why not time? Well, it has been five years since I discovered who I am—what I am—and watched as my mentor was brutally killed. Do you think that time has healed any of that? How about the vile abuse I endured at the hands of moral degenerates at a young age? Nope . . . it is all still there.

I am not sure where the last five years have gone. I have not had much contact with Leah or the Alliance. I have had some run-ins with them here and there; but for the most part, we stay out of each other's way. I am aware that much has taken place in the realm of the Alliance and the Fallen.

From what I understand the Arch Council did not appreciate it or take lightly that Leah did not do what they had hoped for her to do; and that was to ensure that I, the last of the Jerusalem Breed, stayed true to their militant spiritual rhetoric.

To be fair, it wasn't her fault. I mean who are they? They preach about free choice; but then when I fade away into the shadows and choose my own path, they crucify their own?

I am the least of Leah's fans, but truly it was not her fault or choice that I have taken this path on which I travel. If a choice is truly based upon free will, as the Arch Council likes to insinuate, then let it all be! Go seek after your next spiritual lackey and warrior.

Well, anyway, from what I gather, the Arch Council has chosen to place Leah's team on a probationary period; but according to some sources, this has turned into a permanent "back shelf" position. Her team has been unable to accomplish anything. For me, I don't much care, because it has left me with more scum to deal with; and for me, it is the nectar of the gods.

As for the Clans, the Fallen, they have become a disbanded dishevelment of inept gangs of power-hungry buffoons. (You know, I have never used the word "buffoon" before, but I do like it!) They have fallen apart as a whole but have become stronger within each house that is represented. It really doesn't affect what I do at all; but you know, it is where things are.

The House of Hecate has outgrown the Adramelech Clan, mostly due to Arioch's breaking away on his own.

My so-called kindred, the Nephelium, are out and about. They still are the assassins for hire that they always have been but with just a bit more power with Kadar at the helm.

Kadar—ha!—now this buffoon (you see how I did that) is a prick—just saying. He hides within the shadows and is always on the outskirts of what I am doing. I am not sure if he thinks I cannot detect that he is there, but he is like that annoying *mosquito that keeps buzzing just out of the ring of light: you can hear it but can't get close enough to swat it.*

Now, I guess that leaves me . . . what do I say about me? How have these five years touched me? I'm not really sure. I know that I cannot change that I am Nephelium, and I can't change the past; but I sure can do everything in my power to ensure the past is not repeated in the future by seeking revenge in the present. That is them; this is me; and this is the here and now. Revenge is sweet, forgiveness futile.

Chapter One

It was that moment between night and day when the temperature drops just a little bit, but enough, that if the morning is already a little chilly, then the coolness touches one's skin with what she called the cold kiss of death. She stepped off the pavement and onto the well-manicured lawn. The black boots she wore had been well broken in, and they moved with her feet like a second skin. Each step she took barely made a noise. She was dressed in black jeans and a deep red, form-fitting, long-sleeve t-shirt. It was topped off with a black zip-up hoodie.

Of course, her surroundings did nothing to bring warmth to her, either. Her eyes scanned the multiple monuments and stones that dotted around her, all just chiseled reminders that for some, mortality was the same as the moment between night and day: brief . . . and then gone. You could fight it; but in the end, it would win.

She closed her eyes for a moment and drew in a deep breath; at least the air seemed to have a tint of freshness about it. Strange that a cemetery would smell fresh—but hey, mortality was strange.

Once again, with her eyes open, she resumed her memorized trek, bypassing ornately carved headstones that meant something to someone . . . but to her, nothing. Her senses knew where she was headed; it was a place to which she came often.

She soon reached her destination: the backside of a medium-sized, rectangular stone. It was not ornate or lush; but instead, simple and, as some would say, plain. That was alright.

"Just the way you would have wanted," she said as she stepped around to the front so that she could read the inscription. She knelt and traced the words with her fingers: "A simple man who left the world a richer place."

Cry? No, tears were long gone. Tears had been replaced over the last five years by revenge, anger, and a strength that made the guilty quiver in fear and shame. No one would suggest that tears would flow down her cheeks anymore. No, this Nephelium wouldn't cry. To cry would allow the pain to drain from her eyes. No, she needed that pain to pulse through her veins, and it had served her well.

"Alfonso, there is still much to do. I know that this war that rages on would have torn you and me apart. There is no way that I can be a part of any side. That is their battle; I have my own. I do wish you were here, though. There are still so many questions that I cannot answer. There are still nightmares that flash through my mind as a searing arrow—here and then gone—but the feelings never leave."

A black hood covered her hair, which fell down around her face. Her eyes were set and strong. The Nephelium within her had risen to the surface of her mortality and caused an enticing edge about her that she had not had before . . . or maybe that, too, was just the revenge that now seeped through her veins.

She knew that there were several of the Alliance members who visited Alfonso's' grave on the anniversary of his death, but she was a regular. It kept that night fresh in her mind. It allowed her to remember why she had chosen the path she chose. When she stepped out of the shadows, she stepped back into the lives of those who had caused her so much pain. In order to return that pain, she had to remember why she was doing this.

She pulled out a deep red rose and laid it at the base of the stone. She stood up and stepped back. She looked up and out at all the stones and monuments again. There was one more stop that she had to make before she left, and then . . . well, then there was work to do.

She moved quicker now through the cemetery. She needed to get through here and get back to her place to rest before her work for the evening began. She smiled. Yes, the nights were lonely, but they were hers.

Over the last five years, Eve had distanced herself from her Clan, the Alliance, and the Clan Wars. She didn't want anything to do with it. She and Leah had come to a standoff; and at that point, Eve became a shadow to them all. If they really wanted to find her, they probably could. She still had a lot to learn about being a Nephelium. She stayed out of their way, and they stayed out of hers.   True, there was loneliness, but she just added that to her arsenal of reasons to keep doing what she was doing.

What was she doing? She had begun strategically to take out those who had hurt her, stolen her innocence, and brutally used her for their own selfishness and return the pain and emptiness they had given to her.

Alfonso would not have been pleased, but he was no longer here; so, there was no reason to hold back. Did it resolve anything? It really hadn't, yet: the hollowness within her seemed to grow, but she couldn't stop. Maybe once it was all done, she would feel that satisfaction.

She came to her second stop within the field of mortality's trophies. This stone was simplistic, bearing only a name. There was no inscription, just a name: Megan.

She didn't stop with the air of solitude that she had with her mentor, but she did kneel and place her hand upon the top of the stone.

"Girl, I wish you would have listened. I could really use a cup of coffee with you at the café. Wouldn't it have been great if we had truly been sisters? Wow, two female Nephelium waging war on those who destroy innocence!"

The stone indicated that she had passed the same day as Alfonso. That night had burned itself inside the psyche of Eve. She could smell everything, hear everything, feel everything as if it was now. She had gone into The Vortex that night hoping to find both Megan and Alfonso.

She never did see Megan that night as the events of Alfonso's death had wiped all else from her thought. She had forgotten all about Megan after witnessing the death of Alfonso by the hands of Denora. She had only remembered revenge that night when the Nephelium side of her took over and broke forth. She had forgotten there was one other who had needed her help.

She had been told later that Megan's body had been found within the ruins of The Vortex. Eve was told that no one knew if she had been a victim of Arioch or a casualty of the eruption between the Clans. Eve had chosen not to attend the funeral.

She placed a rose at the base of Megan's grave, kissed her hand, and retouched the top. Time to get home. The evening would come soon enough. She smiled. "Death becomes the dance partner within the night's masquerade."

*****

There is nothing else that smells anything like the sweat, oils, and secretions of the human body. It permeates everything with which it comes into contact; it lingers and then becomes a collaboration of toxic smells when there is an attempt to mask it with cheap cologne or body spray.

"Hey, Shitbag," the owner of the horrific stench, as well as a connoisseur of horrific Hollywood biker clothing, spewed. "You are sitting at our table."

The man and object of his focus sat at the untreated wooden table without looking up or turning to acknowledge the conversation or the body odor. He sat with his right side facing the ogre of a man, and his left was up against the smoke- and dirt-stained wall. His eyes were fixed upon the dark stout that so beautifully and magically sat within the beer mug in front of him. It was his third . . . or maybe tenth . . . he couldn't remember; nonetheless, he was sure it was just as stimulating as the first . . . well, if he could remember the first.

"I don't think he heard ya, Derick," the cheap, last decade's halter top-wearing, clown-faced female companion of the wannabe biker stated as she curled up closer to the warthog's back.

She was sneering from behind this annoyance that she called "Derick." He couldn't see the sneer; he just knew: he could feel it. He hated clowns . . . especially over-caked, horror show females like her. He hated body odor more, though.

"I would suggest you open your ears and move," Derick stated as he leaned on the table and picked up the beer that was just asking to be downed and yet savored all at once. With one, not-so-elegant motion, Derick did the former and downed the whole mug and slammed it back on the table.

The figure sitting there still did not move. He just sat there, looking at the now empty mug. There was a moment of silence that began to grow thick, and then he spoke. "Derick, Derick, Derick. Now you see, I had my doubts that you were even half the man you think you are, and I honestly thought for a moment I would let you just continue thinking that you were all the pinnacle of manhood you think you are . . . that was for a moment, though."

The figure looked up at Derick, who was inches away from him and still leaning on the table and breathing like an angry puffer fish in the middle of the desert. "You know what changed my mind?"

"I really don't care," Derick sneered, "All I know . . ."

The figure put up a finger to Derick's lips. "Shhh. You are going to want to pay really close attention."

Derick glared at him in disbelief and anger, but the stranger was holding his own. His eyes appeared to be almost electric blue and appeared to crackle with the same energy. "No real man would have EVER just downed that amazing and sinful beer."

The stranger laughed at the last part of the statement.

"Sinful," the figure chuckled again and for a moment appeared to lose himself in the statement. "Sinful is such a delightful word—and yet so antagonistic." He brought his attention right back to Derick as he reached into the pocket of his torn jeans that he wore, accented by a gray t-shirt with an ace of spade card on it.

Derick wanted to rip this man's head off. He wanted to urinate down his shredded throat and leave him to die, but he found himself unable to move. It was as if the whole world had him glued to the table. His female companion was nervous and stepped back a few steps as she realized that her man was "stuck" to the table.

"Derick, let's play a game." The figure smiled a devilish smile as he placed two chrome dice upon the table. "You see, right now you can't move. You can't even hardly breathe. You feel crushed; and I would imagine you are screaming deep inside, but nothing will find its way to the cavity-infested orifice you call a mouth. Now, being that you have been rude not only to me but also to my beer and my intelligence, I feel I should walk out and let you stay this way. Sadly, I still have enough good inside of me that would not allow me to do this; and besides, it would draw way too much attention to me."

He looked around to ensure that attention had not started already being turned to his direction. The desert dive bar in which he was sitting didn't have too many individuals in it, but those that were there had not caught on that anything out of the ordinary was taking place in the back corner. The old-time country music, mixed with some rock, was still playing on the half-broken jukebox, and beer was still being enjoyed—of course, not with the respect with which it should be, but some people are simply just not intelligent enough.

His attention came back to Derick, who now had more beads of sweat dripping down his forehead. "So, we are going to play a game." He picked up the chrome dice. He felt the cold metal as it touched his fingertips. It was a stark contrast to the heat within the bar. He was a simplistic individual, and yet one of contradiction; so, the balance of hot and cold teased at his senses. He loved it! He felt alive; of course, that, in itself, was yet another contradiction within his existence.

"So, here is how the game is played—very simple, actually. You pick a number 2 through 12, and then I roll the dice. If I roll your number, then I win. If I miss your number, then you win. It really is simple and set to be more in your favor. Understand?"

Derick was able to nod his head and gulp a "Yes."

The stranger grinned from ear to ear. "Awesome! I love this game! So, now pick a number!" He wiggled in his chair like a child who could not sit still in math class. "This is going to be fun."

"Nine," Derrick squeaked out.

It was like slow motion as his hands closed around the dice, and he began to shake them. The man's female companion seemed to hold her breath as he let them go to hit the table. She swore that the music and everything within the bar became silent. The metal dice hit the table top and bounced around, settled down, and then came to rest. He lifted his hand up to where only he could see the dice. "Well, it appears that chance is not on my side tonight. I rolled a ten."

As he spoke the words, he slipped the dice back into his pocket and stood up. He threw a few dollars onto the table and looked over at Derick's female companion. "This is where I would say that you could do better and that you don't deserve someone like him, . . ." pausing as he looked her up and down. "I would . . . but, then again, I am not into lying."

He walked past her as she backed away even further from him as if she had seen a ghost. "What are you . . . the devil?"

"No, Ma'am. Simply a vapor in the breeze. Good day."

As he walked toward the door, he could hear Derick start moving again; and even though there were several explicatives coming from his re-found voice, they were tainted with fear and apprehension.

*****

Michael squinted as the bright sunlight hit his eyes. It took a minute for his eyes to adjust. Anyone who was close enough to see into his eyes would have found themselves puzzled and dumbfounded. His eyes appeared to darken as if he had built-in sunglasses. He walked over to an old, black road bike and straddled it. His body tensed, not in anticipation of the revving of the engine but in apprehension.

"You understand I can smell the scent of home just as much as I can smell the degenerates within that bar." It was a statement more than a question. He didn't even look up. He sat with both hands upon the handlebars of the motorcycle.

"You wouldn't be drinking and driving now, would you, Brother? I hear it is illegal."

He looked up at the silhouette that was framed in the noon sun. "And do you even know how amazing a great beer even tastes?" He sat upon the bike with an air of frustration mixed with disdain. "Why are you here, Michael?"

"Maybe I just wanted to see my brother."

"Oh shut up! You and I know good and well that we have nothing to say to each other!"

"Still bitter, I see, Zarius."

"Really?" He stood up and dismounted the motorcycle. "I should have finished you when . . ."

"When what? You know good and well that you chose to be here!" Michael motioned with sweeping grandeur around him.

Zarius didn't even hesitate; he knew his brother was probably expecting it. However, he also knew that the air on earth was heavier than on Scintillantes; and until an Angel adjusted, it weighed him down. Zarius was pretty sure his brother had not been here long enough to yet adjust. His assumption was correct.

His fist contacted square upon the jaw of the Arch Council member, sending him flying backward about 15 feet.

Michael was able to catch himself and didn't actually hit the ground. He stood back, rubbing his jaw and smirking.

Zarius was seething. "What do you want, Michael? Either lay it out now or go back to your seat on the Council . . . or have they discovered the truth?"

"Truth? You see, Zarius, that is a funny word, isn't it? Isn't the truth what we set into motion as being the truth?" Michael walked toward him with the air of self-confidence that his brother wouldn't have the chance to swing again. "Brother, like we both know, you wanted to be down here among these narcissistic, rat-like beings. You! I didn't force you to make the choices you did."

"You're right, Michael, but I also believed in you—something that I now see was misguided, then again, I guess it goes back to your version of the truth. Oh, if I could get back to the Council!"

Michael walked up and leaned on Zarius' bike. "And what would you do? Nothing, because you know that this runs deeper than just you and me. This goes beyond the ages of this planet and will continue forward even once you and this planet are gone. So, what? Do you think that even if given the chance what you have to say would be considered?"

He walked within inches of his brother. "Do you not think that the real and factual truth wouldn't come out?"

"Oh, and what would that be, Michael?"

"That you fell for her beauty just as I did. YOU were deceived and enticed! YOU chose to make the choice you did because you BELIEVED her; and in the end, she chose *me!*"

"Our story has not fully been written, Brother!" Zarius shoved passed Michael and once again straddled his bike. "Why are you here, anyway? I'm pretty sure it wasn't for a family reunion."

"Well, at least you still have some smarts in that being of yours," Michael said with sarcasm. "I also don't think you have to really ask why I am here. You knew that I would come one day."

Zarius felt his strength drain from him as he started the bike. The bike revved, and he looked straight into his sibling's eyes. "It was lost centuries ago. I don't know where it is."

"Lying, no matter if you are fully not an Eternal anymore, can still set you over into the world of the Clans, Brother."

"Well, I guess you would know more than I, wouldn't you?" With that, Zarius kicked gravel into the air and didn't look back as he roared away.

He knew that Michael didn't believe him . . . well, fully. He also knew that if Michael wanted to, he could have stopped him, but he didn't. This meant that he was testing the waters. He had to figure out why. Why now? What would make his brother take the chance to come out of Scintillantes and come to see him? Well, except for . . . even if he did come for it, then that meant something was in the works.

Michael watched his brother vanish down the road and then walked around the back of the bar and disappeared. There was still time.

Chapter Two

Zarius roared up next to an old sheet-metal building and kicked the kickstand down on his bike. His anger was seething inside. The memories never left him, but to have them shoved in his face was a whole different thing.

The desert heat was not as scorching today as it would be if it was summer, but he still allowed it to dance upon his skin. He soaked it in and just sat on his bike, attempting to collect his emotions. He couldn't walk in with this much emotion.

He wouldn't have to: a voice from the door to his right caught him off guard, and he closed his eyes, not wishing to have to explain anything but knowing he would have no other choice.

"Kicking up a dust cloud that can be seen for miles, revving up your motor at top speeds, and now sitting there with your body more tense than a parachute harness on an overweight skydiver . . . hmm . . . either the bar was out of beer or something else obviously has you angry." The female's voice was strong and clearly had the tone and focus filled with wisdom from the ages.

He dismounted and brushed off the dust from his clothes; it was more of a stalling motion. He had no desire to look up at the weathered, but beautiful, female figure standing in the doorway. "Yeah, you know how I get when they run out of my favorite alcohol."

"True, and I keep telling you that it will be the death of you yet." She held up her hand as he opened his mouth to respond. "Yes, the death of you, because you know good and well that even though you may live longer than any of us mortals, you aren't fully immortal anymore."

He looked into her eyes, and with one look the rush of anger and raw emotion was replaced with an overwhelming desire to grab her and lift her up. He wanted to swing her around and kiss her long and hard. Memories of when that was common brought a smile across his face. "Dang, you are still as beautiful as the first time I met you."

"And you, Zee, are as smooth, charming, and not-to-be-trusted as the first time I met *you!*"

Tanisha was still breathtaking to him. True, living in the desert heat and wind had weathered her skin, and her once long, jet-black hair was streaked with gray; but he didn't care. She stood there in a loose, white cotton, button-up blouse and brown jeans, and he wanted to whisk her away to a fountain of youth.

They had met almost 30 years ago when she was just 25. He had attempted to avoid falling for her, but she had made it impossible. When the time came for him to reveal to her the truth about who he was and what a future looked like for them, she never batted an eye.

"No matter if I have tomorrow or a century of tomorrows, Zarius, I don't want to spend a single one of them without you," she had said to him. And they had never spent a day apart since.

It took over a decade for the difference to begin to show; but even though he appeared ageless to this day, in his eyes she was still the young and energetic 25-year-old. He loved her more today than he did then. Yes, there was a pain that sat deep inside his being knowing that the sands of the ages would blow through and take her away one day, but it also meant that they treasured each moment more than the last.

He walked up to her and wrapped his arms around her waist. Her body was still petite but strong. Strength, both mentally and physically, was required to live out here. He pulled her close and could see a smile break across her lips, but her eyes clearly were stating to him, "You aren't going to get out of telling me what is going on."

He looked at her for a moment, and his lips touched hers. He drank in her kiss and let the world stop. This was home. This was his heaven.

"It seems that what I have always feared would eventually arrive at our doorstep has finally shown up."

She leaned back and looked at him with a look of concern and fierceness. "Your past?"

He nodded, "Yes."

She placed her right hand on his chest and felt each breath he took. "We both knew it would come one day, Sweetheart. You never kept your past—or what it could mean— from me. I chose this path with you with a full understanding of what it could mean. It could have been a month after we met or today. We both knew this moment would come."

"I am not ready."

"Ready? You have been ready since the first time I saw you on the archeologist dig. That was why you were there, wasn't it?"

"I don't mean that. I mean that I am not ready to lose you."

She turned and slipped out of his arms and walked into the building. It was deceiving from the outside. To those who didn't know better, they would think it was an abandoned building made of scrap metal, but inside there were two levels. Below ground was a humble dwelling place that was made up of a bedroom, living room, kitchen, and a few other smaller rooms. The ground floor consisted of a garage with auto parts lying around. Inharmoniously, one corner was dedicated to research of historical artifacts and the study of archeology.

Tanisha may not be working in the field as she once did, but she was still consumed by a passion for ancient civilizations and history. She and Zarius had met on a site in the Middle East. She felt drawn to him immediately. He was a rebel then and still was. She would admit she originally was drawn by lust—lust for his big eyes, thick hair, and the muscular body that filled out his frame. As she began to learn more about him, she discovered a heart of strength, loyalty, and tenderness all wrapped up into an amazing package of a man.

The couple walked in, and Tanisha moved toward her work corner. She started tracing her fingers along the spines of several books that were located on a shelf. She found the one for which she was looking and pulled it out. It was a well-worn journal, dog-eared and stained. She brushed her hand across the front of the cover as she smiled. She then looked up at Zarius and handed to it to him.

"Do you remember this?"

He took it from her. He didn't have to look down at it. He knew what it was. "Of course. You know that I do."

"It is the site journal I was keeping when we met. Little did I know that the notes that I was taking in it would be a roadmap to a life that can only be lived through the imaginations of fantasy writers." He raised his eyes to meet hers as she continued, "You are who you are. You must do what you need to do."

He began to flip through the pages. Words were penned in her beautiful script handwriting, and images that she had drawn in pencil jumped out at him. He could smell the ancient artifacts. He could hear the sound of tools scraping away the coverings placed by time and space.

"Zarius, you will never lose me . . . *never!* Do you hear me? I will always be with you: your memories—our memories!"
A tear began to fall silently down the warrior's cheek. "I am not ready to hold you only in memories."

"Yes, but we both know that if you do not fulfill your duties, there are more lives at stake here than just you and me. Humanity is at stake, and yes, even though you may not be a part of humanity, I am."

"I know."

"What happened? Who was it?" she asked, referring back to what had taken place before he had returned home.

"It was my brother."

"Michael?"

"Yeah, the only brother I have," he scoffed . . . not at her but at the thought of it.

"What if you share what you know with those who need to know?"

He set the book down on her desk and leaned up against it. He stared off into nothingness and didn't speak for a moment. He just thought. Her questions seemed so simple, but the complexity was beyond anything even he could understand. Michael had a point. There would be no way to prove what he knew; and without proof, he was bringing a story that would be impossible for anyone to believe, let alone the Arch Council.

"I can't. There is no way they would believe me. He has them all wrapped around his finger. They have existed with him for longer than any mortal could even understand. He is not only a trusted member of the Council but, I dare say, the *most* trusted member of the Council."

Tanisha crossed her arms and began to pace around. Her humanity may not allow her to fully understand the eternal realm, but her time upon this earth had brought her a lot of wisdom and discernment. "What if you find someone who *will* believe you?"

He looked up with a puzzled expression. "Like who? Dear, you know that most think I am vanquished, and most who know that I am not are those who want nothing more than to make it the actual truth. I have done my best to make sure that no one knows that I exist anymore; and if they do, then they have no idea what I possess!"

"Maybe it is time to come out of the shadows."

"I can't. My role in the War of the Serpents is well-known . . . well, I should say at least the part that my brother has established as truth is well-known."

She walked up to him and grabbed his arms. "That is what I am saying. Maybe it is time to let the truth come out! You know the truth. You know what the leaders of the . . . what do you call them?"

"Well, they were the rebellion, but here on earth they are the Clan Leaders."

"Zee, you know what the leaders of the Clans are hoping to do! You know that they can do it if they are able to get their hands on what you possess! To me, it seems smart to ensure that someone else knows, also! God forbid if they can take you out and no one else has a clue of what is taking place!"

He stepped away from her and walked out into the garage area. "They have known all along what they were doing, Tanisha! The Clans are not for certain I still have it. I know this, because if Michael knew for sure, he would not have stopped at just a conversation today! He would have forced me to give it to him! They also know that if they can keep others from knowing I am alive, keep me afraid of coming out of the shadows, keep others believing their lies, or any version of any of that . . . then, I am hopeless!"

Her eyes flared. "Ok, you can stop right there! I have never known you to be scared or afraid of anything, and the last thing my husband is is hopeless! So, you can stop now! You are Zarius! It is time that you stood up, came out of the shadows, and once again be the warrior I know in your heart that you are!"

"You don't understand! How can you? You are . . ."

Her jaw was set as he stopped mid-sentence. "I am *what?* Human? Are you really going to go there?"

He hung his head; his shoulders slumped. He knew that he didn't mean the words, but he had started to say them. He had found over the years that he was able to "live" like he was just like her. Even though he was able to maintain a feeble attempt at convincing himself, the truth was always there. One of the reasons he had started taking to drinking was to dull the pain and even the guilt that he had for not being like her . . . like her: to know the end was closer than the beginning; to *not* know so much of the universe. How he wished he could be like her.

"I don't know what to do."

"You *do* know, and you will do it. I don't know how, but you, My Dear, have always found a way."

*****

The desert life, especially the evenings, were easier, quieter, and seemed more peaceful than almost anything on this planet. The sky's infinite boundaries couldn't be clearer. The night reached out and touched him, embraced him, and it was the closest he felt to home. Of course, "home" was relevant, because for ages he really had had no home.

He felt his wife's presence even before she touched his back. "I'm sorry. I can't sleep."

"I am not surprised. When will you leave?"

He moved over so she could sit down on the rock formation on which he sat. They both looked out over the landscape. A coyote paused in the distance and looked at them and then moved on. Zarius had wanted nothing more than to never return to what he had left behind. "In a few hours."

She laid her head on his shoulder. "Where will you go?"

"Eden. I have no choice. You were right. I do know what needs to be done, and I know that there is only one that can do it. Eyes will be opened. Either the truth will be believed or rejected, but I have to at least try."

"And that is why I love you." She paused. "Will I see you again?"

"I don't know."

"I do."

"Then why did you ask?"

"I guess I just needed to hear you say what we already know."

*****

"Mistress, he has arrived."

"I know. I felt him long before his entourage pulled up. Have him wait in the foyer, and I will be there momentarily."

"Yes, Ma'am."

Hecate turned and looked at herself in the mirror. This visit tonight was unexpected; and when he had called, she didn't know if she was more shocked that he had called or that he was even here. This would be interesting either way.

She made her way down the hall and toward the foyer. The foyer was large and spacious and held one of two blood-crimson grand pianos: Hecate's pride and joy. They had been handmade for her by a Druid priest and had been strung by Nascente, an underling of Lucifer. Each piano would never lose its perfect pitch, and her fingers seemed to become a part of the keys as she allowed her spirit to flow through these instruments when she played.

The smell of cinnamon and myrrh permeated the air, giving the sense of a sweet strength and, yet, a feeling of heaviness that made one want to move slowly, almost as if in a trance. This was the web of a seductress, and many who entered her lair would not see the light of a sunrise again.

She really missed her estate right now in Europe, but pressing matters here kept her from being where she felt the strongest. The last five years of the Clan Wars had taken a toll on her; but she was pretty sure that her house remained the strongest, and she also enjoyed not having to answer to anyone but herself. True, there was power and strength in the Clans being united, but she had truly discovered freedom in focusing on those who aligned with the House of Hecate.

*****

Her visitor stood waiting for her to make her entrance. He could smell her enticing and enchanting scent coming from the hallway even before she could be seen . . . then, there she stood. He truly wished he was stronger; but of course, he would never vocalize his weakness to her. Why should he? It wasn't like she didn't know and exploited it any chance she got; and as for anyone else, it would not benefit either of them for others to know.

When Hecate spoke, he could feel himself being drawn toward her. "I am sure you still find the atmosphere of mortals crushing and heavy; then again, the bright and light space of Scintillantes is more than I can bear any more."

"True, My Dear, but maybe it is because the longer you stay inside the darkness, the less dark it seems; and before you know it, darkness resembles light."

She chuckled, "Well, you would know that more than any of us. I do believe you may be the only dark spot back home, and to think you still manage to exist without being exposed. Then, of course, there are the 'wise words' that you regurgitate."

He turned and looked at her. "It is my lack of exposure all these years from which you have benefited . . . and what is this 'home' you are talking about? Do you still remember it, or is all you remember simply the *feeling* of it being stripped from you and being exiled?"

Her lips parted in a delicious smile. He remembered the way they tasted. Her dark crimson lips were accented by the hint of elongated white canines. Her skin was pale against the bluish, inky darkness of the night, her silhouette curvaceous and stirring. Hecate was the creator of seduction, dedicated to the refining of such an art form.

This seductress was Queen to her followers, and to her Clan she was the goddess; but to this figure standing before her, she was a necessity, an alliance that had its perks . . . but mostly a respectful agreement.

She walked forward with the confidence of a viper. She drew in close to him, her lips against his ear, her hot breath sending tingles down his spine. "Be wise and gentle with your words, My Dear, for truly you have more to lose in this roughly drawn alliance of ours. Don't forget I am the one already exiled. The stories I could share with the members of the Arch Council . . ." She paused and pulled back. She looked him directly in the eyes. "Phew . . . I believe I may be blushing."

He smiled. She was good . . . and always had been. Before the War of the Serpents they had been more than just Council members, but that had all changed for a while. Today, it wasn't about pleasure but business. A new direction had to be laid out or all the planning and manipulating would have been in vain . . . or as Hecate liked to say, "In vein."

"It is such stories that bring me here tonight."

She stepped back and tilted her head to the side. She gazed upon him. He was still strong and handsome to her, but he would always be a game piece on the board of the universe to her. "Oh, and which stories would that be?"

"You pick."

"Azrael, do I need to remind you what happens when I feel toyed with and feel as if someone is trying to push my buttons?" "No, but I also need to remind you that I am no longer your naive lover; but instead, I have gained a lot more wisdom since you last lay in my arms. Trust me, my bitterness towards your deceit, tricks, and manipulation runs deep."

"Yet, here you are."

"Simply for business, Hecate, simply business. I believe we are at a position within time and space to make our move . . . to put the nail in the coffin of everything that we attempted to do during the War of the Serpents. I also believe that the window of opportunity is very small. If you aren't willing to listen to what I have to say, I can always go to Mantus."

Her face changed, and all allusion of seduction and pleasure vanished. She became cold and rigid. "I said don't toy with me or play me. I have no belief whatsoever that you would appear before Mantus. If you did, it would be the last meeting you ever had; and you know as well as I do that your existence would become merely a speck within any knowledge."

She turned away from him with little flare. "Let's go into the study," she said as she motioned to a door behind them, "before I get weary of this meeting and send you to my beloved husband myself."

Chapter Three

Azrael smiled; he had played her right into his hands. He knew that her "beloved husband" wanted just as much to do with her as Mantus wanted to do with him. He followed her.

The study was a blend of comfort and ancient delight. There were walls lined from floor to ceiling with bookshelves filled with artifacts from the ages that would make an archaeologist drool and a large desk with high-back chairs behind and in front.

Hecate walked around the back of the desk and placed her hands on the back of the oversized chair. "Azrael, so, what are you wanting to tell me? I will give you about ten minutes to keep my interest. After that, if I am bored, you will leave; and I will go back to my planned evening."

She walked over and stood by the lit fireplace. The glow of the flames danced upon her skin and dress. Curled up on the rug was a Demon Dog. These protectors of the Fallen were the source of legends and dark tales. Mortal man told stories of men morphing into wolf-like creatures within the reflection of a full moon. Legend always had a weird way of mishandling truth; the truth was that once a mortal chose to surrender to the status of a Demon Dog, rarely would he ever be seen in human form again, instead staying true to the form of a vicious guard dog.

This particular Demon Dog was especially rare. In a time long ago, this protector had been born with a deformity. Human twins in the womb of their mother, a deformity had joined them. They had been born with two distinct heads but shared one body.

Hecate had discovered the brothers in a gypsy show somewhere in the heart of Europe. Stidoch and Seirbeubar would have been a formidable team separately, but their deformity would eternally bind them as one: two vicious minds joined together by one body.

Hecate had seduced the brothers; and they had sworn allegiance to the House of Hecate, soon making the rare choice to keep their form as a Demon Dog. They had transformed one last time; and ever since, they had kept their canine form. The fear that most had for Hecate's pet was justifiable. Now as one unit with two canine heads, they were her ever-constant protector. Cerberus had taken the lives of too many would-be assassins for his master.

"Azrael, I am not going to keep waiting," she stated impatiently as she watched him staring intently at Cerberus.

He smirked as he helped himself to her liquor tray. "You have spent the last five years attempting to manipulate different power structures within the different Clans, and each time you have failed. We both know that your biggest weapon and tool to success is still splintered with a huge portion trapped away within the dark confines of Mantus' Abyss."

Her eyes flared, and he knew that he had just earned more than ten minutes. "We both know what it would mean for your House if Legion was brought back."

"You are mistaken with your assumption, though," she leered.

"What assumption is that?"

"That I need him in order to rise to power over all the Houses."

"Am I? Is that why you are still struggling to rise to the pinnacle? Look at you, Hecate! The Houses have been in disarray for the last five years . . . and even before that, they were only loosely bound!"

He walked over to her but stopped when he received a growl from the portion of Cerberus that was awake. "Hecate, we are at the perfect time to finally make our move!

Hell, most of the Clans are in total meltdown; many of the Houses have no real organization to them. Familiars are following the *idea* of being part of a Clan but have sworn no true allegiance to any particular House!"

"This means nothing!"

"You are once again wrong! It means everything! If we could unite the Clans behind one House, then the Familiars will identify the strength and power and align themselves with the reigning House. If that happens, then there would be no stopping the House of Hecate! You could finally obtain the seat of Morning Star and reap the benefits and power from the rest of the Houses kneeling before the House of Hecate!"

She gazed into the flames of the fire and held silent as she dwelt upon what he was saying. During the War of the Serpents and before the exile, she had come so close to overthrowing everything and reigning as Queen of the Eternals. So close . . . but then in a blink, everything had crumbled before her like a castle built upon shifting sand. She had not only lost what she had thought would be hers, but all her manipulation had been exposed. Her husband had walked away; her lovers had faded into the shadows. She would eventually lose her only offspring.

She had raged with anger. Her wrath was felt by not only her newly formed House but also by the Alliance, Mortals, and even the Grigori. She had played a key role in their demise. Of course, she had no idea that it would be a Grigori that would eventually get revenge and banish her son.

"What card do you have on the table, Azrael? Not only that, but how would you propose such a thing? You have nothing to offer me but your lofty words and schemes. Where is the power behind your words?"

"You want me to lay all my cards on the table at once, is that it?" he asked. "Come on, Hecate, you know I am not going to roll over like that."

"Fine," she stated with firmness. "Then you can find your way back to the vehicle that brought you here. I don't have time for this." She walked toward the door of the study. "Cerebus, let's go."

The Demon Dog stood up and began to follow his mistress. One head stayed focused on Hecate, but the other zeroed in on his master's guest, snarling.

"Azrael, if you care to share more than just words, then please come back; and I may give you another few minutes of my precious time. However, until then, I would suggest you stay far from any of the Clans. You, Dear, whereas you may have once been close to me, are far from falling upon my friends list now. Don't you believe for one moment that I do not believe you are focused on your own goals, greed for power, or lofty dreams.

"I also want you to know this . . ." She turned and looked at him. Her eyes were far from seductive but instead, those of a warrior, a leader, and full of bloodlust. "I never have, nor ever will, NEED you! I have used you in the past, and I am the master of manipulation. Do not manipulate the manipulator."

"Hecate, you will regret this."

She laughed. "I only regret that within the exiled form of my son there is a portion that comes from you. Fortunately for all, that is a very small portion." With nothing more to say, she exited, followed by her protector.

Azrael stood there quietly. For a brief moment, his face was expressionless, but then slowly a large smile broke across his face. This had gone exactly how he had expected. He knew, no matter the bravado she spoke, he had danced her right into his arms. She was teasing the hook, and soon she would bite.

Time to return home. He had been gone for too long already. He exited the manor and stopped to take in the evening scenery. He did enjoy the fresh air from where he came, but there was also something about the dark nights here within the world of mankind.

There was a bright moon shining above, and the stars of the galaxy where sprayed across a canvas of inky darkness. The smell of the forest touched his nostrils, and he took in a deep breath.

"So sad that all of this has been wasted upon a creation that has no real understanding of time and space . . . a creation that has no inkling of the truth. These poor creatures can't fathom the depth of the lies and cover ups they have lived, all the while having the audacity to believe that their version of life is the truth and that no one can understand it better than them!" he thought to himself.

The driver opened the back door to the black sedan in which he had ridden to the House of Hecate. "Profitable meeting, Sir?"

"It was profitable enough," Azrael chuckled. He sat down and adjusted the tailored suit he was wearing. "I also believe it was a deeper investment into more profit in the future."

"Very good, Sir."

The vehicle sped into the night as Hecate watched the taillights disappear down the long lane that led up to her estate. She reached for a cell phone that was on the small table to her right. She picked it up and hit one of the speed dial buttons. "It's me. I need to speak to Mantus."

The voice on the other line stated something, and she felt her body tense. "I understand that he is busy, but tell him it is urgent. I need to meet with him . . . and better sooner than later."

The individual on the other end responded, and she simply hung up. She hated that Azrael had her wondering if she should have listened to more. What was he planning?

*****

The sun was creeping up over the horizon as Zarius stood in the doorway with a cup of coffee in his hand. He had everything prepared but just wasn't ready to make the final step out the door. So, he stood in the doorway, allowing the aroma of the fresh brew to tease his senses.

"I didn't think you would be here when I woke up," his wife stated as she walked up behind him and wrapped her arms around his waist. She rested her head against his strong muscular back and sighed deeply.

"Really? I don't believe that for one second," he grinned. "You know good and well I would not have left without saying goodbye and giving you a long kiss."

"Well, Mister, you better get busy with that long kiss, because you have to get going sometime!"

He turned in her embrace and held her face in his hands. He looked deeply at her and then bent down and kissed her. Her lips always felt perfect against his. He soaked in the moment and held her close. "Make sure you keep your phone charged and near you. I will call when I can."

"I know, Zee. I know."

He grabbed a backpack that he had placed just outside the door and threw it over one shoulder. "I should be in Eden in a couple of days," he said as he walked over to his bike. "After that, I can't promise what will happen."

"I know," she stated again. "We will take it with the wind. That is how we always have done."

She stood strong and determined. She would not allow him to see her breaking inside. She knew he had to do what he had to do. "By the way, I received an email this morning from Gerault."

"Gerault?"

"The priest with whom I have worked before on a few archaeology sites."

"Oh, yeah, I remember you talking about him before."

"He has something he wants me to check out. He has been working on translating some manuscripts at the church where he has been working. He said that he needs a second set of eyes on something . . . stated if what he is translating is correct, it would be earth-shattering."

"So, you're headed to Europe?"

"We could do it remotely, but since you will be gone for a bit, I thought this would give me a chance to keep my mind occupied." She paused. ". . . And IT IS Europe!"

He smiled and nodded, "Yes, I know."

He smiled one last smile, and then the motorcycle roared to life as he looked back at her and blew her a kiss. With that, he was off. She watched him until all she could see was the cloud of dust that his motorcycle was kicking up, and she walked back in.

Her heart was heavy. Almost from the moment they met, they had been by each other's side. This moment of separation felt as if eternity had begun already. The further he drove toward the horizon, the more separated from him she felt.

She placed a kettle of water on the stove and turned the knob. The igniter clicked once, gas sparked, and a flame roared up, kissing the bottom of the dark kettle. She reached up to one of the shelves that held several glass jars full of different tea blends and pulled down her favorite: orange zest with mint. She measured it out and then placed it in her tea strainer, waiting for the water to heat.

She forced her mind to focus on the email that Gerault had sent her. She and the old priest had spent many years together—he as a mentor and she as a young student—soaking in his passion for ancient text and artifacts. He had expressed his disappointment when she had chosen to leave the field and settle down with Zarius, calling it a waste of a future expert within the field of archeology. He, of course, had no way of knowing all that a life with Zarius had to offer. If he only knew who and what her husband was, he would have just shaken that already-grayed head of his and sat down, loudly stating, "Well, I never . . .."

She completed her cup of tea and walked over to the rustic table that acted as her desk. She sat down, opened the email again, and leaned back, smelling the aroma of the steeping tea leaves and studying some of the photos that Gerault had sent her.

There were several photos of old manuscripts that appeared to be written in a language of which she was not familiar but with sporadic splashes of Sumerian, Aramaic, and some Roman and Greek. For most, including herself, she would have dated each of these within different ages, as well as studied them each separately: different cultures, different times, different languages. The uniqueness and possible link lay in the fact that each manuscript page within the photos had similar contextual sketches. It appeared, with just rough translation, that many spoke of a similar event.

"Of course, that is not unusual," she stated to herself. "Even what would be considered biblical stories can be found throughout different time periods and ancient text. So, why these, Gerault? What are you not telling me?"

She scanned over his email again, and it seemed just as vague as the first time she read it. She opened another tab on her browser and started working on finding a cheap flight to Heiligenblut. Soon she had a flight booked, and she felt butterflies in her stomach. She may not actually be out in the field again, but to be able to once again reconnect with the past while preserving it for the future would be refreshing.

*****

His fingers moved across the old parchment as his dimming eyes squinted at the message that was scrawled there. Years of candlelight vigil had forced his eyes to almost rest in eternal darkness, but the man was determined to not let it stop him from his life's quest. Time had taken the elasticity from his skin and had left it paper thin. His bones, many times, decided they would not move; but his will was still there, strong and enduring.

His surroundings had become his "body." They were as comfortable and familiar to him as the brown robes that had been his coverings now for more years than not. The masonry, though, had begun to crumble with age, ironically mimicking his mortality. Just outside of the flicker of the candles, he knew there was a rat or two; but the cat, Cornelius, would keep them from venturing too far out.

Bookshelves lined two of the four walls; and stacks of different parchments, scrolls, and antiquities lay in different states of disarray, creating almost an ancient catacomb of sorts. He had never been an organizer, but he knew where everything was in the basement of the small gothic church.

He had not really inherited anything organized, either. In fact, most of the things down here had been stored away and had never really been studied. Now in his mid-80s, he had been examining such things for years; these manuscripts had become his addiction. He never could have imagined, as a young priest, what historical artifacts would be left to him and to his protection or the amount that he would acquire himself, working numerous digs over his long life. No one could have imagined, either, the information that he had come to know and what it would do to him. It had not just become his addiction, but it also had begun to spiritually challenge everything he had spent his younger years learning and in which he had been trained. Everything he had kept in journals would become priceless to any who would follow in his footsteps. It brought ages of cryptic writings, hidden secrets, and immortal visions to rest in one place . . . well, several places if you considered each journal a different place rather than a continuation of the one before it.

There were still a few pieces missing, and it made the old priest tremble some as he could only imagine what those pieces meant. The few pieces on which he had been working had puzzled him for years, but he knew they held something; he could feel it . . . each manuscript different and yet the same. His work on all that surrounded him had started out as a simple desire to create a historical chronology of different works and artifacts with which he had been entrusted. Over the years it had turned into something so much more.

The temperature outside was freezing, and the snow had been falling all day. Now, it seemed the evening would continue to be drenched in the frozen tears of the Angels; but maybe the cold, moist air would be just what he needed in order to relax his mind so he could get some rest. He would have to make sure to bundle up. His aged bones didn't handle this weather well, but his spirit soaked it in. In this small area of Austria, known as Heiligenblut, there would be a few people who would most likely call out to him to come inside for a while and talk.

He capped off his inkwell and grabbed the candle as he headed toward the wooden door that would lead him down a hallway, past the crypt of Briccius, and then up the stairs to the main area of the church. The rest of the town was modern—it had truly caught up with the new millennium—but the church had always been about rawness and simplicity . . . so, no electricity or modern niceties.

Chapter Four

The elderly priest walked along the side of the main auditorium and toward the doors that opened to the outside. He smiled as he felt a familiar sense that he was not alone. He paused and then spoke, "Ah, My Friend, I believe that you are arriving a little too late, as this evening I was just about to head out to relax my mind and then call it a night."

A tall shadow moved just to the left of him, seemingly the shadow of someone who blocked the light from the candle but was not visible to the naked eye. A strong and rich voice spoke, sounding like the clearness of a gentle stream. "I am never late; and yet, not held by time, so maybe I am never on time." There was a sense of playfulness as the joking from a good friend.

The priest opened a small wooden door to a closet exposing a long, hooded, brown cloak that he began to put on. "Well, this is true . . . but then are any of us truly bound by time or is time simply a measurement in order to give us boundaries?"

There was gentle laughter from the nothingness, and then the figure slowly began to become visible.

"You always have a way to take anything I say and turn it. No matter the measurement, no matter if time is a creation simply by mortals, . . ." The figure paused as a sincere and deliberate look crossed over his face.

The priest looked up and studied the eyes of the man in front of him. There was nothing but sadness, yet a hint—maybe a gleam—of that same humor possibly because of the understanding that time ended at the curtain of mortality.

The priest sighed heavily as his feeble hands did not even bother to continue to fasten his coat. "You are telling me that I have spent so much time, yet I will not discover the truth?" He paused and sat down on a wooden bench beside the coat closet. "You know I should be upset that you didn't at least allow me to take one last walk. You know it's a full moon out tonight, and the air is that crispness that I enjoy."

"I know; then again, to allow that would be to assume that time is something by which you are not governed but is something that can be manipulated."

The priest grinned. "Uh-huh." He looked around the old church and rested his head against the wall behind him. "You know, to think after all these years, I know less now than the day I first entered into the service of this church."

"Was it worth it?"

"Worth it? In what way?"

"Knowing now that you devoted your life to something that was not what it seemed before you surrendered to it."

"Is there any other way? To sit here now and say it isn't worth it would insinuate that I know of a better way. To do that would be presuming that I am arrogant enough to believe that another way would have been different. I think we all make our choices; and no matter what the choice, we live with it, learn from it . . ."

". . . And die with it?" the figure questioned.

"Yes, but you do so, knowing that any other choice would have still brought you to the same point."

"What is that point?"

"The reason you are here tonight."

The Angel smiled slightly. "True, so are you ready? Everything about which you have just spoken I envy, for it is something that my kind cannot begin to understand."

"What about the journals?"

"You have done what you were meant to do. We must go."

The priest stood up and smiled. "Well, then you lead the way. You are the expert here." The priest looked back one time and smiled as he saw his body resting so peacefully upon the bench. "Boy, Old Man, when did you get old?" he laughed.

*****

"Disgusting!" Victoria said with a condescending tone into her phone as she made the last touches to her hair. She looked in the mirror and noticed that she needed to touch up her lipstick. She reached for it while attempting to keep the cell phone wedged between her shoulder and head. "He is such a pervert. I don't understand why Rachel even wastes her time with him."

She knocked over her makeup bag, and the contents scattered across the ripped linoleum that attempted to cover the small bathroom floor. She cursed as she maintained her juggling act. "I swear when I am able to leave this god-forsaken house, I will; and when I make it big in modeling, I promise that my house will have like five bathrooms twice as big as this!"

She gagged as a roach crawled from behind the toilet and then quickly ran into a crack between the floor and the sink's base. "Maddie, I need to let you go. I have got to finish getting ready. Where am I going? Heading out to The Warehouse with Jason.

There is supposed to be a new band playing tonight. Yeah, I will keep you posted. If it turns out lame, maybe we will go to the Scraper. I haven't been up to the top for a while. Gotcha. Later."

Victoria hung up and slid her phone into the back pocket of her pants. She took one last look, turned the light off, and then left the bathroom. She was unaware of glowing eyes that stayed within the reflection of the mirror as the light went dark and she exited.

"Her mind cannot carry all of us," a voice whispered in the darkness of the bathroom.

"I like her, though. I want her."

"What if she can't hold us? We can't afford to separate any more than we are now."

"She is pretty, though," the second voice stated. It sounded like the voice of a small girl but with the vileness of a deranged madman, a mixture of innocence wrapped within the binds of a straight jacket. "We have no hope anymore of coming together!"

"I will return in full. It is prophecy!"

"We have said that for ages; yet, we are scattered, and a large portion of me is entrapped in exile. So, when? Is prophecy real or just the dreams of ancient ones that, if dwelt upon, becomes self-fulfilling?" the little girl voice questioned.

"Fine! We can see if she can hold us. If not, at least the torment will be entertaining."

A young shriek of demonic glee bolted out of the darkness. "I get to be pretty."

"Oh, shut your fanged mouth! We have had better."

"Yes, but she is young; and it has been awhile since I was young."

Silence fell within the bathroom; only the gurgle of the drain could be heard as water attempted to sink past soap-caked hair somewhere in the pipes.

*****

Victoria walked down the narrow hallway of the apartment. The wallpaper was peeling; and here and there were holes that acted as a war documentary: gaping holes of historical moments when anger flared or even a diary of the maddened mind seeking to escape self-judgment.

She paused for a moment where the hallway emptied into a small living room. She crossed her fingers and bit her lower lip, hoping that her dad would be out on the fire escape or passed out on the mouse-infested, stained couch. She stepped into the living room. She wondered if she was going to be able to get out of the apartment door without an incident or if there would be a battle of words and emotions. Either way, she would get out the door and on her way.

No one was in the living room, and she stopped for a moment to listen. "He must be on the fire escape," she whispered to herself.

"Tori!"

"Damn it!" she swore as she rolled her eyes.

Her dad was calling out from the kitchen. She could either just walk out really quickly, pretending she hadn't heard him, or respond to him. She chose the latter. It may end in a fight, but she also wanted to make sure he wasn't going to run after her. If they argued, he would have his fill of her, say some choice words, and demand her to leave. If she just left, then he likely would follow and yell and scream down the hallway.

"Yeah!" she stated loudly enough for him to hear.

"'Yeah'? I'm pretty sure that was meant to be a 'Yes, Sir.' Right?"

She turned and walked into the kitchen that was off the living room to the right of the hallway. "No, I'm pretty sure it was meant to be a 'Yeah,' David."

She paused outside the kitchen and counted on her fingers, "One, two, three, . . ." and there it was!

"'DAVID'? I AM YOUR *FATHER*, YOU SLUT!"

She stood just out of view from the kitchen and mocked him. She knew he would be through the door at any moment. He was so predictable.

"DO YOU HEAR ME?" He came storming through the doorway and almost ran into her. She startled him being so close to the door, and he stopped for a moment . . . but just for a moment. He grabbed her by the throat and slammed her up against the wall. "Do you hear me? You will respond to me with respect!"

She didn't flinch. The back of her head hurt a little bit from where she hit the wall, but at least it didn't leave a new record within the hole documentary found along the hallway. She had danced this dance many times with him.

"You *are* a slut, aren't you? MY DAUGHTER IS A SLUT!"

"Whatever." She rolled her eyes.

Her father was seeing red right now. She knew it, and she knew what to say. "Well, I guess I'm like my Mom, David. Maybe if you had been more of the stud you think you are, she wouldn't have had to slut around and find someone else to fulfill her fantasies!"

In her head she was counting again. She was pretty sure there was about to be another hole. She got to four this time before she saw it coming, and she moved her head as his fist came past her cheek and into the drywall behind her. She quickly ducked and moved from between her father and the wall. She saw her purse on the coffee table and grabbed it as she rushed toward the door.

"How dare you! You aren't going out tonight!"

She stopped and just stood for a moment . . . then turned. She set her jaw and glared at him. Then the words came flowing out. "No! HOW DARE *YOU!* How dare you not be the father you should be! How dare you REFUSE TO LOOK IN THE MIRROR! How dare you keep a daughter whom you never loved as a father; but instead, you have used me in every mentally twisted way you could to make your lie of a life seem something more than it ever will be! My mother left you because of the pitiful swine you are! The only thing she should have done differently was to take me with her! You are a narcissistic, piss-poor excuse for a human!"

His fist was clenching and unclenching. There was blood evident on his knuckles, and his chest was heaving. She didn't stop. "I will never call you Dad! You may have donated body fluid to my mother, but you have been everything but a dad!"

He bolted toward her. She turned swiftly and made it through the door, slamming it. He was unable to stop quickly enough before crashing against the other side. She didn't wait; she didn't care. That had felt amazing, and tonight she was choosing freedom! She hurried down the hallway, past the elevator that never worked, and to the flight of stairs.

"You see?" a little girl's voice spoke. "I want to be her. I want her to be me! We need her!"

"I already agreed, you annoying Mosquito!"

"Whatever!" the little girl's voice stated, attempting to mimic Victoria's voice.

The young teenager hurried down the stairwell. She was so ready for the night to start. The new band at The Warehouse better be good! She was in the process of switching her mind from the incident in the apartment to the rest of the evening. She was so mentally focused on clearing out the turmoil in her mind that she didn't even notice the dark-haired female who was coming up the stairs.

The two collided, and Victoria stopped suddenly with embarrassment. "I am so sorry!"

"Don't sweat it, but just watch where you are going!" the lady stated as she watched the young teen nod and continue down and out into the evening.

The lady turned and looked back up to where she was headed. She adjusted the hood to her black hoodie so it covered her head once again, then smiled as she started back up the stairs. She made it up a few more floors and then found herself in a rundown hallway with only one light attempting to fend off the darkness and everything that came with it. She didn't need light, though, for she knew exactly where she was headed. Memories of the hallway flashed through her mind's eye, and the acidic taste of revenge swelled within her saliva glands. Yes, she knew this hall all too well and knew which doorway she would be entering.

*****

He was a strong warrior! He stood upon the battlefield alone, fighting off the monsters that threatened the kingdom! The citizens would scream his name! He would be their hero! His sword swung . . . no! Hold on . . . don't go back yet; stay here in this world. It isn't over yet. The smell of cigarettes and three-day-old body sweat reached up into his nostrils and yanked at his senses like someone pulling out a piercing. He could swing . . . and swing hard. He could be . . . no, he was being pulled back. He didn't want to leave his world.

He felt hot and smothered. He felt greasy hands grabbing him. He tried to imagine the monsters again that he had been fighting, but he was feeling a pain that he could not block out. He wanted to run, but he couldn't.

Reality slammed into him harder than it had before. Flash! They were taking pictures again. "No, just let me be!" He hated himself. He hated his skin. He hated the taste that was in his mouth, the taste of innocence being lost.

He swung. This time he made contact. He swung again, and the warrior that he was imagining a minute ago was breaking through.

The room was dim—it always was—but the flashes lit it up. He had the room memorized. It was his cage.

He was on the edge of losing everything or returning to his imagination that would block everything out . . . block all the perversion and vile decadence that had chained him behind physiological walls. Just as he was slipping back to his battlefield where he would be strong and able to defend himself, another flash of a camera caught him off guard. Something was different this time, though. In the flash of the camera, there was something new: horror! It wasn't horror this time on the face of an innocent eight-year-old boy but, instead, on the aggressors—horror followed by something altogether new: the face of a woman.

The young boy felt the weight of the moral- and hygiene-deficient man pulled away from him. In the dim light, he saw others who were present in the room dive for cover as blades began to fly from the hands of the woman in black as if they were being shot from a gun.

The little boy rolled to one side of the bed and hid between the wall and the bed. He wanted to hide, but at the same time he wanted to see this hero, this warrior, this—dare he say—*Angel* at work.

"Look out!" he screamed without realizing it.

The vile sorry excuse for a man who, moments before, had been thrown from the young boy was standing with a shotgun, loaded and aimed.

The lady in black whirled around, her black hair glistening in what little light there was. In one quick and fluent movement, her long coat fell to the floor like the curtain hiding a magician's secret. She dropped to one knee and reached behind her. With one hand, she grabbed the pile of black material, flinging it in the air, surprising her would-be attacker.

She rolled to her right as the explosion from the shotgun resounded through the room. She didn't feel any pain and knew that she had been able to cause enough disturbances to throw off his aim and regain her footage.

The man was slammed violently against the wall as this woman of shadows, in a blurry rush, jammed against him. In an instant, her hand was tight around his throat. He was gasping for precious air . . . not because of her grip, but because of what he discovered in front of him

"Vampire?" he sputtered, coughing.

"No, worse: Nephelium."

She sneered at him, flashing elongated canine teeth. "Every fear, every bit of panic, every turmoil, and every nightmare that you shoved into the minds of those who never had a chance . . .

comes back to you tonight! No more! No more will you steal the innocence of those who have no one to protect them."

"Who . . . what?"

"The 'what' I already told you, and the 'who' . . . well, just tell Lucifer that Eve sends her regards!" With that, a blade flashed as she sliced through his skin and into his fat-laden, oily body. She pulled back as bile, blood, and human filth gave way. "How fitting. Filth for filth," she thought.

Was it right to cheer and be enthralled when evil in the form of humanity met its demise? The boy wasn't sure . . . but what he was sure of, as the greasy, sweaty bag of a man's body was shredded and blood began a crimson wash down his carcass, was that there would be no more need of escaping. He didn't know who the lady was that seemed to be moving in slow motion in front of him, but he did know one thing: she had saved him. That was all he desired to know.

Chapter Five

Eve could feel the young boy's hand in hers. She let go for a minute and removed her left glove and then held her hand out again. He took it and looked up at her. There was still some innocence left inside of him, and for that she was grateful. Rarely did she find a reason to be grateful; but if she was able to rescue young innocence, even if it was just a sliver, then she was grateful.

They walked out of the apartment, hand-in-hand. She stopped in the hallway and knelt down to his level. She could see the tear stains down his cheeks, and yet she could see the young warrior's heart mustering all the strength he could to be strong as he looked at her. "Are you an Angel?" he stammered.

"No, I am not an Angel," she whispered as she touched his cheek. "I don't want you to EVER allow anyone to make you a victim again! Do you understand?"

"I didn't want this."

"I know. This was not you. This was those animals. This was their filth of a soul attempting to destroy the strength and goodness within you."

"They said no one cared. They told me that if I ever told anyone, that . . ."

She placed her finger up to her lips to instruct him to stop what he was saying. "It doesn't matter now. They are gone. You are safe now. You must understand that you are stronger than you think you are, and if there EVER comes a time where you feel as if someone means you harm or attempts to make you believe that no one cares, you remember that those are all lies! Just because someone says it, doesn't make it the truth."

The young boy nodded. "I am Timothy."

"Timothy, I am Eve, and now we need to get you home."

Eve once again took his hand and began to walk down the hallway toward the stairway that had led her to the floor and the apartment. She heard a noise behind her. With one swift motion she turned with a gun in her hand, pointing it directly at the head of an older man.

His eyes were wide in surprise. "Hey now, Lady, I have no beef with you."

"Then you shouldn't sneak up behind someone!" she said with a tone of distaste. She looked him up and down. His peppered hair was in a disheveled mess atop his head, his jeans were unzipped, and his belt was unfastened, allowing it to flop around. His white T-shirt was stained with last year's spaghetti sauce, and he smelled as if he hadn't showered in a few days.

"Hey, listen, Woman, I wasn't sneaking up on anyone. I was trying to find my daughter."

She kept the barrel of the gun pointed at his head. "Young teen girl, all dolled up and dressed in a cheap outfit of gothic or emo style?"

"Yeah, you see the slut?"

"Nope."

With that, she lowered the gun, gave the man a look that highly discouraged him from following, and she led Timothy into the stairwell. They exited the building, and she made her way toward a cab that was waiting across the street. Timothy felt as if the weight of the world had been almost taken off him. It would be sometime before he would be able to look at the scars left behind by the wounds, but tonight was the start of healing.

Eve opened the back door and motioned for him to get in. She then bent down and looked in at the cabbie. "Hey, Mitch, make sure he gets home safely."

"You know I will, Eve; and if you need me anymore tonight, let me know," the cabbie responded. "I don't have much going on tonight. You know I always owe you."

"You owe me nothing, Mitch."

"Yeah, yeah . . . that is what you say, but I would never have my little girl back if it wasn't for you."

She glared at him. He knew she hated it when he tried to thank her. He knew that she didn't want to hear it, but it never stopped him.

She looked in the back seat where the young hero sat. "You take care, and remember what I told you, ok?"

"What do I tell my parents?"

She sighed and took a moment before she spoke. "You tell them the truth, and tell them that you need them to love you."

She watched as the cab pulled off into the maze of the city. She unzipped her hoodie and flexed her neck back and forth. She needed a massage or a new tattoo; both would help relieve some stress.

She looked up at the old apartment building, and memories flooded through her mind . . . memories of when she had been a little girl and no "savior" came out of the shadows to rescue her from hell.

"One more saved; but thousands more tonight will have the light of their innocence forever snuffed out, and yet your precious Alliance is nowhere to be found. I looked up and down the street—even on the rooftops—and there is not even one in sight!"

She didn't even turn. She didn't have to. His voice was still rich like the first time he had spoken to her that night at the café. "Just when I thought I could enjoy my evening . . . I take trash out, and trash comes back."

She turned and looked at Kadar with no glimpse of kindness or a twinkle of friendship. Her eyes were cold as her hand slowly moved toward her waist.

"Oh, I wouldn't even try to reach for any sort of weapon you may have taken from Gideon and Ki's armory, Dear. Do you think I would really come to see you without my own protection?" He motioned around him in a sweeping gesture. "The night. We both love it for the same reasons: the darkness holds so many secrets. Trust me, about a half dozen of your family currently have you in their sights."

"If they were my family, they would have nothing to worry about. The very reason that they are afraid and hiding in the shadows, Kadar, is because they know they are not even close to being my family. They and you have every reason to be scared."

"Tsk, tsk, tsk, Eve. I am crushed," he mocked her as he placed his hand over his heart. "It has been a while since we talked, let alone seen each other, and you hurl insults."

"That is the smallest thing I would like to hurl right now. What do you want, Kadar? Oh, and don't ever think I will be your 'Dear' . . . *ever!*"

She walked up to him and received some satisfaction as he backed up a bit out of reflex. He caught himself and stood his ground. "You may not believe me; but in a way, we are on the same team."

"You are right. I don't believe you."

"Are you worried about law enforcement coming after all the racket you just caused?"

"In this neighborhood? Really? Pretty sure no one even woke up from their sleep . . . that is, *if* they were sleeping."

*****

She leaned against a boarded-up window of an abandoned storefront that had been decorated with graffiti. She reached into her pocket and pulled out a pack of cigarettes. She cursed as she realized she only had one left. She pulled it out and discarded the pack onto the trash that littered the sidewalk already. She placed the end of the cigarette between her lips and looked at the other Nephelium.

"How about that lighter you have in your pocket?"

"What lighter?"

"Come on, Kadar. If you are going to waste my time and threaten me with your lackeys, then the least you could do is give a gal a light."

He reached into his pants pocket and pulled out a flip top, chrome lighter and threw it to her. She caught it and held it for a minute, looking at it. She shook her head and looked up at him. "Really? Are you serious? A skull?"

"What?" he shrugged. "It was at the cash register at one of those gas stations."

"I'm sure." She lit the cigarette and threw the lighter back to him. "So, what do you want, Kadar?"

"Just in case you haven't noticed, there is a Clan War taking place ever since you and your Alliance friends exposed all that stuff going on at The Vortex, and . . ."

"They are far from my friends! Get to the point. We all know the Clans are shattered. We all know they don't trust each other. We all know they are fighting . . . and even some of them are fighting amongst themselves. What do I care?" She blew smoke up into the air and watched it vanish into the night sky. "Here for a moment . . . and then gone."

"What?"

"Nothing. Get to your point."

"We could really use you, Eve." He held up his hand before she could say anything. "I know. I know. I am the last person you want to team up with. I just want you to consider something."

She didn't respond. She just continued to watch the sky above her. She loved the clear winter nights. In all honesty, she just simply loved winter.

"Eve, listen to me. The Clan War has depleted the Clans. We have started hunting them. You know that we never were considered anything but half-breeds, a violation of everything that the Clans and Alliance believe in. They have kept us down. They have attempted to destroy us, use us, and keep us from each other. What is the one thing that neither side wants?"

"I don't know, Kadar. Enlighten me."

"They don't want to see a unified Clan of Nephelium."

She stood up straight, took another long drag, dropped the rest of the cigarette on the ground, and ground it into the cement of the sidewalk with the toe of her boot. She took a deep breath and looked up at him.

"Listen to me now, Kadar. I have given you way too much of my time this evening; and since I listened, you listen now! I am NO LONGER the weak tattoo artist you first met. I am no longer a victim or some sweet, innocent lady. Am I Nephelium? Yes, and I can't change that. However, I *can* tell you that even though I still may not know everything I'm capable of, that I may not fully know where I have come from—my parents or even my history— and that my world may have turned upside down in more chaos than I could imagine," she spoke as she got really close to him, "it is *MY* CHAOS. This war, these Clans, all of this," she stated, motioning outward into the night, "you all can have it! I have my own war, and I want nothing—*NOTHING*—to do with you, the Alliance, the Clan Wars . . . whatever you all come up with! Do you understand?"

She shoved passed him as she finished, not waiting for an answer. He bore his fangs at her, and a growling sound rumbled somewhere deep within him. "You better never shove past me like that again, Eve. You run. You haven't changed in that sense. When things are out of your control, you run from it instead of facing it."

She spun around, her body tense, her anger boiling. "You know nothing about me! *Nothing!*"

"Eve, we could be gods! United, we could become the gods that mortal man has longed for, made up, written about, worshipped in every culture! If not, we lose!"

"I lost five years ago, Kadar. I don't need you. I don't need anyone."

"One day you will see."

She walked out into the darkness, lifting the middle finger to him and to all those within the shadows. "Well, not today. I don't want to see you anytime soon, Kadar. 'Anytime' means never again. Next time, I will cut those canine teeth from that hideous grin of yours."

*****

"Wait up, Jason," Victoria yelled out as she closed the door to his car. She shook her head in frustration as he kept walking ahead of her. "Hey! Wait up!"

"Catch up, Vickie. I don't want to miss any of the music!"

She caught up with him just as he made it to the door of the club. "You know I hate it when you call me 'Vickie'!" she seethed.

Jason rolled his eyes. "Whatever, Tori."

Two bouncers were standing outside the large old warehouse that had been changed into a club last year. It had stood empty for years; and then out of the blue, last year, a company in Europe had purchased it for the asking price. It made the papers; and everyone wondered if the company had plans to raze the building and build housing, office buildings, or something grand.

Soon everyone began to question why a company would purchase it and turn it into a large, multi-level club ironically called "The Warehouse." It seemed to make no sense, but the teens and party goers of the area flocked to it.

It sat in the industrial area of the city and brought a new beat to the redundant club scene. The outside had not been changed much. There were things that had been redone to bring it up to building code and a few lights added, but it really looked the same.

The inside played to the rustic industrial look. There was a large stage that sat in the middle of the club. This allowed a great view of whatever band was playing from anywhere on the bottom floor, and the other levels had areas to look down onto the stage.

Jason gave the two bouncers at the door a big, "how-are-you" hug and indicated that Victoria was with him. They opened the large metal doors and allowed them to walk in.

"You know one of these days they will check my I.D."

"Nah, not as long as you are with me."

"How do you know them, again?" she asked as they walked in and the sounds began to bounce around in her head.

"From here and there. You know, I am all over and know a lot of people. Does it matter?"

She shook her head as she crossed her right arm across her midsection and held it with her left hand encasing her torso in a self-hug. She was excited to be here tonight; but every time she walked into the place, she had a moment of gut-wrenching uneasiness. Jason always told her it was just her social anxiety. She always thought it was the white contacts that the bouncers wore, which made them look possessed.

*****

"Gideon, can you hear me?" She waited. "Gideon?"

Her earpiece squelched a bit, and then she could hear her team leader's voice. "Go ahead, Serenity. What do you have?"

"I have the normal two Possessors at the door, but I am seeing a lot more Soul Slayer activity than we have before."

"Hey, you all, I don't have a good feeling about tonight. I am seeing a lot more activity. I know we call these places nests; but I would say that from what I am seeing, there is so much Fallen activity here tonight that it actually looks like an ant nest getting spun up," Chad cut in as he looked through his set of UV-SAGs.

Ki and Troy had gone into hyper-speed mode with the production of gear that could be used to give them a better advantage of the last five years over the Fallens. Not much different than a pair of shades, these glasses filtered out much of the atmosphere's interference. They were able to pick up the space within matter, where the elements of the Fallen were visible, when it was not able to be seen by mortal eyes.

This had given the Alliance a great advantage by allowing their mortal members to see what the Eternals already could. Through the prototype work, they had stumbled across a way to bypass Troy's destroyed vision and tap into the sensory nerves of his brain. He now was able to view the mortal world once again, as well as the immortal world.

"Serenity, I want you to meet Chad around the north side of the building."

"Copy that, Gideon. Near the old receiving doors?"

"Yes. Don't either of you do anything until I give you orders. You know that we are supposed to only be on a scouting mission."

"Pah," Chad scoffed, "because that seems all we do anymore! Screw the Arch Council."

"Shut it, Chad! DO NOT do anything unless you hear from me. You understand?"

"Roger, Sir. I'm tracking."

Gideon was currently located in the back of a surveillance van in an adjacent lot with the rest of his squad. He understood Chad's frustration. The whole team had the same frustrations.

The Arch Council, for whatever reason known only to them, had pulled back what they were allowing Leah's team to do. Many believed that it was a direct indictment on Leah; but the Arch Council denied that, stating that now that the Clans were warring amongst themselves, the Alliance mission was supposed to be more fact-gathering and scouting. The only thing that made it sit a bit easier for Gideon was that they were not the only Alliance team sitting in the shadows now, just observing. Teams globally were all stating they were being asked to do the same.

"CHAD, STOP!" Serenity's voice screamed through the earpiece in Gideon's ear.

His jaw set. "Serenity, what is going on?"

"Gideon, Chad just went in through one of the side doors!"

"CHAD, I told you not to move in!"

There was the sound of metal smashing against metal, and it sounded as if Chad was being tossed by a giant robot or had walked into a stack of serving trays.

"Boss, you better get in here now!"

Gideon slammed his fist down onto the console at which he was sitting. "Seriously?" He nodded to the rest of the waiting squad as each of them grabbed their "go gear" and began to pour out of the van.

"Chad, what is going on? Chad?" Gideon was seething. There better be one amazing explanation. "Serenity, do you have visual?"

"No. He saw something, then busted through a side door. I am inside the door now but can't see anything."

"Chad?"

"Boss," Chad's voice broke in, "I think we are about to be no longer in surveillance mode!"

"What . . ." Gideon couldn't finish his question. He and his squad stopped yards from the front of the club as the doors opened and throngs of party goers began to pour out, screaming.

Many had visible wounds as if they had been suddenly attacked by a large dog or animal; others were in complete shock.

"GIDEON! WE NEED HELP NOW!"

It was Serenity, and even though there was a strong focus in her voice, her squad leader could hear the change and urgency. "What are we walking into, Serenity?"

He could hear gunfire coming over their comms. He and his team started running past victims as they headed straight into the belly of the beast.

"Gideon . . . there is a reason it looks like a nest . . ." Her voice hit him hard in the chest as they came through the front doors but not as hard as the scene in front of him. "It *is* a nest!"

Familiars, Possessors, Imps, Demon Dogs . . . in a full frenzy! It was as if every member of the Fallen's family tree had just been knocked off all the branches into one big basket. Gideon led his team forward. "Let's roll!"

Chapter Six

He could feel the muscles in her back ripple as her body moved almost in sync with his. They were a good team. They turned in unison, keeping themselves back-to-back as their assailants attacked and then backed off.

"Serenity, we have got to make some kind of move here . . . and soon. They aren't going to keep toying with us all night."

He knew she was smiling that beautiful, knee-melting smile as she answered, "True, but Chad, why would you want to bring this little date of ours to an end so quickly?"

With one hand he racked the chamber to the shotgun he held, at the same time pulling the trigger of the semi-automatic pistol he held in his other. He felt the recoil reverberate back through his forearm, elbow, and into the core of his body.

"As charming as this evening could become, I am not that keen on getting my flesh peeled back by soul lusting, leather-wrapped, white-faced vampires!"

"Demons."

"What?"

"They are demons . . . not vampires."

"All the same to me." He shoved away from her and leaped into the air as he dodged a firestorm of bullets that were aimed to take him out. "No matter, I love me more than they will love the taste of me."

"So, where's Gideon?"

"I don't know. My earpiece is trashed just like yours. The last thing I had heard was that he and the rest of the team had entered through the front doors."

"What made you run in here, anyway?" she yelled at him, as her right heel met the face of a Possessor. She took a lot of pleasure as she watched the separation of the human host and Possessor take place in front of her. She leveled her gun and pulled the trigger, sending the Possessor to his demise within the Abyss.

"You see what is in the next room?"

"Why don't you just tell me?" She winced as she got hit by flying debris. The forces of darkness were determined to snuff out these two. The creatures of evil seemed to pour out of unseen shadows and hiding places. "I think we will be lucky to get out of this shipping bay, so just tell me about the next room," she tossed to him.

"It's a feeding room!" he yelled back to her.

She had to keep herself from stopping dead in her tracks. "Are you certain?"

He was breathing heavily and felt his body's muscles screaming to rest. How much longer before he had no more energy? "If you don't believe me, you can check it out yourself!"

Strands of Serenity's dyed red hair with streaks of black were sticking to her forehead from the sweat that glistened there. Her eyes flashed with a hunger for victory as she kept both arms stretched out, sending a shower of lethal bullets at any who dared to approach her. She felt Chad push away from her and could hear him behind her.

She loved fights like this. She was born for this! Yes, she was mortal. She was one of the very few who really had no complaints about her life; but just like most, there came a point in her life where she had to make a choice. She had to choose when faced with reality to either stand for what she believed to be right or to stand against it. She realized then, that if she didn't make a choice, in her indecision she was choosing.

She stepped through the ash of Fallen and the bodies of Familiars as she tried to make it to the door of the receiving bay. If she could open it, it might allow Chad and her to get outside.

Her nostrils stung with the smell of acidic flesh burning as Fallen were sent into oblivion. Ash fell like snow, and her skin on the back of her left shoulder burned as some of it landed on her bare flesh. She made a mental note to wear something with sleeves next time.

"Where in Jah's name are all of them coming from?" she questioned out loud, more to herself than to anyone. "Who are they protecting?"

Just as she reached the locking mechanism that would allow her to open the large metal doors, it seemed that someone had turned off the supernatural faucet. Everything became quiet. The small number of Fallen that were present vanished into the shadows and were gone.

Silence. Stillness—nothing but two very worn-out fighters, a lot of ash and bodies, flickering lights . . . but nothing else.

"Ok, so does this mean we win?" Chad questioned, throwing up his hands in puzzlement. "What's going on?"

She could feel her chest heaving up and down as she tried to catch her breath. She didn't realize how much energy she had been exerting; she was drained. She leaned back against the concrete wall and just took a moment.

She listened, trying to see if she could pick up any other sounds coming from the rest of The Warehouse, but there wasn't a noise. There was an eerie silence—just silence.

"I don't know. I don't like the silence. You would think you could hear something . . . maybe even the other team fighting, but I don't hear anything."

He nodded as he kicked the crate next to him with the toe of his shoe, trying to shake the sediment off. "Man, these were brand new boots, too; and now they look like something out of a mummy movie."

Serenity scanned several of the bodies that lay around to see if she could see any Clan markings or evidence of who in the world they had been up against. She noticed nothing that was tell-tale.

"I don't know, Chad. I still am not sure what is going on here. There are no markings on any of their wrists. I don't see a single Clan insignia. Who do all these belong to? Ever heard of an unaligned Clan?" She motioned to the bodies of Familiars and the sediment of ash lying in piles. "I am telling you, this is not normal."

He looked around and then shrugged. "So, hey, the way I look at it is this: there are still less of them out there now than us."

"But we can't just go around slaughtering people who are giving themselves up to the Clan."

He looked at her with his eyebrow arched. "And why not? Hey, you're the one who said they have no Clan . . . so, who cares?"

She shook her head. "There is still free will. Do I agree with them? No, but it is their life!" She knelt, taking the wrist of one of the bodies and, turning it over, noticed it was also free of any markings . . . nothing. All the Familiars who had not run but stood to fight alongside their Fallen Possessors were in their teens or 20s, a young Clan. There were lucid signs of ritualistic activity and cutting paraphernalia but nothing else.

"You're right; they do have a choice," he responded, mockingly acting tender and concerned. "I just chose to help make their choice final."

She shook her head once again. She liked Chad and she loved to fight Fallen; but their views on things, most of the time, split right about there.

"Let's go. We need to find Gideon and the rest of the team."

He didn't say anything else. As he turned to follow her, he noticed a medallion attached to a leather filament lying at his feet. He retrieved it and held it in his hand for a moment, looking at it. It was made of bronze and consisted of the Roman numeral XIV for 14 and a dragon with a sun in its mouth. Now was not the time to figure out its significance, but it was the closest thing he had seen tonight to any identifier. He followed Serenity out the door.

As the two moved through a doorway that led them further into the areas of The Warehouse and, hopefully, to the rest of the team, a shadow moved behind them. It was a blur of darkness, quiet and yet steady and unnoticed, overlooked by all except for a young lady trembling in the shadows. She noticed it, but as tears streamed down, smearing the black mascara, she didn't want to be aware of anything; she only wanted to go home. She wanted to wake up. This wasn't fun anymore.

Her knees were up to her chin; and she had wrapped her arms tightly around her legs, trying to keep every inch of her being in the shadows. Her lips were pressed taut, trying to hold in her breath that threatened to either implode her lungs or reveal her hiding place by exploding outwardly. Her skin was tingling in fear. It was as if she could feel every individual hair upon her body standing straight up. Her heart hurt . . . not the type of hurt when it was broken but the type of hurt that crushed through her chest and pounded so hard that she was sure she was going to die.

This had all been just an escape, a way to belong, and a way to get away from everything that had left her exhausted at home. She could feel herself getting ready to panic and lose it. She opened her eyes. Maybe the shadow would be just that: a shadow and nothing else. Maybe she could leave. She would go home and never return. "Just let me live!"

She slowly lifted her head and looked around. There were bodies and ash everywhere; the black she had worn was now an ashen grey, and she could taste the soot upon her tongue as she slowly opened her mouth to allow her breath to escape.

"Victoria," the voice of a young girl called her name through the darkness. "Victoria, are you there?"

She shook her head. She must be in shock. How would a little girl be in here, and how would she know her name?

"Victoria, I am scared. Victoria?"

"Who are you?"

That is when she saw it: it began across the room, turned, and then rushed at her like the wind from a hurricane. If all the fear that an immortal could conjure could be put into the deepest shadow and that shadow have the chance to express itself in a form, it would look like this! Tori screamed! Her flesh became so hot, it seemed cold. She then saw horror at its worst as it penetrated the only living thing left in which it could find refuge. The last thing she remembered in that split second was the inky, vile voice rushing around through her skull, "We are you and you are us, and we soon will be him!"

*****

"You ok, Sir?"

Zarius opened his eyes, and looked at the officer who was standing a few feet away with a bright light pointed right into his face. "I was until you shined that blasted light in my eyes."

"You can't just lie out here, Sir." The officer lowered the light. "There is a rest area a few miles down the road, but you can't sleep out on the side of the highway like this."

Zarius sat up and brushed himself off. "It's ok. I will get on my way."

"Like I said, you can check out the rest area."

"I'm not really all about rest areas, Man. Too many dirtbags hang out there, and I just wanted to catch a few minutes anyway."

The officer laughed. "Yeah, I guess I wouldn't want to really hang around one, either. You have a safe ride for the rest of your trip, Sir."

Zarius shook the officer's hand and watched as he got back into his patrol car and left. He pulled out his phone and looked down at the picture of his wife and then looked at the time. She would probably kill him, but he had to see her. He leaned against his bike as he touched the video call button, waiting as it rang.

It only took one ring before she accepted, and her face filled the screen. He smiled because he clearly saw that she was not in bed or even getting ready for bed. Instead, she was surrounded by papers and books, and he realized she was fully engrossed in some research.

"Hey, Sweetheart! How is the ride? Are you there yet?"

"No, I still have a few hours left, but I just needed to see your face."

She smiled. "Well, I'm glad."

"You look busy."

"Well, after you left, I started looking at some things that Gerault sent me . . ."

"And I dare say that you haven't stopped since that moment."

She looked at him with a mock-offended expression. "How dare you? You don't know me!"

He grinned; he loved her so much. She couldn't be further from the truth, even in her mocked expression. He knew her through and through; and he knew that whatever it was that had her going, she wouldn't stop until she got to the bottom of it. "So whatcha got?"

He felt a switch flip in his being as her face and tone changed. She became serious and very subdued, yet her words began to flow quickly. "Zee, I am not sure . . . I mean, I . . . I don't want to say too much because it is all preliminary, but . . . well, I have to say . . . Gerault was correct when he stated this could be earth-shattering."

"Ok. Can you tell me anything?"

She paused for a moment and then looked at him with a deepness that reached through the screen and held him. "Zee, how much do you know about your history?"

"What do you mean . . . my history? I don't understand."

"What if everything that we believe as truth is truth only because it was what was kept? What if the truth we hold to now is the truth because over time the truth has been forgotten for what those in power at the time wanted to be the truth?"

He didn't understand her. He felt a little bit dizzy, and yet there was a place deep in the pit of his stomach that felt as if a gaping hole was just ripped into it. "You're not making any sense."

"Yeah, I know . . ." She paused. "It doesn't make sense to me, either. If I needed to do some digging into your history, where would I start?"

"Why would you do that?" He stood up and felt his body tense. "What is it that you are looking for?"

"The truth, Zee."

"What? Do you not think that I have been honest with you?" He was getting heated now. They had never argued . . . well, ok, there had been a few times, but rarely. She had struck a nerve within him, though, and he wasn't even ready for the reaction he was feeling. "I have told you things about me that you never would have known!"

She let him blow and then put her hand up. "Stop, Zee. It has nothing to do with not trusting you. I believe that you may not even know the real history." There was a pause, and then she continued, "You know, forget it for now. Zarius, you focus on what you have to do. I will be leaving later today for Austria."

"I'm sorry." He felt his body loosen. "I didn't mean to blow up. I just don't understand what you are asking from me."

"It was my fault. I am not accusing you of anything, yet I can't really talk anymore about any of this. It is only pieces of a puzzle, and I can't seem to see the whole picture. The picture I *am* seeing . . . well, there is something big. I will talk to you once I am in Austria. Be safe."

"I will, and you, also."

He placed the phone back in his pocket, and in a few minutes he was back on the road. His mind was full, and she was right: he needed to focus on his mission and what lay before him, but now he couldn't get her words out of his mind. What did she mean? What was she getting at?

The roar of his tires against the road, the tunnel of the night's darkness, and the stars in the sky blended together into a scene of trance and absorption; it took him deep within himself and brought focus. His wife, at this moment, was behind him, and Eden lay ahead. He took a deep breath and opened up the throttle.

*****

Tanisha watched her husband's face disappear from her phone, and she leaned back in her chair. Her notes were scattered all around her. Usually, her work brought security and peace; but at this moment, the words, papers, and information that lay out in front of her did anything but that. She always attempted, as a student of history, to keep an open mind. She understood that history revealed itself in pieces; and because of that, much of it was left to the interpretation of the one analyzing it.

Years ago she had learned to allow her mind to remain open, but *this* . . . this was so "out there" that she wondered if it was a false narrative. It wouldn't be the first time that a historical find that seemed so bizarre and outlandish turned out to be exactly what it seemed.

"It has to be," she whispered to herself, "but what does your gut tell you, Tanisha?"

She closed her eyes and leaned back. If there was even the slightest chance that any of this could be true, then who would believe her? What did she do with it? Who did she show? She really hoped that Gerault could shed some more light and even more answers.

She needed to get her stuff together. This was going to be more than just a small trip.

Chapter Seven

The only sound that could be heard at the moment was the beeping of the medical equipment and the whirring of the printout on the girl's vitals. Without any knowledge of anything else, one would think that this was just an ordinary hospital room in which a patient slept peacefully; but the figure standing right outside the glass wall, peering in, didn't feel at peace. She felt anger. That anger had been rising for some time within her. It was something that she had been able to package up and use at the right moment in time for the right purpose, but that was getting increasingly difficult every day. Tonight, it was really hard.

She felt she was not only losing control but also losing any sense of sanity and authority. For the last five years, it seemed that more and more the Arch Council was stripping her authority away; and with each passing day, she felt more and more secluded.

"What do you make of it, Leah?" Gideon asked as he walked up beside her and nodded in the direction of the teen girl lying in a comatose state. "Did you see Serenity and Chad's report?"

She placed both hands against the panes of glass and then leaned her forehead in between them. "I did."

"And?"

"I don't know, Gideon. I just don't know. I am so tired. I have been tired before, but this is different." She turned and leaned her back against the glass wall and crossed her arms. She looked at him, her hair hanging down around her face, but he could still see the weariness. She looked at her friend of so long a time and just wanted to let it all go. She couldn't, because she was his leader . . . but she wanted to. She wanted to let him know everything that was in her right now.

"Gideon, from the start of all of this I felt separated from the Council and Scintillantes . . . ever since the whole deal with Eve. Then I felt that they were using me . . . or I should say using *us*."

Gideon had been on Leah's team long enough to know that he just needed to let her talk. He could see the inner struggle within her, and he also knew how dangerous it was for an Eternal to hold in so much; it was the thin line they walked. Questioning was never wrong; but anger, rage, and bitterness could become seeds of rebellion. At that point . . . well, a Clan somewhere would gain a new member, or the Eternal would become a Vapor—something not aligned to the Clans but no longer welcome in the realm of the Eternals. Usually, an Eternal who turned now did not last long. They usually had enough enemies within the Clans, who didn't care if they were Fallen or not, that they would be killed.

"Leah, why all of this tonight?"

She closed her eyes and allowed the rhythm of the medical instruments beeping to clear out her thoughts. "Why?"

She finally opened her eyes and turned to look at him. He would make a great Alliance leader one day—well, that is if he could get rid of the tinge of rebel in him . . . but then, again, maybe that is what made her such a good leader.

"The Council has called me to a meeting tomorrow. They are making the final say on my leading this team."

Gideon stood there quietly, very sober. With everything that had been going on, he had forgotten that the Arch Council was supposed to give their final judgment.

It had been five years since they were given the orders to protect Eve and to keep her from the Fallens. They had done so but to the Arch Council maybe not as well as they expected. The female Nephelium was now considered a rogue, the first Jerusalem Breed that chose not to align with the Alliance or Jah.

It also didn't help matters that her Watcher—one of the last, if not *the* last—had been killed. Since that time, it had seemed that everything they had handed to Leah and her team had set them up for failure, a way to ensure that records were kept to finally have enough evidence to strip her of her authority and leadership . . . an exile without being exiled.

"Any possible clue?"

"No, no one is talking. I have reached out a few times to Nemamiah, but there is a wall of silence. I am worn out, Gideon. I have dedicated the mass portion of my existence for all this," she stated as she looked around. "Don't misunderstand me; I would do it again, but I just don't know how much more I have left. It does not feel as if we have accomplished a lot."

"Yeah, but that is the hard thing about what we do. Many times, it is not about what we can see we accomplished but what we can't see that we prevented. How many generations have been saved from Clan enslavement because we have been the front battlement to a world unknown and misunderstood by the very ones we protect?"

She listened to his words and then exhaled a long sigh as she ran her fingers through her hair, turning and looking back at the young girl inside the med tech room of the Sanctum.

"Changing the subject . . . I read the complete team's report, but I still don't understand why it is I have a teen girl lying inside my med room."

Gideon stood beside her, his dark hair ruffed up and his arms crossed. He was wearing a pair of his most comfortable jeans, ripped at the knees. It accented his smoking-gun shirt. The shirt had been an anniversary gift from Jackie whom he started dating soon after he had rescued her from The Vortex. Many had frowned upon their relationship, one between an Eternal and a mortal, especially one who did not adhere to much of the beliefs that dictated the movement of the Alliance. However, they had pushed through the naysayers; and many who were against it had moved on to other things about which to complain.

"All I know, Leah, is that there was activity in that place tonight, but it wasn't anything like I had seen before. It balanced on organized and unorganized. There were all the signs of a nest: the organized part. I mean, there were cutting instruments, hallucinogens, a feeding room, and Fallen. That is about where the organized part stopped, though."

"Well, none of that is news. We knew it was a nest. Was there any doubt that the property had been purchased by the Fallen? We just didn't know which House. We have our suspicions that it was Hecate but no real proof."

"That is the thing, Leah. We still don't know. There were no clear or visible signs of a specific House. I am afraid that our hunch could be true; we are looking at the rise of the next generation of a new House or a mixture of something more."

The glass doors to the room opened silently and smoothly on unseen mechanics as Leah and Gideon moved into the room. Leah began to take a closer look at the young girl lying there.

She looked like she was about 15 or 16 years old and would have been eye-catching if it weren't for the makeup streaking her face and the scratches on her body. Her hair was long, dyed black and pink. Leah could tell that, even though the girl would most likely deny it, she cared what others thought about her because her fingernails were painted very neatly and well taken care of.

She looked up at Gideon. "So, what was the unorganized part?"

"You mean the part where we know the Clans are now scattered more than ever, but the Familiars are multiplying? Could it be the part where the Arch Council will not let us do anything about stopping what clearly is a reformatting and regrouping of the Houses? Stop me if I am getting close! Maybe it is the part that the Arch Council has clearly just decided that mortal man is expendable, and the place I call home is no longer worth trying to protect. Nope, just allow it all to be fodder for the Clans."

The door to the room slid open again as Serenity walked in to check on the readouts for the young girl. She sarcastically pushed her way into the conversation between the two leaders, "There wasn't a single Clan insignia there but way too much Clan activity for my liking; and if someone can explain the firepower and bloodthirsty creatures, then I would be happy. If anyone would like to explain why it is that activity is at the highest point ever since the Clan War began but we are seeing less actual Clan War and more like a free-for-all bloodbath, that would be helpful."

Leah ignored the sarcasm and looked back at the patient. "All of that we can take a look at, but that still doesn't tell me what she is doing here."

The Alliance leader turned the girl's hand over to check her wrist; but just as both Gideon and Serenity had indicated, there was no Clan insignia. It could be that she hadn't been indoctrinated yet or hadn't sworn allegiance to a Master. She may have only been invited by a Familiar, a friend.

"Serenity thinks she is possessed?" Gideon's voice seemed almost presenting a question instead of an answer. He knew that Leah was going to go off on that remark, but it was the truth.

He was right. "Possessed?! You are telling me that you brought a mortal here who could be aligned with an unknown Clan . . . *and* you brought her into the Sanctum?"

Serenity spoke quick and tough. "Well, what did you want me to do, Leah? If you had seen what I had seen, you would have . . ."

The Angel turned with eyes blazing. "I would have *left* her! I would have made sure that whatever I saw . . . no one else would have to! I would have . . ."

Serenity never backed down from Leah, sometimes walking the line between obstinacy and insubordination. "Kill her? Is that what you would have done, Leah? Is that what you are saying, oh, Angel of Mercy? Is that what your 'years of experience' have shown you? Well, let's just say I'm glad I am the mortal with emotions." Serenity knew she had, most likely, crossed the line with the last comment, but she didn't care.

Leah's jaw was clenched. She took in a deep breath and quietly walked up beside Serenity as she read off the medical charts and recorded them in the file she was preparing. "I don't care why you are here, or even if you are an Eternal, Fallen, or mortal; but as long as you are standing inside this building, you WILL remember that I am the pinnacle of the leadership chain. If that can't be remembered, then you know where the door is: it's the thing on hinges that you walked through to come in here today." She turned her head to the side and saw that Serenity had stopped what she was doing and was just staring at the ceiling. "Do I make myself clear?"

Serenity didn't speak and only bitterly nodded her head.

Leah pushed away from the countertop against which she was leaning and once again began to study the young girl lying in the bed. "So, tell me about her. What do you know? Where are the signs of possession, and why bring her here?" She spoke not so strongly now . . . more of a "let's-get-down-to-business" tone.

Gideon waited for a moment for Serenity to speak up; but when she didn't, he started. "Well, we know her name is Victoria; she is 16 and recently had a birthday. We got that from the driver's license in her pocket."

". . . which could be a fake I.D."

"True," Gideon conceded, "but I don't think so. Serenity and Chad found her in the receiving bay of The Warehouse."

Serenity interrupted, "After Chad and I left the room to find Gideon, we heard what sounded like several Fallen voices all at once. It was almost like they were arguing—yet not with each other—with . . . I guess, her soul," motioning to the sleeping girl. "Did you not see her in the room?"

Serenity shook her head. "No, she was back in the shadows and evidently hiding; because when we left, there was no movement or sound at all."

"Ok," Leah stated flatly, insinuating that she was getting impatient for some facts. "So, if you didn't see her, then we can conclude that there could have been an Overlord also not detected there."

Serenity purposely ignored the sarcastic question and continued describing to her what she could remember. "Chad and I rushed back in there, ready to go at it again; but we didn't see anything. Then suddenly, we heard the worst scream that I have ever heard to come from the vocal cords of any human. I am telling you, Leah, it made my skin crawl."

"Chad described it as the manifestation of horror and insanity wrapped into sound waves and decorated in a shroud of pure evil," Gideon read directly from a small notepad in which he had written quick notes for his report. "He said that at that moment it was as if this girl's body was flung into the center of the room, and . . . well, the best way he could describe it, it was as if there were creatures trapped inside of her, trying to come out all at once."

Serenity shuddered. "Leah, I have seen Possessors try to break free from a mortal, but this was as if there were several at one time. It wasn't like they were trying to break out, but they were trying to stretch her skin in order to make more room! It was like they were trying to . . . well, not just be *in* her but *be* her."

The Angel brushed away some of the young girl's hair from her face and began to silently listen . . . listen as only an Eternal can for the sound of an immortal. There was nothing. She detected no movement or even a murmur below the conscious level.

"Ok, so let's forgo the argument right now on why you brought her here. I understand you felt it was best; but if she is possessed, we must ensure that whatever is inside of her does not escape from this room. We have to bind it to the Abyss, and we also need to get her back to any family that might be looking for her."

Serenity looked up at Gideon, not sure how to proceed. "That is the strange thing, Leah. I have read all the diagnostics that would indicate any activity within her. There is nothing. There is no indication that there is anything supernatural going on here. None of the readouts reveal any double activity that would conclude that there is a Possessor inside of her. It is as if whatever was there is gone."

"Then why is she still here? We need to get her to one of the hospitals where we have a network, and then . . ."

"She is still here, Leah, because none of us ever saw anything leave her. We think that, somehow, whatever is inside of her is deep—almost dormant—and may be waiting."

Leah looked to Serenity for any other words. "Do you have any test showing this?"

Serenity shook her head in disappointment. She knew what Leah was going to say. "No, but that doesn't mean . . ."

"Doesn't mean what? Doesn't mean that we could have something just lying inside this girl waiting for us to turn our back?"

Serenity stared at Leah for a moment and then turned her eyes over Leah's shoulder to stare at the wall. "It doesn't mean I don't know what we saw, but we will get her to a hospital or to one of the safe houses. She is sedated, so she will not remember any of her time here."

"Do it now," Leah stated with authority and walked out, leaving the other two with the young girl.

Serenity turned and, with one hard push, shoved all her paperwork and notes off the small rolling table that she had beside the bed. "I am tired of it, Gideon! This is not what I signed up for when I joined the Alliance. I think she forgets that we mortals have a choice to be here or not be here! I give two flying hoots if she doesn't; but I do, and . . ."

Gideon's voice was strong and steady as he spoke. He knew mortals tended to allow their emotions to rise hard to the surface. Heck, what was he thinking? So did Angels. "Serenity, I don't know what has been up with her lately, but she does have a point. Could she have put it to you better? Probably, but she is right."

She placed both hands on the edge of the chrome table as she leaned over it and just tried to calm herself. She had not only been a great fighting member of the Alliance, but she had used her medical expertise to really add another dimension to the Sanctum and the work of the Alliance.

"I will have Chad drive her to the hospital tonight. A few of the Alliance network should be working tonight, so they will know to take her and not ask questions."

"Sounds like a plan. You let me talk to Leah, ok?"

Serenity just nodded.

Chapter Eight

She closed the door to her living quarters behind her as she turned on the lights. Her body felt worn down, and her mind screamed for an "off" switch that seemed to be hidden within the riddle of existence right now. Leah didn't even feel like loosening the straps on her boots. All she wanted was a shower, bed, and . . . honestly, a chance to hope again.

She lay back on her bed and stretched her legs straight out, throwing her arms above her head. She had to rest, but these days rest was like an elusive wisp of smoke that kept asking for one to wave their hands through it but is never really there.

"To think there was a time I thrived for all of this—a time where I could go days without even taking a break due to the vigor and passion, and now I can't even stop to catch my breath if I wanted to!"

Her mind was all over the place tonight. Tomorrow she was going to be visiting Scintillantes, and she knew that would be an ordeal because the Arch Council was pushing hard on the Alliance members to step back and let things be. Many were doing that; however, she was the one rebel, and that came with threats of being stripped of her leadership.

She felt as though the Arch Council had given up on humanity and decided to allow the Fallen to overrun mankind. She couldn't be upset at the points Serenity made earlier in the med area; she fully felt the same way. She would die fighting to keep that from happening. If she did just give up, then that would mean she had no reason to really exist. Wasn't this the very reason the Alliance was formed?

Her mind played back over the last several years and the rebuke she had received over and over for protecting humanity. She had watched as the Clans were rocked back into the shadows. She had fought to keep it that way and even spoke up to the fact that now was the time to take them out. "Follow them into the shadows, and expose them all," she had told the Council.

She had been held back at every crossroad; and during the moments that she took her team into the shadows, they discovered there was never support . . . they found themselves alone. Tonight, would just be one more checkbox on the Arch Council's long list of unauthorized missions; and yet tonight also showed more than ever that there was a growing, unknown danger that was beginning to peek out and expose itself.

"What is going on?" She sat up and allowed her feet to rest on the floor. She ran her fingers through her hair and then stood up. She walked to a door that opened out onto a metal landing. She had it built about a year ago. She was tired of the stuffiness of the Sanctum, and there were times she just wanted to escape to the outside but still have her privacy.

She looked up at the night sky and realized that the night itself would soon be getting rest. Where had the night gone? Was the morning only a few hours away? She inhaled and held her breath for a moment. If only she could just stop time—even briefly. "Why do I feel, once again, that I am powerless and lost? I don't understand why it is that this feeling never seems to leave me no matter how much I try to stay in front of everything."

Over the last few years, she had learned to truly forgive herself for the moments she had fallen short, for the missions she had not gotten right, and for those she had attempted to protect but may have not been able to. She had grown inwardly quite a bit. She had learned to shed the things that were beyond her control and those moments in the past that she could no longer change. She had to. It had been destroying her.

Her hand instinctively went to the small vial that hung around her neck: Joan's necklace. She had even come to an understanding with herself that the only way to ensure that she did not lose another "Joan" was to make sure her mind was present. She had beat herself up for too long over it, and this moment right here was where she existed.

*****

Chad was careful to ensure the young girl was strapped into the seat of the SUV before closing the door. She was in a medically-induced sleep in order to keep her from waking up while under the supervision of the Alliance.

Several tests had been run on her, but nothing revealed anything supernatural. Of course, that just meant that if there was or had been anything, it was able to stay undetected. He knew that the team had taken some great risk bringing her into the Sanctum without permission from Leah, but it just seemed right.

He walked around to the driver's side and opened the door to get in when the passenger's side opened, and Serenity slid in.

"Oh, come on, Serenity! You know Leah doesn't want you taking her . . . let alone if she finds out it was both of us together."

She smiled that killer smile. "Well, then we better get going before she realizes that both of us are missing and puts two and two together."

"No, I am not doing this; she is already angry enough."

"Chad, you know what we saw! You know there was something going on; and we both know that this girl is either a link to it, or she can tell us what was going on! This is big! There is no way that the Fallen were just chillin' with all that activity."

"Right now," he said as he threw his hands up in submission, "I really don't care. I just want to get back here and get some sleep. I still smell like ash from those vampires' disintegrating."

"Demons."

"Oh, shut up!"

They drove out from one of the bay doors and into the darkness that was making way for the morning sun to peek up over the horizon. The city was waking up, and people were starting to move about. As mortals, both Chad and Serenity often wondered what it was that they couldn't see; then again, Chad knew that it was probably better that he didn't know.

They drove in silence for a while toward the hospital downtown; but he knew the silence wouldn't last for long . . . and it didn't.

"What do you think is going on?" Serenity posed the question. We have Fallen activity that can't be explained, and I have heard some of the other Alliance members say that many of the Clans seem to have gone underground as if preparing for a 'lull-before-the-storm.' Everyone you talk to expresses a feeling of uneasiness, and nothing seems to be right anymore." She looked at him, expecting him to participate in this conversation.

He didn't want to; he sat there quietly.

"Oh, come on, Chad! Stop being a punk! You know you can feel it! Even as a mortal I can feel it in the air! I can feel something is happening."

He shook his head. "Serenity, I don't care. I just want to go kill vamp . . . *demons* . . . and go to sleep. Just maybe I can catch a good flick at the theater and one day have the chance to have a real date. Outside of all that, I just don't care."

She turned and looked at him with a look that said, "There is no way you are that shallow."

He didn't say anything more.

*****

Behind them, the young lady was buckled in, her body still in an induced sleep but only physically. Deep below the surface, voices danced about, and madness screamed at her.

"What is your name?"

"Leave me alone," the girl's spirit sobbed. "Leave me alone. Let me be. You know my name!"

"You chose to be at the gathering tonight. I am here because you chose it."

"No, I didn't choose this. I want to be left alone."

"You were there."

"I DON'T CARE! I don't want you! Leave!" she screamed out within the hollowness of her spiritual existence. "Don't you get it?"

"What is your name?"

Her spirit shivered and trembled, curled up in a dark corner of her mind. She didn't want to speak, and she didn't want to exist;

she wanted to escape. That is all she had ever wanted for so long. Her parents never seemed to care, and her friends never were really true friends. She was alone. She had only wanted some consistency, acceptance, and love . . . not this.

"You know my name! You called me by it. My name is Victoria."

"Some of us know it; some of us do not. Victoria, you are part of us now; and we are a part of you until he comes."

Sobs . . . more sobs. Trembling . . . more trembling. "No, this is a dream!" She began to tear at the skin on her arms. As she did, her body began to shake. Skin began to fall away in ribbons, and just below the surface of her skin were black, centipede-like worms crawling en masse.

"NO, let me go! Let me be!" She could feel the black worms crawling in and out of her skin now, and she could hear voices of different evil pitches laughing. It was as if she was drowning in a well of sulfuric evil.

"You chose for us to be here," a little girl's voice sneered.

"Who are you?" She was full out shaking now. There was no more trembling. This was a soul's last effort to break out of a living horror but unable to shake the bonds that held her. "Wh . . . who are you?"

"We are him, and he is us."

"Who?"

"Legion . . . and he comes."

*****

Chad slammed on the brakes and jerked the wheel to the right as he pulled the car over and leaped out of the driver's side door.

He flung the back passenger door open where the young girl's body was convulsing as foam dripped from her lips.

"What in the world is going on?" he yelled.

"I told you! There is something inside of her!"

"It can't be! You tested her!"

"I know, but I also know what I feel; and I know what we saw at The Warehouse. Chad, be careful! There is something taking her down inside!"

As Serenity jumped out, she flung the opposite door open and looked in horror as the young lady's body bent in unnatural positions against the restraints of the seat belt. Serenity thought she was going to lose it as the girl's skin began to ripple as if there were thousands of creatures beneath it.

"Chad . . . be careful!"

Chad reached into a cargo pocket on his pants and pulled out a plastic vial that had a breakaway tip. He pressed firmly with his thumb, and the top snapped clear. He thrust the tip of the vial between the lips and over the tongue of the convulsing girl. Her eyes shot open and she looked straight at him, but nothing but black could be seen where eyes should be. With inhuman strength the girl shoved Chad, and he felt himself get flung backward.

"Not that easy, Momma's Boy," a voice spat out from the girl's mouth that was clearly that of a man, a man's voice trimmed in the anguish of the screaming of a thousand souls.

Chad was shoved into oncoming traffic. The squealing of tires stabbed at his ears, giving him no room to doubt his mortality. If that was not enough, the smell of burning rubber and the showering of stone and street crud hitting his face as vehicles did what they could to avoid him clearly brought his life into perspective. Horns honked, and he could feel the wind of a truck as it missed his head by inches. He felt a strong hand grab him by his arm and pull him into the air and back toward the SUV. It all had happened in a minute, but it seemed like 15.

The young lady in the car was screaming as she now thrashed at Serenity. The Alliance member had a sedation syringe from a kit she carried on her, and soon the girl was once again out.

Chad brushed himself off as he looked over to the Guardian who had pulled him from the traffic. "Thanks, Man."

"Not a problem," the Angel said. "What in the world do you all have in there?" He motioned toward the vehicle.

"We aren't sure, but what we do know is that we can't take her to the hospital like this," Serenity stated matter-of-factly as she came around to the front of the vehicle.

"Gideon told me to protect you guys if you needed it. I am glad he sent me. He didn't say anything about a Familiar."

"He did what?" Chad asked in almost aggravation. "If he sent a Guardian, then he must have also believed there was something else to this girl."

"Told you," Serenity smirked.

Chad just shook his head and walked back around to the open passenger door and looked at the young lady. "Ok, so what do we do now?"

"You tell me," Serenity stated. "Leah said she is fine . . ."

"Yes, but that was based upon your test."

"Ok, either way, we can't take her back to the Sanctum. That's all we need is to have whatever is in her to decide that being inside her is not as cool as taking on the Alliance inside the Sanctum or, even worse, breaking through Patmos."

Chad ran his fingers through his hair and rested his head

against the top of the door. He looked over to the Guardian. "Any suggestions? You are the immortal here."

He looked just as lost. He didn't have anything to do with any of this. His job was to guard, and Chad was grateful he had done his job well.

"Please, Sir, don't let them take over."

"Where are we going to take her? We can't take her back to the Sanctum!" Chad couldn't think. He was pacing back and forth in front of the vehicle with his arms up and fingers interlaced behind his head. He was lost. He had been given direct orders from Leah to get this young lady to a hospital; but after what he just saw, he knew they couldn't do that.

Serenity sat on the hood of the SUV and watched as the traffic passed. "What ARE we supposed to do, Chad? I mean, come on! We are mortals, and whatever *that* was can for sure be marked as NOT mortal."

He just stopped and looked back at her. She had been a part of the Alliance before him, but they had really grown close. They made a great team, but right now this team seemed to have no clue.

"Let's think this through," he said. "According to your test it appears that there is nothing supernatural within her, but we both saw her body be thrown into the center of the room, and we both just witnessed all that commotion and crazy speaking." He began waving his arms around as he tried to make his point. "If it wasn't for what happened at The Warehouse and that crazy, insane strength and voice, we could say that maybe she is mentally unstable; but that isn't it. Well, I mean, it could be part of it . . . *no offense.*" He emphasized the last part as he motioned toward the young lady as if she could hear him. "But we do know there is something."

"Something that can go so deep within a mortal that it is as if it is part of them . . . or *is* them! This thing is stronger and deeper than any Possessor," Serenity stated. "This thing scares me."

"Well, let's just get a bottle of holy water and throw it on her and leave her here."

"Chad!"

"I was joking! Sheesh, give me some credit. I have to have something to ease this situation."

"Hey, I know where we can take her! Get in!"

Chad looked at her inquisitively. It was never a good thing when Serenity all of a sudden had an epiphany. "Where?"

"To someone who will understand her better than we can."

Chad just stared at her. "No!"

"Got a better idea?"

"No."

"Then get in! I am driving." Serenity jumped off the hood of the vehicle and made her way to the driver's side. Everything in him told Chad this was not going to be good, but he knew that arguing with her would be of no use . . . and she was right: there was nothing better.

He threw her the keys and got in.

*****

"Where are you taking me?" a soft and scared voice asked from the back seat. "Are you kidnapping me?"

Chad lifted his head from where he had been resting against the window as Serenity drove toward their destination. He didn't even realize that he had dozed off. "No, Victoria, we are not kidnapping you. We are trying to protect you."

Victoria sat up in her seat and looked out the window of the SUV. The sun was just breaking the horizon; and from the scenery, she could tell she was far from the city.

"Protect me from what? Who are you?"

Serenity looked back to her left to see if she could switch lanes and then allowed the vehicle to drift in that direction. She was relieved that her two traveling companions had awakened because she herself had started getting drowsy. They had been traveling for a few hours, and she had not slept now for almost 24 hours.

Serenity looked in the rearview mirror at their passenger. She looked normal—like a teen girl who had a rough night—but normal. She could see the confusion on the girl's face. Clearly, this young lady had been through a lot. She didn't show signs of panic, even though she had awakened to find herself in a vehicle with two strangers.

"Going to answer my questions or do I just wait for you two psychos to dump me on the side of the road? Also, how in the world do you know my name?"

"I'm Chad and this is Serenity, and we know your name from your driver's license."

"Well, guess the license can't tell you that I prefer the name Tori . . . and oh, by the way, I don't scare easily."

"Glad you don't, Tori," Serenity stated, "because we aren't trying to scare you. You got yourself in some pretty deep stuff last night, and we are helping you."

"Like what? Did I snort some crank and slash the throat of the mayor's wife?"

They both ignored her questions.

"What do you remember?" Serenity asked as she steered the vehicle down an exit ramp and onto a two-lane road.

"I remember that my mom told me not to talk to strangers!" Even with her brash and protective shell, in all honesty, she didn't feel uncertain or hesitant towards her new traveling companions. Her *body* felt worn down, as one feels after a heavy workout, and her mind and thoughts were fatigued and foggy; however, even with all of that, she felt safe, and that was strange to her. She didn't remember the last time she felt safe; safe was something she was not used to feeling.

She paused for a moment and then cooled her tone a bit. "I remember getting in a fight with my dad. I remember heading out to The Warehouse, which is this new club."

Chad stopped her. "The Warehouse? What do you remember about that?"

"Well, Jason . . . this guy I know . . . took me there. He is kind of like my boyfriend, but we both have agreed not to make it exclusive—too many hot guys out there for that!"

Chad looked at Serenity with a "Ya-see . . . too-many-fish-in-the-sea" look. She rolled her eyes at him.

"What happened there?"

"I don't know," Tori shrugged. She sat there with her arm across her belly and pushed away some of her hair from her face. As old as she may think she was, Serenity still saw a scared little girl. She remembered when she had been there: the world knocking at life's door, yet still wanting to be just a little girl . . . but you didn't want your friends to know.

"You know, Jason knows a lot of people there. It is not a place I usually would hang out at. It is really dark."

"Aren't places like that supposed to be dark?" Serenity inquired.

"Yeah, but not like this . . . hard to explain."

"Dark as in 'it-touches-your-soul' dark?"

She looked at Chad's face as he sat in the front passenger's seat. "Yeah . . . just like that. There are weird things that go on there! Not just drugs and the normal club stuff . . . I mean like dark and really deranged!"

Silence once again fell over the occupants as Tori again turned her attention out the window. She watched as they passed fields and farm structures. She didn't want to talk about any of it, because talking about it made it real . . . and real was not what she wanted it to be. Right now, she didn't care who these two people were or even where they were taking her. She had never seen the wide-open countryside; and right now, anything was better than her apartment with her father . . . or The Warehouse.

"Can you be more specific about what kind of 'weird things'?" Chad asked as Serenity slowed down, entering a one-stoplight town.

"Let's talk about this a little bit later," Serenity suggested, giving a bit of a glare in his direction, indicating he was pushing a bit hard. "I think we all could go for some breakfast."

"Also, a chance to clean up, if that is ok with everyone else. I'm sure I look like a freak show," Tori stated as she sat up and looked at herself in the mirror upfront.

Serenity nodded, "I think we all do."

Chapter Nine

There were a few farm trucks parked outside the large diner, and Zarius could see that the diner was full of locals. He knew that in a few hours there would be a small-town buzz humming around the area, but at this moment things were still fairly quiet.

He shut off the motor to his bike and kicked down the kickstand. His body was stiff, but the long ride had done him good. The miles of roadway had brought focus to his mind, and his resilience was set. He knew the road that lay ahead wasn't going to be easy; and honestly, he had no idea how it all would play out, but he had to go through with it.

The small mom-and-pop diner sat on the corner of a county road and Main Street. The two-story building had been built years ago and hadn't changed much since. The white paint that once looked sharp was now in real need of a repaint. The shutters on the top floor windows had a few slats missing; and the awnings that were once vibrant just above the ground-level windows, the summer sun and winter snows had long worn their appearance.

He walked to the corner and opened the large wooden door to the diner. The expected sounds of morning talk, a conversation about hunting season, and requests for more coffee came wafting over him as the front door closed behind him. There were a few open tables, and his eyes landed on one to his right. The table was mixed in the middle of several tables full of locals, but that didn't bother him. He needed some food, and then he would figure out his next course of action.

The table was just big enough to make four people feel crowded, two feel close, and one to feel like they just had enough space for a big country breakfast. It was covered in a thick, slick tablecloth with a small tear here and there; and he was pretty sure, if he cared to, he could find a complete pack of chewed gum stuck underneath it all. Fortunately, there were no strange stares that focused his way. One always had a fifty-fifty chance in a small town diner of either getting strange glares or not be noticed at all; it seemed the latter was the course for the day.

He chuckled, "Yeah, but give it a few hours, and have a few of the town busybodies to stop by. Then there would be gossip about him all the way into the next county."

With no attempt at etiquette, a large plate of over-easy eggs, three thick-cut pieces of bacon, and hash browns were dropped down on the table in front of him, startling him. "I figured I would keep the menus over by the cash register and not waste my time at pleasantries and just bring out what you would order. Don't worry, the burnt coffee will be right up. Of course, that is unless your taste has changed over the years, Zarius!"

The waitress was a curvy lady in her late 40s, red hair pulled back in a ponytail, and a look spread across her face that would have made any rough country boy shaky in the legs.

He sat back, looking down at the plate. He didn't want to look up; in fact, he really didn't need to. He could feel her eyes boring into the side of his head, and he honestly wanted to just melt away or maybe even stick himself to the gum underneath the table. "No . . . um . . . this is fine, Abby."

"'This is fine, Abby'? That is what you are going to say to me? Really?"

So much for not having the strange stares focused on him right now. He was pretty sure that every eye in the place was focused right at him. There was no escaping any of this. There was no way he could have known that over 20-something years later she would still be working here, and yet he should have figured.

"Always was a small-town girl."

"Everyone," she yelled out, "how many of you have heard about the smooth-talking snake charmer who walked out on me years ago right before my father passed away?"

"Wait!" He looked up at her; and yes, her eyes were as red as her ponytail hair. "Your dad is dead?"

With one smooth motion and no hesitation at all, he watched her hand swing toward his face; and before it registered, he felt the sting and the heat of the smack spread across him. "Yeah," she continued at the elevated volume, "this is the jackass!"

There were several shaking their heads, and a few profane-laced phrases hurled his way; but the patrons quickly went back to their conversation and coffee, which Zarius was pretty sure was, in fact, not burnt.

"Abby, I . . ."

"You aren't going to say anything right this second, ya hear? You are going to sit right there and enjoy your eggs, bacon, and hash browns. You will drink the coffee I bring; and while you are doing all that, you will listen to me as I take my break for the morning. Ezekiel, I'm off the clock for a few!" She pulled out another chair and sat right across from him.

Abby McGraf had grown up here all her life. And yes, she was a small-town gal, and she was also full of a lot of spitfire and kerosene. At 48, she had worked most of her life at the Four Corners Diner. Working there had always accomplished what she needed. She paid her bills; got to socialize with everyone; and, after a while, she became just as much a part of the diner as the worn-out awnings and shutters on the outside.

"Why in the world would you ever . . . especially after this long . . . EVER set foot back in this diner, let alone back in town? Oh, and don't give me any of the rubbish of being some long story!"

"Honestly, I don't know, Abby. I really don't know." He did know why he was back, but he couldn't give her the answers for which she was looking. She wanted reasons, and he couldn't give them.

Her hands were clenching and unclenching. "You know, Zarius, how about we play a game? How about I pick a number 2 through 12. If you roll my number, then you win; and I will get up and not talk to you again. If you don't roll my number, then you answer directly and right away the questions I ask . . . oh, wait . . . or did you lose your dice years ago?"

"Abby, let me talk. " He pushed the plate back and leaned forward. "There is nothing I can say . . . *nothing* . . . and you and I both know that. You can spend the rest of your break and thousands of more breaks, having me sit in silence and you yelling and berating me; and nothing will fix anything or heal any wounds I have caused."

"Heal? *Heal?*" she shoved back. "Is that what you think I need? Healing? Lawd, have mercy, and may the spirit fall down upon me with blessings and healings," she yelled out as she threw her hands up in the air and waved them around as if she was in a Pentecostal revival service. "No, Sir. It is not healing I need!

I healed a long time ago. Yes, it took me a few years to get over it . . . especially when the one man who made me believe that he was different, the one I needed more than anything when my dad passed, was the one man who walked out and vanished without even a word. I don't need healing; I have allowed it to scab over and even scar up. It is a reminder to never let myself be vulnerable like that again. In fact, I guess I should thank you. You allowed me to see that I was strong enough to handle on my own the gut punches life gives."

"I was wrong, Abby, and I'm sorry."

She sat there and looked at him. She never imagined there would ever come a day when she would look up and see him once again walk through the door. When he did, she had actually touched her forearm to the coffee pot to make sure she wasn't dreaming.

"You know, Zarius, maybe I don't want answers. You are right; nothing you can say will make it clear. I won't understand, most likely; nor will I understand how it is that, after all these years, you look almost the same as you did the last day I saw you."

"I'm sorry to hear about your dad, Abby."

"No," she raised her palm toward him, "don't. You don't get to. You don't get to be sorry about his death. He loved you, Zarius. He told me just a few days before you left that if there was ever a guy he would have picked for his daughter to be with, it would have been you. A few days later he swore he would kill you and feed your body to the hogs if he ever saw you again. Be grateful he never did."

Abby stood up and straightened the apron tied around her waist. "I'll get you some fresh food. That was made up from some food that had been returned because someone decided they were too drunk to eat it. I'm not sure why you came back, but do me a favor:" she suggested as she picked up his plate, "make sure it wasn't for me; and for whatever reason, leave me out of it."

"Yeah . . . I can respect that."

*****

As Serenity found a parking spot between a pickup and a black motorcycle, Chad could not help but ask Tori, "What did you mean by 'dark things'?"

"Well, there was the usual stuff . . . I mean, you know, people doing drugs. I don't do them, but who am I to judge if someone else wants to. But the few times I have been there, I noticed that Jason and some of his friends were biting each other's wrists and licking away the blood. I'm sure it was staged but just not my thing. I agreed to go back last night because I just wanted out of my place. Trust me when you have the degenerate for a dad that I do, you will take people playing vampires any day."

She stopped and thought. "You know, I do remember something. Last night was different. I noticed a lot more people there than I have the few times we have gone before. Several seemed to know Jason, but I didn't know them. I noticed that once we went into The Warehouse, Jason seemed to change."

"'Change'?" Serenity questioned. "How so?"

"I don't know. As I said, he is kind of like my boyfriend . . . but not. I respect there are a lot of things about him I didn't really know. But he was connected, so he got me into places."

"But you said he changed."

"Yeah, he spoke in a deeper voice; and his actions just seemed . . . different. I know it may sound weird, but it was almost like someone had stolen Jason and replaced him with a darker version of himself. Not sure how much darker you could get, but he gave off a pretty dark vibe."

Chad sat there for a second and attempted to piece all of this together. He looked at Serenity and wondered what she was thinking. "Well, let's talk about this inside. I don't know about you both, but I am hungry."

The other two nodded as doors opened. They all climbed out into the rays of the morning sunrise. Victoria had the chance to see her reflection in the window of the car and realized how disheveled she looked. "I for sure need to clean up before I sit down inside any restaurant!"

"Chad, find us a booth, and we will catch up with you. We are going to head to the bathroom first."

"Why? We could . . ." He stopped short of finishing his sentence as he caught Serenity's "shut-up" look. "Um . . . why don't I just shut my mouth and get a booth?"

The three were met with the smells of coffee that had splashed upon the hot plate and started burning, as well as the aroma of eggs, bacon, and that smell that is given off by an old furnace. It seemed welcoming and inviting; and that is what they all needed right now, even though for each of them it may have been for different reasons.

*****

Zarius sat looking at the new plate of breakfast that Abby had dropped off. That was all he could do. He missed his wife; his heart hurt for the pain he clearly had caused Abby. Everything about Eden was flooding in on him. The reasons he was here—the past that he had left, the future that it most likely held, and the present that seemed to whip at his soul like a cat-o-nine tails—thrashed deeply painful and treacherous gashes.

He felt the breeze from outside come past him as the door to the diner opened, and he watched as three new patrons walked in: a guy and two ladies. They caught his attention because their style of clothes and their demeanor clearly did not scream, "I'm from around here."

"Well, looks like I'm not the only out-of-towner here," he sighed, pushing the hash browns into the egg yolk. "Of course, I guess to some I am not an out-of-towner, just a prodigal."

He watched Abby as she moved around, serving individuals. Serving . . . she had always had the heart of a servant. They had been in their early 20s, and it was shortly before he had met his wife. He had spent ages attempting to hide and blend in with humanity. He had kept his distance from real relationships; then again, Abby had been so full of life and such a gentle spirit. She had reminded him so much of a time when life was simpler.

He had come to this small town, drawn to it because of what it held, even though no one within the small farming community could ever have imagined it. He had hoped with everything in him that he would become free, and in some ways he had. He had learned about a path he could choose to follow of which he had never before been aware. That path had made him who he was today; but in doing so, he discovered a world beyond even what his mind could understand. His destiny began to grow; and for every truth he thought he had known, more was revealed. His understanding of existence had begun to unravel.

He thought about what his wife had asked him a few hours earlier when they spoke. She had asked him what he knew of his history. He had bristled at that. A feeling, long buried, had begun to swell in him . . . one from which he had run years before.

In fact, it was questions like those his wife had begun to put forward that caused him to run from here the first time; now it seemed the very same questions brought him back.

Abby had been such a part of his existence here. He had never intended to hurt her; yet it was clear that when one runs from questions they may not want to face, it leaves others to face them . . . others who should have never had to face them but were forced to and, in doing so, were drawn in like a hangman's noose to the point of choking the life out of them.

Yep, he was done. He couldn't stay here. He had to focus. He had to move forward. He couldn't let the fears of yesteryear become the bullet in the assassin's gun for anyone else . . . not this time. He downed the last bit of coffee in his mug, stood, and threw a tip onto the table along with enough money to pay for his breakfast. He headed out the door, past the three who had just come in. He needed to ride a bit more . . . ride and think.

*****

The girls made their way quickly toward the ladies' room as Chad made his way toward one of the small square tables. He quickly chose one next to a few older men in trucker caps and overalls.

He sat . . . or actually plopped . . . down and let out a long sigh. "What are we doing here?" he pondered. "I know Gideon has to be wondering about us by now, and just wait until Leah catches wind of this."

"So is that your boyfriend?" Tori asked as she pushed open the off-white, worn restroom door that displayed the traditional silhouette of a thick woman in a dress and a perfectly round head.

Serenity laughed out loud as she followed the teen and looked at herself in the mirror that met them straight on. "No, we work together."

She turned to Victoria and held out her hand. "By the way, I am Serenity, and that guy out there," nodding her head back toward the diner, "his name is Chad. I know we already told you, but I wanted it to be less like an interrogation."

Tori took her hand and shook it, but the smile turned quickly to tears. "What is going on with me, Serenity? I actually do have a lot of memories from last night, but I am not sure if they are real or more of a nightmare. I mean, you would think that the biggest worry that I have is that I am with two complete strangers in a really whacked-out, 'horror-film-style' diner, but I . . . I am so scared."

"We are going to find that out, Tori. But first we need you to finish telling us what you remember. Also, what about any family that may be worried about you?"

Tori turned on the water faucet and splashed water in her face as she let out something that sounded like a blend of a laugh and a cough. "Good luck when it comes to family. My mom left us; and shortly after, she passed away. My dad never knows where I am and couldn't care less. He should have been jailed a long time ago, but the system only protects those that it wishes to. To them, I am just another statistic." She began doing her best to straighten any tangles in her hair by running her fingers through it. "I have been pretty much on my own since I was ten."

Serenity put a hand upon her back as she began to see more of the soul of this young lady come forward. "Well, you are not alone, anymore. Chad and I are a part of something a lot bigger and safer than that 'club' you were in last night, and we specialize in those who are alone." She almost said that last part with a grin, thinking, ". . . more than you will ever know."

The teen girl looked at herself in the mirror one last time and then back at Serenity. "You know, I can feel it. I can't explain it, but I can feel it in both of you."

"That's good . . . now, let's get something to eat!"

"Lead the way!" The young girl smiled as she motioned toward the door. They both headed back into the main diner area and toward food. "By the way . . ."

"Yes?" Serenity replied.

"I think Chad likes you."

Serenity just smiled.

Chapter Ten

"You ever miss being away from here?"

"You mean, do I miss humanity's existence?"

Gabriel smiled at Metatron's minimalist description of what she was asking.

The two members of the Arch Council were sitting together in a secluded area just outside the Hall of Heroes. They both gleaned needed strength from each other.

"I know you were speaking more rhetorically, My Friend, but that is a hard question to answer," Metatron stated as he looked over at her.

"Really? Why do you think so?"

"Since my ascension, my mind has been opened; and I have seen a clearer and larger picture about existence itself. If a mortal man holds a small mouse inside a cage from the time the mouse is born until its later years and then the mouse is let go into a field, does the mouse miss the cage?"

"I guess that's why I am asking you, Metatron. I don't know. I was formed into the world where you sit. It is a world that cannot comprehend the matter of time that was designed after our kind was made. Jah created time after the War of the Serpents, once it was realized that when one has everything they could desire within an infinite space, what should be valued is not. Scintillantes and this existence are what I know."

Gabriel looked around her at the vibrant landscape and architecture that could only be dreamed of outside the scope and hindrance of a human mind. "Ages had to come and go—even time within the world of mortality—in order for me to consciously learn to appreciate and value what I am given. At times, I feel as the mouse you described; but I am a mouse who has been allowed to roam free. I have spent my existence fighting predators. At times, I believed I was the pinnacle of beings. But then, watching humanity, I ponder what it would be like to know there is an end and then to appreciate what I have before that end vanishes me into nothingness."

Metatron contemplated on what Gabriel had just said. He could hear the pureness in her statement, and he could understand some of the emotion tied to her words. The truth is that he had stood on both sides of eternity. He had been the mouse within the cage and the mouse in the field. He had felt like steam rolling inside a pot but then felt as though the lid had been taken off. He understood the feeling of vapor rolling free; but once outside of what appeared to be captivity, that steam became a part of a larger atmosphere and vanished into nothing of its previous form. It became part of a larger picture by changing its structure and, ultimately, vanishing.

"I remember what it is like to be mortal, as well as immortal, Gabriel. What I know is that our existence, here or there, is about more than existence itself. If we can truly appreciate that we are all a part of the one before us and the one after us, we will go further, live happier, and discover that your original question would not matter."

"Why is it hard to understand? Here, I have known only an existence not limited by time; yet, mortals are bound by it. Both find it hard to just simply 'be.' Why is it hard for us to just live in existence as you state?"

Metatron laughed. "Gabriel, it boils down to the truth that the intoxicating hunger for power and control are deeply embedded in the evolution of matter. Humanity feels the burden of time weighing down on their every move. Is this going to be the last ride I take, the last individual I fall in love with, the last experience I am going to have? If it is, then how long will I be remembered? Will I regret how I lived it . . . or, in essence, how I *controlled* it? Those who were designed and came into existence before the constraint of time still feel the need to rise up. Instead of taking that hunger and using it for what it was intended . . ."

"And what is that? Why do we all have this insatiable desire for control and power?" Gabriel asked as she looked at Metatron, not even sure if he would be able to really answer her question.

He cocked his lips to one side and thought for a moment before answering. "I believe it is misunderstood and has become twisted. It is intended to grow within us and have us build each other up. It was meant for you to not be satisfied with where you are but to remember from where you have come. You then begin to see others who are where you used to be, and you begin to invest in them with your understanding and knowledge. The more one does this, the more empowered they feel, for the pure form of that need is the need to power others forward. If each person would do that, we all would become unified in conscience under a sense of joint empowerment."

She raised an eyebrow and looked at him. "You just lost me."

"Let me think . . ." How could he explain it more clearly and in a way that would not water down the point? "Simply, every aspect of existence is about balance. When darkness begins to be tapped into, it will then become unbalanced over light. What was supposed to be then becomes misunderstood, and soon what is misunderstood becomes what generations think to be fact. This is the poison of existence itself. This, then, can only be overcome by a deliberate focus on oneself to understand their true role. If they can discover that, then they can re-establish the balance and purpose. Power then does not become something wielded out of control but, instead, something administered out of pure desire to see the better in others."

Gabriel wasn't sure if she was really understanding his point, but she also knew that he would probably not become any clearer. She decided to drop the conversation and just spend time later dwelling on what he had shared with her.

"So, any thoughts on the council meeting today?" she asked as she stretched her legs out and leaned her head back.

"I think we all know what is happening."

"Sometimes, I do; and sometimes, I wonder if we are not just paranoid. We know that Michael is passionate about the Alliance members, their mission, principles, et cetera."

"Do we?"

She leaned her head forward and looked to see if he had any sign of joking; he did not. "What do you mean?"

"Do we know that? What is our role? Why are we supposed to have five council members?"

"Guess it goes back to balance and what you were saying earlier. Our role is to maintain balance within our existence and Scintillantes and to act on behalf of mortals before Jah. We have five members to ensure that we maintain the balance of free will and existence. Five is the number that indicates no fixed foundation. We are to maintain a free-flowing existence."

"Do we do that? A better question may be 'Does Michael allow us any of that?' Hasn't he kept us from filling the empty seat on the council?"

"I know that you and Michael don't see eye-to-eye on many things. I know that he, at times, can act aloof due to your former existence as a mortal, but what you are suggesting . . . I really can't see. He has tried to fill the seat, but we haven't found someone who is able to fulfill the duties of the Council."

"What is it that you believe I am suggesting?" Metatron laughed.

"That Michael has lost focus, that he is trying to run his own show, that he does things contrary to our original reason for being formed into the Arch Council."

"Now, you see, *you* just suggested all of that . . . not me."

Gabriel slapped Metatron hard across his chest. "You know I hate when you do that!"

"But you did! I didn't say any of that."

"So, you believe that he has it out for Leah, and he shouldn't? You believe that he is purposely setting her up for failure in order to replace her?"

"Again, *you* said that."

"Seriously, Metatron!"

He leaned forward, placing his elbows on his thighs and shaking his head. "I don't know. I know that something doesn't feel right. Each member knows that Michael has had it out for Leah. Why? That is what we don't know, but we know he does. Up to this point, we have been able to really keep her protected from his desire to take her from her team, but I fear that we may have run out of protection. My question is 'for what end goal?'"

"You mean what is his purpose for his going after her like a watchdog?"

"Yes. It makes no sense. Usually, if no sense can be made from it, then there is something that is missing; and I fear what that something may be. There is a sense that this is bigger than Leah and even bigger than us as an Arch Council. I don't know how but just a gut feeling."

"Let's hope you are not correct. I don't know what it is you are thinking this may be a part of, but I, for one, am ready for things to be smoother and not so complicated."

He looked at her with a "did-you-really-go-there" look and then stood up. "Speaking of meeting, I would imagine that our focus of that meeting should be here by now."

They both began to walk down the path toward the Great Council Hall. Gabriel knew she felt similar to what he had shared, but he also hoped they were both wrong.

*****

Water rushed over her body and traveled its course from the top of her head to the soles of her feet, splashing off every curve and point that it could find and wrapping her in a sheet of purity and serenity. This was something she could understand from mortals for even she could appreciate the tranquility and celestial aptitude of just letting go and letting the shower take control. Steam rose up around her and encompassed the small space in which she stood, and she could feel the tile of the walls change from cool to warm as everything succumbed to the water.

Leah closed her eyes and inhaled, allowing her chest to rise and then fall. Was she strong enough for this? Could she face the Arch Council without her team really knowing the reason for which she was going before them? Would they forgive her? Was this really it? Could she do this, or would they actually do something this time and she could stand proud to be a part of all of this?

"That would truly be a day when Hell froze over," she spoke softly to herself. She leaned back and allowed her wet hair to fall around her head. She wiped the water from her face. "Please forgive me for this," she whispered, wishing she could tell each of her team members to their face. She couldn't do that. If she did, they would try to stop her or join her; and this had to be solely her.

She opened the door to the shower and grabbed a white towel that was lying just in arm's reach and allowed it to unfold as she buried herself in it. She felt it whisk away the moisture from her skin; and she just stood there, breathing. Her body felt as if it was held down with heavy weights.

There were soft chants being piped into her room through hidden speakers, much like those within Patmos; but it did little to soothe her this morning. "Girl, are you sure you know what you are doing? You understand there is no turning back from this," she silently spoke to herself. "I know that. I know that more than anything, but this has gone on too long. Someone has to stand up for those who can't; and if my position here holds me from doing that because of the gains or losses of those in power, then I have to do something."

She went to her closet and pulled out the white hoodie that had become her "Arch Council Uniform." She laid it on her bed and walked just a few steps to a dresser where she pulled out a black tank top and allowed it to embrace her body. She followed it with a white pair of pants and then completed the ensemble with the hoodie. Once she was dressed, she took one more deep breath before leaving her quarters.

*****

The inner workings of the Sanctum were operating smoothly; Alliance members, both mortal and immortal, were coming and going. To most, it was just another very early morning. She needed them to feel this way: to concentrate on the different tasks at hand. They would still be here, and their missions and reasons for being here would all continue. The less they knew, the better for all . . . especially for her and her command team.

They had made so many improvements over the years to this place, it truly was the envy of many smaller Alliance groups. None of this mattered, though, if it were not for the people. They were the heartbeat of holding back the Fallen and ensuring the well-being of mortals.

"Mankind will never fully know what we do for them. How blind is mortality to truly believe they are the beginning and the end? It is as if they are a child really believing the sheets of their bed will hold back the evil in the closet."

She moved toward the conference room that had been the cerebrum of her leadership pinnacle here at Sanctum. She walked in as she slowly drew in a deep breath, smiling at the two old friends that sat there waiting for her. If she didn't know better, she would have thought she was trembling just slightly.

"Good Morning, Guys." She spoke in a warm tone. "I hope that you both slept better than I did last night."

Ki and Troy, with stoic strength etched on their face, bluffed that they did, even though all knew that none of this trio had slept even a wink.

Troy stood up and walked toward his leader and buried her in a hug. His prior military background always kept him at arm's length from his leader out of respect, but this morning she was a friend first . . . and a close one.

Leah accepted it. There was no need right now for rank. They were friends; they all had actually become even deeper than that: they had become family.

"I see that your implant is working," she expressed with some joy. "What exactly does it do?"

Troy, who had been blinded in combat by an IED, had been left with his life and the ability to only see the spiritual world and nothing of the physical. He had been working with Ki to create a computer implant that would move past the destroyed nerves and into the portion of the brain that would register images.

"It is working enough, but Ki thinks he can get it better. Right now, I struggle with three dimensional, and a lot of times it makes things appear as if I have a bad connection . . . kinda fuzzy. You won't hear me complain, though," he chuckled.

"So, what's the word, Boss?" Ki asked inquisitively. "Any possible chance you already know the outcome of this hearing?"

Leah's thoughts rushed in on her quicker than she expected as she began to think about how much this team had done together and how she never could have imagined that she would be facing the Arch Council to deal with a possible demotion. She shook her head and made her way to the head of the long conference table. This table had been gathered around by so many: Trinita, Alfonso, Isaiah, Gideon, Ki, Troy . . . even Eve had once sat here.

She sat down in her chair. Leaning forward, she placed her arms on the table top and just looked into the eyes of these two warriors—one mortal and one immortal. How fitting it seemed; it was the epitome of everything the Alliance stood for, everything for which she had fought throughout the ages.

"I don't know. All I know is that I am to appear before them in a hearing on the effectiveness of my leadership and the ability I have to continue to carry out the will of Jah without question, even if that means to allow the Fallen to gain ground against mortal man." The last part came out with inky bitterness. "Before we head into Patmos, I want to express to you both my heart. You both are warriors and true leaders.

"Troy, you have served both in the Army of mortals and alongside immortals. You are very aware of those individuals you would trust always with your life and with whom you would, without hesitation, go fully into battle. You are one of those men. You have shown strength beyond what many Fallen have even shown. We know how relentless they are," she laughed.

This brought a little joviality to the stiff air that was hovering over them. They each had good memories upon their thoughts, and she wanted them to stay that way.

"Ki, no matter what happens with the Council today, you know what needs to be done. You know what is going on around here, and you also know that someone needs to follow up with Isaiah. I believe that Alfonso's work with us lives on through him, and I think he may be onto something. Alfonso never did anything just to do it, and you can be sure if he sent Isaiah his notes . . . and on a trip into Hecate's territory . . . there is something to discover there."

Ki nodded but said nothing. He wouldn't right now. His stoic heart was steady as he prepared to walk with his leader to Patmos.

"Well," Leah said as she pushed herself away from the table, "let's do this."

The three were silent as they made their way into the center of the Sanctum to where the room, or gateway, known as Patmos was located. They were all familiar with the traditions and protocol that went with the usage of this gateway into Scintillantes. It had become second nature to the trio and, even under these circumstances, each step was followed to the exact requirements.

Soon they were inside the circular room; and Leah closed her eyes, longing for the music that filtered through Patmos to sooth the tempest within her. She ached deep inside her center. She hadn't felt this before; the pain seemed to be increasingly spreading outward, and with it, she felt anxiety and even anger.

She knelt on the cushions that circumvented the shaft of light that was found in the center of the room stretching from a white cubical altar to the ceiling. There was a sweet smell of incense that teased at her senses. Briefly she felt a warm, gentle breeze touch her skin. A peace seemed to linger, then vanish.

The troubled Angel opened her eyes and allowed her gaze to fall on her partners. They were in meditation, so she knew that the gateway would be opened. It required a link of meditation and prayers to stabilize for anyone to travel through the gateway.

She stood. She took in a deep breath, pulled the hood over her hair, closed her eyes, exhaled, and then stepped into the path of light.

Chapter Eleven

The rush of eternity in just one moment is something that can never really be understood until it is experienced. "In a way nauseating," Leah whispered to herself as she stepped into the Hall of Heroes, the other end of Patmos.

She pulled the hood back from her head and allowed it to hang down. Her crimson hair flowed down from her head, over her shoulders and the hood, and halfway down her back.

She scanned the corridor. She had heard rumors about an addition to the statue collection and wanted to see if they were true. Her steps echoed off the colorful marble as she left the corridor in which she had arrived and headed to the center. Any time an addition to the Hall was made—which it had been some time since that had happened—the new statute would be placed for a time in the center rotunda near the large fruit-bearing tree and then would be moved to its permanent space along the wall of one of the corridors that stretched out like the spokes of a wheel.

"There you are, Old Man." She smiled as she looked upon the statue of a much younger-looking Alfonso, younger than when he had been taken by Denora's torture. The image was most likely from when he first was chosen as a young man to become a Watcher. "How I hope that your eternity is beyond your imagination. You were so much to more people then you will ever know."

She kissed her fingertips and touched the cheek of the statue. She took one last look and turned and headed toward the doors that would lead her to the outside and closer to her meeting with the Arch Council.

*****

The Hall of the Arch Council was buzzing with activity as everything was being prepared. Nemamiah had arrived early in order to mentally prepare herself for what lay ahead. Inwardly she was in much turmoil over all that would be dealt with in this meeting, and the Council was well aware of her disagreements on it all. She knew she would have the chance to voice her opinions when the time came, but she was also certain that nothing she said would sway Michael. She paced the hall as she went over in her head what her argument would be. Her fingers traced the smooth curves of one of the seven clay pots that lined the room; she could almost feel the vastness that was within those pots.

"Leah, Leah, Leah, did I not warn you? Did I not tell you that you were your own enemy? Can I protect you this time?"

Others were moving in and out of the room as they were setting it up, but another female's voice spoke out over all the commotion, "You can't save those who don't wish to be saved, Nemamiah." It was the voice of Gabriel as she entered and spotted her fellow Council member.

"Do you think she has been given a just cause, Gabriel? Honestly? When did we reach out to her after Joan? When did we really give her a chance to heal, and then we threw her Eve? Is it really her fault that we lost Eve or was it the free choice of Eve?"

Gabriel raised her hand, stopping the Archangel from continuing. "This isn't the time. There are too many people moving in and out of the hall, and you know we are not going to settle anything between us."

"No, but maybe I can get you to understand what I am trying to say; and we can save one of our best Guardians."

"That is why we are having this hearing today." It was Metatron. He had just walked in to catch the end of the conversation between his two counterparts. "You are right, Nemamiah. She is one of our best; but, no matter, we must ensure she is still one of our best or if she has fallen short."

"How? By crucifying her?"

Metatron motioned for everyone else to leave the room as he closed the doors. "I am not here to crucify her. I am here to finally put an end to this Jerusalem Breed issue and help all of us move on. If by chance, in this, we discover that she did not perform her duties as a leader of the Alliance in her area . . . well, we will deal with that as it arises. My hope is that it won't, and we can all leave here with a better understanding."

"Pardon my choice of words here," Nemamiah spoke softer but still agitated, "but I smell a witch hunt here. It has been five years since Eve chose to walk her own path. Five years, and now we are hoping to ensure someone takes the fall for allowing the only Jerusalem Breed left to walk away from the table and become a renegade. I only fear that, in finding someone to blame for such a mistake, we will discover we have been the author of yet another one."

"A mistake?" This time they all turned as the last of the Arch Council members walked in. Michael walked in with authority and strength. He was not looking forward to today, but he also was a warrior. A warrior never relished battle but understood necessity was necessity.

"No, Michael, not a mistake, although one maybe could label it that. It is making another renegade."

"Do you think that is what will happen if today's Council does not go in Leah's favor? You think she will choose that?"

Only silence met his question as none of the Council members wanted to admit what they all were thinking. Maybe Nemamiah was correct. Maybe this was just a façade to pin some crucial mistakes on one who seemed fragile, anyway; however, not a single individual was talking.

"So be it," the brawny Archangel stated solemnly as he sat down at his place behind the Council table. "It will be her choice. We will not be the ones to put her there. I know that is not anything any of us will offer as a solution to all of this, but none of us can stop her from any choices she will make."

"We can't?" Nemamiah protested. "Really? So that is the way we work? You can live with yourself knowing that when we have needed her to do something, she has done it even if she did not agree to it . . . no questions asked?"

"She has done it?" Michael's voice was starting to rise. "*She has done it?* Really? So, when we told her to step back from Joan and allow the Fallen to take her, she did? So, she protected Eve as much as she could with the resources we gave her?" His fist came down upon the polished stone table. "Shall I go into how we have told her over and over to allow the Clans to fight amongst themselves and to stay out of it, yet continually she has stepped into the paths of the Fallen? To my understanding, she even had her team enter a nest last night!

"Do I need to remind you that each of us has made costly choices; and, in an attempt to fix the repercussions of those choices, we needed Leah to just do a simple thing: FOLLOW OUR COMMANDS? Is there anyone within this room that is willing to just step forward and admit to the mistakes we have made since the War of the Serpents; or are we determined to ensure we can fix those mistakes at our level?"

"And," Nemamiah quizzed, "are we not to stand against the onslaught of the Fallen, Michael, or have you forgotten who we are and why we even exist? Sure, we asked Leah to step back from Joan; yet when she didn't and Joan was still lost, we blamed her!"

Michael was standing again as he leaned forward over the table, eyes flashing. "Do not question me, Nemamiah, or my actions! You forget that I am the head of the Council here! Don't YOU forget that I was the very one who stood staring the Morning Star in his eyes daring him to take me on during the War of the Serpents! I am . . ."

"'I am'? 'I am'? 'I am'? I do recall those very words falling from the lips of one who once sat in your very seat, Michael . . . or was it more like "I *will* . . . 'I *will* ascend'? Yes, I think those were the words Lucifer stated in this very hall before his counterparts stormed the hall to kick off the very war of which you are speaking!" The hall fell silent as every head turned toward the Angel standing right inside the doors, her hair framing her face, and her white hoodie slightly unzipped. "But please, don't let me stop you! You were being so eloquent in your statements."

Leah stood there, not flinching and showing no emotion to the four members of the Council. She was there not to make friends, and she was pretty sure that the majority of them—if not all of them—felt the same. This was no "kumbaya" meeting.

*****

The Arch Council was seated, and Leah took her place in a seat in front of the Council table facing her peers. Her jaw was clenched, and she had to keep reminding herself to loosen her fingers from the tight fist into which they were balled. She was ready for a fight.

How ironic that it had come to this: fighting her own. Were they not the ones she should be looking to for help, leadership, and guidance? How was it then that they were the very individuals who, for their own "sake of power" (as she saw it), were now looking to turn her into an example for any other Alliance leader who would stand for the truth, even if that truth seemed to go against the Council?

Michael had several organized stacks of notes, but he didn't even bother looking at them. She was sure he had planned this out very strategically, and he would attempt to orchestrate it all like a conductor would a symphony.

"Leah, you are aware of why we are here today, correct?"

She nodded, refusing to give him the satisfaction of a verbal answer. They would draw this out for as long as it would take to make them feel good, and then the gavel would fall. "Has the thirst of mankind's religious power bled into the hearts of the Council?" she thought with a hint of sadness.

"Leah, I know that you believe we are out to get you. You have thought that for so long, and nothing this Council has been able to do has kept you from assuming you knew our intent. Sadly enough, your own paranoia has brought us to where we are today."

"And where is that, Michael?" Nemamiah asked, leaning over so that she could better see to her right where Michael sat. "I know that Leah states that she knows why she is here, but I want it officially stated here. I want it in the records why we brought one of our best leaders—one that we, at one time, considered to even sit alongside us—to this inquisition."

Metatron reached over and placed his hand on Nemamiah's. "Careful, My Friend, let the process balance itself out. You are not the only one here who stands for justice."

Nemamiah's hands trembled as she managed to keep her cool, but her eyes were flashing with anger and determination. This was wrong!

Michael pulled a piece of parchment from one of his stacks and began to read out loud. "On the basis of clear and open disregard to orders to stand down from specific areas of operation of the Fallen, Leah, you are being brought before this court to determine your status as an Alliance leader. It is to be determined if you have acted upon your own will and not on the will of Jah. Further, it is to be determined if there are any signs of the darkness within you that has caused so many of our brothers and sisters to become what is known as creatures of the dark, the Fallen. Further action will be based upon the findings of this Council.

"Furthermore, if it is determined that you are not guilty of any of these charges, all dealings in these matters will be closed and forgotten."

"By whom? The will of Jah? Who knows even if Jah's will is even what drives anything? What about the will of the almighty Council?" Leah whispered to herself.

Metatron was writing something down as Michael read from the decree. Leah had always felt that Metatron, a keeper of records for so long, really should understand her struggle with the Arch Council; but at times, she felt a dark cloud between them. He looked up from whatever it was he was writing as Michael stopped, and he looked at her. His eyes were set, and she could not determine how he felt about this.

Metatron indicated that he wanted a moment to speak. As he did so, he reached down to one side and grabbed something. "Michael, we are here to determine if this gallant leader has been faithful to our cause and to determine if she is still loyal . . . correct?"

"In certain terms," Michael responded, "but, not meaning any disrespect to what you are about to say, Metatron, there is a process to this, and we are getting ahead of ourselves."

"Oh, forget the process, Michael! Can't your stiff, analytical, by-the-book self just give this a break?" Metatron raised his voice as his fist slammed down. "We are not strangers here, and we all know that this is nothing less than a lynching!"

Leah's eyebrows raised as her eyes became round with surprise. She had come here with the belief that she would be the one standing with anger and raised voice, defending herself. She wasn't sure what to make of what she was hearing.

"Stand down, Metatron!" Michael raised his voice to match the tone of his fellow Council member. "Do you not see what this whole situation—caused by her rebellion—is doing to us all? Here we are now, fighting. Is this not what rebellion and her choice to go against our orders bring?"

"Disregard? To whom, Michael? You? What is it that you have against her? I have records here from Watchers who have stated nothing but the opposite . . . showing she has been nothing but a stellar leader and warrior!"

Gabriel gasped in disbelief as Metatron threw what appeared to be a book of antique fashion on to the table. "Where did you get that? Eternals are not to have access to the records of the Watchers! You know that!"

Nemamiah pushed back from the table as if the book itself was the disease of the Fallen. It might as well have been, for pride was one key that would open the door for the darkness to take root in the being of an Eternal. The records of a Watcher were never to be seen by an Eternal but were only for the purpose of ensuring historical accuracy and for mortals to discover the mysteries of Jah on earth.

Every eye was upon Metatron as he stood there, his chest rising and falling with anger as he looked at Michael. "Why should it not be here? Forget who gave it to me . . . but why not? Will the truth be seen, or is this Council here to burn this soldier of the Alliance upon stakes of hypocritical notions of what is right and wrong for our own power? Is that of Jah?"

Leah couldn't breathe. She had stood up and was looking at the book that was only a few feet from her. An Eternal rarely laid eyes upon the cover of the record of their existence. She knew that, even though it seemed to be one volume, this most likely was a compilation of many different things and not the detailed records that would be fully hidden until needed by Jah.

She watched as the Council members stood in disbelief and almost horror at what Metatron had brought before them. Michael's eyes were flashing with anger and rage as he stood there. Leah didn't know if he was angry because of what the book may say or the fact that Metatron was standing up to him. Then

153

again, the fact that Metatron had defied the very historical law that an Eternal was not to have access to such information also brought a new meaning to defiance and rebellion.

"What have you done, Metatron?" Michael was seething. "You have just sacrificed your position upon this Council by your act of rebellion and possibly have sealed your fate to exile . . . and for what?" He was angry. There was a reason that weapons were not allowed in the Council chamber, and right now Michael's fingers were itching to grasp his sword.

Leah could feel mixed emotions welling up within her. A crushing blow deep within her threatened to bring her to her knees as she realized that Michael was accusing her defender of treason to Jah and to the Arch Council by his actions. He had clearly gone against all the rules in order to protect her!

Gabriel was in tears. As strong as she was, she couldn't believe the darkness that was flooding the Council Hall through the breakout of emotion and anger that rushed from Metatron and Michael. "Stop! Both of you! Control what you are feeling right now!"

Leah knew she had to do something. Whether or not she was guilty of what Michael had accused her, she could not allow everything she had fought for, stood for, and stood with for ages fall apart. Sacrifice was exactly that. She knew the times she had "fallen on the sword" for those whom she led; and because of it, they stood even stronger behind her. She could not watch as Metatron stood being stripped of everything he was because he stood for her.

"Why, Michael?" she yelled out. "Why? Are you scared of the truth? Are we not defenders of the truth? If I am guilty as you have stated, and this is not your way of finding a pawn to place the blame on for the last of the Jerusalem Breed acting upon her free will, then what is it that you are scared those pages will reveal?"

"Shut up, Guardian!" Michael's warrior spirit was borderline crossing from anger to darkness. "You will stand down, and . . . *YOU*," pointing to Metatron, "will also stand down and be quiet! You are no longer a part of this Council!"

"By whose authority, Michael?" It was Nemamiah, now. "Whose authority? Yours?"

"We will deal with this after we have completed our first reason for being here."

Then he still has the right to speak. If he has not been officially removed properly, then he is still part of this Council."

Michael gritted his teeth and shoved his chair back. He needed to calm down. What was going on? Was this not clear evidence that by Leah's very presence darkness bled out?

He could feel the darkness, and he knew that she had been going against the authority of the Council to meet the Fallen on every front! True, it was for the protection of mortals, but even the most heartfelt action done in wrong was still wrong.

"You want me off this Council, then so be it!" Michael turned in disbelief as Metatron's voice broke through his emotion. "So be it!" he repeated louder. "I cannot be a part of what this Council has become! This is not what we were formed to be."

Nemamiah's being sunk in her chair as she watched Metatron pull from his finger his ring, a symbol of a Council member, and place it upon the table. It was not supposed to be like this . . . not like this.

"Mark my words, Michael, what has taken place here today is only the start. You cannot fathom what has happened here; and there will come a point where you will fall to your knees, wishing you still had her," he stated as he pointed to Leah, "as one of your leaders."

The Angel walked from around the table and, in just a few steps, was standing in front of the Alliance Leader. His eyes were still ablaze with strength and determination, but his voice was gentle and in a whisper that only she could hear. "You do what you will. There is turmoil within you. I know, because it has been within me; but each of us must make a choice. It is not the choice that will cost us but the *consequence* of that choice. Choose wisely."

"Thank you," was all she could whisper back.

He wrapped his strong arms around her and held her for a moment; and then, without even looking back at the remaining three members, he left the hall, the closing of the large door echoing through the now-silent room.

Chapter Twelve

The inky darkness that had burst down deep within the being of the Alliance leader began to turn into a grayish inky substance; and as she took a deep breath in, she knew that for what she had originally come here still was the right thing to do. Metatron was right: the choice never costs us anything, but the consequence is what we pay for.

She took in another deep breath and held it. She could feel it fill up her lungs; and then she slowly let it out, rushing past her lips. She lifted her head and looked straight at the stunned and silenced Council.

"There is an understanding that goes beyond mortal and immortal: it is the understanding that the manipulation of belief to gain power starts inside the soul of good intentions found in the heart of good leaders. It grabs root in the weakest ground within the spirit and begins to feed like a parasite. There is a plant, a parasite of sorts, which is lush and green. It is called kudzu. To those with great intentions, it is a lush, beautiful vine; however, once it is planted, it begins to cover everything in sight. It is only a matter of time before everything that once stood stately and true is covered with this lush, green curtain of power. Oh, it still looks beautiful and almost enchanting; but beneath the outer green is a world of shadow and decay, for it blocks out the light and nutrients to all that is longing to live beneath it.

"I have stood by for too long, watching as the good intentions of a few have transformed into the manipulation of the truth and has left a path of 'green growth' in the name of power, but everything under it is truly gasping for life and hope. We have had that chance to be the messenger of that hope; but we, who mean well, have found ourselves overgrown in our own kudzu.

"No more. I step away from it all with the belief that truth is still out there and will break through into the light of mortals' souls. I believe the Clan Wars that we have not stopped are nothing but another small vine. The real destruction is to come, and mortals must believe there is hope and understand the Fallen can be held back. There is a war taking place, and it is more than just what is in this Council room. There is a war for the very embodiment of truth and existence itself."

She unzipped her white hoodie and allowed it to drop to the floor. She stood with her black tank top revealed, arms bare. But it was not the clear message of conflict between the white pants and black top that brought the clearest of messages: it was the katana, no longer hidden by the hoodie but strapped to the Angel's back. She stood strong and confident, head held straight and eyes not wavering.

"Today you set out to place the blame of so many mistakes and loss of lives upon the shoulders of an innocent. I stand today as the Protector once again of the innocent and the Defender of the balance of truth!

"Michael, mark my words, this Clan War is just a tremble of an earthquake that will reach to the very heart of the Arch Council. I can feel it. The blame will fall upon your shoulders; and the voice of the innocent will scream in your ear, and I will be their Champion!"

"Leah," Gabriel spoke. There was no persuasion in her voice or pleading. She knew this was past that . . . it was just a straightforwardness from genuine care. "You do know what this path you are choosing means? You understand what mantel you are placing over your shoulders, right?"

"I do, Gabriel, and my only regret is that I didn't do it before innocent people, such as Joan, Alfonso, and so many others, were lost. This Council meant well, but the kudzu of good intention is killing the light of truth. I understand that the consequences of my choice today will cost me so much, but years of standing by have already almost cost me myself."

Michael said nothing. He sat stunned and crushed by the heaviness the words of truth that this strong warrior before him had said. Had they been blind? In the desire to protect that which was good and true, had they opened the door for darkness to gain footholds through their own intentions?

The air seemed thick and unmoving, the way it does when one enters a room that had not been occupied for a very long period of time. What could be said? What could be done?

"Leah," he paused, seeming to struggle for words, "you understand what you are asking, then?"

"Michael, I can't put it any clearer than this: I choose the path of a Vapor."

*****

Leah looked down at her hands as she turned them back and forth, looking at the skin structure and feeling for the first time what mortals felt, as no longer did immortal blood course through her veins. She closed her eyes as she tried to focus on the sounds around her as she stood in the center of the Sanctum. Tears brimmed at the edge of her eyes as the weight of a mortal world began to flood in through emotional portals that she had never fully understood before due to the lack of not having that mortal connection. She wondered what the full effect would be and if it would cost her her own existence because of making a mistake that she wouldn't have made earlier.

She was trembling; she couldn't help it. Had she only gained her strength from her Eternal structure? Could it be that fear would hold her to where she was? How many times had she expressed to a mortal that it was about "faith," trusting in that which you do not know? Now, she felt shackled.

Leah couldn't bring herself to take a step toward anywhere that would bring her to meet any of her Alliance, though they would not be "hers" any longer. What would she do now?

As she began to focus her thoughts, the feelings and emotions that had exploded in her meeting with the Arch Council began to deluge her mind; and she could feel her anger coming back . . . but this time it was different: it was as if she was a vessel with a capacity that was small, and she felt that she was only filled now with the desire for revenge. She could taste it . . . like the salt that remains on one's lips after eating a handful of pretzels.

"Leah?"

She did not turn but kept her back to Troy. She could tell by the sound in his voice that he could already sense that something was different. She wondered what he was "seeing" with his spiritual sight. What would a Vapor look like to him?

"What happened?" Concern and hesitation marred his question, and she could tell that he was more than just puzzled.

"What do you see, Troy?"

He didn't say anything. He didn't know what to say. His blindness was only physical. Even with the implants, his gift of spiritual sight was still strong; and he had never seen anything such as what stood before him. He couldn't explain it.

"You are wispy."

It seemed strange, but it was the only way he could describe it. He saw her as a ghost, not clear as he would see other Eternals and even different than a mortal appeared with the sight afforded him by his implants.

"You are like . . . what I would imagine . . . a ghost reflected in a mirror."

She didn't realize, until now, she had been holding her breath. She let it out, and at that moment realized it was time—time to move forward. How? They would all figure it out, but she knew she would not be able to stay here long. She would not allow her choice to affect the Alliance any more than what it was going to already.

"Troy, gather up Ki and Gideon and anyone else that you can think of that would normally need to know key decisions. I want to meet them down in the motor area in about 30 minutes."

"Everything all right?"

"I will let you all know together what is going on. I have to get a few things from my quarters, and I will meet you all down there. Make sure Chad and Serenity are there, also."

He just nodded and, without another word, walked away to get everyone gathered up.

"Ok, so, let's put all of this together: there are still Fallen to take down, innocents to save, and now a new me to discover. One thing at a time . . . I think I'm going to need something stronger than coffee," she told herself.

She didn't even know where she was going after all of this. She made her way to her quarters and then to her bed where she knelt and pulled out a military-style duffle bag and opened it. Taking it over to her closet, she threw some clothes into it. She made a mental note to stop by the Sanctum's armory before she headed down to the meeting. She knew that Ki and Gideon would keep her supplied; but she didn't even know what she was going to do later tonight, and she wanted to make sure she was prepared.

She wasn't going to take much. There would be too many memories attached to a lot of the things that were here, and it would just be better to keep it all in one place—and that one placing not being with her

She zipped up the duffle and grabbed another backpack that she slung over her shoulder. She took one more look around the room, grabbed the wooden box that held Joan's necklace, and started to walk out. This last glance revealed so many memories. She knew that she was changing, and she knew this all would just be another niche in the centuries of her existence.

She headed down the hallway, down a few flights of metallic, grated stairs, through a door, and then turned right into the arms room. She went to her weapons cage and opened it. There hung another katana, a crossbow, and a set of pistols. They all had been made to specifically fit her body and her style of fighting. They had taken out so many Fallen, and they had come to help her truly be a threat to any who lurked in the shadows.

"Michael, you and the Council have no idea what you have lost, yet!" She stopped and thought for a moment about Metatron and how he had stood up against everyone for her. She wondered what would become of him. Would he be exiled or just shunned from the Council?

"I have got to find a way to talk with him." She was trying not to think of the Watcher's Journal that he had, supposedly marking many of her works; but she would be lying if she didn't admit she wondered what all had been written. If only she had one chance to look at it! How wrong would it be for her to just take a look? She was already a Vapor.

She stood outside the metal cage that surrounded the armory. Her head was pounding, and her chest felt constricted. She had heard of Angels who had either been forced to become a Vapor or, like her, had chosen it. Many did not last much longer, for the Fallen destroyed them before they realized what powers they no longer had. They were not angelic or mortal; they were simply there . . . and many for a short time. In fact, there was even mention of them within the Scripture: "We are vapors, here today but so quickly gone." It was a secret epitaph of sorts, something that mortals never understood.

She stepped back and closed the door, ensuring that she locked it. She really didn't know why because she had taken everything she needed from there, including a few grenades and a satchel of throwing blades. "If the Clans want to take this Vapor out, they won't do so without a fight!"

She made her way toward the motor pool where the rest of her leadership would be. What would she tell them? How would they take this?

She did not doubt their capabilities. A true leader always trained their subordinates to replace them. A true leader was never fearful of power being stolen from them, for a true leader understood they served those they led and believed in them, thus, earning their respect and loyalty. With this form of leadership, those who followed carried the legacy of that leader with them in the form of their own leadership.

She saw them before they saw her, and she never expected the lump to catch her in the back of her throat. There they stood, all except Serenity and Chad. Troy, Ki, and Gideon were her trinity of leadership. They had been through so much, and she had watched this group grow.

She remembered Troy's anger and resentment when he had first come to them—something to which she could relate and was able to step back just enough to let him work through it without going the way of destruction. She had watched as he began to understand that the anger he felt devastated him within and that if he would embrace forgiveness and face his demons, he would shine brightly. Maybe she should have taken some lessons from him.

Gideon was still young, in Eternal respect, and had so many things to still experience and opportunities to rise through the ranks as long as he kept his emotions in check over Jackie. He was stubborn, but she had watched as he used that stubbornness to work for his team and not against them. He would excel in leadership.

Then there was Ki. She had come to love this Asian Eternal like a brother. They had done so many things through the years; and many times he could have sought his own team to lead, yet he chose to stay beside her. He had proven himself invaluable so many times.

She refused to let the tears start. They still had a lot to do. She may not be at the helm, but their mission was still as serious as it was yesterday when none of this loomed before them.

There were several others who had gathered on news that there was a big shift in operations taking place, and that anyone in charge of any form of leadership or operations needed to be present for this meeting. This Alliance team had become so well-oiled in the beauty of diversity.

She spotted the tall, slender figure of Trinita's sister, Yara. She had taken over the covert operations division and her sister's work after Trinita's passing. So many times, her Latina flair brought such a spice of festivity to the Sanctum; so much like her sister, the pain of the loss of Trinita had been dulled some.

Standing beside Yara was her intelligence chief, Faheem. He had spent most of his time here within the mortal realm working in the heartlands of what had become known as the Arabia territory. Their history together dated back before the fall of Babylon.

They all allowed her to take "center stage" and surrounded her as they stood solemnly. None of them could truly fathom the impact of this meeting. They knew she had returned from a meeting with the Arch Council, and several noticed that she appeared to be dressed for a full onslaught.

She turned to look at all of them straight on. Her face was set, firm and noble. They were her family, and she was theirs; some things would never change.

"I am leaving." The words seemed to come out without her moving her lips. They were just there . . . no explanation, at first . . . just there.

There were a few gasps, and then Yara expressed vocally what everyone else was thinking, "What do you mean? Leaving? Leaving . . . as going on a trip? Leaving like . . ."

Leah turned to look at her. She was shaking inside out of anger toward the Council for bringing her to this. "Leaving, Yara, like I am no longer allowed here."

"Says who?" Ki vehemently expressed through clenched teeth. He thought he knew the answer, and he could feel anger coursing through the fibers in his arms. Nothing prepared him for her answer.

"By my choice," she lied. True it had been her choice, but it had been coming. She couldn't afford them to fully comprehend the struggle between her and the Council. They all couldn't follow her, and she knew they would if given the chance.

"Your choice?" Troy was puzzled. "I don't understand."

"*You?*" Faheem questioned Troy. "Look around. I dare say none of us do!"

"Shhh . . .." she hushed all of them. She stood in the middle, feeling every set of eyes upon her and starting to feel the fatigue of the burden she had accepted. "I have chosen to go the path of the Vapors."

"No!" Yara expressed almost in a sob. "No, Leah!"

Ki couldn't speak. He stood there feeling as if the death blow of a Fallen had sliced through his core, and he was waiting as the shadows took him into their embrace. He couldn't move. His hands were numb, and his tongue felt swollen. "This could not be! This was a test! Not Leah!" he raged inwardly.

It was times like this that Troy hated his humanity. He had no idea what they were talking about. In his time with the Alliance, he had heard of the Vapors; but it was something no one talked about, and he dared not really ask. He understood enough that they were not Fallen or mortal.

"No!" Ki exploded. The muscles in his face quivered as his anger blasted outward, eyes glazed over in frustration. "This was not your choice but theirs, wasn't it? They forced you!"

"Who?" Troy asked looking from Ki to Leah. "The Council?"

Leah grabbed Ki by the shoulders, her fingers gripping tightly against his skin, and pulled him face-to-face with her. "Shut it! Do you hear me? Stop it now! You don't know what you are talking about, and I need you to control everything you are feeling right now! This team needs you, and *I* still need you!"

"Oh, so we don't need you? Is that it?"

Even though he spoke in anger, his words were like a punch in the gut to her. She knew he had every right to be angry, but that was dangerous. It could cause him to cross over.

"I chose this! I ask all of you that if there has ever been a time you have trusted me, PLEASE let it be now! I do not expect you to understand, and it is something that will hurt; but it was something I had to do."

"So it is," Faheem stated. The even tones in his deep voice seemed to reach out and bring quietness to the group. "We cannot change what has been done, no matter how much we may want to or not understand it. It is simply just so. Leah, I don't know why it is that you have chosen what you have chosen; but you have always been there for us, and we will still be there for you."

He turned and looked at the others. "The Fallen are still out there, and there is still a lot of activity that is unexplained. We cannot afford something like this to tear us apart when the mortal realm needs us now more than ever."

Chapter Thirteen

The aroma of the pancake batter, burnt bacon, and peppered eggs had all been lost in the middle of Tori's all but inhaling her own breakfast and indulging in four glasses of OJ. She normally found herself grabbing a snack cake, maybe "quick-handing" a donut from the corner store. She honestly couldn't remember the last time she sat down to a full breakfast. Her traveling companions ate in silence, allowing the teenager to fully ingest this morning feast. It was the least they could do.

There was a lot still to discuss, and there was also the matter of what was going on inside of this young lady and what they would tell Leah. Serenity was very surprised they had not received a phone call yet from either the Alliance leader or Gideon. It would surely come at any moment.

She and Chad had not had the chance to really discuss this "thrown-together" plan and what the repercussions may be. Right now, it didn't seem to matter. What mattered is they just follow their instinct or the guidance of Jah, depending on how one looked at it.

It seemed they had been on the road for a long period of time; but, in fact, they had only been traveling from the city for a few hours. Dawn had already broken, and daylight was full blown.

Their destination sat only about two miles away, but neither one of them seemed to want to move.

Neither really knew what lay at the end of today nor even if there was hope for Tori, but they had to believe in something. They both knew that Tori would be asking more questions in a minute, and they had to have some answers—answers they really didn't have.

The teen used the last of her toast to sop up the egg yolk on her plate. The texture of the toast whisked up the yellow substance, and she relished the last bit of flavor as it sat upon her taste buds.

At this moment she felt as if her worries, cares, and burdens were gone. She was on the mountaintop, and the world lay at her feet. She sat with her head still, her eyes closed. She breathed in slowly, ignoring the obvious scents in the air but remembering the clean, crisp scent of the winter air outside. She wanted to be free . . . free from any nightmares and outbursts, free from a feeling of captivity and depression. She wanted to be strong . . . strong like what her companions seemed to be like . . . and, yes, there was always love—like the way she saw Chad look at Serenity.

"Tori?" it was Serenity's voice tapping on the window of her conscience. She opened her eyes and lifted her head. "We think it is time to let you know a little bit of what is going on and what we are doing out here in this deserted place."

Tori sat up and leaned forward in her seat. Her eyes were bright with anticipation, and her heart was beating quicker . . . the way it does when one is reading a great novel and can tell that something big is about to happen. The only thing was that this time it wasn't a novel, and the feeling was about something of which she was truly a part.

"This is the raw truth of it all," Chad expressed as he fidgeted with his fork and knife. He adjusted them on his plate and then re-adjusted them, clearly showing he didn't know what to say. "There is a darkness that threatens everything we know each and every day. Call it demons, vampires, ghouls—I don't care—but it is real, and we are a part of it. Actually, everyone is a part of it whether they know it or not. Those of us who do know about it, believe it, and fight it, try our best to ensure that those who do not know stay not knowing. Sometimes that doesn't happen, because individuals get too close to things that they don't fully understand."

"Like me, huh?" her voice held as if she was making a statement, and yet a question all in one. "Those things really were vampires, weren't they?"

"Yes."

"No."

Both Chad and Serenity spoke at the same time. Chad threw up his hands slightly as if to say, "Come on!"

It was Serenity who spoke though, "As Chad stated—call them what you like—the truth is that they are dark, evil, and out to take down anything mortal and make it their own."

"Am I one of them?"

"We are not sure."

"But I didn't get bit."

"It doesn't work that way, Tori." Serenity almost whispered with regret. "There are myths and legends that have been passed down through the ages that have made these creatures even more dangerous because it has made what they do unbelievable."

"People don't know what to really believe . . . the difference between reality and fantasy," Chad interjected. "What better way to make prey vulnerable than to make them not truly understand your existence and the true danger?"

"So where does that leave me? I mean, what I saw in The Warehouse was real! I saw it, and I heard it rush at me; and then the fits and voices that I am having and hearing . . . I know those are real! Am I . . . *possessed?*"

Serenity just sat there, not sure how to explain what she also did not understand. "On the way here, you went into a fit and attacked Chad," Serenity explained, trying to see if Tori remembered any of what had happened. "Do you remember any of that . . . anything at all that might be able to help us?"

The young girl sat in silence, her chest moving with her breathing; but nothing else showed that she had even heard the question. It seemed like ten minutes . . . time seemed to stretch outward past the trio. She felt as if cold water was dripping down her legs, and her arms were itching. Memories were trying to peek around barriers that her mind was building up as fast as it could.

She *did* remember—but didn't want to! That voice, the visions, the pain, and soul anguish had been too much then; and her self-preservation was kicking in, refusing to return. What if they were still inside of her, or maybe she was just mental? What then?

Chad and Serenity watched patiently and attentively. They didn't want a rerun of last night's incident, but they needed her to provide as much information as she could. The young lady began to fiercely scratch at her arms as if she was riddled with bites; her head hung down, and her hair dangled around her face.

"Tori, what do you remember?"

"Worms and pain! They were eating at my skin, and I was scared like I had never been scared before." She paused, and Chad noticed that her hair was taking on a shine as if she was sweating.

He reached across the table and took the one hand that he could reach and held it. The young girl trembled slightly. Looking up, she had a worn-down, crushed appearance about her. "Who is Legion?"

Chad and Serenity just sat there. Nothing. They looked at each other, but neither of them seemed to have an answer.

"Is that a name you heard?"

Tori nodded her head at Chad's question. "They said it was his name . . . no, *their* name."

"'*They* said'?"

"There were so many voices, but they spoke almost as if they were one voice. They were all there, yet it seemed it was one shadow, one creature. I can't explain it. I don't want to." She was now shaking very visibly.

"You don't have to," Chad spoke with strong, soothing tones; and he kept a hold of her hand. It was cold and clammy, the way it would feel if an individual was going through shock. "You don't need to right now. Hopefully, we know of someone who can help out."

Tori just nodded her head.

✶✶✶✶✶

Denora eyed Hecate as she walked in and sat down in the chair across from her. She wanted to hate her—the way that one thirsty for power hates another who has it—but it was because of what Hecate represented that did not allow for hatred from Denora. Hecate did represent power and strength. She had been wielding it for so long, and Denora could not help but admire the skill with which she did it.

"Welcome, Lieutenant," Hecate stated with dripping sarcasm. "Thank you for taking time out to meet me."

"Shut up, Hecate," Denora snapped. "You know that I haven't held that rank since your escapade at The Vortex."

Hecate reached over and plucked an almond from the bowl that was on the small circular table that was beside her chair and quietly put it in her mouth. She began to chew on it as she thought to herself how she was going to approach the reason for having Denora here. She paused, smiled, and then asked, "How is your Master these days?"

There was no response right away. Hecate's visitor knew that she was trying to bait her. For what reason, she wasn't sure; but she knew that Hecate's question was meant to get a specific response. She wouldn't give it to her.

"I am my own Master; but, then again, I'm sure you are attempting a futile inquiry into the status of Arioch."

Denora leaned forward in the tall, antique chair in which she was sitting. She was dressed in dark, ripped jeans; a printed, rock T-shirt; and black leather boots that were laced to her mid-calf. Not much had changed over the last five years; but one thing had changed, and that was her ability to control the dark fire that burned within her soul. She had actually learned the virtue of its control by watching the lady before her.

"I still am not sure what your motive was that night at The Vortex, and I am fairly sure that what The Alliance did that night was not part of your plan; but being the skilled manipulator you are, you were able to still use it to your advantage."

"*My* advantage?"

"Don't play coy with me, Hecate. It is no secret that as the different Houses have fallen in disarray, your Clan has actually grown in strength and numbers."

She could not deny that even if she wanted to. There was no way to hide that she had been able to not only bring fresh Halflings and Familiars into her ranks, but she also had pilfered very nicely from the broken Clans. She could never have planned such a shattering of the different Houses if she had tried. After the division and fighting among the Clans following the incident that night at The Vortex, many Clans had broken into a civil war. Overlords found themselves having to defend their positions from within their own Houses. Arioch's plan to create his own Clan from out of the shadows of the House of Marduk had fanned the flames of a flickering ember of dissent that burned just below the surface in many of the Clans.

"You have renounced your Clan ties; but I am still an Overlord to mine, and you are in my house. You also will do well to not forget who has been in my position from the time of exile and even before the War of the Serpents," Hecate stated with an authoritative tone that demanded no argument without repercussion. There was a low growl from where Cerberus was lying in the corner.

Denora reached down to the top of one of her boots and, with one finger, partially pulled out one of her blades. "I can tell you this, that he . . ." she cocked her head in Cerberus' direction, "may maul me into eternity, but I can guarantee that he will struggle to haul around one dead head."

Stubborn, disrespectful, and obstinate would all describe Denora; but vicious, violent, and bloodthirsty were the characteristics that Hecate knew had drawn Arioch to Denora, and these were the things that Hecate needed right now.

"Denora, the truth is no matter what you think of what I have done or not done, I know what you are capable of; and I need you."

"Did you just say you *NEED* me?"

"I know that is something very few have ever heard come from my lips throughout all the ages of our existence, but you just heard me say it." Hecate stood up and began to walk around the study in which they talked. "You are right when you assume that I have plans. I have always had plans. It was my plan that set the War of the Serpents in motion . . ."

"Was it your plans that got our kind exiled?" Denora scoffed.

"Even the best thought-out plans have unforeseen setbacks and consequences, Dear. At the same time, a good leader will take those unforeseen moments and capitalize on them; and you will do well to learn this. This is one of those moments, Denora," She turned and looked at her.

"I can see you are hungry for power and authority. This is what drove you to side with Arioch, and you served him well—maybe with misguidance—but well. Now, I am going to give you the chance to rise beside me, and I promise you that beside me you *will* rise. There is no mistake there.

"Before you ever thought of belting out the first tune with your band, before you tasted your first drop of mortal blood upon your lips, I had things in motion; and both mortal and immortal have danced to my tunes. I *do* need you; and if you will be my dance partner, you will discover that you will also be unstoppable!"

"I have heard similar speeches before, Hecate. Personally, I am tired of grandiose speeches from figures in power who always have a backend, hidden meaning that usually requires a lot of sacrifice to the ears that hear and no return for the hands that perform." She stood up and threw up her hands. "Speaking of 'performance,' I have one to get ready for. My band is starting our European leg of shows, and this is taking up too much of my time."

"What if I offered you Scintillantes?"

Denora didn't know how to react to this. "What do you mean?"

"The place where you have not set foot for ages . . . that place to which humanity strives a small lifetime to be able to go . . . yet of which you spend eternity only hearing stories."

"Get to the point, Hecate."

"You come on board with me, and I can promise that you will do more than just hear about it: those laced-up boots of yours will actually walk upon the grounds of Scintillantes . . . and do so with power and authority."

"What is the catch?"

"Just follow my lead."

Denora thought for a moment. She really didn't know of what this mad mistress of darkness was talking, but she also knew that she really had nothing to lose. Denora had always been about "what is in it for me?" and never had an issue with stepping away on her own terms. She knew that Hecate was more devious and viler than anyone with whom she had teamed up before, but she wasn't scared of her.

"Sure, why not? You got me," Denora casually answered.

*****

Michael walked quietly alone through the halls of the Arch Council. Scintillantes had not changed much over the ages, but there had been subtle changes here and there. The Hall of the Arch Council was one spot within Scintillantes that still looked as it did the day the Council had first been held. Scars from the War of the Serpents could be seen here and there, but overall it remained a citadel of eternal justice and tradition.

Michael walked out through the pillars and started down the stairs as he looked out over the evening sky. He had to chuckle at how many mortals would cite quotes about there being "no night" in what they perceived as their eternal home. "They believe so many things are shaped to mimic Jah but then come up with bizarre statements and beliefs like that? If their existence has night, then why in the ages would we not have a night?" He just shook his head and looked out over the vivid constellations above him.

His right foot barely stepped off the last step before he felt something that was not normal with where he lived: a cold sense of darkness. He stopped and just looked straight ahead without turning one way or the other. "Who stands at the 14th gate this evening?"

"You are keenly aware that I am able to be here and there at once, Michael."

The Archangel turned around and looked back up the stairs into the shadows of the pillars. He faintly could make out the silhouette of a very unwanted guest. Michael paused at the bottom of the stairs, looking around to make sure no one else was around. He made his way back up to the figure standing within the shadows. "Dumah, how dare you show your face here! Do you realize what this could do if you are seen? How would that be explained? What extreme situations would arise?"

"Not my issue. I can handle myself just fine, and I am not the one hiding within the shadows of something I am not." He laughed a minute at the irony. "Mantus wants to meet with you."

"Why?" Michael questioned.

"I really have no clue. All I know is he sent me to tell you and to see what you are up to. He would like to know why you went to see Hecate."

"Hecate? If he is worried about me around his wife, then maybe he should spend more quality time with her; and you can tell him that my business with her is exactly that: with *her*."

Dumah leaned against the pillar, chuckling. "Would love to see you tell him all of this yourself. Remember how that has gone in the past. This world needs more than just one Angel of Death, so I would hate to see you leave me with that sole responsibility!"

Michael started to rage, his body flooded with adrenaline as he got up in the face of Dumah. "Don't threaten me! It would be just as sad as it would be to see only one Angel of Death left, and I have no issue being the only one."

Without notice, Michael felt the tip of a blade nick his abdominal area. "You forget, Council Leader, that I have no problem shedding blood upon what others believe is sacred ground. I willingly gave all of this up for the taste of blood spilled upon the grounds of this very building."

Michael put his hands up and stepped back. "I know you are only doing this because your brother sent you as his little messenger pigeon . . . and as a good messenger, you can return back to your handler and tell him that next time he wants to breach the grounds of the place you both use to call home, let me know. I will make sure that I have a battalion standing by as a welcome home committee."

"I'm sure he will thrive on the words I share with him about you." With that, Dumah vanished in a haze.

Michael stood for a moment, still shaking. He quickly regathered his composure and headed into the darkness himself.

Chapter Fourteen

She watched as a forest full of trees flew by as they drove. They had not returned to the highway after breakfast but had headed into the wooded part of the state. Before, she had only seen thick, green foliage like this in books. She had dreamed as a little girl of finding where the concrete ended and the land of dreams started but had never really been out of the city. Now as they drove, she felt she had stepped literally into a fantasy novel; and she expected any moment to see mythical creatures step from between the tree trunks that hugged closely. She hoped that if they did, they would be the type of mythical creatures that one would *want* to see such as elves, unicorns, and maybe even a centaur; she could do without anything more of evil and darkness.

Her traveling companions had grown silent and just sat in front, watching the road and likewise viewing the landscape, lost in their own thoughts. They had not told her where they were going other than to say that they were taking her to someone who might know more about what she was going through.

She had lived so long depending on no one and growing up faster than a teenager needed to but not having a choice. It had been the norm to her; most of her friends were the same. They had all joined together and had become their own "little family." They didn't need their parents; although Tori knew deep inside she was lonely and that there were times at night that the loneliness was almost suffocating.

Tori leaned her head against the cold window as she watched them turn right into a small lane that took the trio off the main road. Her mind felt a weird mixture of anxiety and peace. She couldn't really describe it. It was almost as if her mind was telling her she should be anxious and concerned but her heart was resting within her chest, beating an even rhythm of contentment.

The narrow lane they were on now was overgrown on both sides with evergreens that seemed to meet just a few feet above the level of their vehicle, creating a natural tunnel of sorts. She turned to watch as any view of the sky above them slowly became blocked from sight as the tunnel stretched out behind and before them.

"Where are we?"

"A place that not many really know about . . . or at least its true reason for existence. I'm hoping it is a place where we can find some answers, because that is something we are running really low on right now," Serenity stated with a hint of concern in her voice.

"Have you been here before?"

"Once."

Tori still could not see anything through the trees or anything up ahead. "What for? Why did you come here?"

"Well," she hesitated. Did she really want to unlock that door again? She knew the subject may come up, but she had hoped not. That had been a few years ago, and she had changed . . . life had changed so much. Serenity was normally a very private person, and not too many people knew she had been here. She could feel her skin flush as she held her breath for a second.

She didn't have to say anything, though, because just as she was trying to figure how much she needed to say out loud, the wooded drive they traveled opened; and there, sitting before them was a stone complex that looked like it had been built ages ago.

"Eden," the teen girl read out loud from a sign that was framed by pillars made from similar stones from which the complex was built. "It is breathtaking!"

"Yeah," Serenity quietly stated, "more than you even know."

They followed a drive leading up to a place that was clearly for incoming vehicles. The house had flavors of a medieval castle mixed with the warm feeling of a stone cottage. It was three stories high and had several windows that were accented with small drifts of snow here and there upon jutting rocks and window panes. To describe it as "enchanting" did not even do it justice. It truly seemed an "oasis" after everything this group had recently seen.

Tori stepped out and was taken aback by the purity of the air that filled her lungs and the tingle of the crispness about her. She felt lighter, as if all her cares and burdens had been left back somewhere in the tunnel of trees.

"Let's get inside. No one is expecting us, because we didn't think it wise to let anyone know where we were headed," Chad expressed. He was nervous still that they had not heard from Gideon or Leah, wondering of their whereabouts. He also was wondering if or when Tori would have another spell like before, and he wanted experts to be there for the next one.

The three entered the building through heavy, wooden doors that had a carving of a large tree that took up both sides. The foyer was breathtaking and almost mystical. Accented in dark wood of which none of the three were familiar, it held a magical atmosphere. Lined with large display cases holding strange artifacts, the architecture of the room was smooth with strong curves, all bringing the focus of anyone who entered toward the center where a shaft of natural light from outdoors shown down onto an ancient-looking tree. It took the teen's breath away.

"I . . . I have . . . I mean it is so vibrant! What is it?" She could barely speak. She couldn't even explain what it was she was feeling or what it was she was even really seeing. She walked forward, her head going back some as she walked to take in the whole image. She turned for a moment to look back at Serenity and Chad . . . but only for a second. "What is it?"

Serenity walked up beside her and took in the view. She didn't answer for a moment but just allowed the immortal beauty of the tree to permeate the young girl's soul. "It is known by many names, but it is called *Etz Chaim* or the Tree of Life."

To attempt to even describe the tree to anyone who had never laid eyes upon it seemed impossible, not only to Serenity but also to anyone who had made their way to Eden. Its trunk was thick and was the deepest, darkest, and richest wood that one could imagine. The wood seemed polished with natural oils, glistening glass-like. The branches reached out in the regal glory of natural perfection: lush with leaves that had no sign of insects or disease or lacking natural nutrients and radiant in vibrant greens.

The splendor of the tree did not stop there, for the leaves were not just an expressive green but seemed to glisten with a hint of a prism, seemingly changing colors as one moved about it. It embodied the essence of a child ready to climb to safety, a lover longing to find romance beneath its branches, or even rest for a weary traveler. It stirred one to much emotion that centered on fulfillment and peace.

"I am in Heaven!" is all the young girl could whisper as she circled the tree.

"Not really . . ." Chad was cut off by a stern and glaring look from Serenity. He knew what it meant: "Continue and you may not be able to speak for a long time after I am done with you."

"Victoria, there will be more time to look at it and everything else here, but right now we need to get some answers." Serenity hesitated with her words, not wanting to take away this moment from her young ward; but she knew that time may not be on their side. If she was possessed by something they could not fully understand—let alone detect—and if the name she gave was any indication of what this may be related to . . . then they needed to do something sooner than later. She also was aware that "Heaven" was far from what this young girl was about to go through. She would be longing for Heaven while screaming from hell.

A door opened to their right, and an older gentleman stepped into the foyer. His hair was a beautiful white, and his eyes seemed almost to burn with fire. He walked with a firm and demanding gait that required attention, yet did not demand anything that didn't seem to come naturally. Dressed in a simple sweater and a pair of dark khaki pants, he came off as a very professional man but one who could be a grandpa and make one laugh at the very way he told stories or the way he fell asleep when the day became a bore. A very personable and genuine smile broke across his face as he walked up to meet the trio with hand outstretched.

"Serenity, Chad, so great to see you both. It has been too long." He smiled, grasping each of their hands respectively as he spoke. "It must be something of great importance for you to come here without any word beforehand or without Leah knowing. I am sure she doesn't; thus, I received no word beforehand," he laughed to himself.

They both looked at each other, wondering who should go first; but the older man saved them the hassle as he turned toward Tori. "My name is Gene, but many just call me Professor. Although some of the younger ones around here have been known to call me Old Gene," he chuckled. "I think they mean it as a new title of respect. May I ask who you are, Young Lady?"

Tori felt warm and safe. She shook his hand, and then, to the surprise of her traveling buddies, she hugged him as if she wasn't going to let go. He smelled of pipe tobacco and aged leather. She wasn't sure why, but this brought a great sense of safety. "My name is Victoria, but most call me Tori."

"It is nice to meet you, Tori." He turned to the other two. He could see the look of eagerness mixed with desperation on their faces. "I take it that this is a meeting full of information and desperation. Maybe we should go into my study," he suggested as he motioned toward the door from which he had just entered.

They both nodded and followed him. As they headed in, Tori noticed two young children looking down at her from a banister to her left. She smiled and gave them a little wave. They both giggled and ran down a hallway out of sight.

*****

Gene sat with the same grandfatherly look with which he had first introduced himself to Tori. She sat, wiping tears away with a white cotton handkerchief Gene had given to her somewhere in the middle of the conversation where Serenity and Chad had explained what had brought them to Eden. Tori had not said much, feeling very sure that this man would turn them away once all was revealed.

He was not turning them away, though . . . at least not yet. He was sitting there with genuine concern etched within the wrinkles of his face. His fingers were interlaced, and he was looking toward a window in front of which were numerous picture frames sitting upon the windowsill.

"Serenity, would you and Chad do me a favor and give me some time with young Tori alone? Would you allow me that, Tori?"

She simply nodded.

The duo nodded, as well, and got up to leave. Serenity stopped for a moment and put her hand on Tori's shoulder. "You are not alone anymore." She and Chad then left the study.

As they walked out, Chad spoke first. "How is it that someone like her gets wrapped up within the darkest elements of what we fight with every day? I chose to fight these creatures!" He sat down on the bench railing that encircled the tree. "I chose to deal with the sewage of the spirit world . . . but her? Honestly, Serenity, how is it fair?"

She sat down beside him; and she wasn't sure why she did, but she leaned her head onto his shoulder. It just felt comforting and right. Yeah, he was annoying, but he was . . . well, he was Chad; and he was always there. He rarely opened up like this, and this truly was a rare moment.

"That is the other side of free will, Chad. Everyone wants it, but no one wants to accept the responsibility of it."

"Responsibility? She had no clue what it was she was getting into! You think she chose this? You think this . . .," he asked, pointing toward the doors behind which Gene and Tori were meeting, "is free will? How can Jah hold her accountable for choosing to be somewhere that she could never fully comprehend what it would hold for her? You saw her! She is a scared, abandoned teenager who now could literally have the weight of the demonic world upon her shoulders!"

"That is the part that is not fair, I agree. I am not saying I necessarily agree with how you look at it, but . . ." she stopped for a moment and thought hard. "Free will—free choice—always was an Achilles heel to humanity. Mortals wanted it, pleaded for it, fought for it, but so many refused to accept what came with it. So many refused to accept responsibility and the understanding that each action within free will sent out a ripple that touched others. Those ripples collided with each other; and in that, the outcome became even a new ripple far from the original."

"The other night when we found Tori?"

"Yeah."

"So, that night before we met her, she had a choice. She chose to go to what she thought was some kind of weird nightclub."

"Sure."

"So it was her choice to go. No one forced her. Yes, situations before that may have caused a hole in her heart that was looking for fulfillment. We each have those holes. We have that longing to be a part of something bigger and stronger than ourselves. I understand that more than anyone, but what we fill that with is our choice! Our response to that is our responsibility; the outcome of that response is something we then must take ownership of. To not do so is only accepting the part of free will and choice that benefits us."

"So, you are saying it is her fault that she now may have part of one of the vilest demonic beings trapped within her body?"

She wanted to carefully choose her words. This was something with which she had struggled for so long herself: responsibility for the choices we make and understanding that we are also dealing with our choices colliding with the choices of others and the repercussion that must be faced . . . good or bad.

"Her fault? Yes," Serenity ventured.

He could feel his blood rising inside. "Really? Her fault? Just that point blank?"

She lifted her head from his shoulder. With her left hand she took his face and made him look at her. "Chad, fair? I never said that. Easy to swallow? I never said that. It is not even easy to understand." She paused and took in a deep breath. "You caught on earlier that I had been here before, right?"

He nodded. He had never seen her look so vulnerable and open as she did right now. He saw deep within her eyes a look that this beautiful warrior friend of his had never revealed. He felt a connection that reached out and touched the inner segments of his soul. Maybe it was the atmosphere of Eden, or maybe it was sitting beneath this tree; but whatever it was, he was seeing Serenity in a different, vulnerable light.

Chapter Fifteen

"I was Tori."

"Come again?" Chad questioned.

"Before the Alliance, before med school, before all the self-defense classes—before all of it—I was a teenage girl who was alone. I was a young girl whose boyfriends used and threw away. I was a young teen who wanted to belong but whose parents were too busy and whom other girls bullied. I was the one who allowed boys to do what they wanted because they said they loved me and showed me attention. Eventually, I was a young girl who was called a whore."

Chad felt angry.

"Yeah, you think that was part of my free will? No! Tell that to a young teenager, though. Tell that to a young girl whose family member told her that if she hadn't looked so beautiful, he would have not had the feelings he had for her. Tell that to a teen girl who developed faster than a lot, and on whom all the boys in high school placed bets as to who could get her to sleep with them."

"Serenity, you don't have to . . ."

"No, I do, because there is a point to this; and it is something I want you to know about me. I want you to know where I was and why I am where I am today. I want you to see where Tori is and where I believe she could be."

He nodded for her to continue as he turned more to face her head on. He wanted to reach out and hold her hands; but he also knew that at this moment she just needed to be heard . . . nothing more, nothing less.

"I had boyfriends who raped me more times than I can count. I became an angry teen girl. I began to believe that the only power I had was my sexuality. So, I used it! I used it to get whatever I wanted because men were all pigs in my book!"

"No one could blame you for that feeling."

"Maybe," she stated calmly, "but I was choosing to self-destruct. Did I choose what happened to me? No, I was a victim. No one had any right to do what they did to me; and yes, the mortal mind can only take so much in before it begins to self-destruct. Self-destruct is exactly what I did."

She took a deep breath and sat in silence for a moment as she collected her thoughts. Sitting once again within Eden brought so much flooding back to her.

"So, where does this fit into free will? I don't understand. You didn't choose to have that happen."

"No. But, you see, yes . . . every choice we make ripples out to affect others, and we are affected by the choices made by others . . . but have you ever seen a ripple hit a rock in the middle of the pond?"

He nodded.

"What happens? Does the rock move? Does the rock create a new ripple?"

"No, it stops the ripple."

"Exactly! You see I allowed the actions and choices of others to change me. I allowed them to infect me. Revenge was all I could desire, seek after, and embrace. I, in a way, became the very vile essence that had attacked me. No, I didn't rape people; but my choices and desire for revenge on those who had treated me in whatever way they wished was destroying me and destroying others. I started sleeping with men whom I knew were married and worked at destroying their marriages. Why? Because I felt vindicated! I used men! Why? Because they had used me."

"Yet, in all of that, seeking revenge for the choices of others, you were choosing to continue the ripple; and nothing was resolved or satisfied. The guys from high school were still winning each day."

She smiled. "Now you're catching on!"

"So, when did you discover you needed to be the rock and not the ripple?"

She winked at him. "You are a fast learner! All those things I have said to Gideon about you, I take back."

"Uh-huh . . . I doubt it."

"So, I finally came to a point where I was gone. The hole in my spirit was swallowing me up. The darkness was bigger than anything I could imagine. I hated what I saw in the mirror. I hated who I was, but it was all I knew. I continued to blame everyone else. I blamed anyone and everyone I could, except for the one person who had the free will to continue to be the ripple or to be the rock."

"Yourself."

"Yes, myself," she agreed as she nodded. "One night I was at that old club that Leah and they talk about, The Vortex."

"Yeah, I have heard them talk about it."

"It had become one of my regular hangouts. One night I was wasted! I don't remember too much, but I remember this beautiful lady who was kind of standing in the shadows. She seemed to be watching me, and it kinda freaked me out."

"Why? Because it was a lady checking you out?" he laughed.

"No, because it seemed she was calling to me . . . like in my head!"

"Yeah, that would freak me out."

"So, I finally walked up to her and was about to confront her. Just when I went to say something, she spoke first. She called me by my name and asked if I was tired. I asked, 'Tired of what? You checking me out?' She smiled this most genuine and beautiful smile and said to me, 'No." Then she asked, "Are you tired of living excuses instead of living life?"

"That's pretty weird and deep."

"Well, those words hit me like a hot iron straight out of the fire onto bare skin. I couldn't think. I couldn't breathe. I felt like I was going to cry and break down. It was as if I had been waiting for someone to ask me those words all my life! All I could do was nod. She told me her name was Trinita and that she was there to show me what life was really about."

Chad's expression changed quickly. "Wait! Trinita? Like Yara's sister?"

She nodded, "Yep, that would be her. One of the most amazing beings, caring beings, and loving beings I have ever met! That night I left with her and passed out in her SUV."

"Let me guess . . . you woke up here?"

Serenity looked around as she smiled. "I had the same expression as Tori did when I first walked in. I can't explain the feeling! I felt the same as she did! I felt I had walked into Heaven. It was as if every burden just fell from me as I walked in through those front doors! The first time I saw this tree, . . ." she spoke, looking at the branches that glistened above her, "I fell to my knees and cried. I have no idea why! I just felt as if this tree was my freedom. I felt as if it breathed life into me."

"So what then? I mean, how did you go from the person you were to the person I know you are today?"

"Gene and many others showed me that, in the compass of free will, we choose our response. Our response is our responsibility. My response to my parents' never being there for me or to all the men and the situations of my life was my responsibility. What they had all done to me was not my fault, but my eventual response was my responsibility. I chose that if I was going to continue to be the victim, let them win."

"Be the ripple or the rock?"

"Yes," she nodded. "I fought it for so long. Society cripples us so much by desiring free will without helping us understand that we may deal with the repercussion of someone else's free will; but I also have the free will to stand strong, to stand firm, and to rise above my circumstances! I was a victor, not a victim. I could allow those moments to define me or I could define my life by exercising my own free will and changing the course of it all!"

"Just like Tori?"

"That is why I wouldn't give up and just let her go to the hospital and wash my hands of her. Leah may have just seen yet another mortal, but I saw . . ."

"You saw yourself and the chance to change the course of the ripple in her life," Chad interjected.

She smiled.

"I guess I can see it better now. Not easy, as you said but truly deep and true."

*****

Zarius sat on his motorcycle where the road turned into the lane that led to Eden. It had been too long. He wasn't ready for that to change, either. He wanted nothing more than to be back at his ranch with his wife and let the world go to hell. He had almost been able to forget that he actually cared. What had caring done for him? No, the only thing that had ever really paid off was being considered dead, gone, vanished, and living with Tanisha.

His phone began to buzz in his backpack. He pulled it off his back and sat it in front of him on the gas tank. He reached in and pulled out the phone, hoping it would be his wife. His hope sank when he realized it was not.

He swiped to answer, "The last person I ever thought would use this number, and yet you did."

Zarius listened. He knew this conversation, just because it was happening, was not to catch up.

"Yes, I understand. Are we sure we want to do this? If she sees me, she will know things that have been hidden for some time; and that could lead to more questions—questions to which I really don't think answers need to be known right now."

He listened a little bit more. "Yes, I get that. Ok. Give me a little bit of time, and I will make sure it is done."

He hung up the phone, took another look at the driveway to Eden, fired up his motorcycle, and turned around and headed in the opposite direction.

*****

Gabriel stood within the Hall of Heroes, gazing up at its new addition. She had never known Alfonso, but she knew that he had meant a lot to so many people, something he had proven in his life and even more in his death. It had been rumored that he was on the path to discovering a lot about prophecy and the future. Angels were not all-knowing, so even they didn't know what the future held. They discovered it like everyone else: as it happened or through the interpretation of prophecy.

"What secrets did you die with, Old Man? What are we up against? There is something we are missing, and I think you were on to it."

She ran her hand against the cold marble and closed her eyes. Her emotions had not fully recovered from the Council meeting: the outburst between Metatron and Michael involving Leah and Leah's choice to walk the path of a Vapor. Tears moistened her eyes, and she leaned her forehead against the statue. She had always been strong. Ages upon ages had built walls of fortitude and strength within her being, but she was getting tired. She had considered walking away from it all, and now she was angry at herself for starting to harbor jealousy toward Leah for being able to do exactly that: walk away.

She remembered before the War of the Serpents how everything just fit. Life was simple then—true and straightforward—and not full of conflicting ideas, requirements, and ideals. All of that had changed when Lucifer had attempted the overthrow of not only the Arch Council but also the whole authority concept within Scintillantes. From that time forward it had been a constant struggle, and the Fallens' vileness had deepened and darkened. Some days it just felt that this was a losing battle that would never end.

Approaching footsteps brought her back to reality, and she stood up and looked past the statue toward the entrance to the hall. She didn't feel like talking to anyone right now. She just wanted time to figure out things and reset her mind.

Metatron entered the hall and stopped as he saw her. "I'm sorry, Gabriel. I didn't mean to disturb you."

"You didn't," she stated. "I was just taking some time to walk amongst history. Sometimes I fear we forget all that we have seen, been through, and the struggles we have already faced. Within that, we seem to face the certainty that we will walk right back through it all."

Metatron reached up to touch the statue of Alfonso. "So, I have been thinking about your question earlier; and I must say my time upon earth, at times, seems less burdensome than my time as an immortal."

She was puzzled. "How so?"

"As a mortal, I understood that I lived but a short time. Yes, there were consequences for my actions . . . there were consequences for my *lack* of actions.

"As a mortal, though, I comprehended that my time was short. I dare not waste that time in wrong actions or lack of actions. I needed to learn from them; put countermeasures into place; and most of all . . . I needed to just live!

"As an immortal, I think that is something we lack because what is time to us? We exist on a different plane than our mortal counterparts. We make a mistake, and then we think 'oops.' Do we really stop and think about the consequences? Do we think about the need to learn from it, fix it, and ensure that we don't do it again?"

"That makes more sense now," Gabriel responded. "Take what you shared before and all of this, and I am starting to understand. What I know is that we may not be bound or controlled by time, but it seems that time is seeping into our existence . . . and time is destroying us. I fear that Leah was correct. We will discover that we need her, and at that time will she be there? Will she even survive as a Vapor? She was one of our best, and now what are we left with?"

"I can't predict the future. I can tell you elements of what I see and can tell you where I believe we are headed but the finite details of it all . . . I cannot. I can tell you that she is not alone. She was given the same choice as all the Vapors before her were given."

"Who was it that met her?" Gabriel asked.

"I sent Zarius."

She spun around and looked at him with surprise. "Zarius? Wait . . . he is alive?"

"Ah, now you are starting to see even more, My Friend . . . that all things are not always as they seem . . . nor people as they seem. Trust me on this."

"So you called in a favor? You called in a favor to a 'thought-to-be-dead' traitor?"

"I did, but it was more than that. Even though you may know and remember him from his actions before, even immortals can change. There is more to Zarius than you could ever imagine. The most important part is that Zarius doesn't trust Michael. He believes that there is something a lot larger than you and I can see: the Arch Council and even the expelling of Leah."

"What do you mean?"

"He wouldn't explain, but he believes that Leah is a key to something bigger; and I didn't have to ask him twice."

Gabriel sighed, "I am fearful that everything we have known over the ages is coming to an end."

"A new age?"

"Possibly!" She paused for a moment and then looked up at him. "Are you leaving Scintillantes?"

"I don't know. I believe you are right when you state there is a new age upon us. I think the time for the Arch Council has come and gone. We are holding on to old ways that are shackling us. The truth will always be the truth, but I believe the truths we have been set aside to protect now are to be carried on into a new age and by new messengers."

"Like?"

"Mortals and immortals . . . but not us; leaders like Leah and mortals like . . ." he spoke quietly, looking up at the statue, "well, like Alfonso. The truth we stand for will be ageless, but our time is coming to an end. I believe we will do more for the sake of Jah, Scintillantes, and mortals by joining them on their level."

"You believe war is coming again, don't you?"

"I don't think it ever ended, My Dear Friend . . . it never ended." With that, he bowed deeply and walked, not toward the doors that led back out into the light of Scintillantes but toward the alcoves and the path to the mortal world.

She ran her fingers through her hair. "So it begins . . . or continues . . . but how will it end?"

Chapter Sixteen

The door of the Sanctum closed behind her, and she just stood there. She had ordered that none of the team follow her out. She knew she needed to do this alone, if just for the sake of not dragging it out and the chance to start somewhere in understanding now what she was to do.

Leah was not aware of anything about the Vapors; and, in fact, she didn't even know really what she had chosen. She knew that within the manuscripts that the mortals held there was a reference that stated, "We are but a vapor . . . here for a short time, and then vanishing." Many of them had taken that to explain the soul of man; and it was true that it could be a very strong interpretation, but anyone on the other side of the curtain understood what it meant.

After the War of the Serpents and the Fallen had established themselves, there came a time where many Eternals, for different reasons, chose to leave their realm, their understanding of existence, and embrace that of mortal man. They did not fall, for the dark shadows of the Fallen, the virus, had not overtaken them. They had simply chosen to step over.

Once that was done, most faded into the mortal realm, never to be heard from again or even traced. That was why they had become known as Vapors: here today and gone tomorrow.

Periodically, one or two would show up on the radar helping the innocent or doing something "miraculous" then slipping back into "nothingness."

No one really knew anything about them, for they were in many ways the forgotten. Most Eternals never understood why any would make such a choice. Leah had once been one of those. She had, for so long, failed to even really recognize that the Vapors existed; but now here she stood: a Vapor.

"Wow," she let out the air she had been holding in subconsciously, "I guess we are kind of like the Nephelium."

She looked down as she realized her hand was shaking. Was she scared? "Jah, do you still hear the voice of a Vapor? I may not understand your ways; but that doesn't change that right now I really feel alone, and I don't know what to do."

This was new ground for this once-fierce warrior. She had been stripped of her angelic glory and strength. Right now, she wasn't even sure of what she was capable. It was as if she was being reborn . . . starting brand new, hungry, and naked. She closed her eyes and held back tears. Mortality was a heavy blanket that was starting to lie upon her shoulders.

Leah was surrounded by concrete, metal, and graffiti. For the first time in her existence she felt small and insignificant. She began to realize all the times she had inadvertently looked down upon mortals for what she took for weakness. Now her heart broke for them, for she, for the first time, could understand them. She could feel it all: every burden, heaviness, and feeling of hopelessness.

She dropped what she was carrying and fell to her knees. What was this? Was this why you never heard from a Vapor . . . because they couldn't survive the change? There was no way for her to know that the first few hours of a Vapor were critical to their existence. The mantle of humanity was heavy. Their understanding of the true strength and hope of mankind would save them, and yet the opposite would destroy them.

"Jah, I need you! Do not let me fall here. Do not forsake me in this time where I wish only to help those who can no longer help themselves. Do not allow me to fall prey to darkness!" She wept. She had never felt so weak . . . even after Joan she had not felt like this.

The sound of a motorcycle's engine drowned out the rest of her prayer. Exhausted, she looked up to locate the source of the engine noise. She saw a rugged looking guy catch sight of her and turn down the street. She stood up as he came closer. He pulled his black motorcycle up beside her. He placed the kickstand down and took off his sunglasses, revealing vibrant blue eyes.

"So, ready to ride?"

She stood there for a second. What in the world did he mean was she ready to ride? She was confused.

"Ready to ride?" She questioned. "You must have me mistaken for someone else. I actually live right here. I'm not looking for a ride."

He grinned. "Yeah, ok. If that is the case, then I guess I will just wait for you to head on in so I know you're safe."

"Who the heck do you think I am?" She didn't like his nonchalant attitude. She picked up her gear bag and fidgeted quietly with a snap that would allow her access to one of her handguns.

"Well, let's see," he said. "If I am where I was told to be and at the time I was told to be, then I would say you are Leah, once the leader of the Alliance group; yet the keyword to it is 'once.'

You are no longer that because you chose to stand up for what you believe in and for those you believe in; and, in that, you have become what many know as a Vapor."

She stared hard at him. She had no response. She had nothing to say.

"If you are, in fact, Leah, and you are, in fact, a Vapor, then you need to get on board with me, because we have a long road ahead of us; and you have to realize that this journey of yours has just begun. You have a lot to learn and a very short time in which to learn it, because if the whispers through the networks are true, there is a war coming; and you are going to be needed."

"And who are you?"

"My name is Zarius." He held out his hand to shake hers.

"Zarius?" she gasped. "Raphael?"

"Well, yes. I haven't gone by that name in beyond ages . . . but yes."

It all hit her. Everything was flooding in on her. She had just become part of something so much bigger than what she thought. She realized that just as the Alliance and the Fallen were considered myths to most mortals, that there were even truths that they themselves had chalked up to myths and legends. She now started to realize that just because there was something unexplainable, unseen, unknown, and not understood did not mean it did not exist.

"I really don't understand." Her voice was gaining strength.

"Leah, you will. You may not believe it, but you have more friends on your side than you know. I was sent here, diverted off my own journey, to pick you up by one of those friends. You just must accept right now that there is a lot you may not understand, but it doesn't mean it isn't going to be true or even take place. I am here for you if you will accept help. Every Vapor is offered the same opportunity as you. Not all take it, and if you decide not to, then no hard feelings; but you have come to your moment of truth . . . you have come to a point to choose."

She grabbed her stuff, threw her leg over the back of his bike, and held on as he stood the bike fully up, kicked up the kickstand, and headed out . . . to where, she didn't know; but she could feel strength starting to increase inside of her. The moment she chose to get on that bike, something started building inside of her. She was a Vapor, and she was not alone.

*****

Hecate rolled over, allowing the sheets to fall and drape where they may. She had been awake for a few minutes, but she didn't want to rush anything. Her day was just starting. She paused for a second, remembering that she had been sharing the bed . . . and now the other half was empty. She adjusted herself lying on her back and lifting her head to look around the room. Suddenly, she realized that she may be alone in the bed but not alone in the room . . . and that the individual standing near her bed was not the one with whom she had shared her bed the night before.

"Are you kidding me?" she spat out as she sat straight up.

"I see that you have grown less cautious over the years, Dear. I also see your taste hasn't changed when it comes to the desires of the flesh, except you normally don't sleep with our kind. I thought mortals were more your taste."

"Shut up, Mantus!" There would be heads rolling for allowing him to get this far into her residence without any alert. She stood up, her bare skin visible within the limited lighting in the large room. She walked past him with a slight pushing, knowing that he would be gazing at her. He had never been able to resist; then again, very few could. "Next time I expect a little professional courtesy . . . and speaking of my interest, where is she?"

"I didn't do anything to her if you are really concerned. I dismissed her."

"It is my concern; and no, it is not your concern. So, what causes my husband to leave his ever-growing underworld to grace my humble estate?"

Mantus kept watching her, not really because of her beauty but more out of not trusting anything she was doing. He knew his wife. He knew that every move she made and every word she spoke was calculated. Never had there been a time where she was not working on some ploy that would, she hoped, place her on top. He had to give it to her: she was always hungry, but hunger can soon overtake the mind and make one lose control.

She grabbed a black robe off the back of a tall chair. "How is our son?"

"You know how he is, Hecate, so no need to even go down that road."

"Oh, I do. I know that he is still chained and tormented every day within YOUR realm that YOU have control over . . . ah, but *no control* over the chains that hold him or the creatures that torment him."

There was a rush across the room, and Mantus had her by the throat. His hands squeezed tight.

"You do not have authority over me or what I control, and we sure as hell are not sleeping together. This, of course, means that you and I are equals, and I do not tolerate anyone who attempts to talk down to me!"

She laughed. She could feel his hand clenching tighter, but she also did not fear him. Yes, if there was anyone who could send her to the Abyss, it would be him; but she also knew that he would rather not have her within his realm but, rather, as far away as possible.

"So, Dear Husband, what brings you here?"

"I was told that you wanted to talk with me; but I knew not to believe that you would actually come to me, so I came to you."

"Took you long enough," she spat as he let go and she shoved him backward.

The door opened and Denora walked in, glaring at Mantus. She walked past Hecate and into the large master bathroom. "I don't care what you both have to say to each other, but since I was rudely kicked out this morning," she snarled at Mantus, "I at least would like to take a decent shower." She shut the door behind her.

Mantus sat down, laughing and shaking his head. "Wow, so your new lover is just a young version of you; now, isn't that total narcissistic irony?"

"Again, none of your business. Now, if you would like to follow me, I need at least one cup of coffee before dealing with you this morning; and then we can start talking."

He waved his hand toward the door. "Lead the way, because we know I don't trust you to my backside. I prefer not to have sharp metal things protruding from it."

They made their way to a small alcove where coffee was brought to them. Mantus' face was set. Dressed in black dress slacks and a black, button-up shirt, he looked formidable to many. His face was covered in a very large, but well-groomed, black beard; and his head was shaved, revealing tattoos down both sides of his scalp. He rarely had to demand anything, for most followed his deep voice out of fear.

"Hecate, cut straight to the point. I don't have time for coffee and niceties. I have things that need to be taken care of back home."

She stirred a cube of sugar into her coffee, tapped her spoon on the side, and then laid it on the saucer. She slowly took a sip and then placed the coffee mug down. "There is something on the horizon. I am not sure exactly what just yet, but I sense a stirring; and I believe that we could, together, work it in our favor."

He put his hand up to stop her. "Wait . . . so you brought me here for some lofty idea about something that MAY happen—something you DON'T know about—and yet want ME to join with you to use this figment of your imagination to our favor, which—let me add—usually means *YOUR* favor?"

"Michael came to see me."

Of course, Mantus already knew this, but he did not let on that he knew. He always kept a few cards in his back pocket. He wasn't attracted to his wife's cunningness for nothing. "So?"

"He suggested that he had a way to release our son from his imprisonment."

"Oh, he did? How does he plan to do that?"

"We didn't really get that far," she smirked as she picked up and took another sip of coffee. "I wanted to talk with you first. What do you know about Legion's exile?"

There it was. It was like a poker player who played the cards they wanted the opposing players to read and then set them up for the final throw down. She had been doing this for so long that she didn't even realize that what once was a strength had become a predictable flaw.

"You already know the answer to it."

"I think we all do," Denora stated as she walked up and stood beside Hecate. "Legion was banished by a Watcher . . . well, a Grigori . . . who had been given the supernatural gifts of Jah. As he was banished, there were segments of him that were able to escape into the mortal world and what could not be bound for eternity within the realm of his father . . . well, from what I hear, one of his fathers."

"Easy, Underling," Mantus growled.

"Due to the laws of the Eternals if he is banished and bound within the Abyss by an Eternal, then he is there until released by the sacrifice of free blood, blood given freely by the owner. Seeing that no Eternal, Fallen or not, would sacrifice himself for such a Clan member, he is cursed to be tormented for eternity."

Mantus threw up his hand as if to say, "There you go."

"What if there is another way?" Hecate's question was almost a statement. "Even within our existence we are continually finding new ways that the laws of existence are bending. Maybe he found another way."

"If he did—and it is insanity that I am even having this conversation with you—what would it be?"

"I am not sure."

"My follow-up question for that is what is he wanting in return?"

Hecate tapped her finger to her forehead. "You see, I think I may know the answer to that. I believe that he has seen the writing on the wall. Sure, all the Houses are in disarray; but he also knows that his role within the Arch Council seems to be growing weaker. His role as Michael is harder to hold together, and the position of Azrael is threatening to take over his being."

"Still doesn't answer any of my questions."

"So, what if he can't release Legion? We already have believed for ages that our son will never become whole again. What if we are able to find a vessel strong enough to hold what is left of Legion? With Legion, we could unite the Clans. You know that most believe him to be the one to unite the Houses. With Azrael beside us, we would gain access to Scintillantes. We would be able to accomplish what we attempted to do so many ages ago."

He sat silently for a moment and then began to roll up his sleeve. He exposed his right arm and laid it across the table. There, very visible, was massive scarring from a burn that went from his wrist up past his elbow.

"Do you know what this does for me, Hecate? This is a constant reminder that I once stood within the halls of the Arch Council. It reminds me that I once followed you, Azrael, and Lucifer into something you had convinced me was winnable. Each day I see this, each day I feel this, I am reminded of the War of the Serpents and how, from the very beginning, you were twisting every single player into believing we were righteous in what we were doing! Each day I breathe the sulfur of that which I command and hear the screams of the tormented, I am reminded of the beautiful skies of what used to be my home."

She smirked as she sat back. "Ok. I don't blame you for any of that."

"*BLAME ME?* It was *you* who set off the War! If was *you* and your deceit that betrayed all of us . . . *YOUR* lust for power!"

"So, what are you saying, Dear? Are you saying that you won't consider any of this?"

"What I am saying is that you haven't been one time to see what is left of our son! You have not once learned from your mistakes."

He paused for a moment. "Actually, you haven't learned what you should have. You learned each time how *not* to do things, but you haven't learned that this lust of power is what has destroyed all that we are! I may be a Fallen; and yes, I see the anger toward Jah and those who live and exist daily where we have come from. Yes, I am dark to my very bone . . . but a lust for power . . . that was always *your* thing."

She slammed her fist on the table. Coffee went everywhere, and her spoon fell to the floor. "You were always weak! Here, the greatest general of our kind—and dare I say *still* the greatest general even now—and yet one who is afraid to fight!"

"Afraid? No, you mistake what you see! I fear no one; but I also understand that you do not blindly run into a battle that has no way to be won, built upon fantastic notions and chances that are not even a possibility!"

He got up and checked to ensure that he had no coffee splatter on his clothes. He looked first at Hecate and then to Denora. "Denora, you have fun with her. Soon you will see that she loves only herself; and in the end, you will be left holding drifting sand that has no foundation."

He shook his head and walked away leaving Hecate furious and Denora sneering.

Chapter Seventeen

Hecate sat pondering. She had to stay in front. It was going to take something big, something drastic to keep ahead of her husband. She wasn't sure exactly what he would do, but she did know he was not stupid. He would start seeking out what she was doing; and if she wasn't careful, he would have roadblocks in place before she could even travel down this road.

"Denora, I need you to do something for me . . . actually two things."

"Sure, what are they?"

"I need you to follow and keep tabs on Mantus. I want to know what he is doing and whom he is talking to."

"Ok, and second?"

"Send out a message to all the Clan Houses, old and new. No, send a message out to all hierarchy. Let them know that we will be holding a gathering. I want it as soon as possible. It will be here. Apologize for the short notice. I want to make sure that we don't give Mantus a chance to find out anything. If I can flip the switch and align the Houses, then we ensure that he will not stop anything I decide to do moving forward."

"The last time we had a gathering, it didn't go very well; but I will get on that right away," Denora responded.

*****

"Twirl amongst the bile of denial and wash yourself with the filth of the human excrement. Madness is heaven and death, denied in the never-quenching flames," a voice dripping with intestinal echoes of degradation laughed out. It came in and out from all directions in a circle of insanity. "Oh, Great One, you still are held as nothing. Look about you; see the waste of mortal lust and burned tendons tied to the copper stones of your Abyss! Is this your throne?"

The Malebranche's long tongue dripped with acidic, inky ooze as he scoffed at a figure that looked to have once been a mighty warrior; however, now serpentine creatures with mouths of razor-sharp teeth ate holes into his being, creating festering cavities that would burn with black flames, never healing. His face was hollow with bulging eyes. If there ever had been eyelids, they had long been peeled away. His lips had become drawn and cracked from lack of moisture, exposing teeth that seemed dull and without any threat—all except a set of pointed canines.

The Malebranches were his tormentors, and these creatures that dipped below the horrors of imagination were enthralled with their duties. They were created with no intellect but simply for the purpose of torment and lining the bottom of darkness.

A Malebranche never had a true definition—to define one was contrary to its very existence. Eyes, large and without symmetry, were set within a scaly and leathery face. A head covered in tumors and tufts of course hair all sat upon a body of bony protrusions and grotesque disfigurement. Even with all of this, they had come forth out of evil for one purpose: torment. They did it well.

This particular one was half of a team who had been given control over the figure that now was captive before him . . . a pile of what looked to be waste. "Oh, Great One, tell me how you roused the majestic Jah!" A strain of wheezing and spewing came forth as if the creatures were attempting to laugh. "Or please tell us how within you flows the source of the Clans: their Great Hope, their Dracon!"

The captive had long stopped showing any signs of life or fight. Ages had passed; but deep in the inner conscience, a crimson light flickered, waiting for the kindling that would reignite the rage . . . a rage that would rip the jaw from the Malebranche and make it his weapon. His time was coming. A new body he would gain—maybe even a young one—and there could always be the chance for more than one.

His tormentors looked up with shrieks and hisses as they felt a presence begin to take form within the confines of the rocky cell of their prisoner's existence. "General Mantus! He comes!"

Mantus stood looking at the being who had almost become one with the rock walls that held him. "Son, how I despise your mother and all she has done."

An utterance, hardly even able to be called a groan, sounded from Legion's chest. His ability to look at his father or even speak had left so long ago. Mantus wasn't even sure if there was full comprehension anywhere within his son anymore.

He remembered the day that his son had been cornered by the Watchers. Legion was complete then, all his multi-levels of existence embodied within one mortal shell; but it was his defiant stubbornness that had been his downfall. Legion could have fled. He could have existed to rise up and lead the Clans; but instead, his obstinance kept him where he was: facing down the Watcher embodied with the power of Jah.

Legion was banished. Only segments of him had been able to escape the banishment. The day that his son had appeared within the Abyss and bound by an Eternal was the day that Mantus started questioning everything they had done.

There was no real account of how Legion had come about. It was known that he had appeared, as it seemed, from nowhere sometime after the War of the Serpents. He was the epitome of darkness and horror. He was the protégé of the Morning Star and the signature of the seven Overlords of the Clans. He was of no Clan, yet of all the Clans. It was as if he was a combination of the essence of the Fallen embodied into one manifestation. Hecate had made Mantus believe that he was the sole father of their son, but later it was discovered that the seed of each of the Clan leaders had been a part of his creation. It was Hecate's way of looking to be the mother of the Fallen and use Legion as the son she could control.

Centuries would see the fingers of Legion, the Dracon, torment mortals and become intertwined into legend. The Order of the Dracon would give birth to the rise of one Dracul or Drăculea.

Probably the most highly recognized Fallen—or at least Vampire (the manifestation of the human mythology dealing with the Fallen),—Drăculea, embodied the largest collection of segments of Legion at one time since his banishment into Malebolge. It was at that time the Fallen believed they were the closest to Legion's return; in fact, they were not far off on their assumptions. A prophecy by the Watcher John stated that Legion, in his full power, would return; and mortals would struggle to survive . . . even to the point of extinction.

Mantus was torn. He longed for his son to be free, yet had become tormented with the thought of what it could mean for both mortal and immortal if he was fully brought together again. He reached up and placed his palm upon the disfigured forehead of his son. His mind was racing back to his conversation with Hecate. He knew not to trust her, but what if the things she suggested could free his son? What if he would not have to rule this realm knowing that his son was one of those being tormented within the nine circles of his domain?

"Brother?" Dumah had come up behind the general. "She got to you, didn't she?"

"No, not like she had hoped." Mantus turned to look at his brother. "She tried, and she was able to hit me a few times; but her influence over me has waned through the years. I know her all too well."

"What do we do?"

Mantus motioned for his brother to follow as they left Legion to be handled by the Malebranche once again. "I do believe she is right when she states something is starting to take place. She knows something . . . or *thinks* she knows something."

"And Michael's role in it all?"

"I'm not sure. Hecate sounds really confident that there is a way she can break Legion free. If there is, then it is something I am not aware of."

"And if she does?"

"I don't know, Dumah. I really don't know. I am torn."

"We have been separated for so long from the fight, Mantus. Yes, we both know that being given this area to control was, in essence, the same as being banished to here. We both have had long conversations regarding our role within the War of the Serpents and what we would do if we could do it all over again."

"I know. I also am aware that we really have no recourse. Who can we trust . . . and better yet, who would trust us?"

"Then do we just sit back and watch it all play out, hoping that in the end we have an alliance with the winner?"

Mantus could feel the heat rising from the pits around him. Most days it was like a second skin; then others, like today, it was a constant reminder of where he was now. He had served for so long as the head of the protective forces for Scintillantes . . . that was until the day that he had been swept into the current of Hecate's enticing spell. The scars of her grip were not only within his mind but also physical. He looked down at the burn marks upon his right forearm. He ran his fingers along the scar, a constant reminder of what it meant to believe in love built upon deception.

They both entered into a large, polished black stone room and sat down at a conference table. "I think we need to look at this from a few different angles, Brother. We need to keep tabs on Hecate's new toy, and then . . ."

"Toy?"

"Yes, she seems to be using and grooming Denora now for something; and I would imagine if we can keep track of her, then it will give us insight into more of what Hecate is up to. Also, I think I need to speak to Michael directly. He needs to be reminded of his status in everything."

Dumah laughed, "That will be interesting to see how that goes down. Who do you want me to attach to Denora?"

Mantus sat quietly for a moment pondering that question. He knew that if anyone from his ranks was assigned, then it would become obvious. He wasn't scared of Hecate finding out, but he knew it would make it more complicated if she did. "Hmm . . . what if we hire someone?"

Dumah knew exactly to what his brother was referencing, and he really didn't like the idea. "So, you are suggesting taking one power-hungry individual, who is known to not be trustworthy, to keep tabs on another one, who is just the same?"

"Kadar and his kind may not be trustworthy, but they also do not pretend to be trustworthy. At least when it comes to his small group of misfits, we know what we are getting; and he will flat out tell you to your face what he is up to if you ask."

"True. Let me see if he is willing to make a deal."

"Oh, he will . . . if the price is right."

*****

Tori was not sure what would come next amid all that had taken place, but she knew that her body felt like it was floating on a cloud as she lay down upon the bed that was in her new room. She felt—dare she say it—completely peaceful. She wasn't sure the last time she had felt this way . . . or even if she had *ever* felt this way. It was nice.

After her meeting with Gene, she had been shown a room and had been told that she needed to feel free to make herself at home and encouraged to rest. Chad and Serenity were somewhere on the property, and they had assured her they were not leaving.

She wanted to sleep, but she was also very anxious and worried about what would be on the other side of her eyelids. Would the creatures be back? Would they take over again, and maybe she would never wake up? What if they took over and not let her go? Would she ever even know?

There were giggles coming from outside her door; and as she rolled over, she could see children's fingers sticking through the crack between the floor and the bottom of the door. They wiggled with glee and then vanished, but she could still hear the whispering of children on the other side. She quietly got out of bed, tiptoed to the door, and then quickly pulled it open. The twins, whom she had seen before, almost fell at her feet.

They both jumped up quickly and stepped back. Both had playful but shocked looks on their faces and acted as if they didn't know if they should run away again or stay.

"Hi," she greeted them both.

The twins were a boy and a girl about four or five years of age. The little girl had pigtails, but her brother's hair was shaggy. The little girl waved, and her brother slapped her hand down.

"Hey now! That isn't nice!" Tori chided playfully.

"Lado! Lada!" A female voice rang from down the hall, followed by quick footsteps.

Both of the children squealed and ran in the opposite direction. Tori poked her head out and looked down the hall in the direction of the lady's voice. She saw a slim-figured lady with long, black hair pulled back into a ponytail, walking her way with a very motherly and stern look on her face. The lady spotted Tori, and her expression turned to a carefree and loving smile. "Hi! You by chance didn't see two little fugitives come this way?"

Tori laughed and pointed in the direction of where the twins had disappeared. "I believe you are getting hot. They ran that way."

The lady rolled her eyes and sighed a playful sigh as if the world was so heavy. "They better be glad that I love them!" She held out her hand and introduced herself. "Hi, I'm Ann."

"I'm, Tori," she stated as she shook the lady's hand.

"Welcome, Tori. If my children bother you too much, let me

know. They love to see new faces here, and sometimes they have more energy than they know what to do with."

"They are cute! I'm an only child, but I love being around kids . . . well, little kids," she laughed.

"Well, feel free to wear their energy levels down as much as you can. Sure will help me!"

"Deal," she stated. "So, you three live here?"

Ann took a quick look down the hall to see if she could spot her children and then leaned against the wall. "We do. Home, sweet home."

"It is a beautiful place to live! Is Gene your dad?"

Ann laughed at this. "Oh, no, Dear. I am just another former lost soul you can put on the tree of those Gene and Eden have set on a different course within their life. I actually don't remember my father too much, and my mother . . . she was what horror stories could be written about."

Tori shook her head in understanding. "I can so relate . . . except more my dad than my mother."

"Well, let me know if you would like a tour of the place. It is quite big; and I still swear after five years here, that this place actually grows on the inside, no matter how it may look on the outside. I still can find myself lost in here."

"Thanks. I think for now I'm going to lie down. I'm pretty beat."

"And I should find my little hellions."

Tori watched her leave, heard a few more squeals from the twins somewhere down the hall, and closed the door. Sleep was going to come even if she didn't want it to; she needed it. She could feel her body's energy levels depleted.

She lay back down and soon felt her eyelids begin to close. She wanted to fight it; however, she knew that it would be hopeless, so she allowed the warmth of the room, the comfortable bed, and peace wash over her as her body gave way to exhaustion.

*****

Both riders placed their feet down as the motorcycle engine was shut off. They were parked right where Zarias had been just hours before. Leah swung her leg over and stood up. Her body was sore, and she still felt heavy. Her back ached from carrying her two bags during the ride. She extended her arms over her head and felt muscles stretch that she was pretty sure she hadn't used in a long while. Her mind was still swirling from everything that had taken place within the last several hours.

"So, anytime you would like to share with me where you came from, what is going on, and how you know about me would be perfectly amazing for me!" she stated as she used her fingers to make an ill attempt at fixing her windblown hair.

"Well, who *hasn't* heard of you? You tend to leave a lot for discussion, Leah."

"You know what I mean!" she stated, frustrated. "Let's not start with how is it that a traitor from the past, thought long-dead, shows up outside my residence—sorry . . . *former* residence!"

"Traitor is pretty harsh coming from someone who, hours ago, was standing before the Arch Council, basically being accused of similar."

"Really? Nothing . . . I repeat . . . *NOTHING* that I have done within my existence comes close to what you did to turn your back on everything good, betray those who believed in you, and help set in motion a catastrophic set of events that would cause and still to this day *is* causing destruction to all that is! I served *others!* You served *yourself* . . . not to mention, again, that you are supposed to be *DEAD!*"

"Oh, you served others? Let's look at that! So, everything you have done as a Guardian and an Alliance leader was for others? You didn't do any of it out of seeking glory for yourself?"

She was angry! She felt a flood of anger that she had never felt before . . . before . . . well, before becoming a Vapor. Before there had been a wall against what her anger would dash, but now it seemed as if there was nothing holding it back. She swung her fist, and it connected with the side of Zarius' jaw. He stepped back, more out of attempting to avoid it than anything.

He stepped forward, chest to chest with her. He stood several inches taller than her and did not give her any forward ground. "I will say this: due to a lot of unknown things taking place right now in your life, I will let you get away with that; but keep in mind: that one was a freebie. Next time you swing on me, I won't be as reserved!"

"Bring it! I could care less!" she seethed.

"You have no idea of what I am capable or of what you are no longer capable. So, I encourage you to figure out a way to get your point across without taking it out on the side of my jaw! May I also suggest you start acting more like the former leader you were and less like a teenager?"

Chapter Eighteen

Leah bit down hard on the inside of her cheek. She felt the heat rushing up her neck into her face. She wanted to lay him out . . . well, at least *attempt* to lay him out!

He leaned against his bike. "I can't really share a lot about myself, and that is more out of safety for you and others. I am sure much will come out soon; but until then, I reserve the right to not share it. I can tell you, obviously, I am not gone . . . never have been. I can also tell you that I would rather have stayed away; however, just like your current situation, something must be done."

"What do you know about my current situation?"

"That will be an answer to another question of yours. Metatron is the one who let me know what was going on with you and where to find you and told me to pick you up."

"Metatron?"

"Yep. Like I said, you have friends in more places than you know, Leah. Sometimes we can get so wrapped up in our own little niche of the universe that we become blinded by it. We forget that there are a lot of other things taking place out of our scope of vision."

She nodded. "Yeah, I guess I can respect that. Why, though?"

"Now, *that* I don't know. There are very few people in the world that know I exist . . . although I believe that is about to change . . . and even fewer for whom I would drop everything to do a favor."

"And Metatron is one of those," she stated.

He nodded. "Yes, he is. He told me what happened at the Arch Council. He told me to get you and bring you here." She looked around, puzzled. "Here . . . 'out-in-the-middle-of-nowhere' here?"

He nodded in the direction of the beginning of the drive. "Well, actually up that way; but this is where our paths collide even more, and we are sitting here more so for me and not you."

"What?"

"This is Eden, Leah."

Leah's eyes widened. She had heard of Eden. She had sent people to Eden. She had talked with people from Eden, but Eden was a place to which she had never actually gone. She knew what it held and its purpose but had never actually set foot inside.

"Why here?"

"Honestly, because this is where I am going; and since you are along for the ride, this is where you are going."

She took it in for a moment and let it mull around in her mind. "So, what do I do? If this is where you are going, what is my role in all of this?"

He shook his head. "I wonder sometimes if I acted this stupid when I chose to be a Vapor."

She knew he had insulted her, but his words hit her like a ton of bricks. "Wait! *You're* a Vapor?"

"Guess you can say I'm your daddy."

"That's one thing I will not say!" she scoffed. "What do you mean by that, though?"

"I was the first Vapor. As I said, there are a lot of things I really don't want to get into; but the fact is, that yes, I was the first to walk away from it all . . . neither a Fallen or an Eternal. In fact, it was my lips that uttered the phrase about being like a vapor; thus, the name stuck."

She felt she was getting a headache. "The world really needs to slow its roll right now and give me a chance to process all of this."

"Get on," he stated as he straddled his motorcycle again, starting it up. "Let's see what the world has for us. My thought is we ride this out and see where it takes us."

She didn't say anything more. She got back on, and they made their way down the drive.

*****

Serenity had managed to rest for about an hour and then got back up to see if she would have a chance to talk to Gene alone. So much was in chaos right now, and she knew that she and Chad would need answers for Leah back at the Sanctum. She had checked her phone a few times to see if anyone had questioned where they were yet, and she thought it odd that there were no messages or missed calls.

She made her way down the staircase positioned to the left of the tree. She was hoping that Tori had managed to fall asleep. This would allow them time to figure out a plan moving forward, as well as allow the teenager to recoup the energy that she surely would need soon.

As she walked down the staircase, the front door to Eden opened; and she watched as a tall man walked in . . . and then she froze. It wasn't the man who made her stop but the fact that right behind him walked in her leader.

"What in the world is Leah doing here? Did she figure out where they were?" her thoughts raced. She attempted to walk quietly backwards up the stairs, hoping not to draw any attention to herself; however, just then the sound of small, running feet echoed down the stairs. Both the man and Leah looked up, and Serenity's heart sank. She was going to hear it now!

Leah looked just as shocked to see Serenity as Serenity was her. "What the . . ." Leah almost squealed. "What are you doing here?"

Now, of course, this puzzled Serenity, because she figured that she and Chad were the reason that her boss had shown up. She wasn't even sure what to say. Was this a test of some sort?

Serenity felt her mouth dry up like a sponge on a desert rock. Her mind raced trying to find a reason that Leah may believe but nothing came out. They both just stood, looking at each other.

Finally, Zarius spoke, "Well, I guess you both know each other. So . . . um . . . that is good."

"Seriously, though," Leah questioned, "why are you here?"

Just at that moment, from Leah's right, Chad's voice came bellowing out in some sort of attempt at rapping, "Rata-tat-tat, vampires go splat, as I come in, knocking them flat. I . . ." his voice trailed off as he walked into the foyer and spotted Leah. Then out of the corner of his eye, he caught a glimpse of Serenity on the stairs with a "you-are-an-idiot" look on her face.

"Chad?"

"Um . . . hi, Leah!"

"What is going on?" she inquired. "I . . . wait . . ." She paused as pieces started coming together in her mind. "Did you really bring that girl here? After I told you to take her to the hospital?"

Serenity finally found two words; but as they came out of her mouth, she almost gasped, wishing she could grab a hold of them and pull them back in. "I quit!"

Chad and Zarius stood with blank looks. Zarius felt like he was on a hidden camera show; and Chad felt like Serenity was an accomplice in a heist and had just handed him the bag of jewels and walked away.

"You what?" Leah felt her head spinning. "WHAT IS GOING ON?"

"Um, I think what she meant to say was she quits . . . hiding what we are doing?" Chad looked at Serenity, still standing frozen on the stairs, with a "come-on-I'm-trying-to-save-you-here" look.

"No, I really mean *I quit!* I quit the Alliance. So, why I am here is no concern to you, and what I did with the girl is also no concern to you! I mean, come on, Leah, now you don't have to worry about your Alliance or your reputation."

"My what? Wait . . ." Leah threw her hands up, indicating everyone needed to just stop for a moment. "No, *I* quit!" she stammered

Now both of Leah's former warriors stood, blank-faced. There was enough confusion to fill a whole room full of smoke and mirrors.

Zarius just stood looking at all of them and started chuckling. "Well, I guess that leaves me and this guy," motioning to Chad, "who *hasn't* quit . . . unless you are next?" He questioningly looked in Chad's direction.

The young man didn't know what to say. He shrugged his shoulders. "Sounds like the cool thing to do, but I honestly am not sure what I am doing right now. I was just going to go make a sandwich, and suddenly I found myself walking into a sideshow comedy act!"

*****

"What the hell is a Vapor?"

Serenity and Chad were leaning up against a tall table inside Gene's study. The older man was behind his desk, and Zarius and Leah were sitting in chairs across from him. They had just spent the last 30 minutes or more listening to Leah share her story about the Arch Council and her decision before them. Now both still had blank looks on their faces.

"So, this means that if I don't quit the Alliance, you don't get to show your authority over me?" Serenity asked with plenty of sarcasm pouring out of her mouth. Chad hit her in the side with his elbow. "I'm just saying!"

Leah looked over at her. She was calm, and her senses were about her. She knew from where the sarcasm was coming, and at other times she most likely would have gone off; but she could understand the meaning behind the words of Serenity's question. "Listen, I get it. I was hard on you, and we didn't always see eye-to-eye."

"More like *most of the time* we did not see eye-to-eye, Leah." This got another jab from Chad.

Leah paused for a moment and then continued. "What I am trying to say is this: I have always believed in you. I was hard on you because . . ."

"STOP!" Serenity put her hands up. "Just answer the damn question, Leah. I have to say I liked the belligerent Leah better than this soft one. Where do we stand?"

"Careful, Serenity, because I can promise you that I did hold back a lot more than you know; and now nothing is keeping me from unleashing on you. So, if you would allow me the chance to finish . . . I'm sorry. I don't know where we go from here. I am starting to think there is a larger plan in motion than any one person, and we are all going to need each other in the end."

"I couldn't have said it better myself," Gene quietly stated. "Now, if you all are done with this catfight, we can move forward!" He looked at both of them. Neither appeared to have anything more to say, so he moved on. "Now, Zarius . . . I must say I never thought I would ever see you here in Eden again."

"There are people who never thought they would see him again . . . period," Leah muttered under her breath but continued no further.

"I had never planned on being here again, Gene. Even now I would rather be somewhere other than here . . . with my wife."

"How is Tanisha?"

"She is currently on her way to Austria, I believe . . . something about helping a priest there. The last time we talked she started asking me questions about my past."

"Hmm . . . interesting. Like what?"

"I don't remember, really. I was tired and actually felt like she was accusing me of lying."

"Well, seems like accusing a dishonest being about lying isn't news!" Leah knew she had pushed the envelope, but she was feeling irritated and hungry . . . not a good mix.

"Leah, you are free to walk out at any time you like. You may have been the leader in *your* house, but here *I* run the show. I am pretty easy-going . . . but still . . . *my* house."

"Understood."

Chad raised his hand as if he was in middle school, and Serenity put her palm in his face. "Really? I guess we raise our hand now?"

"Ha! I have no idea what we do now, but I do have a question." he retorted.

"What is it, Chad?" Gene asked.

"Can we just slow everything down for a moment and catch up all the players? Like, who is he?" pointing to Zarius. "And again, what is a Vapor?"

Zarius shifted in his seat. He knew the questions would come; and he knew, just like he had shared with his wife, he would have to expose himself to the world. Hopefully, it would be with small doses at a time.

"I can explain the answers if you want me to, Gene."

"That is up to you. I do not tell the stories of others; that is up to them . . . or maybe a Watcher . . . which I am not."

"I will share with you as much as I feel you may need to know, but I ask that you respect my wishes in not sharing anything that I say here with anyone else. If Leah is right and the future has our paths going in the same direction, it is only fair that you all know who you are working beside. What I have to share is not known by many and is also personal. I am a private person and would have liked to remain that way, so please respect that."

They all nodded.

He took a deep breath. "Time to come home," he thought to himself.

*****

She could feel the cold Austrian air begin to fill the cabin as she stood to retrieve her carry-on luggage from above her. Her muscles were tight from the long, 13-hour flight; and she was excited to get to her room and rest before meeting Gerault in a few hours.

The cabbie was talkative and, fortunately, he didn't need her to carry on the other side of the conversation. She didn't bother letting him know that she had been here once before and let him go on and on about all the different things she should do while she was visiting.

The drive from the Klagenfurt International Airport had taken only about 45 minutes. Soon the car came to a stop, and she stepped out while the driver retrieved her bags from the trunk.

She took in the view that surrounded her. There were no words to describe the breathtaking, surreal, and inspiring landscape. Even in the light of the moon, it was clothed in shimmering beauty. From where she stood, she could see mountains and the valley without even moving. She loved her desert, but she now realized how much she had missed traveling.

She looked over the roof of the taxi at the Gasthof Zirbenhof, a comfortable, dark wood building with orange and green accents. There were flower boxes dotting the windows, and there was a sense of an "at-home cottage" feel to it.

She tipped the driver and took her bags from him and then walked the short but clear path to the small hotel. She thanked a young cheerful couple as they held the door open for her. There was an inviting fire that was crackling in the fireplace across from the reception desk. She was tired but felt a thrill to be once again in a different country, getting ready to do what she loved doing.

After receiving her room key from the slender and attractive Austrian, who seemed to be in her mid-30s, she made her way up a flight of stairs, down the hall, and to her room. She felt a sense of relief come over her as the door closed, and the room embraced her. She could just sit for a few minutes and try to take all this in.

Her room was made of lightly-stained wood. It held a hand-carved double bed and a green wardrobe. In one corner were a bench seat and table. This would allow her to spread out her notes and research if she needed; but then again, she had a hunch that most of her time would be spent away from the hotel.

From where she sat on the edge of the bed, she could see the pointed bell tower of her final destination lit up with several beams of light. The church was one of the centerpieces for historical researchers who would venture to this small slice of heaven. A building of gothic accents and a tall, slender bell tower that could be seen from miles away welcomed tourist and pilgrim alike.

The room smelled of old days gone by and new wood polish. She began unpacking her bags and putting away her clothes. She figured if she was going to be staying for a while, she might as well make herself at home. She pulled out a picture of her and Zarius and placed it beside the bed. Missing him would be the biggest downside of this trip, and knowing that he was facing some big challenges ahead for which she could not be there made it even harder.

Chapter Nineteen

"My hope is that in sharing this I will be able to keep things straight and clear," Zarius started. "There is a lot to it; but if it is not all shared, I can promise you that we will end this conversation with more confusion than when we started."

He looked at Chad and Serenity and then to Leah. "I promise you this: what you think you know, you do not know; and what you do not know is everything. I know that may seem a ridiculous statement right now, but trust me on this. You need to open your minds to the possibility that both mortal and immortal have been deceived.

"Yes, I betrayed my kind at the start of the rebellion or what has become known as the War of the Serpents. Why I did or the reasoning behind what I thought I was doing is neither here nor there. I did, and I accept responsibility. What happened several ages after that is what we need to talk about.

"Many ages ago the Eternals, both good and bad, began an open conversation. The Clans had become weak . . . much like today, and many were wanting to seek a way to return to what they knew before the exile. An agreement among mortal man, those Eternals who had not been exiled, and the Clans had been reached to hold a council to see what form of arrangement and penance could be achieved. This meeting was known as the Council of Shammah.

"For several days there were debates, talks, and a lot of arguments and disagreements; but on the sixth day, it seemed that an agreement had been reached. Many who had been exiled would be allowed to return to Scintillantes. Many of the Clan leaders would not be allowed back right away but a pathway to their returning had been discussed. The Council Hall was full, and the power of the ages was to be restored."

Chad stopped him. "Power of the ages?"

"Everything that exists is formed from energy, Chad," Leah explained. "That energy was generated from two deltas. Imagine two pyramid-type stones that were made to balance perfectly upon each other, point-to-point. Together they formed almost an hourglass shape."

"Wait . . . I thought all was formed by the existence of Jah . . . or something like that."

"In a way: Jah created the deltas," Zarius stated. "As I said, you will need to forget what you know and embrace what you do not know."

"Sorry," he apologized to Zarius. "Please continue."

"One Delta remained within the care of the Arch Council. Leah, this would be the Ancient Ones, not the Arch Council you know today."

"I have heard stories about the Ancient Ones but nothing of value. It seems no one will talk about them," she stated.

"And for good reason. To talk about them would expose more than those in power wish for anyone to know, and there are only a few who do."

You are one?" It was as if a lightbulb went off in her head. "That is why you chose to remain hidden throughout the ages?"

"Yes."

"Please continue, Zarius," Gene softly spoke as he sought to keep the conversation moving forward. "As you stated, there is a lot to share; and I will say that our time is limited."

"So, to show unity, each group represented were to join their deltas. There were three: one for the Ancient Ones, one for the Clans, and one for mortal man. When joined together, the two for the Eternals would balance point to point, one upright and one pointing down. This was to show equality. The one for mortal man was clear and hollow. It was larger and would encase the other two. This was to show that mortal man, when joined with Eternals, created a complete fullness of all that existed.

"Paschar represented the Ancient Ones. He came forward into the center of the room where there was a black onyx pedestal. Interwoven around this pedestal was a glowing, blue light. On top were grooves that indicated where the Ancient One's delta was to be placed. He placed it pointing upward; and as he did, there was a hum like one chord of a grand musical being played. The blue light began to overtake the delta, swirling around it and making it glow.

"I remember Mantus was next . . ."

"Mantus?" Leah interrupted. "You mean the Overlord of the Abyss?"

"Yes. He came forward with the delta that had been taken by the Clans during the War of the Serpents. He turned it with the point facing downwards, and it balanced perfectly upon the other. The glowing blue light from the pedestal began to move upward and engulfed both deltas. The song became fuller and harmonious.

"At this point, Climitriaus, the head of the Brotherhood of the Grigori, came forward with the third Delta that would encase the other two. Paschar stopped him, though, and stated that in order for the other two Deltas to become unified, they must be sealed with the blood of the Ancients."

"Grigori?" Chad asked.

"They were the predecessors to those you know as the Watchers," Zarius explained.

"Yeah, so I'm already kind of bored and yet weirdly intrigued. I mean, are we talking about a bad fantasy novel or can we skip some of the history lessons?" Serenity asked. "What does any of this have to with us now?"

Zarius realized that his wife's passion for antiquities may have rubbed off a little too much, so he thought for a moment on how he could shorten his story.

"Something went wrong. It is believed that the vial used was not a mixture of blood from both orders, the Ancient and the Clans. You see, if only one type of blood was used, then whatever blood was used would create a different, unbalanced reaction. The blue light turned red, like fire; and there was an explosion. Almost everyone was killed or seriously injured."

Leah's faced showed an expression of bewilderment and yet of understanding. "That is why we have the Arch Council we have today? The Ancient Ones did not survive?"

"Michael and Gabriel were the only Ancient Ones from the Arch Council that survived . . . they and almost every Clan Overlord. Mantus was severely burned but survived. That also was when it was believed that the Brotherhood of the Grigori ceased to exist.

We now know that a few survived, but they went into hiding; and the sect grew from there in secret."

"So, what you are saying is that the Overlords switched the vial of blood; it was only the blood of the Fallen that was poured over the Deltas?" Chad asked. "That is why the resulting reaction took place and most walked away without injury?"

"Yes, I believe so."

"But wasn't Pashcar an Ancient One? Wouldn't he know what was in the vial? Why would he use it?"

"You are right, but it is my belief that Michael was the one who gave him the vial."

"Wait! What?" Leah sat up straight. "Why would he do that?"

"You are talking about Michael the Archangel, right? I mean like the big guy that so many people here think is close to Jah?" Chad asked.

"Chad, I am . . . and to answer your question, Leah . . . because he is not who you think he is."

"What do you mean by that?" She couldn't believe she was wanting to defend the very member that had made it his goal to put her away in a corner, but to listen to someone who had betrayed everything she had fought for insinuate that Michael was working with the Fallen was beyond anything she could stomach. "Do you even know what you are saying?" she fumed. "You are talking about one of the greatest who has ever served on the Council! For ages, he has mentored so many Guardians and has kept the Fallen from destroying mankind!"

"I do know, Leah. If there is anyone who should know, I should."

"Oh, really? Why? Because you can clearly remember what

home is like? You can remember what everyone was like before you threw it all away?"

"No . . . because he is my brother."

The room went deathly quiet. No one said anything as the words that Zarius had spoken sank in.

"Ok, so, didn't see that one coming," Serenity stated as she walked over to a table that held different whiskeys and scotches. "On that note, I think I'm going to pour myself a drink! Anyone else?"

Chad held up his hand. "Yup . . . maybe even a double."

Leah sat stunned. Things were starting to become clearer. It all started to make sense. There was a reason Michael had held the Alliance back so many times. There was a reason she had felt as if they were behind the eight ball at times. If what Zarius was saying was true, then all this time they had been dancing to the music of the Fallen; and no one even knew.

"What you are saying is . . ."

"Unbelievable?" Zarius finished her sentence. "I know. He has relied on it all this time . . . relied on its being unbelievable. He also was relying on me to stay in hiding."

"Why now? What made you come forward now and then to think we would even believe you?"

"I didn't think anyone *would* believe me, and I still question if those who need to believe me will. Why? Well, because I believe he may be forcing my hand without knowing it."

"How so?" Serenity asked.

"The Deltas are powerful beyond mortal understanding. The one that mortals held, the casing, was ceremonial. You don't need it, but if someone were to get the other two and have the vial that was supposed to be used that day, . . ."

Leah gasped, "They could open up a way for the Fallen to overtake Scintillantes!"

Zarius nodded. "Oh, even worse than that!"

"What is worse than that," Chad asked, "or do I dare even bring that up?"

"I believe that with both Deltas in the wrong hands, life can be created. It would be created within the image of the one holding the power of the joined Deltas."

"Wait!" Leah was starting to see a picture that she did not want to think about. "With the right blood, Legion could be freed! The prophecies!"

"Legion? Like the voices and creatures inside Tori?"

Now it was time for Zarius to look confused. "Tori?"

"We found a young girl who appears to be possessed, yet unlike anything we have ever seen before, and . . ."

Serenity interrupted her partner. "The name Legion keeps coming up when we are dealing with whatever it is that seems to be inside of her."

"If Legion was freed and he had the Deltas, then it would mean the end of everything we know. We could not stop the Clans!"

Leah gasped. It seemed as if she had not even heard anything past her portion of the conversation over the last minute or so.

Gene sat back. As he spoke, his voice was calming, steady, and strong. "Each of you be quiet for a moment. Chaos creates confusion. Confusion creates fear. Fear creates a void that is very hard to overcome. Stop for a moment and breathe. We can change nothing at this point. What we can do is plan. What we can do is work together. What we can do is focus."

"Gene is right," Serenity spoke as she sipped from her newly-poured glass of whiskey. She handed Chad his. "We keep talking about the Delta-whatever things . . . these comic-book stones of power . . . and the fact is, we don't know if they are even around anymore!"

Zarius laughed a little bit as he grabbed his bag that he had earlier placed beside him on the floor. "Actually . . ." He reached in and pulled out a pyramid-shaped black rock with ancient carvings on each side. He placed it down on the desk in front of Gene.

"AND OF COURSE HE WOULD PULL OUT A MAGICAL PYRAMID!" Chad groaned.

"This is what I meant by Michael forcing me out of hiding without really knowing he was. He believes I have it, but he is not sure. He came to visit me to test the waters. I don't think he believed that if I did have it, I would expose myself. I have no doubt that my brother would kill me for this."

"Well, now that we have gone all Cain and Abel," Serenity laughed, "anyone else want to confess to anything else?"

Leah sat quietly. She was focusing. She needed to know more about being a Vapor. What she did not know about being a Vapor, she made up in knowing how to take on the Fallen. She may have lost a lot, but there was even more she had not lost. War was coming, and she knew that she had to be ready. Sure, she may have lost her team; but she could feel around her another team growing.

"My suggestion," Gene said as he leaned forward, "is for us to take a break. Most of us just heard things that we never knew, and others are worn out for sharing things we may not have been ready to share. We take a break. Let me check on the comings and goings of Eden, and then we can get back together. There may be nothing we can do right now. Much of what we have discussed has been speculative, but we need a break."

They all agreed and slowly left the study, each in their own thought.

*****

Eve wasn't sure on whose car she was sitting and, frankly, she didn't care. She kept a watchful eye on the building in front of her . . . more specifically, the second-floor window to the left.

She had stopped and got a deli sandwich about an hour ago, but that was long gone. She looked down at the wrapper and then reached over and stuffed it in between the windshield wiper and the windshield. "Technically it isn't littering," she laughed.

The front door to the building in front of her opened, and a young man in his late 20s with sandy hair and beard walked out. He was looking down at his phone and then stopped as he looked up. He shook his head and walked across the street to where she was sitting. He looked over at the food wrapper. "You?"

"What?" Eve responded. "I don't recognize it."

"Uh-huh."

"Well?"

"I haven't heard anything from his apartment today. I would imagine he is passed out again. He had a pretty bad rage moment yesterday."

"When?"

"I told you! Yesterday!"

She jumped down and hit his shoulder. "Come on, Byron!"

"Brian"

"That's what I said, Byron."

"Eve, seriously! Most people would have given up on him a while ago and just let him be."

"You have known me for . . . how long?"

"Well, you did my first tattoo about seven years ago."

"And in that seven years, have you ever known me to be like 'most people'?"

"Nope, that is why I like you."

Eve laughed and poked a finger in his chest. "And that, Byron, is why I like you."

She spun around with her back toward the building and looked him up and down. He had hit on her a few times, but she never could find the attraction. He was a nice guy and all but just no real attraction. Then, of course, that was all before the whole supernatural stuff came forward. He didn't know about that, and she planned on keeping it that way.

"Well, I'm late for work and you have a drunk man to save." He gave her a hug and headed down the sidewalk.

Eve watched him for a moment. He was a guy who would treat a lady right, but she didn't need any distractions . . . and there was that attraction thing: it just wasn't there.

Eve headed across the street, walked in, and then walked up to the second floor. She paused at the door on the left and listened for a moment. There was nothing but silence, and she was pretty sure she already knew what she was going to be walking into. She reached above the door, found the "hidden" key, and then unlocked the lock.

*****

Michael stood looking at the minimal furnishings scattered around Tanisha's desk. He flipped through a few of her journals but found nothing that caught his eye. One thing for certain, it did not appear that anyone was coming back in the near future. "Where are you two?"

He had to find his brother . . . well, actually find what he believed his brother *had*. "I know you have it, Zarius. I can feel it. I saw it in your eyes when I talked with you."

He moved around the room a little more, and a notepad sitting beside a coffee machine caught his eye. There, in Tanisha's handwriting, was a checklist: "Book flight – Austria; Email Gerault notes on the manuscripts; Book hotel room."

He smiled as he recognized the name of the old priest. "Well, how close you were to letting secrets out, Old Friend. Won't she be surprised when she arrives and finds you no longer there!"

He sat down on the couch and thought for a moment. "If she is in Austria, then where, oh, where art thou, Brother? Maybe there is more than one way to get you to appear. I think my sister-in-law needs a visit. I'm sure she will be heartbroken to find her dear old priest is no longer walking among the mortals."

Chapter Twenty

"Eeny, meeny, miny, moe, how do you catch a snake when you don't want him to know?"

Michael didn't move. He knew it didn't matter, anyway. Mantus would already have an attack plan ready for him if he tried anything. "Your breath smells like a fire pit, Mantus!"

The Overlord walked out from behind a metal partition and leaned against it. Michael could hear movement behind him. He was certain it was more of Mantus' minions, the general's way of showing power.

"Azrael! Really? That is all you can think of saying? When you spoke with my brother, he led me to believe your words had more bite than that; but then again, you always were one who preferred to fight from the shadows, never really from the front.

"Your wife wouldn't say that about me."

Before he could say or do anything more, he felt a thick wire go around his throat, pulled tight and upward. His eyes began to bulge, and the color of his skin began to change as he fought back, trying to regain even the slightest breath. Mantus slowly walked over and looked straight into his face. "You say something like that about her again, I promise you it will be the last thing you say. True, she is a whore; but she is my wife . . . and a whore."

Mantus looked up at his lackey and nodded. The restraint around Michael's neck was loosened.

"You are a fool, Mantus!"

"Maybe."

"Why are you here?"

"Well, here is where you are, so here is where I am. I do believe you made it clear to Dumah that if I wanted to talk with you without being taken in by your battalion of troops, that I better do it in an area where I was safe. Can't say the same for you."

Michael moved to where he could see all of those present in the room in order to keep a better eye on any chance of another attack. "What do you want, Mantus?"

"Speaking of my whore of a wife, you visited her recently. After you did, she got a hold of me."

"Well, that is great! Look at me: bringing families together. Maybe I should consider marriage counseling!"

"Possibly, but I think it is frowned upon for you to sleep with someone else's spouse whom you are counseling."

Michael smirked and thought of something to say, but his hand went to his throat and he thought better of it. "If you are really here because I went to see her, then maybe she told you that she refused to talk with me."

"She didn't really say that; but I figured as much, although I do believe you piqued her interest. In fact, you piqued it enough for her to call me; and now *my* interest is piqued."

"It was nothing. I thought I may have figured a way to set things right, set things the way they were supposed to be if we had succeeded at our overthrow; but when she wouldn't listen, I realized it was futile."

Mantus moved around the room, looking at everything he could see. "Why here, Azrael? Whose place is this?"

"We all have our vices, Mantus; and the mortal female is mine."

Mantus picked up a shirt of Zarius' and threw it at the Council member. "Hmm . . . does her husband know?"

"What I do here and who knows is no business of yours. Are we done?"

"No, in fact, we are not. I have a proposal for you."

"Oh, do you now?"

"Sure, I will defend Hecate—more out of spite to you—but we both were used by her. I will never allow you or any of the other Clan leaders to claim Legion, but we also have a common enemy in Hecate."

"I'm listening."

"I think, even if you have given up on whatever it was you were thinking about doing, that Hecate has decided that now is actually the time that she can prey upon the weakness of the Clans. Unlike her, I do not make promises; but I also believe that if she would rise to any form of power or figure out a way to unleash the power of Legion, then we all will be doomed. I love and despise my son all in one breath.

"The Clans, on the other hand, are steeped in prophecy and tradition. That could be their downfall. They would follow Legion out of obligation to prophecy instead of thinking on their own."

"So, what do you want me to do?"

"I believe we can call her bluff and reveal to them who she truly is."

Michael pondered this. He didn't really trust Mantus any

more than he trusted Hecate, but he felt there was a chance that Mantus may trust him more than the general should.

The Archangel knew his time was either up or coming close to it. He didn't know where his brother was now; and without that knowledge, it put him between a rock and a hard spot. If, by chance, Zarius did have the delta and he was able to get it from his brother, there was still the matter of finding the other one. To do that, he was pretty sure he would need help. It would be a gamble; but if he could find one of the deltas without Mantus' knowing, then just maybe he could use Mantus to find the other one. Why wouldn't he? One delta is not worth anything, and if the Overlord didn't think the other one existed anymore, . . .

"Ok, I am willing to entertain the thought; but at any time I think you are trying to double cross me, I'm out. If at any time I think you are jeopardizing my cover with the Arch Council, I'm out."

Mantus laughed. "Ok, although I'm not sure how much cover you have left back home, Azrael. I can't believe that questions aren't starting to come up on why you are making the decisions you are making. If it is time for the Houses to come into power, then you will be revealed. If it is time for the Clans to rise, then we also must come together and stop Hecate."

"I think that is something on which we both can agree."

Mantus smiled, nodded to the group he had brought with him, and they walked out. Michael sat back on the couch, rubbing his neck and sighing a big sigh of relief that he was able to keep Mantus from realizing the goldmine in which he had been standing. If Mantus discovered that Zarius was alive, there would be a lot more questions that would come up; and Michael was sure that he would be smart enough to realize the real reason for Zarius' maintaining secrecy all these years.

*****

There was a foul smell as she opened the door to the apartment. Eve couldn't tell exactly what it was, but it made her stomach turn. She tried the lights and, of course, they did not come on. "Pay your damn light bill!" she muttered.

She walked into the living room. On her way to the blinds, she had to step over empty liquor bottles and takeout food containers half full of food. Many of them had been knocked over onto the floor, and her boots stuck to the carpet.

She twisted the blinds to let the light in; and there he was, lying half on and half off the couch. She went over and kicked him, but he just grunted.

Eve looked around the room at the mess. Among the knocked-over bottles and trash, she saw a cardboard box full of papers, photos, and notes. Sitting on the top was a photo of a husband and wife and their little girl. She went over and picked it up. She just shook her head. "I'm so glad they can't see you now. Of course, if they were here you may not be like this."

She knew the rest of the contents of the box. She didn't have to look. He had shown her the night it was delivered. She remembered his looking confused and even scared. "What does all of this mean? What am I supposed to do with all of this?" he had asked her.

"I still don't know," she whispered. "The old man had a reason for having it delivered to you." She pushed one of the flaps of the box down and saw Alfonso's handwriting and the words, "Deliver to Isaiah," written in beautiful cursive.

She happened to spot a plastic cup filled with a clear liquid. She picked it up, smelled it, and determined it was water. She walked over to the passed-out Nephelium and emptied the contents on his face.

He awoke with a yell. He sat up, trying to get the water out of his eyes and off his face. "Are you kidding me, Eve? I was just sleeping!"

"Now, that one has gotten way too old! At least if you are going to keep lying to me about your quitting drinking and keep passing out on me, you could at least come up with a different lame excuse as to what you are doing!"

She threw him a shirt that seemed to be the cleanest of several that were lying around and a pair of jeans. "Do me another favor: if you are going to get drunk and pass out, please either do so dressed OR get some boxers. The 'tighty-whities' are not flattering."

"Can we close the blinds? The sunlight is killing my eyes!"

"Well, you are in luck! Give it about an hour, and it should be setting. Then once again, you can embrace yourself in your dark cocoon!"

"You know if you weren't just about the only friend I had right now, I would kick you out!"

"Well, you are lucky you even have me as a friend. So many other things I could be doing other than babysitting a drunk preacher."

"*Former* preacher. Now . . . well, I'm a drunk demon."

She swung around and slapped him hard across the face.

"Guess I deserved that."

"Yeah, ya did. I warned you if you ever refer to our kind as demons again that it would be coming your way."

Isaiah stood up and waited for the room to stop spinning. He pulled on the pair of jeans and the shirt and then fell back down onto the couch.

Eve didn't even know where to sit. She really hated him right now. It had been a year after the incident at The Vortex and Alfonso's death when the box had been delivered.

Isaiah had felt he had lost everything the night he chose to reveal to his friends and the Alliance that he also was a Nephelium. He had lived the lie for so long, trying to blend in; but that night he could not watch the innocent be destroyed any longer. Many had turned their back on him. Then when he received the box from Alfonso, even though Eve had been hurt that Alfonso had not sent it to her, she had hoped it would bring new life back into a former warrior of a man. It had not.

Since that night at The Vortex, they had begun to understand each other a lot better. Troy had tried to mend his relationship with Isaiah, but he never could get over what he felt was a betrayal.

After a while, Isaiah had felt more and more eyes on him; and he felt that more of the Alliance were questioning his actions and talking behind his back. Soon he began to understand why the Fallen considered any Nephelium an outcast.

Eve's actions that night at The Vortex had been daggers to his heart; but time moved forward, and soon they only had each other. No, he didn't believe she was any different than her choices that night had made her. Her bloodlust for revenge was more than he could understand. He knew that the darkness of the Fallen danced upon the cellular structure of her being, but she had been able to keep it from consuming her so far.

That day when the box had arrived, he had asked her to come over. They had sat together in his living room as he opened it. Together they had looked at all the notes, personal writings, journals, et cetera, that lay out in front of them on his floor. For a moment she believed he felt that sense of belonging return. As he read the letter scribed in Alfonso's handwriting, the full impact of it all hit him like a semi-truck hitting a concrete barrier. The more they dug into it, the more she watched as he closed himself off again. The understanding of what was being asked of him was too much. The letter had expressed that if Isaiah was in possession of this box, that it meant that he had been appointed by a Watcher to succeed him. Alfonso had given clear directions on what he was to do.

They argued for so long after that night. She was angry because she knew how important it was to Alfonso that what he asked would be carried out. She knew that the belongings within the box were important, but Isaiah refused to even look at them again. He stated that his time had come and gone.

She tried to go over the things in the box with him. For over a year she studied and went through all the notes that the old Watcher had penned for so many of his years. She was able to finally get Isaiah to at least look at them. They learned of books of prophecy and ancient text that had not been understood by mortals, but the Watchers had ensured that they were not lost. Stories of demonic lineages and evil manipulations . . . re-interpretation of things that mortals had thought so true for generations . . . now had new meaning within their conscience. The deeper they went, the more they began to realize what a thin line of balance they all were walking.

Much of it was new to Eve, but she could tell that it bothered Isaiah a lot. When she asked him about it, he would shut down and start drinking. One night, when he was wasted, he explained that so much of what he had preached behind the pulpit and to what he devoted himself was all lies.

There were stories of battles throughout the centuries in which so much of mortal man's very existence had played out beyond the curtain of reality. Finally, they opened and read what they believed was Alfonso's last letter or journal entry:

"Isaiah, when you have studied what I have given you, and you have begun to see the picture emerge, then, and only then, you must go to the church of Saint Vincent. There you will continue your learning under the watchful eye of the Watcher there and become the Guardian of the Vial."

– Alfonso

There were a lot of questions Isaiah still had. He made excuses as to why he would not be able to carry out any of the old Watcher's request.

They had learned from Alfonso's notes that the Brotherhood of the Watchers was far from gone; however, the exact number was not known and, out of respect for the Brotherhood, was never discussed. The most important fact they had learned was that the Watchers had been doing everything they could to hold off a prophecy from being fulfilled: the prophecy of the return of the Dracon . . . or Legion.

*****

The sun had started to go down, and Isaiah had sobered up some. Eve lit a few candles and heated up water on the gas stove to make some coffee for Isaiah to drink. "I'm not cleaning any of this up again."

He huffed, "Yeah, I don't expect you to."

"So, what was it this time? Brian said you were raging last night, and by the fresh holes in the wall I must believe him."

"I want to, Eve, but I just can't. I'm scared. I can rush onto the battlefield; I can face demonic hordes; but this, . . ." he said, pointing to the box, "*this* scares me!"

"Yup, we have been down this road before. That doesn't answer my question. What sent you over the edge this time?"

He looked at her and then grabbed his phone. He activated the screen, did a few swipes, and then handed it to her.

She took it, puzzled, and then looked down at the screen. She couldn't believe it! "You bought tickets?"

"I did. As soon as I did, I regretted it; but now that I did, I guess I'm going to Austria."

She normally would not hug him, but this time she did. "You got this!"

"*We* got this!"

"I know. I told you that I have your back. That is why I am here, yet again, in this filthy, dank apartment, waking up your drunk self!"

"No, I mean . . . I also bought *you* a ticket!"

She looked back down at the phone. She hadn't seen it before; but sure enough, there it was: two tickets purchased.

"What? No! I'm not going! This is *your* journey . . . *your* mission! I have things I have to do here!"

"Eve, we both know that I can't do this alone. There is no way. I will land there and find the closest pub and drink myself to death. I will most likely make the news for being some drunk American veteran in a foreign country taking a leak on some ancient landmark."

She shook her head. "No."

"Why? Because of your revenge mission? Is this what he wanted for you?"

She glared at him. "Don't go there, Isaiah!"

"I *will* go there; and you can slap me, hit me, kick me! I don't care! Maybe the reason he gave me the box is that he knew that, if the time came that he was not around, I would understand that I needed to reveal to you who I am. He knew that you had no one else but him; and if he was gone, then you would need someone. We need each other."

She could feel her muscles tightening, her fist clenching, and her jaw setting. She hated him right now. She wanted to go off on him, but something deep within her knew that what he was saying was probably right. Alfonso had a way of always being several steps ahead of everyone else, and he had always made sure she was taken care of.

She didn't need anyone now, though. He had been the last one she needed. When he was killed, she realized that she was to be alone; and she embraced it.

Chapter Twenty-One

Isaiah reached over and pulled out an envelope from underneath the pile of stuff scattered across his coffee table. He handed it to Eve. "What you don't know is that inside the box there was something else. Maybe it was wrong of me to hold on to it, but I did. I don't know what is in it; but I felt that it may be something directing you to make me go through with all of this, and I didn't want to have to fight you over it. You are all I have, and I also knew that I wasn't ready for all of this."

She took the envelope. She didn't know what to say. There was her name written by Alfonso. She was angry and hurt all in one breath. "How dare you! You had no right."

"I know. All I can say is that I am sorry. Nothing else, Eve. You have done nothing but right by me; and for me to hold onto this . . . well, it was wrong."

She took the envelope and turned it over in her hands. Whatever was inside was from a man she had loved more than any other man or person in her life. She could feel his power and love as if they were coming off the envelope. There were tears starting to brim up in her eyes. She stood up and walked out of the apartment.

She found herself having a hard time standing. Her chest hurt, and her hands shook. These past five years she had done everything to bottle up the anguish she felt as she had held his bleeding and mangled body in her arms. So much had changed that night for so many; but for her, everything had ended. The Eve that she had seen looking back at her in the mirror for 20-something years was no longer there. She had died within that room of The Vortex.

She carefully opened the sealed envelope. She didn't want to just rip into it. He had taken care to seal it just perfectly. Her mind was racing to see what was inside; yet her heart was pleading to slow down, embrace this moment. A small sliver of the old Eve ignited past the dark inkiness of the Nephelium that had taken over.

It was a letter . . . not written on lined paper. He always hated that. He felt letters were to be written on blank sheets. "A blank sheet with only memories and deepest thoughts placed upon it," he would say.

She felt tears start falling when she noticed a small coffee stain in the upper righthand corner. She lifted it up and smelled it. Yep, it still smelled like coffee.

My Dearest Eve, My Daughter,

I am not going to placate to the art of sympathy and all the words that can be shared about how if you are reading this, what it means. No, I will not taint this for you in that fashion.

Instead, I will make an ill attempt to do what I have always desired to do: express my pride, love, and instruction to a woman who once was a young girl, now a lady who has taken on the weight of the world head-on with such tenacity and fortitude that you have allowed an old man the opportunity to swell with such waves of pride.

From the day that I saw you inside that booth, I knew. I instantly had no doubt that you were placed into my life, not just for your sake but for mine. As a human, I knew that you could accomplish greatness, and as a Nephelium, I knew that the world would be hard for you. I worked diligently to keep you protected and loved. I wanted nothing more than you to live out your existence on this earth knowing that you had been loved more than my own life.

There are two roads, My Daughter, that lay before you. One is the road that leads to revenge that your heart will, in anger, scream out for. This road is the road to destruction. It is not the way I desire for you, but I am not the one to choose your journey—you are. If you choose this road, know that it will not diminish any love that I have for you. If I was there, it would break my heart to see you travel down this road that has no real reward or end, but my love remains.

The second road, if I could choose, would be the road I would choose for you, My Dear. It is the road not so easily visible, but the best roads rarely are. It is the road that will lead you to fulfillment. Oh, there will be heartache on both roads. There will be rough times on both roads. The second road, though, is one where you take all that I have poured into you and invest it back into others. This road—ah—this road, my dear Eve, will swell up within. It will embrace you. It will nurture you, as I have; for in nurturing others, we find true nourishment within ourselves.

Farewell, My Daughter. I am never gone, for as long as you are, there I am also.

Love,
Alfonso

As the tears flowed freely down her face as if a dam, which had been in place for so long, finally broke, she felt a hand on her shoulder. She leaned her head against it. "You were wrong in holding this from me, Isaiah; but I also believe that if I had received this back then, I would not have read it the way I do tonight."

"I know, Eve. I hate to see what you have become . . . what we *both* have become."

"You can change your path still, Isaiah . . . but I am not sure that I can. I chose my road, as he says in this letter, years ago. Revenge feeds me every night. I cannot run from its tentacles. It holds me tightly and comforts me in the darkness when my mind's demons confuse me to what is real and what is only in my imagination."

"Come with me. Maybe we can cut those ties together."

She looked up at him. His smile accented his dark skin. She had not seen that smile in a very long time. "I will go with you; but not for me . . . for *you*, Isaiah. Eve, Alfonso's daughter, died the night he did."

*****

Denora was cursing at Hecate right now. She wasn't sure how Hecate had discovered that Mantus was meeting with Michael, but here she was sitting in the middle of the desert trying to make heads or tails of the Overlord's meeting and movements.

The night was starting to fall, and a chill was setting in. Mantus had just left, but Hecate had instructed her to keep tabs on Michael. He seemed to be camped out inside a very non-glamourous dwelling.

"Who would think the desert would be cold?" she griped as she looked through a set of binoculars to see if she could see anything worth remembering. A pack of coyotes was starting their evening hunt, and a bobcat had hardly given her notice as he walked past about 30 minutes ago. "Light the place on fire; dance naked, for all I care! Just do *something!*"

Denora was sitting at the base of a Joshua tree, stomach growling for food and her mind frustrated. In the flash of one breath, she caught a sense of someone beside her and felt a blade pressed against her neck.

"Don't move! Don't look around . . . and whatever you do, I beg you to go for that blade you have tucked away!" It was a male voice, one that she believed she should recognize but just couldn't pinpoint it.

"Ok, I hope you understand who I am and what I can do if you choose not to run that blade across my neck," she spat defiantly.

He laughed. "Well, it has been a while, but let me see if my memory is still as keen as I think it is. You are Denora, former Lieutenant of Arioch, a former member of the Clan Adramelech; but of course, that is only because Arioch wasn't successful in his bid for his own Clan. Grant it he has his own now, but that is a story for another time. I believe now you may be with the House of Hecate."

There! She recognized the voice. She took her hand slowly and placed it against the double-edged blade, pushing it against her neck until she could feel the pain of it cutting her skin and her hand. She then removed her hand and licked the blood from the cut. "Kadar, half-breed, wanna-be assassin, hired gun, and self-proclaimed leader of the Nephelium Clan! It has been some time!"

Kadar removed the blade from her neck but kept it pointed inches away from her as he moved around to her front. "I'm flattered!"

"Don't be," she said in disgust. "You are far from home, Castaway."

"I could say the same about you; and I also could think of a few other choice names to call you in return, but all those are such childish things."

He wiped the blade and returned it to its hidden sheath. He plopped down beside her and looked out in the direction of Zarius' house. "So, what are you doing?"

"Straight to the point, Kadar?"

"Well, would you like for me to pull out a picnic? Maybe snap a selfie?"

"Maybe. I am starving."

He reached into his pocket and pulled out a piece of unwrapped jerky and attempted to hand it to her. "It is my last piece, but I'm willing to share."

Denora looked at it in disbelief and pushed it away. "No, I think I will go without."

She never understood how poised he could be and so relaxed. He actually lay down and propped himself up on one of his elbows. He looked down at the jerky in his hand and took a large bite out of it. The rest he used as a pointer toward the house. "So, we on a stakeout or something?"

"*WE* are on nothing. I work alone, and *YOU* just happen to be here for some bizarre and freaky, stalker-type reason."

"Hey, I'm not the one with binoculars!"

He had her there. No, he was just the one who seemed to appear out of nowhere, thousands of miles from where she was used to seeing him. She really did despise him. Sure, he was attractive; but she couldn't get past the part where he was an outcast, a half-breed. "You never do anything, go anywhere without a reason, Kadar.

We both know that neither of us is acting on our own; and most likely, neither of us want to be here. So, let's cut to the chase."

He took another bite of jerky and waved it around indicating that she should continue.

"Hecate has me watching Mantus and Azrael. For some reason, they just had a meeting in there." She pointed to the building. "I have no clue why; and honestly at this point, I really don't care."

"You ever get tired of all of this?" he asked. "What are we really doing all of this for? Over and over we find ourselves like bad remakes of the same movie, and we continually get a supporting role!"

"Nope, not going to join anything you got going on, Kadar."

He feigned hurt. "I can't believe you would even insinuate that!" He paused, and then laughed. "Ok, so don't hate on me for trying. I'm just saying."

"You still haven't told me why you are here."

"You are right." He got up and stretched. "What I can say is this: I have always told you to be careful the game you play. I'm serious, Denora. You are one hell of a fighter, and you have a great strategic mindset. There are not too many who I think could give me a run for my money, but you are one. Don't get me wrong; I would still leave you hanging on a fence post, gurgling in your own blood and choking on your own tongue, but it would be a good fight.

"Think about it, though. You come from a lineage of hierarchy and strength! Your father, Paimon, a loyal lieutenant to the

Morning Star, still to this day is revered as one of the fiercest of all the Houses. You should be controlling things, yet you continually play second fiddle to others."

"Why are you here, Kadar?"

He started to walk into the darkness of the night. "I miss you, Denora . . . I missed you."

She reached for the knife inside the top of her boot. It wouldn't kill him, but it would sure stop him. She reached around, looking down to see if she could see it sticking out.

"I will send it to you, My Friend. I would rather not have it in my back," the assassin yelled out to her.

"Curse him!" she muttered. She should have realized he had swiped it.

*****

It was dark enough outside where she was able to move up to the house without having to worry that the barren landscape offered barely any cover. She pressed up against one of the walls and tilted her head so that she could look inside the window and not be seen.

She observed and listened for several minutes and could tell the place was empty. "Damn it!" she cursed. "Michael must have slipped out while I was being taunted by Kadar!"

She made her way to one of the doors and let herself in. Standing in the center of the living area she stopped and focused. There had to be a reason why Mantus and Michael were here; there had to be some sort of value to this place.

She closed her eyes and allowed the energy of the area in which she stood flow through her. She tapped into the threads of time. Kadar was right: to some, she was royalty within the Clans. She had gained certain traits from her father, and one was the ability to stand between mortal and immortal where the strings of the concept of time stopped and eternity began. Many mortals may consider this a form of time travel; then again, that would indicate that time was a real thing and not just the curtain of measurement created by mortality.

Blurred visions of a woman walking around with a cup of coffee and a cell phone came to her. She sensed that she was a part of the fabric of the place. Denora watched her as she went over to a desk and began to write things down inside a notebook. Denora mimicked the vision and walked to the desk. The journal in which the lady was writing was not on the desk, but Denora kept focused. She watched as words began to form in her consciousness.

"Artifact," "Vial," "Ancient Text," she spoke each out loud. She began to sense another presence, so Denora turned. There was another figure, but he seemed different. She felt like she was seeing him as a reflection within a bathroom mirror covered in steam. "Why are you not coming into focus?" She sensed there was a conversation going on, but she could not hear it. "Voices . . . where are their voices?" she questioned to herself. "Strange," she pondered.

The lady in her vision was still writing, and Denora looked back down and gasped. The lady was drawing now. She was sketching out a pyramid-shaped stone and writing out the dimensions of the stone beside it.

"A delta? Where are you getting this information?" She continued to watch as the vision faded and came back. Now the woman was writing down a few more things and a name. "Gerault?"

Denora felt she had enough to take back to Hecate. She wasn't sure what it all meant and still wasn't quite sure why Azrael and Mantus had been there. She had not seen them in her vision, and who was the male figure? She wasn't sure; but what she did have, she hoped Hecate could make sense of it.

Chapter Twenty-Two

"Can we talk?" Leah had walked up beside Serenity as she was standing, looking out at the snow that was starting to fall.

"I will try; but to be honest, Leah, there is a lot going on in my head right now, and I'm not sure I am in a good head space to talk."

"That is fair. I just need to share some things before we get caught up again in whatever all of this is," she motioned around her.

"Sure."

Leah felt vulnerable, and that was new. She didn't like it, but there wasn't much right now she was going to be able to do about it. "I'm sorry."

Serenity turned and looked at her with some confused puzzlement. "About what, Leah? What exactly is it that you are sorry for?"

"This isn't easy for me," Leah said, putting her hand up to stop her counterpart, "so, could we forego the sarcasm?"

There was no response, just silence, so Leah continued, "Since you came to the Alliance, I have not been myself." That sounded more like an excuse than an apology. She was growing frustrated. "Listen, you are great at everything you do. You are great at looking at things differently than those around you, and that makes you vital!

"I hated being stood up to, but I also admired that from you. Honestly, you kept me in check and even probably saved all of us from making some stupid choices. I appreciated it and hated it all at once.

"You were a constant reminder of many things. Your voice reminded me daily of what I was supposed to be, who I used to be. You reminded me often of why we do what we do, even though many times I just wanted to throw it all to the wind. You also kept reminding me that I was slipping away. My anger, my stubbornness, and my personal vendettas were eating at me, clouding my judgment. For all of that, I am sorry and grateful for you."

Serenity took in everything that her former leader said. She didn't respond right away but just chewed on it. After a moment, she responded, "Leah, thanks. I'm pretty sure I know how hard that was for you. Not really sure I could have done it, and not sure I can. I'm sure I owe you an apology, also; but right now, I just don't care. Why you are a Vapor or whatever you are doesn't matter to me. What matters is that young girl. What matters is that we get all this right.

"I can't promise a friendly end to all of this. I won't promise to send you Christmas cards or go out for drinks when everything is said and done. What I know is that mortal man has been a pawn within the web of immortal deceit. We have been treated no differently than ants inside one of those stupid little ant farms.

"Yeah, you may think you helped us; however, all you really did was rearrange the sand to make us believe that our world had changed . . . and sometimes for the better. The whole time we have still been sandwiched inside some small glass cosmic container. You don't get a medal for refusing to hold a magnifying glass up over our lives and burning us with some holy ray of light."

"You are right, and I have nothing more to say," was Leah's response. She didn't. She was lost between two worlds, and that is where her new world now was being built.

Serenity just shook her head and walked away, leaving Leah standing alone. She felt cold, almost dead. She couldn't clear her mind. It seemed like so many voices and sounds were screaming and having an argument inside.

"I just wish I could find silence and peace! I wish the voices would just shut up," she stated out loud.

"I can totally relate! You can hear them, too?"

She looked behind her and recognized the young lady whom the team had brought in from The Warehouse. She had walked up from the opposite direction in which Serenity had gone. She was the same girl, yet different. She looked . . . well, she looked alive for one thing but also not as troubled.

"Hi, I'm Tori." She held out her hand.

"I know." Leah smiled and shook her hand. Twinges of guilt stuck at her like small pinheads. The team had been right; she had been willing to just throw this young girl to the wolves. Had losing so many really become like thick scales over her empathy?

"How did you know?" she quizzed.

"Well, my name is Leah, first off."

A small cloud passed over Tori's face. "The same Leah that wanted to just have me dropped off at a hospital?"

Yep, there was the sledgehammer. "Guilty as charged."

"Hmm . . . I was expecting some old, crusty hag who was just grumpy and hated people. You seem like someone pretty cool."

This made Leah smirk a little. "Well, actually you were not far off. I'm older than you may think; I do tend to be grumpy; and slowly I have begun hating people. Thanks for the compliment, though."

"Why did you want Chad and Serenity to take me and just dump me, though?" She walked up and sat on the windowsill beside which Leah was standing. She felt the cold glass through her shirt and enjoyed the contrast to the warmth of her body. "If it was because you hate people, what did I do to you? I have never met you."

"I don't know, Tori."

"Is it because of Legion?"

Leah wanted to say that it was and, of course, that *was* the reason she used originally; however, if she was honest, she knew that it had nothing to do with the young girl's possessor. It was about Eve; and yes, it was even about herself.

"I think it was because I knew I was just done with everything— done with fighting; done with filling my role; done with trying to just be the one who sweeps in each time to make things better. I didn't want to admit that I have failed and didn't want to take the chance of failing again."

"So, who asked you to be that person?"

"What?"

"Who asked you? I didn't ask you to come in and fix me or my situation. Did anyone else?"

"You were lying in my medical room of my building!"

"Was I? I mean, there weren't other people that work there or reside there?"

"I'm not following."

"Probably because you are old and stuff." She laughed while Leah just rolled her eyes. "My point is that there is not one single person in this world or universe that can handle everything, for everyone, by themselves. When my home life sucked, I couldn't change it. I lived there, and it affected me; but I couldn't change it. When my boyfriend dumped me, I couldn't bring the prick back. Nope, I had to call a girlfriend to talk me off the proverbial ledge. I had to rely on my friends for a place to stay and encourage me when my life just sucked. I didn't rely on just *one* friend! Come on! Even on my social media apps, I make sure I have lots of people to hit up, because we are not about a solo act. It takes the whole cast of your life to bring about that life and to write the screenplay."

Leah tried to follow the young teenager's logic; and the more she talked—even though confusing—it seemed to make sense.

"I mean, I don't know why I am here. I don't know why I got the demonic lord of the universe tapped into my chakra or whatever. I have no clue why Serenity and Chad chose to not just drop me off and forget about me. Doesn't matter, right? I mean we all still end up in the same place: here. Why? Eh, who knows? But I do know that there is not even one of us that has it all down.

"My grandpa on my mom's side once told me that a bow with a string is just a stick, and a stick with a string is a bow. But without the arrow, you will still go hungry."

Leah sat down beside her. "You know, that is some pretty deep stuff there."

Tori looked at her and smirked. "Yep, and they don't teach you that in some damn hospital."

Leah laughed. "Touché."

*****

She sat, surrounded by antiquities, a library of manuscripts, melted candles, and one stupid cat. She was fairly sure there were no more tears to pour over her eyelids and down her cheeks.

Tanisha had awakened that morning full of energy, excited to see an old friend and start helping him decode and translate whatever it was for which he needed her. Hours later, she was alone, broken-hearted at the news that her friend had passed away inside the foyer of the church; and now she was feeling lost. "I don't even know where to begin! Why? Why now?"

She looked around her at the mounds of information. Would she even be able to find what he had sent her photos of? She had already looked around his desk, and nothing looked even close.

She got up, felt badly that she kicked the cat, and walked out of the study. She walked over to the crypt of Briccius. If she could have her way, Gerault would have a crypt right beside this one; but of course, no one was about to put her in charge.

"If the legends are true, I could only imagine the burden that you felt, Briccius, as you made your way here! I don't know if the legends of the vial of blood are true; but if not, I am sure you thought what you carried was truly a holy gift! I cannot imagine carrying a burden so heavy, so secret, and so precious . . . a secret that is unable to be shared with anyone and the burden almost too much for one man to bear!"

She thought of her husband and how through the ages he had kept such a secret; and even now, she wondered if new information would knock him into further self-exile. She loved him. She loved him more than she realized that one person could love another, and yet even in that love there was a chasm that seemed too much for love to cross.

Her thoughts were interrupted by the sound of footsteps echoing above her. Someone must have come into the auditorium. She bent and kissed the crypt and headed up the stairs.

As she reached the top of the stairway, she opened the door that led into the front of the auditorium. She saw a man in his early 60s standing toward the back. He was dressed in a long, gray, wool coat with buttons down the front. He wore a fedora on his head, and tucked neatly under his left arm was a leather satchel that seemed to be stuffed with papers or a large book . . . she couldn't tell.

"May I help you, Sir?"

He took his hat off and held it in one hand as he extended his right hand out to her as she walked toward him. "Well, I hope that you can."

"Not sure if I can. I am new here, and . . ."

"Yes, and Gerault sadly was taken from us a few days ago."

She looked at him inquisitively. "Did you know him? Were you a friend of his?"

"Yes, and yes, I believe would be the proper answers to those questions."

"So, then what could I help you with?"

"Well, I guess the first proper thing to do, Tanisha, is to introduce myself."

She was taken aback. "Wait . . . how do you know my name?"

"There is a great deal that I know; but your name . . . well, I took a gamble. Our mutual friend expressed to me that you were coming; and since, sadly, he is unable to no longer keep you company, I have taken it upon myself to do so."

"Were you helping him?"

The man smiled for a moment as he placed his satchel down in one of the pews. He unbuttoned his coat and proceeded to hang it and his hat inside the closet to his left. He then sat down on one of the church pews.

"Yes . . . yes, you could say that."

She waited, realizing that he had not actually gotten around to telling her his name.

"My name is Enoch, and I have known Gerault for a long time."

She tried to think back to a time where their friend may have mentioned Enoch; but if he had, it seemed to escape her memory right now. Of course, she wasn't surprised: she was sure he had known so many people with all his traveling.

"I haven't been able to find out much about what happened to him," she stated.

"From my understanding, he passed away quietly right over there." He pointed to the bench near the front entrance. "I had spoken to him that evening, so it had to be later in the night."

Her gaze fell on the bench. She could picture him sitting there as if waiting for a longtime friend to stop by and talk. "He probably was getting ready for his evening walk. He was religious about that!"

Enoch nodded. "Yes, I know."

He reached over and unbuckled the strap on his satchel. He carefully pulled out a leather-bound journal that was filled with a lot of loose pieces of paper. "I believe these are for you, Dear. It was the last thing he had been working on; and it is what he was working on when he contacted you, to the best of my knowledge."

She took them from him and began to sift through the pages. "Yes, these do look like what he had sent me photos of."

"So, you are familiar with them?"

"Only from the photos and emails he sent me. He didn't go into much detail. He just stated that he thought he had uncovered a pretty big historical find but needed some fresh eyes and some help with some translations."

"So, is that your expertise?"

She nodded, "It is."

Things were quiet for a moment as she found herself immersing herself in the paperwork. Her visitor coughed a little bit to catch her attention. "Would you mind if I stopped by . . . maybe tomorrow . . . to see what you come up with? His work always interested me."

"No, not at all! It also would be great to have another face around . . . other than the cat, that is," she laughed. "I'm still dealing with the news of his death, and sitting here without really knowing anyone makes it feel even sadder."

He pointed to her wedding ring. "Did your husband travel with you?"

"No. I wish now he had. It would be nice to have him here. He has a way of bringing comfort like no one else."

"That is good! It is good to have someone like that . . . someone you can trust and grow old with."

"Are you married?" she inquired. She could not see a ring, but she didn't want to be rude.

"I am not. I guess you can say that I have been married to my work for too long to even entertain the thought."

"Now, *that* is sad. Finding someone to embrace your passions makes things so much better!"

"I have had a love in my life before, but sometimes things are not meant to be. Well, that or you get burned really badly . . . badly enough to know you never want to feel that again."

"Ah . . . I see," she stated. "I have been there."

He ran his fingers through his thinning gray hair and stood. "Well, it was nice meeting you in person, Tanisha. I need to get going, but I will stop by tomorrow."

"Thank you so much. I was afraid I wouldn't know where to begin. I will see you tomorrow."

He retrieved his coat and hat from the closet. "Take care, and we will talk again." With that, he walked out the door, leaving her once again with only the cat.

Chapter Twenty-Three

Hecate's fingers ran through the fur upon one of the heads of her pet, while the other head of the animal looked about in ever-constant alertness. She was fuming inside from the news that Mantus had met with Michael. She could only hope that nothing had come from their face-to-face. She also was gloating in her profound move to call a gathering. Her hope was that it would set Mantus back on his heels, and that way maybe he would just give up and settle in for the ride. He didn't have to join her; but for sure, he better not try to stop her.

The room was silent, and not a single individual stirred. If one closed their eyes, it could be easily believed that the room was empty . . . but that was the furthest thing from the truth. She had called out, and she knew that none would resist her. Even though each House was strong in its own right and, most likely, there was not a single Clan that held the upper hand, she did hold the charm. That was hard for them to resist.

She had enticed each of the warring leaders to join her. She held the power, their counsel; and right now, they were sitting in her realm. She understood how to balance the power. That was the beauty of being a seductress: use the needs of your opponent to control in a way that they give up themselves willingly.

The room was full! Clans of Ancient origin, who for ages had refused to acknowledge any of the New Generation Clans and their ways, had shown up tonight. Seats of the Ancient blended, she believed, for the first time with the Houses of New Generations.

Rules of the Ancient and New Generations had fallen to the side over the last two years with the warring of the Houses. All ceremonious rituals had been forsaken, and it had become every Clan for themselves. She knew that attempting to convince them to join once again—and some for the first time—as a unified force would be nearly impossible.

To her right sat one of the original Overlords, Elisheth Zenunim. Hecate believed that most of the Overlords present today may have never laid eyes upon him. He had refused to grow as the Clans grew but, instead, adopted new rules and organization standards on how many Clans there were to be and how new Overlords were chosen. His Clan had chosen to grow their evil and havoc outside the norm and constriction of the rest.

They were the last Clan to have joined into the Clan Wars. Drawn into the merciless slaying of over a hundred of his Clan, Elisheth rose up out of fury; and soon all the Clans knew that one of the few Ancients who still had a Clan was now a force with which to be feared and reckoned.

He sat in silence. He hated the young blood that had risen up, and he could taste the immature stupidity that puffed up around him. "Cough it up, Witch!" Adramelech spat. Surrounded by his Darkins, he looked almost as diabolical as Lucifer himself. This was the first time he had come out of seclusion since the fighting amongst the Clans had begun. He had spent the last two years orchestrating the growth and attacks of his House. He was darker and viler than Hecate had ever remembered him before.

She loved the look of seething anger he had shown as Arioch had entered the meeting room with his entourage. Arioch had noted it, also, and smirked. His Clan had risen in numbers quicker than anyone had expected. No one knew whether it was because Arioch had them waiting in the wing the whole time or if his influence and smooth swagger drew in the younger crowd who were hungry for the darkness that they did not understand.

Hecate had noticed that Arioch was flanked by his two lieutenants: Crow Shadowfire and Lestra. The addition of these two had brought new blood into his Clan. Crow Shadowfire had been a religious leader of a cult that had thousands of followers. Lestra was a High Priestess of Wiccan. He was the one Overlord who had no Darkins; he never had trusted the order of Darkins. He felt many worked for their own good, somewhat as if it was their own personal Clan.

She did not respond right away to Adramelech's order. She knew that he was pushing and was attempting to flex his muscles, but she wouldn't have any of that.

There were still a few seats vacant at the table. This table had been hand carved from one solid piece of blood red quartz and held around the edges many intricate, ritualistic designs, knotwork, and carvings unknown to mortals. It was her table of power.

"In due time, Melech." She stated the Hebrew name with detest and sarcasm, her eyes daring him to provoke her. She knew that he was aware he was the weakest within her lair; he was outnumbered here. "We still have empty seats, and I must be sure that all are represented here. If we do not, then our meeting is futile."

Arioch looked around as he took his seat. He questioned within himself, "For whom are the extra chairs?" He could feel a small pressure within his head, and he turned his head slightly to look in the direction of Hecate. He was not disappointed: she was looking straight at him. He knew she was attempting to draw out of him what he was thinking, but he had never given himself over to her; thus, she had no power there. He looked at her and slightly shook his head. She just smiled and poured herself a drink from the dark bottle that was to her right.

The noise of the large, wooden doors opening drew her attention from what she was doing to the left side of the room. The expression upon her face remained the same, but inside she was laughing: they all had answered the beckoning of her call. She had more control over them than they realized . . . either that or they were just all that confident in their own strength. Either way, she would use it to her advantage.

Hecate may have been able to keep her composure, but that was not to be said about the rest of the room. Overlords, Darkins, and Clan members alike began a large commotion as several figures walked into the room, stopping just enough inside as to allow the doors to close behind them.

"*NEPHELIUM?*" angered voices, dripping with distaste, echoed around the room. Darkins reached for their individual weapons and moved to stand closer to their Overlords. Arioch and Adramelech each clinched their jaws and stared hard in the direction of Hecate. Elisheth spat onto the floor as he uttered a curse.

"I demand to know what this is about!" Adramelech slammed his fist down on the flat surface of the table. "What are you doing, you whore? Have you aligned the House of Hecate with the outcast in order to destroy the rest of us? It is antics like this that started us fighting each other to begin with!"

Kadar stood solemnly, not flinching or even muttering a single word. He had three other Nephelium standing about him. None of their weapons were visible, but then the weapons of an assassin are never visible until it was too late. He had not been too certain about this meeting when he had received Hecate's invitation, but how ironic it seemed that everyone was as much in the dark as he. Nonetheless, with Adramelech's protest, he had just given power to the Nephelium. The others thought this was a setup by Hecate. That meant they were just as clueless as he but didn't know it. Oh, how he loved this!

"Evening, Mistress of Shadows, Mother of Magik," Kadar spoke with much eloquence as he nodded his head in Hecate's direction. "Please accept my apologies for being late."

"Fashionably, if I may say so," she noted.

"Of course." He and his troupe made their way around the side of the table and took their places on the table's right side, just down from where Elisheth sat. Kadar noticed that she had left the side of "prestige" for the Nephelium, the Outcast Clan.

Right behind the Nephelium leader entered a few fledgling Clan leaders . . . clearly not Overlords yet, as their Clans were small and usually paid allegiance to a larger Clan for whom they fought.

"Oh, how clever she really is," Arioch was thinking to himself as Kadar and his group entered and sat down. "What is going on in your mind, Hecate? What are you conspiring? Why now?"

Adramelech was seething. He was starting to think he had walked into a trap, and he was feeling an itch to just finish it here and now.

Since the Clan Wars had started, factions of "would-be" Clans had attempted coups . . . some successful and others destroyed. Familiars played among the different Houses, and everything the Fallen had worked toward had started falling apart.

"Now that we are all here, it is time," Hecate stated smoothly. "All of you are sitting here with your thoughts, apprehensions, and concerns; and I understand them all. Much of what I am about to say may even bring *more* concern, but I ask you to hear me out."

Her voice was almost melodic and hypnotic. She stood up; and her pup walked quietly away, curling up in the corner of the room. Her presence and demeanor captivated most in the room, and she had their attention.

"The time has come to put our differences, if not to rest, at least to the side. We have something that is rising that is much bigger than each of us individually; and if we are not careful, we will miss it."

She moved about the room, showing to them that she had no Darkins or any of her Clan present. She had come by herself. True, they were in her domain; and with one word she would be surrounded . . . but that was not the point.

"Tonight we must put it all on the table and once again join together as a family. Even the weak and wretched mortal families fight but are able to come together when it means for the good of the whole."

"Are you asking for us to just 'trust' again?" Arioch laughed, "Are you serious, Hecate? For what?"

"Is there ever really trust amongst us, Arioch?" she laughed. "I am asking for us to find a common reason to walk beside each other and together hold the weapons of destruction . . . at least until we can see if we are able to rise once again to our rightful place."

A burst of deep laughter broke out. Hecate turned and glared at the person who seemed to mock her.

"Kadar?"

"*We?* You keep talking about 'we,' yet you forget that 'we,'" indicating the Nephelium, "are still not accepted as an official Clan within the family. Why is it now that you are asking us to be a part of whatever it is that you are scheming?"

She nodded. "True, Kadar, and even now I hesitate because there are none of you that are true Fallens . . . merely half."

"Is that considered flattery?" he questioned, almost mockingly.

"Hear me out!" She snapped, placing both hands on the table and looking at him intently. "Let me explain it all to everyone. From there we can begin to work out the fine details. To all of you," she continued, "I ask only one thing: to hear me out. Let me lay the reason that you are *ALL* here," placing an emphasis on "all" as she looked hard at the Nephelium leader. "Then you decide what part you wish to commit to. I have promised all of you safe passage to here and back from where you came; so, if you choose to walk away from it all," she paused, "you do so without any fear that you will not return to your Clans."

Arioch took a long drink, finishing the contents, and held up his glass. "Then let's hear it! I have already grown weary of all of this. I feel like some bored chairman in a stock meeting instead of a leader of a dark and gothic Clan."

Hecate knew she had them all right where they needed to be. They wanted to know and yet were not ready to trust each other. This was good because the one thing they all had in common was the desire for the information from her. She had them. Now it was time to drop the guillotine.

*****

"In the last five years, we have seen more division between the different Houses represented here than ever before. We didn't even have this much division at the time we were exiled." They all were listening to Hecate with intent. "Elisheth, even your House was unable to keep from the division that has threatened us."

The Ancient Overlord's eyes raged. "How could we avoid that which we wanted no part of," he responded as he glared at Adramelech, "when well over a hundred of my House were murdered in a cowardly effort to destroy that which was established from the start?"

"Careful, Old Man . . . those are words and insinuations that will only escalate the fury that is already brimming to almost the tipping point tonight!" Adramelech stated with no emotion.

Elisheth pushed back from the table and stood. He was tall, and his frame was chiseled with time. Arioch had heard of this original Overlord, but the stories could never have done him justice. He truly understood his power, his place, and his strength. He feared no one; this was evident.

"Please!" Hecate soothingly but firmly spoke, "This is not going to get us anywhere. This is exactly what has kept us from gaining any ground within the mortal or even immortal realm. We should be gods ruling with authority and confidence . . . not schoolyard bullies fighting for what section of the monkey bars we will hold to!"

Elisheth leaned his massive frame over the table toward Adramelech. "I will sit and listen to what she has to say. I may even agree tonight to go along with whatever cockamamie plan she devises tonight; but I will ensure one thing:" his fist clinching on the table as he spoke, "you may have been my brother at one time, but nothing except your blood will ever pay the debt of those your Clan murdered of my House . . . your eternal damnation!" He sat down and motioned to Hecate to continue.

"My Brothers, we all have come from the same family. We all have shared the same burden of this mortal realm and the crushing blow of the exile. Together we have vowed to return to our home and from there control the mortal realm in the fullness for which we have always fought. You are just as aware as I am that we had one joining power, one force, that allowed all of us to come together as one united movement . . ."

"Are you kidding me?" Arioch spat. "I have heard the stories of your bastard child for ages. I have heard how the original Overlords all gave up blood to save this bastard child . . . how all the elements of each Overlord grew within him and how he was to be the hero."

Hecate was seething, but Arioch continued, "Yet, where is he? Oh, yes, I forgot . . . he is with his daddy in the Abyss, isn't he?"

"Silence, Arioch!" she hissed.

"No . . . wait . . . please! I'm getting to the good part," he scoffed. "I guess he isn't with his daddy because no one has ever proven that Mantus *is* his daddy. In fact, maybe it was Elisheth here . . . or Marduk . . . or was it . . ." he spoke, feigning a gasp, "a miracle baby?"

Chapter Twenty-Four

"You will silence that babbling rat trap of yours now before I rip that lower part of your jaw away and leave your serpent tongue flapping uselessly!" a booming voice spoke with warrior finesse. The door to the meeting room had opened; and everyone in the room, including Hecate, sat stunned and unable to move.

"Good evening, Dear! I'm sorry I must have not gotten the correct time to the meeting on my invitation. So please, excuse my tardiness."

Immediately, without even having it to be suggested, every lieutenant and underling at the table stood and moved back to ensure that the unexpected guest could choose whatever seat in which he wished to sit.

Hecate was the first to gather her wits about her as she stood to face her husband. "Mantus, I did not believe that you would be interested in attending a meeting of the Clan Overlords." She emphasized the last two words of her sentence.

Mantus was one feared by many, yet many within this room had never laid eyes upon him. As he had taken the reins of command within the Gates of the Abyss and Underworld, he became a presence within the Fallens that no one wanted to cross or even see. The Abyss or Underworld was not a place where Fallens wanted to be or with which they wanted to associate.

Mantus walked to the head of the table where Hecate sat and reached down and grabbed the goblet from which she had been drinking, spitting into it. As he swirled the excrement from his mouth inside the liquid, he stood glaring down at her. "Ah, my darling whore of a wife, could it be that my invitation did not make it to me because of your fear of what I may bring to the table?"

She held his gaze. The two had been so volatile before, yet such a force with which to be reckoned. She would not allow him the satisfaction of seeing her skin crawling and her heart racing. This truly was not expected. What had brought him here? No one in this room would have told him about this meeting, so there would have been no way of his knowing . . . right?

He placed the goblet down and made his way toward where Kadar sat, flanked by the Nephelium who had stood with the other underlings when Mantus walked in. As he reached him, Kadar stood and bowed slightly. "My Lord, I am grateful that, in fact, you did receive my invitation as my guest of honor here before the families."

"Kadar, I have never believed until now that your kind was needed or desired. You, in fact, with your invitation have proven every thought I had about the half breeds; but also, with your invitation you have shown me that you are more cunning and brazen than any of your kind before. I never stand in debt to any within the families, but I will say that your actions will not go unrewarded."

As Mantus finished, Kadar stood and gave up his seat at the table. Hecate could slit his throat with one move if she could reach him right now! How dare he! To be outwitted by this . . . this piece of garbage that she had invited only because of the exact cunningness of which Mantus was just speaking. She had underestimated him for sure, but she could guarantee that wouldn't happen again.

"So allow me, if I may, pick up where you, Hecate, so eloquently left off and where Arioch's rotting breath attempted to fill in." He looked with a side glance at the now tight-lipped Overlord.

In fact, none of them looked as if they even could find their tongues . . . all but Elisheth, who was leaning back with ease and comfort. He had truly underestimated the young Assassin and his Clan. He was impressed. It had been way too long since the last time he sat in company with Mantus; and to watch Hecate squirm and the young, overconfident leaders sit in silence was golden!

"What my darling wife was trying to state was that we have waited too long, allowing the Alliance, the Arch Council, and even ourselves to destroy any chance that we have to rise to the level of authority that we all used to have or believe that we should continue to have. If we have a chance, yes, it would be through Legion.

"As you are all aware, there is only one way that we would be able to bring him back to his full essence: through the lifeblood of an immortal willingly sacrificed for another. Well, as I am sure that none of you are willing to stand and volunteer or, of course, my taking your blood *from* you . . ." he stated these last words looking over at Arioch, "would not meet the requirements. The only way that we can see that this will happen is if we are able to obtain the vial of blood that was saved from the death of Jah's son . . . or one of you must willingly take one for the Family.

"Now, there is something else of which I believe you all should be aware . . . and I am not sure if your gracious host was going to share this part."

Hecate was shooting visual daggers at him with all the effort she had within her. This was not the way this was supposed to go, and if he thought that he could waltz in here and . . .

"As you are aware, there were many segments of Legion that were not fully put into captivity within the Abyss. Since that time, the elements of him have wreaked havoc upon mortals through the ages. Many of you have benefited from it, but what you are not aware of is that your host here has started secretly sending members of her House and her Darkins out to start bringing about followers of Dracon . . . or Legion. Her desire is that once he is released, the elements of him will already have a Clan following. Then with one swift move he will become whole and will already have a force to stand beside his mother's Clan. Which of you would be able to stand? Which of your Houses will be able to withstand an onslaught of such force?"

Hecate let out a scream and leaped across the table at him. Kadar jumped between her and Mantus and felt the nails from her right hand cut deep into his face. Blood began to flow; and with a strong right uppercut, he felt his fist crash against the open, screaming jaw of the Enchantress.

Hecate fell to the side of the table. Before she could get up, she heard music to her ears as the vicious, violent, and savage raging bark from Cerberus blasted through the room. She felt his body fly over her, and the commotion that rang out after that was beyond chaos.

Kadar's assassin instincts kicked in from the moment his fist collided with Hecate's jaw. As he felt her fall to the ground, he shoved Mantus backward and ducked as Hecate's protector came flying at him. One of Cerberus' heads missed its mark . . . but blast that second one! Kadar felt the jaws clamp down upon his arm that was protecting his head. He held the desire to scream out in pain and, instead, channeled the feeling of agony into his alert conscience. He was grateful that they had not frisked for weapons beforehand. He thrust upward with his legs from a squatting position; and at the same time, his left hand pulled a thin but sharp blade from a hiding place within his clothes. He thrust his hand upward with such force that he felt the underbelly of the creature part and the warmth of the inner contents swallow his hand. The blade was so sharp that it cut through with ease.

Kadar felt the mouth of the mongrel loosen as the dog's blood poured over the stone table. Kadar, for effect, jerked his hand the length of the body, gutting the dog from neck to hind end.

Hecate could do nothing but look on in shock and horror, her appearance changing before the very eyes of all who were within the room. The picture of the alluring Enchantress was now gone, replaced with the enraged appearance of the dark, evil creature she was! Her canines were elongated; her hair became disheveled; and her eyes were completely inky black. She stood with fury and anger. Blood would be the only thing that would quench her thirst! She screeched as she lunged for Kadar; but instead, she felt strong hands pull her back and hold her firmly where she was.

She turned, ready to lash out at whomever it was who dared restrict her and came face-to-face with Elisheth. "I don't think so, Hecate. You created this tonight. You will be the one reaping from this tonight. All the trickery, pain, and anguish that would have come upon the Houses represented here tonight is now on you!"

"You stand against me?" she screamed at him. "*Me?* You stand with this half breed and against one of the Originals? You owe me your life! I am the one who rescued you from death and instead got us exiled . . . a way for us to once again plan to return to our rightful place!"

"You are wrong, Hecate! You are wrong, and I told you that if you double-crossed me again . . . then you would lose!"

Her eyes widened in horror as a voice spoke from somewhere behind the chaos. There was no way! No! *She* was in charge! *She* was the Enchantress! *She* controlled them! *She* pulled the strings!

Elisheth released his grasp as Hecate turned to face the crowd. It was not all the faces of the Overlords that were blanketed in anger and satisfaction that made her fall to her knees. No . . . but it was the face of Azrael.

"What? I don't . . . how?" She could not finish a complete sentence. "This is treason!"

"Yes, you are correct but not in the manner to which you are inferring," Mantus spoke. "*You* are the traitor here. Now is the time for you to stand trial among the Clans. The truth will be known to all, and all that you have done through the ages will be exposed."

"You need me!" she seethed. "Legion will not follow you . . . *any* of you! He is *my* son!"

"Maybe. Just maybe you are right, but the fact still remains that he was infused with the lifeblood of each of the original Overlords!" Mantus stated authoritatively. "And I venture to say that if he will listen to anyone, then he will also listen to his father."

Clasping her arms to her chest and rocking back and forth, she threw her head backward and laughed out loud . . . laughed with great fervor at this statement. "And who do you suppose that is?" she spat.

She stood up from where she had fallen to her knees,

attempting to re-obtain some form of dignity and strength. "Who do you believe is his father? You, Mantus? Maybe you, Azrael?"

She looked at Elisheth. His eyes were stern, almost daring her to make the accusation. His glare did not cause her to falter in any shape or form. "Elisheth, have you not shared what the others have? So, could he not be yours? The one fact is that you do know he came from *my* body! You are aware that *I* am his mother, and if he will listen to anyone before any of you . . . it will be to *me!*"

*****

The room had cleared except for the leaders who had been attending the meeting, as well as Azrael. Hecate refused to have anyone come in to clear the body of her deceased pet. The animal's body was in a heap upon the table where he had been slain. His blood dripped off the edges of the table, and his former master paced back and forth beside the corpse. She was seething with rage that filled every ounce of her body and existence. They were all going to pay. They may think they have the upper hand, but she would regain it.

"So, Dear, how does it feel? How does it feel to be the one standing double-crossed?"

She refused to respond to Mantus' mocking question. She glared at him and then snarled but refused to respond.

"Care to explain all of this, Mantus?" Elisheth asked.

Azrael answered before Mantus could respond. "We are done. Everything that immortal and mortal have known has run its course. Mortal man has fallen so far from the truth and are so narcissistic in their thoughts and actions that they are like children without parents. We have become so shattered that there is only a shadow of our former glory and power that dances when the spotlight shines just right.

"We have the chance to rise up. We have a chance, this very moment, to put down our differences, stop fighting each other, and become the masters for which mortal man is begging, even if they are not even aware it is us whom they desire."

"How?" Adramelech asked. "Look around you, Azrael! None of us trust each other. Even tonight we have shown that there is not a single one of us who believes another will not cut down our Houses without a second thought." He looked over at Elisheth for confirmation of his statement. He was ignored.

"Adramelech, we all are aware that all that exists is bound by a thread that, at times, seems to unravel; but when it does, it never does so all the way. It loosens to allow a new experience to come forth.

"Mankind is more divided with hatred and self-inflicted wounds than ever before. They are longing for power and leadership, and most believe myths over truth already. If we are able to capitalize on that and become those myths exposed, we will be the gods they seek."

"I hear all that you are saying, Mantus, but I don't see a solution. I don't see the actions that can be taken to make this work."

Azrael sat down at the table and motioned for the rest to do the same. "Please, everyone, have a seat. Of course, don't let the blood of this poor creature get all over your clothing." He looked mockingly at Hecate and then shot an approving glance at Kadar.

Everyone had a seat . . . everyone, that was, except for Hecate. She stood with her back against the wall, sulking.

"As much as I don't want to admit it, Hecate has some very valid points. Where she and the rest of us would part ways was that she has one desire: raise her House to the top of the pinnacle of power.

"We can come together . . . but alone we will not only destroy our chance at this, but we will also divide ourselves in a way that we may never recover again. Trust me, if any of you know or believe history, you are aware that Mantus and I have no love lost between us. Neither of us really trust each other, but we have talked. We believe that there is a moment— call it prophecy or destiny or even both—that is upon us. If we do not seize on it, we may not survive it." Azrael looked at Mantus. "Care to share more?"

"There is no need to pull punches right now," Mantus responded. "As much as we all may hate Hecate for what she did with the creation of Legion, her original plan of creating one from all may actually be our salvation. What will *not* work is for one House to claim the authority that comes from him . . . *that* will not work."

"What happens if we are able to restore him and he chooses to claim that authority himself?" Elisheth asked. "That could very well happen and understandably so. None of us have the power . . . and I mean *NONE* of us . . ." he said sternly, eyeing Hecate, "will be able to stand against him. Why, after all these years, would he not seek to gain the top seat?"

"You are right, and we don't know that. Therefore, Azrael and I offer an alternative."

"Oh, and what would that be, Dear?" Hecate spat.

"We don't release him."

Confusion buzzed all around the room. Everyone suspected

they knew where this was going, but no one imagined that Mantus and Azrael would suggest leaving Legion in captivity.

Kadar shook his head. "Then if that is your plan, why are we all here and how does that differ in any way, shape, or form from where we are today?"

"Because we use what we have. Not all of Legion was captured and exiled. We all have seen what the segments of Legion have been able to do over the ages; yet each time, his mother, for her own hunger for power, attempted to manipulate the being that encased Legion."

"Yes, and every time, it did not end well."

"You are right, Arioch, but the one constant was Hecate and her desire to rule alone. I believe that if given the chance to join us as one of us, Legion would do so. He has no desire, from what I can see, to reign as supreme; yet, he also has no desire to be a puppet for anyone."

Elisheth leaned forward. "So, you are suggesting to find the part of Legion that is not held captive, forget about the broken wretch that is trapped within your realm, and negotiate a joining of all Houses?"

"I propose we return to the old ways; and I believe in doing so we may even have the chance to overpower Scintillantes and return to what is rightfully ours," Azrael stated calmly.

They all sat in silence for a moment, and then Adramelech spoke up. "This sounds rough, at best. I also don't understand the benefit of any of this. Ok, sure, the Clans calling a truce . . . we all could win with that. I am not sure how strong it would hold because of the lack of trust. We all have done things to each other that has caused deep-seated hatred; and to believe that will just vanish overnight . . . well, I don't think any of us are that naive, but why do all this other stuff? To what end?"

"Look around you, Adramelech. What do you see? I don't mean here in this room, but out there . . ." Azrael answered as he motioned outwardly, "an existence in chaos. Trust me, I have ensured the power of the Arch Council has been diminished. The Alliance . . . when was the last time they felt as if they were accomplishing anything? They are on the verge of fighting amongst themselves.

"Mortals are weak. It was already stated how they believe they are superior in existence. Everyone in this room understands the ebb and flow of it all. We are very aware of the order and place in which each segment belongs, but we also are aware that we are not at the top of this food chain. We need to get back there."

Mantus leaned back and began to stroke his beard. His mind was going all over, but he was also very focused on the overall goal. They needed these leaders to buy in to what they were attempting to sell them.

"So, the lowdown is this: if we can come together and bring Legion to the table, with Azrael's connections within the Arch Council, we have the chance to launch an assault and take back what is ours, including authority over humanity. We must work together, though." He paused and looked around the room. "We *all* must be in."

There was mumbling around the table for a bit, and then one-by-one they each nodded their head in agreement.

"Hecate?"

"Dear, you seem to leave me no other recourse; so I must be in to survive."

"Good!" he responded as he pounded the table. "We need to meet again soon and put together a plan."

"And Legion?"

"Azrael thinks he may know where Legion is, and it will be up to him to bring him to the table."

"Why would Legion listen to him? Does Legion even know that Azrael is with us?"

"Leave that to me," Azrael answered. "We are just getting started. At the end of this, nothing will look like it was. Revenge will be sweet."

Chapter Twenty-Five

"Tori, I wish there was an easy road ahead of you," Gene stated as they all sat in a circle inside his study. Leah, Chad, Zarius, and Serenity were all there. Each of them looked worn down, and each seemed to be deep within their own thought.

"We have no idea of the power of Legion inside of you; but what we do know is that however much is within you, we can't leave him there. He will destroy you and, in the process, most likely will destroy others."

She could feel her anxiety rising inside. "I guess living like this is not an option; then again, if not, is living an option?"

"It isn't easy, but I never said it is impossible. This is Eden; we are all about the impossible. I just want you to know that all of us are here for you, and we desire nothing more than to free you from this possession."

She looked around at all the assuring faces that were nodding in unison. "So, what do we do?"

"It is going to take a powerful Eternal to bring him out and to take him on."

"Like you?" she asked, looking at Leah.

Leah shook her head. "Even if I wasn't a Vapor, in my strongest days I would be no match for Legion . . . even in his smallest existence."

"Then, who?"

"Leah is kind of correct," Zarius spoke up, "but not fully. It would take a member of the Arch Council or Jah himself; and since it seems that neither is an option, it is going to take two of us."

"No . . . there is no way, Zarius!" Leah shook her head. "You and I together would still be no match for him."

"Correct, but you and I . . . and then we have two others here at Eden who could join us. With their skill set and lineage, I think we could do it."

She jumped out of her seat. "No! They are too young; and we have no idea what they are capable of, not to mention their mother has been very clear about protecting them from who they are."

"Maybe it is time they find out!"

Gene held up his hand for silence. "Leah, we all hear you and understand; but in the end, it will be their mother's choice. You both are correct. Leah, we don't know what they are capable of; but, Zarius, you are correct that we will need all the help we can get if we are going to go through with this."

Chad, Serenity, and Tori simply sat there. They all felt they were out of the loop on this.

"You are talking about the twins, aren't you?" Tori asked.

Gene nodded, "We are."

"Wait . . . the twins are not mortal?" Serenity asked.

"Half," Leah whispered as she sat back down. She leaned forward and placed her face in her hands. She felt nauseated. This was not going to work. There were too many unknowns and too many "what ifs."

"Half?" Chad asked. "Come again?"

Gene looked at Leah for the explanation.

"Five years ago their mother was rescued and brought to Eden. When she was brought here, she was pregnant. We did not believe that the baby—because we had no idea she was pregnant with twins at the time—would survive. We also were not sure if their mom would even survive."

"You are talking about Ann?" Tori asked.

Leah paused and then nodded. "Well, of course, all of them did survive . . . including an extra baby."

"Doesn't explain the 'half' part," Chad commented.

"Their father was a Fallen."

"Wait . . . so, Ann is a Familiar?" Serenity was so confused. "I am not following this at all."

"We can't share everything, because the fewer people who know the full story, the better it is for her and her children."

Zarius leaned forward as he cut in, "Ann and her kids are here for their safety and the chance at a different life. Ann wasn't really a true Familiar but was dragged into a world that she was not ready for and, in that, became entangled in it beyond her control. Certain circumstances allowed her to be rescued. Her existence is not known by many, and even fewer are aware of the existence of the children."

"So, in a way, she was a lot like me?" Tori asked.

"Yes," Leah explained, "very much like you. The reality is that the twins are not fully mortal. If you want to get technical, they would be like Eve; but due to the fact their lineage is not traced back to the Nephelium, they really are not Nephelium, either."

"How about Vapors?" Chad asked. "Wouldn't they be like you?"

"No, Vapors are immortals who have *chosen* the life of a mortal. These twins have neither a Nephelium lineage or have reached an age to choose; and with that, we are not even sure if they have carried forward any powers of their father. They have also not reached the age of understanding. They are young and innocent and have not been put in the place to make the choice as to whether they will follow the Fallen or stand for right." Leah looked at Gene. "That is why I am very worried about going through with making them a part of this exorcism."

"Your concerns are noted and legitimate, Leah, but I am afraid we have no other choice. It has been pointed out that we have no Arch Council member that would be a part of this, and you and Zarius do not have enough strength between you."

She hated this. Her prayer, since the birth of the twins, was to help them and their mother steer as far away as possible from the darkness that always danced upon their doorstep. Why was it that it seemed darkness always won?

"Have we asked their mother yet?"

"Yes, and I don't have an answer yet." It was Ann. She walked in as they had been speaking and was standing just inside the doorway. "I thought my days dealing with all of this was long gone, but then I also can't bear the thought that I could help Tori experience freedom from the shadows that threaten her mind. I was given that chance, and what if it was for this moment here? What if my children were brought into this world for this reason? Who am I to hold them back from what they were created for?"

Tori felt tears, yet again, come down her face. For so long she wanted to belong, feel as if she was loved, and feel as if there was someone out there who would give everything for her. Now, it wasn't just one person but a group of strangers who were willing to risk so much—including everything—for her. It was overwhelming.

"What if we *don't* do this?" she asked. "What if we just let whatever is inside of me stay. You can put me in a cell or restrain me on a bed . . . do something that would make sure I didn't hurt anyone."

"We could do that," Zarius said, "but there is not even one of us that is ok with that option. We are all here for specific reasons, Tori. We were given a mission when mortal man was created. I wish I could say that I have lived up to that mission, but I betrayed it years ago. Since becoming a Vapor, I promised that I would do everything to make that right, even if it meant giving up everything."

She looked at his wedding band. "Even your wife?"

He looked down at his hand and twisted the band around on his finger. Tanisha was always very present in his thoughts and heart. Who knew what all of this would bring? Even she knew that each has a calling; and unless they follow that calling through to the end, they only live half their life.

"Yes, *everything*. It is a part of me; and for her to love me, she must love *all* of me. We both understand that."

"And you, Ann?" Tori continued. "You would take the chance that the lives of your children will forever be altered? For what? For me? You don't even know me!"

Ann sat on the arm of the chair in which Tori sat. She looked into Tori's eyes as she held back tears of her own. "As a mother, my world *is* my children, but if we are unable to look beyond ourselves . . . our own fears . . . we may lose the very world we hope to protect. Life is a gift that is given to us so that we can live it to the very best possible. When we become so focused on ourselves, our wants, our own desires, we fail to truly live. Life is only truly worth living when we understand that it is the investment in others that makes it priceless. It is what we invest into others that will move on long after we are no longer here.

"It has taken me forever to understand that. For too long I lived my life simply for myself; and if I can help my children, even at a young age, learn that lesson now . . . well, it would be worth it."

"Tori, if you are willing, we will get things moving along tomorrow. You will need a lot of rest, and I want to make sure you get that tonight," Gene stated in his grandfatherly voice.

She nodded, and they all realized that this meeting was over. Tomorrow . . . and maybe even the next few days . . . was going to be something that would take every ounce of mental and physical fortitude that they all could muster.

*****

Mantus and Azrael stood outside Hecate's estate. The rest of the Overlords and members had gone, and Hecate had made it her personal mission to walk both of her former lovers out the door . . . and with flare, she locked the door behind them.

"She has no idea," Azrael stated as the cold night embraced the duo.

"There is no way she can know. Are you sure you are wanting to go through with all of this? It is going to be like putting a thread through the eye of a needle . . . not much room for error or it will all come crumbling down on us."

Azrael watched as his breath could be seen in the cold. He

didn't know how to answer that question. Mantus was right; it was risky. He also wasn't sure if he truly trusted Mantus, either.

He did believe that the general had no desire for ultimate power; but again, like the other Overlords, Azrael couldn't see how this would all play out. He felt that Hecate had already amassed too much power, and the only hope was to set the reset button— but who knew if that would actually transpire? It relied heavily on a lot of individuals trusting each other who had not done exactly that in ages.

"What makes you believe you can trust me?"

Mantus laughed, "If you believe I do, then you are more foolish than I ever imagined. I don't trust you . . . not one bit. Now, you can trust this: I have my stop safes in place. You will never know what hit you if you attempt to go against me. I have my ways, and I have my allies. As long as we continue in the same direction, we will be good; but you deviate from anything we discussed after our little meeting in the desert, everything you have ever known will come crashing down on top of you."

"That is fair, and I would expect nothing less from you. Just when I thought you may be getting soft, you show me that you are still the same."

"Azrael, the fire of my home toughened me harder than you could ever fathom. I lost everything so long ago, and you know . . . never play roulette with someone who has nothing to lose and everything to gain."

They both shook hands and went their separate ways into the night.

*****

Azrael sat in the back of the car as the driver drove them away. He was angry inside but also pleased. They could not have pulled off tonight any better.

He thought back over the offer Mantus had given him over the phone after they had met at Zarius' house. He knew that Mantus could sense that he had something up his sleeve that he was not revealing, but Mantus had taken a gamble.

"Nothing to lose, Mantus?" he spoke out loud. "You are right; and you forget that, in reality, I also have nothing to lose."

He still had to find his brother. If Zarius still had possession of the Delta, then it would give him an ace with which to play.

Mantus had proposed that instead of working against each other, they could work together toward a common goal of ensuring that Hecate did not take over control.

She had played right into their hands by setting up a gathering. There was no way she could have known that Kadar was working with Mantus; so, once the invitation had gone out, her hand had been shown.

Of course, it also revealed to him that Kadar was in Mantus' pocket, and that also showed a little of the general's hand. As far as he could tell, he was still the only one with hidden cards to play.

His phone rang, and he looked down to see who was calling. He smiled. "Ah, speaking of aces in the hole!"

He swiped and answered the call, "Yes?"

"Not sure what information will be more beneficial for you," the female voice on the other side of the phone stated. "She is in Austria."

"I already figured that. Do we know why?"

"Not really. I'm sure you know that she was called there by Gerault."

"Yes, and I already took care of that. She should be walking in blind without him."

"I thought so, also; but it seems that someone provided her with a collection of notes from the old man that got her geared up."

"Who?"

"I don't know. My sources tell me that there was an older gentleman that showed up with a journal of sorts."

He sat back for a moment and just thought. "Who would have that information? Who could have access . . ."

His mind went back to the Council meeting for Leah. Images of Metatron throwing out a Watcher's Journal onto the Council table came over him. No one had actually looked at the journal. Everyone had just expected that what Metatron was stating was the truth.

"Well, I'll be damned! Well-played, My Friend . . . well-played. That wasn't Leah's history at all. Gerault had a backup plan; and of course, he would go to you. He always trusted you more than anyone else."

"Are you still there?" the voice asked.

"Sorry," he responded. "I think I know who our mysterious savior is—something I am going to have to investigate more. What else do you have?"

"Your brother is in Eden."

So, the wheels turn . . . and they turn fast! Had Zarius finally grown a pair? He would have never thought his brother would return. If he was in Eden, that meant that he was exposing himself; and if he was exposing himself, there would be only one reason:

he had the Delta, and he was initiating his own safety plan in an attempt to keep Michael from getting it.

"How long has he been there?"

"About a day, I believe."

"Interesting. You did well. Can you head to Austria without drawing a lot of attention to yourself?"

"I may be able to do that. Give me a bit to think of a way to twist it so that she doesn't suspect anything."

"Do that, and then get back with me. I need to see if I can figure out a way to find out what my brother is up to and maybe give him a visit. We need to keep Mantus off our backs, also."

"I think I can do that. Kadar offered me a proposal to work with him and Mantus. I did not give him an answer, but I believe now would be a good time."

"Great . . . but, Denora . . ."

"Yes?"

"Don't forget who you are working for, because I could start questioning if you aren't working for yourself with all the brands you have in the fire. Remember what happens with that many brands."

"Oh, and what is that?"

"You pull the wrong one out at the wrong time, and you get burned."

"Understood, Azrael . . . or should I say Michael? I have learned from some of the best manipulators in the field."

He ignored her sarcasm with the name. "I know you have, and sometimes that is what worries me the most."

Chapter Twenty-Six

Denora could hear Hecate's screaming from down the hall. She smirked at the thought of what those in charge of cleaning up the dead two-headed monster were going through. She paused for a moment from outside the door, just listening at all of the commotion, and then opened the door and walked in.

"I don't care how heavy he is! You have no idea all the dangers that he has protected me from! He didn't deserve this!"

"Hecate?"

She turned around and saw Denora standing behind her.

"Do you see this? Kadar will beg for mercy when I get the chance to filet him with his own blade!"

"I am so sorry," Denora said with empathy oozing from her tongue. "He will deserve everything that you can do to him!"

"Oh, he has no idea!"

"Let me make this right, Dear! Let me handle Kadar."

"And how do you propose to do that? How does that satisfy the taste for revenge upon *my* tongue? Please, I pray . . . tell me *that!*"

"Oh, I will let you have him, Hecate. Let me bring him to you."

"So, I let a lackey go after one of the best assassins that we have ever seen, and I am to believe that you can bring him to me."

Denora bit her tongue. She didn't even wince as the blood from the bite trickled down her throat. Oh, how she wished she could pull the rug out from under this lady of diabolical charm to show her that her time had come and long fizzled out! She couldn't though . . . not yet.

"I am just offering."

"Fine, I don't care. Go sacrifice yourself to him. I can always find another lover, another protégé." She waved in Denora's direction as if she was swooshing a fly that was annoying her.

"I will keep you posted." Denora exited quickly before she lost her cool and brought the whole castle of sand down around them. She hated Hecate with such fervor. She had spent the last five years strategically planning each move that had brought her into the trust of the Enchantress. When Denora had stated she had learned from the best, she had not lied; but now the student had become the star, and she loved it. The power of manipulation was just as intoxicating as the power for revenge, and she was tasting from both cisterns.

She blamed Hecate for much of what had happened at The Vortex, as well as over the last several years. After everything had fallen apart, Hecate had begun to masterfully dismantle—many times from the inside out—the different Clans. She had played upon the weakness of Arioch and had Arioch believing that he no longer could trust Denora.

Arioch accused Denora of not being strong enough, even after she had disposed of Alfonso. He had mocked her, stating that the old man was the only thing that she was able to take out and insinuating that if she had actually been half the lieutenant that he needed, she would have taken out more of the Alliance that night . . . or died trying.

She was left with no Clan . . . no family. None of the other Houses would consider her because of her role in attempting a coup against Clan Adramelech. She was marked. Of course, when the time was right, Hecate had started courting her. She wasn't stupid.

She knew this had all been Hecate's plan. She didn't know it then, but as things began to take shape, Denora could see that she had been a pawn in a bigger scheme. She had started receiving word that the House of Hecate was secretly amassing Familiars but not asking any of them to swear allegiance to the House or even become marked with the Clan insignia.

She had confronted Hecate, and that is when she started realizing that Hecate had bigger plans than just being the Overlord to her own House. She was looking for the top power over all the Clans. That moment is when Denora started strategically inserting herself within Hecate's plan. The queen of seduction was so self-absorbed and looked at Denora with such disdain that she never saw the fox in the chicken coop.

She was no one's lackey anymore. Kadar did have words of wisdom when he challenged her to remember from where she came. Sure, she didn't like him; but she could feel a sense of camaraderie with him. He and his kind were outcasts, and quickly she had found herself on the outside. The difference was she would find her way back in; and once they realized she was there, it would be too late. They all would understand, one day, that she was once the daughter of the Fallen. They never showed her mercy; and on that day, she would remember that with vengeance.

She now had a trip to take.

*****

She hated crowds, and the crowds at the airport had left her wanting to hit someone . . . then again, she almost always felt that way.

"So, what do we do? Just knock on the door?" Isaiah asked.

"Well, Preach, you are the former reverend here. I would think you just try the door; and if it is unlocked, you go in. I mean, it is a church, right?"

Eve and Isaiah had landed earlier. Even after touching down, she had to talk him out of just getting back on a plane and heading home. She told him to at least go to the church and see what happened from there. Now, they both stood in front of St. Vincent. He tried the door and found it unlocked.

"Of course, it would be," he thought.

They both walked into the foyer and stood at the back of the long, narrow auditorium.

"Do you just yell out, and a priest appears?" Eve asked.

"They are not genies, Eve," he laughed.

"I don't know this stuff. I have never been about all this religious, power-hungry stuff. You know, there is an overpowering God who is waiting to strike you down if you get too many tattoos or enjoy too much carnal fun!"

Isaiah shook his head. "Yeah, I get that . . . although I don't buy into all that, either . . . didn't when I was a preacher and still do not. There is a lot more to it."

"Oh . . . like say a magic prayer, and some religious guru appears to grant you answers?"

"Yeah—no!"

They didn't stand there long before Tanisha entered from the other end. She had gotten annoyed hearing people upstairs. All she wanted to do was research and silently questioned if it was ok to lock the doors to the church. What would it hurt? Wasn't like there was a priest or preacher here anymore!

"Can I help you?" she asked.

"Wow," Eve said looking at Isaiah. "I guess we are looking for a priestess and not a priest!"

"Excuse me?" Tanisha questioned, clearly annoyed.

Isaiah shot Eve a look and then introduced himself, "My name is Isaiah, and this is Eve. We were hoping to meet with the priest who is over this church."

"Are you friends of his?" she asked.

Eve rolled her eyes. "Well, if we were, do you think we would have asked for 'the priest' . . . or maybe we would have used his actual name?"

Tanisha was not having any of Eve's sarcasm. She wasn't in the mood nor did she have the time. "Well, since we clearly have left our 'friendly pants' at home, let me be blunt, also. Gerault, who was the priest here—oh, *and* a friend of mine—passed away a couple of days ago. So, sorry for your lack of timing, but I'm sure you aren't looking for someone to show you the door that you just walked in."

Eve's demeanor changed with Tanisha's comeback. "Ohh, . . . I like her!" she thought.

"I would say that I am sorry for my friend's attitude; then again, if I did, she most likely would take it out on me. So, I won't; but I will say that I am very sorry for the loss of your friend. I guess you are right: if he is not here, then we don't have any real reason to be here."

Secretly Isaiah was thrilled. He could at least say that he tried, found nothing, and then returned home. He turned to leave; but as he did, he could feel the firm grasp of Eve's hand on his arm.

"Actually, I'm not sure how good a friend he was and not even sure if any of what I am about to say makes sense; but you know, I personally don't care." She turned Isaiah back around. "My friend here used to be a priest."

"A *preacher*," Isaiah retorted.

"Ok, whatever it is. My point is that we have a mutual friend that also passed away, leaving my other, soon-not-to-be friend—if he keeps up the weak-kneed attitude—with a lot of papers, notes, and instructions."

Tanisha was not prepared for this bit of information. She stepped forward, clearly showing interest now. "Ok."

"Well, I will not let him go home until he figures out what they are all about and why he was instructed to come to see your former— now deceased—friend, Gerault, or whatever his name was . . . may he rest in peace." She made an ill attempt of crossing herself.

"What kind of papers?"

Isaiah pulled off the backpack that he had been wearing and pulled out a pile of things that had been inside the box that Alfonso left him. "Honestly, I am not sure what any of it means. Like Eve said, no offense; but I'm not even sure I'm supposed to be showing you or anyone these things."

Tanisha walked over and looked at the leather journal, very similar to the one that Enoch had given her earlier. "Did you know your friend well—the one who gave these to you?"

"He was like a father to me . . . so, yes," Eve stated emotionless.

"These belonged to a Watcher," she whispered as her fingers traced the embossed Watcher symbol on the front of the journal.

It was now Eve and Isaiah's turn to be shocked.

"You know about the Watchers?" Eve asked, her tone now friendlier and without the blatant sarcasm.

"Yes, Gerault shared information with me about them. They are a secret organization meant to protect historical artifacts and accounts that deal with the world of the supernatural."

Neither of them knew what to say. They both felt as if they had walked into a weird reality show but right in the middle of it. They weren't sure what had happened before, but now they were a part of it and were expected to understand it all.

"So, do you know anything about these?"

"I'm not really sure. This type of stuff is what I have worked on with him for years and is why I am even here right now. I just got here myself."

"Well, I guess we all are a little late to the show then!" Eve quipped. "I don't believe in destiny, but I guess this could get someone questioning it."

"Don't worry, I don't either," Tanisha stated, "but I do believe we all have a purpose; and if you call meeting that purpose in the right time and place 'destiny,' then I guess I can believe in that. Why don't you both follow me? I do believe there is a reason we all are here right now, so maybe we should figure that out."

"Fantastic!" There was Eve's sarcasm again.

"Do you have anything to drink?" It was all Isaiah could think to ask.

Eve slapped him across the back of the head. "Really?"

"I meant non-alcoholic, of course." He shrugged his shoulders at her. "Hey, I got habits, you know."

"Yes, I do know."

*****

Eve and Isaiah were in awe as they stepped into the old library. Neither knew what to say at the stacks and rows of things that were everywhere.

"No one better ever knock my housekeeping again!" Isaiah said as he looked at Eve.

"Well, if you had old things stacked everywhere, I would take that over the used takeout boxes and empty bottles of liquor."

"Ok, that is fair."

Tanisha sat down at the desk and offered a place for each of them to sit, although space was limited. "What are you willing to share with me?" she asked.

They both looked at each other, and Eve shrugged her shoulders. She had given up on the whole secrecy thing a few years ago and figured that if you were breathing, you should know the truth. She didn't buy into this whole thought pattern of keeping the two worlds separate, unless things required you to expose mortals to the immortals.

"Ok, so the way I look at it is this: people like you already believe in the freaky, horror movie stuff; and I have no idea why it is that everyone is so fascinated with it but you are. So, let's jump in."

She couldn't understand why Tanisha looked so amused at her statement, but she didn't care. "So, neither Isaiah nor I am really human. I mean, we kind of are . . . but not. We are what you call . . ."

"Vapors?"

Eve stopped. "Come again?"

"Vapors? You are Vapors?"

They both looked at each other, confused.

"Vapors? Um . . . what is that?"

Tanisha thought for a moment at their reaction and then guessed again. "Well, if neither of you is aware of what a Vapor is, then you must be Nephelium."

Again, both were speechless. There was obviously more to this lady than either of them originally suspected. She knew about the Watchers—and even the Nephelium—and of something called Vapors, which neither of them had a clue was.

"Maybe I should start. Since you brought me a Watcher's Journal and you both are claiming to be Nephelium, . . ."

"I didn't claim to be anything," Isaiah said quickly. "*You* said that."

"Am I wrong?"

"Well . . . no, but I didn't claim it."

"What I was saying is that I am a part of your world. Don't get me wrong; there is nothing supernatural about me, and I don't profess to know a lot; but on the other hand, I am married to one who is known as a Vapor."

"And again . . . what is that?" Eve questioned.

"Ages ago, you may be aware, that within the world of Eternals there was a war, a rebellion?"

They both nodded, so she continued. "My husband was one of those who fought in that rebellion."

They both looked at each other, and Eve slowly began to move her hand toward a knife that she had hidden in her waistband. "So, your husband is a Fallen?"

"He was, and . . ." she said, looking at Eve, "he taught me many things, including how to hold my ground in a fight. So, you can relax and stop reaching for a weapon until I am done with what I have to share. Then if you so choose to pick that battle, you can try me."

Eve stopped and held her hands in her lap.

"Yes, he is what we call a Fallen. He never aligned with a Clan, though. After the rebellion, from what he tells me, he realized he had followed a deceitful path. He took responsibility for his actions but still realized he had blindly and faithfully followed those who sought out power and, in doing so, had deceived himself and many others. He could not continue forward. He found himself stuck between all the worlds. He was not a Fallen, per se—no longer a part of the world he had always known—nor was he human.

"What I am sharing with you needs to stay with you; he is believed to be dead. He chose to vanish into nothingness."

"Like a vapor," Isaiah stated. "That is where the name came from."

"It is. There are ancient texts that briefly mention them."

He rubbed his forehead as a light bulb went on. "Wow . . . again, things that we have so misunderstood."

"Zarius, my husband, says that frequently."

"So, what does all of this have to do with anything?" Eve asked.

"So, Zarius didn't fully vanish right away. For a while, he made a vow to protect what he could here on earth from the destruction of the Fallen, his kind. He knew that he couldn't reveal himself to the Alliance."

"Why? Because of his role in the rebellion?"

"Let's just say, for now, it is because he knew too much about a lot of things that have been hidden."

"And, obviously, seeks for it all to remain that way."

"Yes, Eve, for now . . . not for any other reason than each of us have a story to tell that is our own, and it should be the story's owner who shares it."

"Fair enough."

Tanisha continued, "So, he became the guardian of *Etz Chaim*, which is one name it is called by; but you would know it as the Tree of Life or the Eternal Tree."

"Wait . . . it is *real* . . . the tree?" Isaiah asked.

"From my understanding. I have never seen it, but my husband was its guardian for ages . . . not only the guardian for it but for all of Eden."

"Eden?"

"Not the Eden of mortal man. Again, that is a misunderstood writing. Eden is not necessarily a designated place. It is wherever the tree is . . . the tree and its planter."

"The planter?" Isaiah was sitting on the edge of his seat. Eve held back a smile. She did not want him to see how happy it was making her as she watched the flicker of the old Isaiah he once was start growing within him.

"No one knows where he came from or much about him. He was at the beginning of mankind, although he is not mortal himself. From my understanding, many believe that he is the very energy of life itself, embodied in a human form. He planted the tree and, in doing so, it became the life energy source that created all we know today within our world."

He sat back with his jaw open. None of this made any sense when dressed within the closet of religion, yet it all spoke deeply into the depths of his soul. He felt as if he had just found the outlet that he had been trying to plug into while searching in the dark.

"So, you said he used to guard it . . . your husband?"

"Yes. He became lonely, though. Time became his enemy. Ages passed; and he, a wandering warrior at heart, could no longer stay in one place. He chose to step away from his position and dove deeper into this evolving world of a Vapor. It was rumored that as ages moved throughout time, there were others, mostly Alliance members, who chose to step away from it all. They were not exiled but could no longer walk the path that they felt was full of just as much power-starving leadership as those within the Clans. So, they stepped out and became Vapors, also.

"My husband began to travel the world, searching for each of them. He, of course, had to reveal to them he was alive; but he spent time focused on building a network behind the scenes that would allow them the opportunity to become part of a world that neither wanted them or could understand them . . . in essence, allowing them to vanish into the world of mortal man."

Chapter Twenty-Seven

"How did you two meet?" Eve inquired.

"I am an archaeologist," Tanisha began. "I was working at the site of what we believed to be an ancient temple. We uncovered what we thought to be an altar room. It was like a round auditorium with seats surrounding the outside and a black onyx pillar in the middle.

"There were inscriptions on the pillar and throughout the room that we had never seen before. I am usually very good at translating ancient text; but this . . . this was something different. There was not even one of us who had seen it before.

"Gerault, the priest you came to see, came to the site at my request. As soon as he saw what we discovered, he turned as white as a sheet. I had never seen that man scared of anything in my life, but he was truly scared. He told me not to allow anyone back into the dig, and he was going to notify a friend to come and see if he could provide more information."

"Why? What scared him?"

"I didn't know at the time. A day or so later, this amazingly handsome and strong stranger, whom I had never seen on any of our sites before, showed up."

"Your future husband?"

She blushed a little bit as she nodded. "He and Gerault spoke for a long time alone, and together they went down into the dig. Shortly after that, the country we were in banned us from returning to the site . . . or so we were told. Even to this day, it is closed off. I found out later that it was a site that had been used for a large gathering, a council meeting of mortal and immortal. There were Fallen and Alliance, as well as mortals, who had been there."

"So, why the secrecy?"

"Again, without sharing more of my husband's story, what I can say is that the council meeting did not go as hoped; and the rift between each faction grew. In fact, that is where it is believed by most that my husband was killed.

"I discovered later that the land is protected by Guardians and not a government now."

Both of the Nepheliums sat without speaking. Their world seemed to continuously be growing before them, and they each wondered if there was ever an end to this rabbit hole.

"So, here we are now. Why?"

"Good question, Eve. I do know that Gerault—without anyone else knowing, including my husband—took things from that site. What all he took, I do not know; but he has been studying for years old manuscripts, text, and even artifacts. He also was a Watcher; and this week he messaged me saying he believed he had found something, but he needed some help with some translations. He believed that whatever it was he needed help with may unlock a whole different interpretation to all we have known."

"Well, that seems to be happening a lot," Isaiah laughed. "I have no idea what to believe anymore."

"That is the beauty of existence, though. When our world of knowledge is challenged and we open our minds to the understanding that others, most of the time, have dictated our beliefs, then we are free to re-establish who we are. We become free to see the truth in its raw form and not through the prism of someone else's interpretation."

Isaiah saw a pitcher of water sitting on the desk, along with a glass. He helped himself to it and then downed the water. His mouth felt like cotton, and he could feel a tightening in his chest. He felt shaky. It took him a moment to realize that he had not had a drink of alcohol for over 24 hours, and most likely he was having some withdrawals. "This would be a great time for three fingers of whiskey," he thought to himself, but he also was excited that he had taken at least one step forward in leaving that version of himself behind and embracing a new version of his old self.

"So," he said out loud, "here we are . . . all of us here."

"Took you awhile to figure that one out?" Eve jabbed at him.

He rolled his eyes. "What I mean is, that we are *here*. We each have some puzzle pieces; and maybe together . . . along with what Gerault has here . . . we can figure out what it is he thought he stumbled on."

"That is what I was thinking, also," Tanisha said very simply and straightforward.

"Yeah, me too!" Eve rattled off. "Well . . . ok . . . not really, but it sure felt good to say it."

Isaiah just shook his head. He sure was glad she had pushed him out of his free fall. She had given him a parachute without even knowing it. Sure, she probably felt as if she had jumped out of the same airplane without one, but he saw a pathway now in front of him . . . and a purpose.

*****

"Metatron! I have been looking for you!"

Metatron turned and saw Michael walking his way. "Well, not very hard, I assume. There is not a lot of places I tend to go."

"Funny that you say that." Michael caught up with the other Council member. "I looked in the Council Hall; you were not there. I stopped by your residence; you were not there. I looked out by the water, and guess what?"

"Well, let me see . . . I was not there. I only guess that because I wasn't."

"So, that is why I said that I have been looking for you."

Metatron stopped and turned toward Michael. "Here I am, Michael. What do you want? What is it that makes you need to find me so badly, and what makes me feel like there is a point that you are trying to make? The reason I am where I am is because of its seclusion . . . because I wanted to be *alone*."

"We haven't really talked since the Council meeting over Leah."

"And I would say that is probably a good thing. I have nothing more to say. What I said in there is on the record, and I got everything out that I needed to get out. In the end, she made her choice, although my personal opinion, if you want it, . . ."

"Sure."

"She saw the writing on the wall, and she just ensured the ending was in her control and not yours."

"Hmm . . ." Michael's arms were crossed as he listened. "So, her choosing to leave . . . you still blame me?"

"I do and I am not the only one; then again, it doesn't matter now, does it? She is gone, and she made that choice."

"You see, *that* is the key! You stated that *SHE* made the choice, and she did. I did not."

"Shut up, Michael! It has been so clear . . ."

"What has been clear Metatron?"

He wanted to just unleash on the Council leader, but he maintained his composure. "As I said, it is probably good that we have not talked since then; and honestly, it may be best we don't talk for a while."

Metatron turned and started to walk away. He was done with Michael. He knew that there was something going on, but he didn't know what. Until that time, he would just keep his distance.

"Oh, one more thing . . ."

He turned back around. "What?"

"How did you come to get your hands on the Watcher's Journal on Leah?"

"It was given to me."

"I understand that but by whom?"

"Why does that concern you, Michael?"

"Well, there are a few reasons, not to mention the number one reason: that it is forbidden for you to have it."

"That has already been discussed; so, what are the other reasons?"

"I'm glad you asked." He walked up next to Metatron. "You see, I really was concerned that we have been getting away from the foundations and laws that govern us. If we do that, then we lose everything . . . we lose our very selves. Would you agree?"

Metatron felt like punching him hard in that smug face of his.

If there was anyone that should have that speech given to him, it would be Michael himself.

"Get to your point so that I can disappear again; and hopefully, the next time you go looking for me, it will take you a lot longer to find me."

"You see, what you may have forgotten, My Friend, is that as the leader of the Council, I have access to many different things. I also have the liberty to make decisions when it comes to our kind."

"Ok?"

"Well, what you would not have known is that some time ago, after the death of Joan when Leah refused to obey our orders, I had her records destroyed."

Metatron felt his stomach turn. Michael was right; there was no way he would have known that. In fact, he was pretty sure there was no one that was still alive that knew that.

"What are you saying, Michael? Of course, her Watcher would have them."

Michael looked up at the sky for a moment as he enjoyed the look of shock and even slight panic on the face of his counterpart. "Ah, true! Sadly . . . because no one could know that I had them destroyed. Let's say that another reason Leah looked so shocked when you pulled that little stunt of yours is that, for years, Leah was certain she no longer had a Watcher documenting her world."

"Because she didn't, did she?"

Michael shook his head. "Nope. Sadly, her Watcher couldn't stand the thought of his actions that betrayed poor Joan and crushed Leah. Shortly after the young witch was burned at the stake, he hung himself. Sad."

All the color drained from Metatron's face. "Why are you telling me this, Michael? You know that I would not keep any of this secret."

"That is true, and I don't expect you to . . . although I don't expect that you will have time to tell anyone . . . and if you do, who then will believe you?"

"Are you threatening me?"

"Take it how you want. I do believe that you have shared with at least one Council member that you were not sure if you would stay any longer here in Scintillantes. So, who then would question if you seem to just vanish?"

"Your time is drawing to a close, Michael. I don't know everything; but I can promise you that I will find out what it is you are a part of and, in the end, you will answer for what you are doing and what you have done!"

Michael laughed. "So stoic! So poetic! Sounds as if you are standing on a stage, performing for an audience. Sadly, today, that audience will no longer listen. Your curtain has closed, Enoch."

Metatron fumed at the use of his earthly name. "I would suggest you make your exit, Michael. I will not stand by any longer, watching as you pretend to be something you are not!"

"Ha . . . coming from the once-mortal who was chosen to stand within the halls of that which he could never understand! Dumah, my friend, do you mind?" A figure stepped out from behind a large sculpture near where they were standing.

"TRAITOR!" Metatron shouted at Michael, as he recognized the Fallen warrior that now stood within arm's reach. "You called me by my earthly name, and now I will call you by the name that has been rumored for far too long within the ages of time: Azrael, your time will come!

"Dumah, you can take him now. He is words only. Per rules of the Council, he is not armed. Metatron or Enoch . . . whichever name you want . . . you meddled in the places only meant for Eternals. Now, you will become trapped within the place originally meant for mortals but then became the darkness for immortals. It is a place where, no matter which side you are a part of, you will find torment."

Dumah unsheathed his sword. "Know that I do not care if blood is spilled here; so, do not attempt to resist me. I will take any reason to dismember you here!"

*****

The early morning sun touched the snow-covered landscape. Everything looked clean and innocent. Tori sat with her knees up to her chin and her back against the headboard of her bed. Even though the outdoors seemed inviting, her soul was tormented. She was scared. She had slept fairly well; but as she woke up to the realization that she had no idea what the day would bring, she felt fear begin to sweep over her.

There was a knock on the door, and then it opened just a bit. "Mind if I come in?"

"You're good."

Ann walked in with a tray of fresh fruit and two glasses of juice. Her smile did little to calm the teen's mind, but Tori was grateful for the company.

"I figured your stomach would be in knots, so I didn't think a heavy breakfast would look appetizing. So, I cut up some fresh fruit." She sat down on the bed, cross-legged, in front of the young lady. The tray had fresh strawberries, melons, kiwi, and some heavy whipped cream to dip it all in.

"I can't do this, Ann."

"I know you feel that way, but that is why I wanted the chance to talk with you before everything got crazy." Ann handed her a napkin and motioned for her to help herself. "I don't talk a lot about my past, Tori. I would rather live in the here and now, and I would love nothing more than to forget all that I have gone through. The problem with that is that if I do forget what I have gone through, there is a chance I will never fully appreciate where I am today."

"That's understandable."

"With that being said, I did want to share with you a story that I hope will ease your anxiety."

She nodded. "Ok. I will take anything right now."

"When Leah brought me here, it meant that everything that was a part of me before was gone. The old me was gone. I couldn't return to who I once was. If I did, it would mean that I wouldn't live very long. My old life was dead, just as those inside that life believe that I am dead."

"Wait . . . you have people who think you are *dead?*"

Ann smiled. "Yes . . . and, in all honesty, I am. Ann is not the name I have gone by all my life. My old self . . . the person I once was . . . she died before I was brought here. In fact, when Leah brought me here, as she stated, they didn't think I would live. It was only by a miracle my children and I are alive.

"What I wanted to share with you is this: when I first got here, I was in a coma. I didn't even know I was here . . . but I did."

"How so?"

"This place . . . Eden . . . it is alive. It is unlike any place you have ever been to and ever will go again. It wrapped me up, even in my dark and devastated physical and mental state. While I was in a coma, I remember a vision or dream. I don't know . . . maybe it was even real. It was Eden. She came to me."

"Really? You mean Eden is a real person?"

"No, I think Eden is an idea or maybe even energy. I think Eden is whatever you need Eden to be for you.

"Anyway, a lady, who told me she was Eden, came to me. I was sitting in a field of the most beautiful wildflowers, and I saw her coming toward me. When I saw her, my heart leaped as if I had seen an old friend for the first time in decades. I ran to her and hugged her. She was wearing a beautiful, baby blue dress; and she had thick, long-flowing, red hair.

"She spoke to me and told me that I would become the mother of generations. She explained to me that motherhood would be a burden, also. She stated that I would find myself in a desolate area, looking for my children; but that in the end, the desolation would become green like the very field in which I was standing and that my children would thrive as the wildflowers that were bringing me joy at that moment.

"I tell you this because I know you are worried . . . not just for yourself but for my children. I can't thank you enough for that. That shows that you are a beautiful person inside. You carry the weight of evil within you, and yet that evil does not consume you. If it did, then my children's wellbeing would be the last thing on your mind.

"They will be ok. I know they will, because Eden has told me so . . . she promised."

Tori looked out of her window. "Funny how quickly life changes. If you had shared that story with me just days ago, I would have asked what drugs you were on . . . and then probably asked you where I could get some. Here I am though, sitting in a place that you claim is alive, being told I have the spawn of hell somewhere in my gut, and that in order to rescue me, we must use two young children and two angelic beings. Anytime someone wants to wake me up, they sure as hell can feel free to do so."

Ann reached out and took her hand. "Just know we have you. You are no longer alone."

"Yeah, I get that. Still doesn't make any of this normal."

"Normal is funny, though. Normal is a figment of our imagination and the way that our brain is programmed to accept what we see around us. What is normal to someone who has grown up in one part of the world is not necessarily normal to someone on the opposite side. So, you take that and plant it within the universe of existence. To believe one thing is normal and reject another is a form of extreme self-centeredness. It means that we are in full understanding of ourselves and the universe at any given point."

Tori wrinkled her nose. "Wow, now that is pretty deep and out there, but it clicks in my head. I can understand that."

Ann picked up the tray that now had only a few things left on it. "I will see you downstairs in a few."

"Thank you for sharing with me your story. Maybe Eden will speak to me."

Ann smiled. "Maybe."

Chapter Twenty-Eight

"Lano and Lada, what are you going to do once you fall asleep?" their mother asked them as she knelt between the twins. They each were comfortably sitting in recliners. There were heart monitors attached to each of them as well as I.V. lines.

"We follow her!" they both said with young enthusiasm as they pointed to Leah.

"Good job! What if you see something scary?"

"We still follow her," Lada said as she wiggled around in the big chair.

"Also, if we see something funny, we still stay with her." Lano was not about to be undone by his sister's answer.

Ann laughed, "You both are right. Remember what we talked about. There may be all kinds of things you will see and experience, but you stay with these three." She pointed to Leah, Zarius, and Tori.

"Now, there may be some really scary things that could take place with Tori. Trust Ms. Leah and do as you are instructed. You also may find out that there are some really crazy things you can do while you are asleep. Don't be scared about those things, ok?"

"You mean," Lada asked, "like when Lano pulled a booger from his nose and ate it?"

"I did not!"

"You did! I saw it; and that is crazy . . . right, Momma?"

Her brother crossed his arms and pouted at his sister's story as their mom attempted to not laugh. "Well, if it did happen, that is pretty crazy; but I'm talking about like crazy, super powers!"

"WHAT?" They both had been surprised and had excited looks on their faces. "We get to be superheroes?"

"Maybe . . . we are not sure, but again . . ."

"We know!" they both said in unison. "Follow her."

Leah was watching all of this from her recliner as she was getting prepped for what surely would become one rough day beyond the curtain of reality. She wondered, now that she was a Vapor, would she have children? She also looked over at Tori who was reclined back with her eyes staring straight ahead at the ceiling.

"I'm so sorry, Tori, that I didn't offer you the chance that Ann had," she whispered.

Serenity was hooking up the I.V. to Leah's arm and overheard the whisper. She reached out and touched her shoulder. "Leah, I have a lot of shit in my head; but I do want to say that although you may have turned your back on Tori earlier, right now you haven't."

"Thanks, Serenity. I feel like I owe her this, and also . . ."

"Yeah?"

"Thank you for disobeying my orders on taking her to the hospital."

Serenity smiled a little bit. "I'm pretty good at disobeying your orders."

"Well, maybe it is because you and I are so much alike."

"Whoa! Don't push it too far, Leah. Remember, I am in charge of all the stuff that is going to bring you back from the other side."

Leah just smiled and winked. "I'm in good hands, then."

"So, how does this work? Everyone says prayers or something over me, throw some holy water on me, and watch me twist like a pretzel?" Tori asked.

Gene walked in as she was asking that question. He sat down on a rolling stool and slid between her and Leah's recliners.

"Nope. Kind of like vampires and werewolves, mankind has taken the truth and twisted it to seem more over-the-top. Now, don't get me wrong; this will be no walk in the park, and we don't know the outcome, but it isn't like what you said at all."

He addressed everyone in the room but, most specifically, Leah, Zarius, and Tori, "You will find yourself drifting off to sleep. You then will feel as if you wake up; however, in reality, you will be caught between the threads of existence. Everything that happens there will be real. I mean *everything!*"

He looked over at the twins and motioned for Ann to place headphones over their ears so that they could listen to music and not have to hear what he was about to say to the rest of them. Once he was assured that the young ones could not hear him, he spoke again. "It is hard to explain where you will be. Reality is a curtain; time is a measurement of that curtain. You will be outside both things. You will actually tap into the soul energy of Tori.

"Everything that exists does so with threads interwoven within each other. The connection is sometimes hard to find, and others are so clear. It is that sense of kinship that you feel with someone right away whom you have never met . . . or even déjà vu. Everything is connected.

"This could look like anything and everything. It may look

familiar. It may look like something only familiar to Tori and, on some very rare occasions, you all may see different surroundings."

"Wait!" Zarius sat up. "How does that work if we are all supposed to be going after this thing?"

"And all while keeping the twins safe?" Leah interjected.

"Well, yeah . . . that, also," Zarius finished.

"Think of it as two people being in the same room. One of them is wearing glasses that are crystal clear, but the other has some oily liquid smeared on his. Same room but different view. The turns and twists, rooms and hallways . . . they are all the same but just look different to each person."

"Yeah, let's hope that is *very* rare, because that doesn't seem right at all." Zarius shifted some in his seat.

"The key to all of this will be an understanding that you are facing a demonic being that can divide himself into numerous entities. It will be like taking on several Overlords at once, but each part of him knows what the other is doing. He is a master of trickery and deception."

"I must say this sounds less and less like something I want to do!" Tori was starting to tremble.

"Tori, if you do not do this, this being will shred your mind until you no longer recognize anyone; and no one will recognize you. Once he has devoured your very identity, he will then leave you as a shattered shell."

"Maybe this is a stupid question and I'm the only one who doesn't know, but once we take Legion on, what do we do then?"

"Our hope is that he will manifest himself *outside* of Tori and, in doing so, he can be restrained. Once manifested, I will restrain him; and we can figure out from there."

"And if he doesn't manifest outside of Tori?"

"That is when it gets trickier and, honestly, harder. You will have to gain control over him where you are and, in doing so, exile him to the Abyss."

"What if he doesn't go?" Tori asked.

"The ancient rites will not allow him the choice if he is beaten. He must surrender to the one who bested him."

"Oh . . . yeah, like I understood any of that."

"Basically if you all win against him, he has to do what you tell him to do," Serenity stated as she turned down the lights.

"Well, that was easy to understand."

"Each of you will need to put your headphones on. You will hear my voice in them, and I will be counting backward. I want you to relax, close your eyes, and breathe deeply." Gene's voice took on a smooth and even tone.

Serenity made sure she was next to Tori. She placed her hand on Tori's forehead so that she could feel that human connection. She could feel the trembling, and Tori's pulse was racing. She reached down and gave the young lady's hand a reassuring squeeze, and she heard the monitors for each of those in the recliners begin to even out.

"They are all asleep," she stated very matter-of-factly. "So, what now?"

"All we can do is wait. This is not Zarius' and Leah's first rodeo with darkness . . . maybe their first in this fashion, but they are both well-seasoned warriors."

"Can I touch my children?" Ann asked.

"Yes! In fact, I want you to! Hold their hand, caress their forehead! You never know when the love of a mother will chase the darkest of evil away."

Serenity checked the monitors and then walked over to Gene. "Can I ask you a question outside?"

He nodded, and she followed him out into a hallway. "What is it?"

"I have a question about what you said back there when dealing with Legion if he manifests himself."

"Ok, what is it?"

"You said we would restrain him. How are we going to do that? I didn't see any equipment for that inside that room. I also know that if I was back at the Sanctum, there are many different weapons we could use to take him out, but again . . ."

"You see nothing in there."

"Right." She waited for an answer. His expression never changed. He just continued to look at her.

"Well?"

"I already answered you, Serenity."

Her eyes widened as she realized that he had answered her, using her words back to her. She covered her mouth, scared she would be too loud in her reaction, "You don't have anything like that here!"

"If you think I let them go in blindly, let me assure you that I did not. Leah is aware. She knows that there is no way that Legion will manifest himself. He, even in his weakened state, believes himself unconquerable."

"What about Ann?"

"She knows. We have a way of pulling the twins out if we need to, if things go south fast."

"You should have told everyone."

"Maybe, but I didn't."

*****

Leah could feel herself waking up. She opened her eyes and was startled by two pairs of eyes looking down at her. "Momma said to follow you."

She sat up and looked around. The sky was dark with streaks of orange and red, and she was lying next to the charred remnants of a one-room building that still smelled of smoke and ash. She could not see Zarius or Tori, but she had enough wits about her to remember that her real self was asleep in a recliner in Eden.

"Take my hands, both of you," she almost barked. She winced because she had to remember she was dealing with children and not hardened warriors.

She knelt down in front of them. "Listen, I want you to tell me about anything weird that you may see, anything strange you are feeling. Do you understand what I am saying?"

They both nodded. Continuing to hold their hands, they began to walk. She had no idea where to. She needed to find the other two before going too far.

The small, smoldering building was in the middle of a field. There was a tree that had large scars in the trunk of it and no leaves, which stood about ten yards away from the house.

The coloring on everything was . . . well, strange and dark. The tree itself seemed to have hues of purples and gray, and the grass that was under their feet had grays and greens. She didn't recognize any of it, so she knew that this must be the threads that were connected to images and moments within Tori's mind. This, of course, didn't mean anything. The shack itself could be a metaphor for an empty shell of a memory or could truly be a shack.

She had to find Zarius and Tori.

*****

"Tori, can you hear me?"

Tori opened her eyes and found herself sitting up with her back against a large rock formation. She looked to her right; and she saw Zarius several feet away, standing up and looking at her. Her mind was foggy, and her body felt drained. "What happened? Is it over?"

He walked over and reached out his hand to help her stand up. "No, My Dear Friend, I don't believe it has even begun. This is the in-between . . . that part that Gene was saying is like an energy network of threads. Do you recognize any of this?"

She looked around at the rocks against which she had been leaning and up at the dark-colored sky. "Should I?"

"I don't know. Try to think abstract . . . like if your life and thoughts were placed out as images but not clear images."

"Well, that helps, because all I see is a field in front of me, and woods with rocks behind me. Sure, Zarius, looks like home away from home within my brain."

"Ok, so yeah, guess that was an unfair question. Do you see Leah or the twins?"

She shook her head. "I don't see anyone or really anything. Yay, go, team Demon Slayers, for not even being on the right playing field!"

"Shhh . . .." Zarius motioned for Tori to be quiet. "Did you hear that?"

She shook her head.

"I thought I heard children laughing. It may have been the twins."

They both listened, and then Tori could hear it. She motioned out into the field. The grass within the field was about waist level, but there were places where it appeared the grass had been cut short.

"Sounds like it is coming from out in the field. Maybe the twins are playing in the taller grass."

Zarius stood on his tiptoes, trying to see if he could spot them but was unable to.

"I don't know. Leah should be with them; and if she is, we would be able to see her, at least."

"I guess we could start walking that way. We do have to find them; and unless you have a better idea, that way is just as good as any."

There was a hot breeze blowing across the field. They felt it on their skin as they stepped away from the rock formations and the tree coverage. It felt as if every bit of moisture was being wicked from their skin with each step.

Off to their left, they heard children's laughter again and saw some of the grass moving as if something was running through it. They still had no visual of the twins or of Leah.

"That has to be them," Tori said as she quickened her pace toward the movement and sound.

"Tori, wait," he stopped her. "So, nothing looks familiar to you?"

"I already told you that it doesn't."

"I know you did, but this just doesn't seem right. Something seems off. I don't like that we can't see Leah if that is the twins."

There was the laughter again. This time it sounded closer, and they could see movement again in the grass. The movement looked as if it was advancing towards them.

"You have heard Legion talk inside your head, right?"

She nodded. There was a knot forming in her stomach as he

said that. She felt clammy and as if she was about to faint at the thought of the voices that had been so crystal clear.

"Did they ever sound like children?"

Her face went white. "Are you saying that . . ."

"Stop! Just answer my question."

"Maybe. They always sounded different. I do remember a little girl, I think."

"So, listen to me really closely, Tori. Are you listening?"

"Yes."

"While we are doing this, I need you to be focused on what I say; and I need you to try your best to not let your emotions feed into your mindset. You got me? It is important! A good soldier has emotion but does his best to keep those emotions walled up until after the battle."

"I'm not a soldier, though, Zarius. I'm a teenager."

"Today . . . at this moment, you are both."

She began shaking. She was trying to keep control of her body but she couldn't. She felt stomach acid singe her throat.

Zarius looked on the horizon and saw lightning flash across the sky. He then looked over at his partner. "Well, you may not recognize any of this place, but this place sure does recognize you!" He pointed to the lightning. "As soon as you started shaking, that lightning started flashing over on the horizon."

"Fantastic! So maybe if I puke, it will start raining on us?"

"Can we do me a favor and not test that theory?"

"Tori, come play with us!"

She screamed and jumped back. A boy and a girl's voices rang out. It sounded as if she could reach out and touch them, but she could see no one.

"Legion! Listen, I am Zarius, former Guardian of *Etz Chaim*. I demand you come out of the shadows and face us!"

Childish squeals of glee rang out. "Silly Boy, we want to play with the girl."

"She is under my protection!"

"We just want to play games!"

The grass moved near them, and Tori grabbed Zarius' arm as she caught sight of the heads of two small children. "Zarius, right there!" she pointed to her left.

Two young children emerged from the grass. As they did, Tori screamed and jumped behind Zarius. "Those are *NOT* the twins!"

The little girl had just eye sockets where her eyes should have been, and her sibling was missing half of his scalp. Their fingers were twice as long as a normal adult, and they each had four feet. "Play with us, Tori!"

Their voices began to change from playful, childlike voices to a deep feral voice. "We are a part of you! You are a part of us!"

Zarius was not one to freeze when it came to battle, but he found himself like granite. These were kids! Sure, they were demonic and horrid but still kids.

"Get it together, Zarius! They are projections of what he wants you to see," he chastised himself as he stood there.

"Hey, so you want to play?" He reached into his pocket. He felt the cold metal cubes. "I love playing games. Let's play a game!"

"We love games," they growled in unison.

"I have two dice. You both agree on a number from 2 to 12. If I roll your number, I win; and if I don't, you win!"

"What do we win?" the voice kept hovering between childlike and a cruel horror flick.

"If you win, then Tori gets to go play with you."

"Wait . . . what?" Tori looked at him in disbelief.

He turned and looked at her. "Trust me," he mouthed in her direction. He looked back at the children. "Do you want to play?"

"Yes! We choose the number 12!"

He began to roll the dice around in his closed fist. "Are you sure? Once I roll, you can't change your answer."

The dice bounced around in his hand. Their feel against his skin allowed him to start focusing on the dice and not on all the fears and anxiety that seem to be attacking his mind.

"We want 12!"

He overturned his hand and allowed the dice to fall toward the ground. Just as he hoped, both children looked down; and for a moment their attention was diverted from him and Tori. Without hesitation and without allowing the thought of their being just children clouding his mind, he reached back and pulled out a large-bladed knife. The blade was curved, and he had trained for years to strike fast and accurately with it.

Before the dice could hit the ground, there were two young heads on the grass, looking up at both of them. Zarius felt the hot blood splatter across his face and hands. The two little bodies crumpled to the ground. For a moment the children's eyes fluttered, and then the remains turned to ash. Tori burst into screams and tears. He grabbed her and held her tight against his chest. He said nothing but allowed her to sob. She was right, she wasn't a soldier; she was a teenager.

"They were not real, Tori. You need to understand that. They were segments of Legion. His games have just begun."

Chapter Twenty-Nine

Both, Lano and Lada heard the screams coming from close by. Each of them held tighter to Leah's hand. "What was that?" they both asked.

"It is ok. That sounded like Tori. Maybe she is screaming to help us find them."

"Momma says to never scream unless you are in trouble. That way when you do scream, people will know you are being honest," Lano stated nonchalantly.

"That is a good idea, and maybe we can tell that to Tori when we find her and Zarius."

"Ok," he smiled.

Inside, Leah was feeling frustrated. The Alliance leader in her yelled at her to run to the screams, but she had no idea into what she would be leading the children. She knew that Ann allowed them to go with her because she trusted Leah, but when does trust given become trust broken?

There was always the chance of her giving the signal for the twins to wake up, but they also had just begun. If they did need them, as Gene thought they would, then it would be useless to keep going if she woke them up.

She listened for a moment and did not hear any other noises.

"Well, I guess there is always the choice of drawing attention to us. I just hope it isn't unwanted attention!"

"Zarius!" she yelled out. "Tori!"

The children thought it was their turn to also help, so they joined in with their small yells, "Zarius! Tori!"

Leah sighed a heavy sigh of relief when, a moment later, she saw her two lost companions walk toward them. She pointed them out to the twins, and they both took off running in that direction. Leah figured she did not have even close to the energy as both of them. She decided to walk.

There were plenty of hugs to go around, and Leah couldn't help but notice the red eyes that Tori had from crying. There were also a few spots of blood splatter on Zarius' face that he had missed wiping off. She motioned for him to walk with her.

"You missed a few splatters on your face."

He used his sleeve to get them off. "Yeah, so that happened!"

"What did?"

"Demonic twins that he formed himself into. I could go my whole life without having to take a blade to any children, again, no matter how demonic and horrid they are."

"So, what now?"

He crossed his arms across his chest and just looked at her. "I was hoping you would tell me. We can't just sit here waiting to be picked off by pieces of that thing."

"Well, your guess is as good as mine. I agree with you about not waiting, but the only thing I can think of is calling him out."

"Sure! Why not do that? I mean he could appear before us like a summoned genie, or we could have an army of rotting children."

"Any idea where we are within Tori's spiritual world?"

He shook his head. "I could guess. This field seems to stretch on forever. If you go back the way we came, you will run into thick forest that is too thick for us to even think about going into and rock formations that are unclimbable . . . at least without anything to climb with."

Leah looked around and took it all in. She felt she should be able to decipher this; and in doing so, it may help them to figure out a way to draw Legion out into the open.

"Just let me think out loud for a moment."

"Okay"

"The fields are endless because no matter how much she has been through, she finds hope. The coloring here is because, even though there is hope, that hope is dying. The color palette of her life is changing. It was most likely bright and beautiful at one point, but it has grown dreary."

"The patches of cut grass?"

"Again, she has attempted to bounce back each time in her life, but after a while the proverbial plot of land will not grow back after being cut down so many times.

"I saw a burnt building. That very well could be a metaphor for a small area within her hope in which she protected thoughts and memories; but after a while, like the grass, it was finally destroyed and abandoned."

"Sounds right to me," Tori quipped as she walked up into their conversation. "When my mother left, I tried to maintain control. I would go through a daily ritual of remembering all the things we used to do together. They were memories that I could hold onto, and they would get me through my day. After time passed and she stopped contacting me, I began to realize that those memories would not keep me forever. I had to move on.

Leah turned to her. "Tori, when you feel Legion's presence coming on strong, what are you thinking? What are you feeling?"

"I don't know."

"No, you do; and I'm sorry to push you, but you must go there . . . wherever that is that you are avoiding. You must take your mind there right now."

"Because that is where he is going to be most concentrated!" Zarius spoke up.

"Exactly!"

Tori didn't want to. She just wanted to go back to Eden. She wanted to pretend that none of this was real. She didn't want to feel as if she had no control anymore. She just wanted to be . . . she wanted to be herself. "I can't."

"Come on, Tori! We will go wherever you go!" Both of the children stood on either side of her. In their faces was innocence but also strength . . . supernatural strength. She knelt between them, and they each hugged her. She felt healing strength and courage begin to flow through their bodies and into her heart and soul.

Tori looked up at the other two. "He used those twins earlier because my mother had a baby boy after me. He died during birth. I believe it was his death that caused my family to break apart.

"She used to blame me for it, even though I wasn't even anywhere near the hospital. She would tell me that as a toddler I was impossible. My mother told me that it was because I caused her so much stress that her body couldn't handle giving birth to him.

"My father had always wanted a boy; it devastated him, and that is when he started drinking so heavily."

Tori began to break down as she recalled her past. "I began to make believe that my mother truly loved me. Later, she did in her own twisted way; but I made up a version of my mother in my head that never really existed. All I wanted was parents who would see me as their world. If I could have brought my brother back to life, I would have; but I couldn't. I also could never live up to being enough for the two people who should have loved me unconditionally!"

"So where would Legion be, Tori?"

"Here in this version of who I am? I don't know."

"Ok," Zarius spoke with strong compassion in his voice. "Imagine this being your everyday life. Where would he be?"

"He would be at the toy store."

"Toy store?"

She nodded through her tears. "I would always go find a toy store. My parents didn't have a lot of money, so I never had any real toys to speak of. I was pretty much left on my own, so I would find my way to a store where I could find stuffed animals or dolls and pretend they were my brother. I would then act as if my brother and I were on a shopping spree with my parents. I did this until I was about 11. It helped me believe in my hope of having a family that was whole and complete."

"We are going to a toy store?" The twins jumped up and down. They were ready to go now!

"I'm afraid if we find a toy store out here in the middle of existence while looking for a demon, it will not be one that any of us will have fun in," Leah stated.

Her body was worn out. Her heart hurt for this young girl; her heart hurt for her former team. She felt sadness unlike she had felt in a long time . . . not the shadow of it but true, deep-piercing sadness.

Tori stood up and gave the children another quick hug. "I know where it is."

"Where?" Leah asked.

"It is going to be in that burnt building you mentioned."

"That building is half gone."

"Remember, though, nothing is as it seems." Zarius started walking in the direction from which Leah and the kids had come. "We aren't looking for a literal toy store."

"Tori said earlier, though, that the building was a place that kept her hopes and dreams protected." Leah paused. "But her dreams and hopes stopped when she was 11 and she gave up. That is when she stopped protecting her memories."

"Ah, now you are catching on! Now, catch up," Zarius stated over his shoulder.

*****

The sky began to rumble overhead, and Zarius wondered how much turmoil they were about to face. He knew that Tori was fighting more of an inner battle than any of them understood; but at the same time, they all were about to experience it.

They all could see the charred remains of the little shack out in front of them. He was still in the lead, and he could feel Tori dropping further behind. He wondered if he would have to pick her up and carry her into the ruins.

"Zarius, wait," Leah stopped him. "It has changed."

"What has?"

"All of it." She pointed toward the building. "It is more built up than when I woke up here; and look, there are old toys scattered in the yard. Those were definitely not there before."

"Tori is losing the ability to hide her emotions and fears. I would bet money that these things were here before, but she had them hidden within her subconscious; and now, she is not able to do that so easily. She has begun to open herself up, so the things she had hidden are being exposed. It worries me what we will find inside."

There was music from a jack-in-the-box playing somewhere inside, and a doll that was lying outside kept making noises, laughing and repeating the words, "Silence is golden; silence is golden; silence is golden."

"I swear, mankind makes the creepiest things for their children to play with. Trust me, I have seen some dark things in my existence but toys that move and make noise . . . those scare me more than anything."

"Agreed!" Zarius responded to Leah's analysis.

He looked back and noticed that Tori and the children were several yards behind. The twins had begun to hold back, also; and he could see that their version of a "toy store" and the reality of what they were standing in front of was not the same. He wasn't sure if they were holding Tori back, or if Tori was having to pull them forward.

He turned to Leah, who was now standing beside him. "I'm not sure how we are going to do this. There is no way they are going to be able to be worth a damn in this fight."

"We don't know that. Mortal history is chock full of the young, afraid, and unskilled rising to the height of heroics when faced with a challenge of overwhelming odds."

"You should write that down and claim it," he laughed.

The other three now stood beside them. Tori leaned up against Zarius' tall frame. "Do I go in first?"

"I would imagine, but 'first' is relative. I mean, most likely, this is where Legion is, so he is first. You will lead the way; but we will be behind you . . . so, are you really first or are we all together?"

She rolled her eyes. "Ok, so that may have made me laugh when I was ten."

"Oh, come on, it at least made you smile!"

"That is true."

*****

Tori felt the building calling to her, pulling her in. She could feel it reaching out and teasing her with safety that it could no longer offer. It called her, and yet at the same time mocked her for her childhood foolishness of believing in something that could not be.

She stepped forward and, as she did, stepped on a small toy frog that squeaked. She jumped, and Lada shrieked.

"Sorry," Tori apologized.

The building had most of its four walls now in place. There were segments that were burned through or had fallen; but for the most part, the whole building was now a complete structure in front of them. There were large gaping holes in what was left of the roof; and window frames were there, but there was no glass left within the windows themselves. The front door hung off one of its hinges, and it stood halfway open.

"I hated that music box!" she said angrily as she continued to slowly move toward the front door.

"Music box?" Leah questioned.

"Yeah, the one playing."

Leah looked at Zarius and the children. They all had the same blank look on their faces as she did. "Tori, you hear a music box?"

She nodded. "You don't?"

They all shook their heads.

"It is so loud! How do you not hear it?"

"Must be something that Legion is using to toy with you—no pun intended," Zarius said. That got him a decent punch to the back of his arm from Leah.

The young teenager was watching the front door, but then something caught her attention at the window. A figure of a female appeared just inside its shadows. She could barely make the lady out. Tori took a quick glance at the rest of her team and realized that they showed no reaction to the lady. She figured she was probably the only one who could see her, just as she was the only one who could hear the music box. She stopped and turned around. "I have a feeling that this may be something I am going to have to first attempt myself."

"Come again?" Leah shook her head. "There is no way that is going to happen!"

"Listen to me, Leah. This is me . . . about me. True, whatever happens here . . . sure, it could have some kind of an end-of-the-world type consequence on all of mankind . . . and even those who aren't mankind. Right now, this moment, here . . . this is about me. I can see it now. I may not have realized I was welcoming him into my life and existence, but it doesn't change the fact that I wasn't doing what I needed to do to keep from being his victim.

"Today, I can't be his victim anymore; I won't be! He is using my fears and anger against me. That is what has allowed him to dig so deep inside. I swept all the exposed areas of my life clean from what I thought could hurt me. The truth, though, is all I did was lock it all away in the recess of my soul. I didn't clean anything out. I just gave it the appearance that I did. I see that now. So, he had a wide berth to sweep in, possess me, and then use me against myself as his security system.

"Sure, you all may have the experience, the brawn," she looked at Zarius when she said this, "but I . . . well, I have me. It is me whom he is using. It is time I take back control of my life, my existence, and even my future. I have lived as a victim to my circumstances already for too many years . . . and come on, I am young! I sound like I should be in my 60s. I can either stay a victim to all of this, let it eat at me, let him or some other creepy dark matter steal my joy and life, or today I can face him and all that has held me back."

Neither of them could say anything. Leah stood there, shocked. This was not the young lady who had been rescued by her team; she was turning from a teenager into a warrior in front of them.

"Well, I . . . I . . . hell, I got nothing," Zarius stammered. "You want us to just hang here?"

She nodded. "You can babysit," she laughed as she pointed to the twins. As she did, she only saw the little girl. "Um, Lada, where is your brother?"

The little girl shrugged her shoulders. "I don't know. He told me not to say."

"Lada, you need to tell us!" Leah gritted her teeth. Yeah, she was a lot better with adults and ordering them to do things, not young children. "Where did your brother go?"

"He said that the singing lady told him it was ok to go with her. I told him Momma said to stay with Ms. Leah."

"Singing lady? Did anyone else see a lady?"

Tori raised her hand a little to Zarius' question. "I did, but she wasn't singing."

"What was she doing?"

"She was standing inside . . . OH MY GOD! NO!" Tori's scream could have pierced eardrums. Nothing could hold her back. Zarius attempted to grab her, but she slipped past him as she ran full throttle toward the doorway.

"Tori! Tori! Wait! What are you doing?"

Leah looked toward the building. She could not see anything that should have caused that reaction.

"NO, please *NO!*" Tori's screams continued. She was running toward the door, but her focus was on what she could see through the window. There, in the broken and burnt window was the lady once again, but this time she was not alone. She stood holding a crying Lano. One hand was over Lano's mouth, and the other clutching the young boy. The lady was smiling but it was as if her smile literally went from one earlobe to the next; and rows of horrid, razor-sharp teeth were clearly visible.

The two Vapors watched as Tori vanished inside the house, neither of them able to see what she could see. "What do we do now?"

"Not on my watch. No more am I losing anyone!" Leah scooped up Lada and started running toward the door. She didn't know what they would find inside; and she wasn't sure how to fight while holding a child, but the thing she *was* sure of was that this was a team commitment.

She heard Zarius' heavy footsteps behind her. "Maybe we should get the twins out of here," she heard him say to her.

"Sure! That would be a great idea! If we only knew where BOTH WERE!"

"And there is that."

Chapter Thirty

As Tori entered the one-room building, she felt her equilibrium begin to waver. The house around her began to move. She looked to her left to where the lady and Lano should have been. She caught a quick glimpse; but before she could move, two burnt walls came down from the ceiling, creating a hallway. She attempted to slide underneath it but was not fast enough. As she stood up, the floor spun in a counterclockwise direction; and she found herself facing a mirror.

She caught her balance as she fell against the mirror. As her body contacted the glass, the glass became liquid; and she fell through, screaming. She lay on the floor, her body covered with dark streaks from the soot and ash. She looked up, disoriented beyond belief. It seemed the room was backward; but the floor had spun her around, so it was as it seemed when she first walked in. She had fallen through the mirror, though, correct?

She got to her knees and looked in the mirror. There she could see the reflection of the front door that was to her left. It opened, and in rushed Zarius and Leah, carrying Lada. She turned her head quickly from the reflection in the mirror and looked at the front door to her left. It was still closed. She looked back, and there the three were. Lada was looking over Leah's shoulder toward the mirror and waved.

Tori pounded on the mirror; but it appeared as if not only could the other two not see her, but they could not hear her. Lada was pointing, and Leah turned and looked; but there was no recognition that she saw Tori on the other side.

There was a knocking on the front door; and Tori turned, walked over, and flung it open. The fields outside were in flames, and lightning was flashing violently across the sky. A strong wind was roaring and creating fire devils across the landscape.

She looked down at her feet and saw a baby carrier. She could not see if there was anything inside, because it was covered with blankets; but she could hear crying come from underneath them. She grabbed the carrier and pulled it inside. As she did, the wind caught the door and slammed it shut.

The crying became louder, and she reached down and pulled back the blankets. Her hand went to her mouth and her face twisted in a strange contortion as she looked down and saw a rotting baby boy inside the carrier.

She pressed up against the mirror, attempting to get away from the baby carrier. Hands reached through the mirror and pulled her through. She kicked and screamed . . . fighting with all she had to get away from whomever it was who had grabbed her. The hands let go as she crawled several feet away on all fours and turned to get a look at who it was.

She was sobbing and shaking. Her heart was racing, and she couldn't breathe. As she looked up, she half expected to see Leah or Zarius. Instead, she saw a radiant woman with blue hair and a dress that seemed to flow like the wind. Her eyes were piercing but peaceful. Her face held the wisdom of the ages and the youth of life itself. She made Tori feel calm almost instantly . . . made her want to jump up and give the lady a hug. This was not what brought the biggest surprise, though. From out behind this image of peace and beauty peeked a small girl.

"Lada?"

The little girl held her finger to her lips as if to indicate to Tori not to speak and then giggled and gave a little finger wave to the teenager.

"It's Eden!" the little girl whispered in a loud, child-like whisper.

Tori stumbled to her feet and looked at the figure in amazement. "You did come."

"Oh, Tori, I have always been here, but *this*," she said as she motioned around her, "has been so dark and burdensome to you. You created a place that you believed would bring you safety; but instead, it became the prison of your nightmares. You had to face all of this before you were able to break through and see me."

"He has Lano. He has the other twin," she quietly stated. "I can't let him take her brother like mine was taken!"

"That is not your responsibility, Dear One. You cannot rescue those who are not yours to rescue. Your intentions are right but your heart is not. You rushed into Legion's arms, as he knew you would, to rescue a little boy that you associated with your own brother . . . your own feelings of pain, guilt, and loneliness. In doing so, you placed yourself and others at risk."

"No, I didn't mean to do that!"

"I know you didn't. Like I said, your intentions were good. Yes, the threads of your existence and Lano's connect here at this moment and time, but his thread is not for you to follow. You are to follow your own.

"Legion is a part of you; and because of that, he knows your darkest secrets and fears. Everything you are seeing and experiencing is his manipulation of it all. You must stand against him. You must understand, as you stated before, you get to choose if you will be a victim or the victor today."

Tori looked down at Lada and then back up at Eden. "Where are Leah and Zarius?"

"They are here . . . but not. Legion has created the twisting of the threads to make it where you are both in the same place but just different views."

"How can Lada see me, then?"

Eden bent down and picked up the little girl. "She is special. Her innocence has allowed her to stand outside of what most understand. She doesn't even realize it. To her, it is just the world as she sees it; but to others, it is strange, weird, abnormal. Tori, we must leave, but you . . . you must face him. He will not leave you alone until you do."

*****

"What is she looking at? Someone needs to tell me what in the world is going on!" Leah stammered as she watched Lada, standing in the middle of an empty building. They had rushed in to help Tori but had found nothing but the empty remains of the burned building. Leah had sat Lada down as they looked and called out for Tori.

Leah then turned and watched as Lada had reached her hand in the air as if she were holding the hand of an invisible entity. She did not seem afraid or scared but, instead, had a smile on her face.

Both she and Zarius watched as the little girl looked as if she was hiding behind something and then place her finger to her lips and whisper something. Then to the shock of both of them, she appeared to be picked up. It looked like she was sitting on something in mid-air. She never said anything that either of them could hear, and she appeared to be looking into the middle of the room. Neither Leah or Zarius moved as they watched her come back to the ground and put her feet under her. She then waved and turned around and came almost skipping back to them.

"Lada, who were you talking to?"

"Tori, Silly!" she giggled.

"Tori? Where is she?"

The little girl pointed toward where she had just been standing. "She is right there."

Zarius knelt down beside her and looked hard at where she was pointing but could see nothing. "Can you still see Tori?"

Lada shook her head. "No, she just went into the other room."

Leah's eyes felt like they were going to pop out of her head as she stared hard at the empty space in the middle of the one-room ruins. "Another room?"

"Yup, she is going to find my brother and Legion."

"GREAT!" Leah threw her hands in the air. "So, what do we do now?"

"Maybe it is time we wake up."

"Are you kidding me? Leave her and Lano here?"

"I don't like it either, but how are we supposed to help someone we can't see, maneuver through something that we cannot understand, and fight an evil that we cannot get to?"

"I don't know."

"I can show you," Lada smiled.

Leah stood pondering. "Remember what Gene said! That there are rare times that we are in the same existence, but nothing looks the same. There is a reason he had the twins come with us! Lada is right; she can show us!"

"How? Look around you, Leah! We are in a small, ruined building with just what you see; and she is going to lead us through rooms that don't exist?"

"Faith, Zarius . . . faith."

He shook his head. "Whatever. This should be really interesting."

*****

There was an eerie silence surrounding her now. She jumped as a few large spiders crawled past her. As she walked, the building changed. She clearly was in a maze.

"I have to stop and think for a moment. I must face what I have not wanted to face. That is a common theme that keeps coming up. If this is all within my existence, then I should be able to find Legion and Lano with no issue."

The house began to look familiar; suddenly, it hit her why: "This has turned into our apartment." She stood in the living room where she and her family had lived, and her Mom had left. There was no furniture, and the walls were still burnt; but the layout was the same. She could see the doorway to the hall that led from the living room to the bedrooms.

She approached it and could see one door that would represent where her parent's bedroom was and one where her bedroom would be. Her mother had locked herself away for so many hours in that bedroom.

Tori felt strength start growing . . . strength and resolve. "Was your speech to Leah and Zarius just a speech, or did you really believe it?" she asked herself out loud.

"Tick tock tick . . . don't worry about walking quietly and carrying a big stick. We know you are here because we are here," multiple voices spoke at once.

"I'm here . . . not because you are here, but because I chose to be here! I may not be an Eternal or a Vapor. I may not have any form of supernatural instinct; but what you fail to realize is that, as a human, I understand what it means more than anyone to rise from the bottom and to stand up from off the mat before the bell is rung. You . . . you, Legion, saw someone weak, someone hurting, someone without hope that you desired to control. You were right, then; but you are wrong now."

She squared her shoulders and began to walk toward the end of the hall with her head held high. "I am Victoria! Today, I forgive my mother. Today, I forgive my parents. Today, I forgive myself. I did not choose this life; but I did choose to continue to allow the pain, anger, and abandonment control who I was. No more. I forgive myself for all of those things; and today, I stand reborn from the ashes of my past into a powerful and victorious woman."

As she walked past the door that would represent her room, she caught sight of something out of the corner of her eye. She turned and looked. There in the center of the room was Lano.

She wanted to rush to him, but she was cautious. He appeared to be unable to move. His eyes were bloodshot and swollen from crying, and he was breathing heavily. He looked at her, and all she could see was fear! He tried to speak, but all he could do was mouth words. His throat was raw from the crying, and he seemed to not have the strength to get any words formed.

"Are you hurt?" she asked him.

He shook his head.

"Can you move at all?"

He once again shook his head. He tried to speak again, and she put up her hand to stop him. "It's ok. You don't have to talk. You are going to be ok."

"Make the bad monster go away, Tori!" He finally was able to speak the words in a sniffling, heaving, and exhausted voice.

"I will, Lano. I promise." She did not go up to him or enter the room. She felt that was the very reason Legion had placed the young boy there. She turned and saw a light from under the doorway at the end of the hall. "I will be back, ok? Just try to breathe, and know that you are not alone."

The little boy nodded his head, acknowledging that he understood, and watched her vanish from the doorway. The closer she got to the door at the end of the hallway, the more her skin felt like it was crawling. She felt itchy, and every breath seemed to be hard to draw in and even harder to exhale.

"Not today, Satan . . . not today!" She laughed a little bit. "I have always wanted to say that and mean it."

*****

"Go this way," Lada said proudly as she led Leah by the hand.

Zarius felt ridiculous. He was pretty sure that two grown Vapors were being led in a game of make-believe by a young girl just old enough to start learning how to write.

"Watch there. There are spiders. I'm not scared of spiders."

Zarius' whole body shook as he jumped back. "Are you kidding me?"

"What?" Leah turned around quickly to see what the fuss was all about.

"I actually felt a spider!"

Lada giggled, "I told you!"

Zarius looked around where they had been standing. He rubbed his eyes. Everything started to become fuzzy.

"Leah, anything happening to your eyesight?"

She didn't answer right away because, indeed, her vision was blurring. "I think we are changing views, Zarius."

Sure enough, what they had been seeing began to fade away; and soon they were standing inside the hallway in which Tori had been when she saw Eden.

"Lada, tell me what do you see around you? Can you touch what you are telling me?"

"Yes!" The little girl touched one of the walls of the hallway. "I'm touching a wall."

"Ok, and what else do you see?"

"A doorway." She pointed to the doorway which the teen had taken, leading her into the area that replicated her family's living room.

"Great job! Give me a high five!"

Little Lada gave Leah a hug instead.

"How can we see it now?"

"I would imagine that Tori is gaining strength in herself. She is opening doorways that only she can open, and now they are stronger to her. Because they are stronger to her, they are stronger here where we are."

Leah pulled a small, handheld disk out from one of her pockets. She pushed a button on it. There was a noise that came out of it, and it began to glow blue.

"Uh . . . and do I get a cool, little, glowing disk?"

"I want one." Lada ran over and tried to touch it. Leah pulled it from her quickly.

"You have your wits and blade with which you are clearly experienced. This was a small parting gift that I took from the Sanctum when I left. I guess you could say it is like a supernatural sticky bomb. It should do the trick of taking Legion out."

"Hope you have an accurate throwing arm, because I am not wanting to get close enough where either of us can reach out and touch him to make sure it sticks.

I also have a strange and bizarre question."

"What?"

"How do we know that he is going to be all in one place? We already know he was banished once and that a large portion got away, and now we are dealing with that part of him."

"We don't."

"OH . . . now, that is honest and not encouraging at all!"

"Lada, can you do me another huge favor?"

The little girl jumped up and down. "I'm doing good!"

"Yes, you are. You have done the best! So, now it is mine or Zarius' turn. I need you to stay between us while we are walking. Can you do that?"

Lada immediately obeyed, placing herself between the two Vapors. "Just like this?"

Leah nodded. "Yes, Ma'am . . . just like that."

She took a deep breath and looked at Zarius. "Well, the good thing is I don't hear any screams. The bad news is I hear no noise at all. I guess it is time to end this."

Chapter Thirty-One

Tori's hand turned the doorknob. She started to push the door open; but as she did, it was yanked from her hand. The door flew off the hinges, and she was pulled into the room. There were arms and hands reaching at her, pulling at her, scratching at her.

Screaming. She had heard it before. It was the same madness that had slammed into her the night she hid inside the back area of the club . . . right before Chad and Serenity had found her. She was not that same girl, though! She had to be strong.

"You are nothing!"

"Oh, Mommy didn't love you! Mommy left you!"

"You have no real purpose! Everything you touch, everyone you try to love is ruined! It is because of you that others find themselves feeling sick and nauseated!

"You are worthless! You have no real value to anyone for anything!"

"Give up! You have never won! You have even lost at your own life!"

It was madness. She could hardly see anything past the rushing dark creatures into which Legion had broken himself. They were beyond maddening and horrific.

There were qualities that were similar, but each had distinct differences. There were some with eyes that bulged and looked in every direction but straight. Others had long tongues that licked at her face, and the foul breath was more than her stomach could take. Some of the creatures had small bodies but longer arms and legs that seemed to be able to twist and turn almost like tentacles. All their voices were different pitches and tones, but the unifying message was death, evil, and destruction. She could feel skin being torn open, and the pain was so intense that she had to concentrate on not passing out.

She felt her body fall and slam against the floor; and each of the creatures moved backward but did not stop surrounding her. Tears flowed freely, but so did anger. She rolled over and attempted to move her body so that she could stand up.

"Ah, child, did you believe—truly believe—that I, an Ancient One, would be able to be bested by a faint pep talk within your soul?"

She could taste blood filling her mouth and feel it running down her face. Her hands were almost raw meat. There was a gash upon her arm that, without even having to lift her head, she could see within it fatty tissue, torn muscle, and even bone. Every move she made brought waves of agonizing pain. She tried to formulate a thought, but her mind screamed at her to let go and just die. She managed to turn her head so she could see the source of the voice.

There, about two feet away from where she lay, a figure stood. Take the artistic and cinematic renditions of an Ancient vampire, blend it with a charming, demonic Overlord, and dress him in black pants and no shirt . . . one would have the embodiment of Legion.

"Damn!" Blood spattered from her mouth as she spoke, "You are one, ugly dude."

He squatted down so she could look into his eyes. "You are one, stupid and foolish, young mortal."

"Was all of this worth it?"

"*You* did this. *This*," he motioned in a sweeping gesture, "is all you. Lano, and what he has experienced . . . that was you. What I will do to the small group of friends who have every intention of destroying me tonight . . . yes, all you. Your own demise, Tori . . . that is also your fault."

He moved the matted, blood-soaked hair back from her face. He touched his fingers to his lips and tasted the blood that was on them. He listened to her gurgling as she tried to move. He thrived on the anguish of humanity.

"If you even knew half of what I have done through the ages . . . all the names I have gone by and the historical accounts that are written . . . you would have never attempted this madness!"

"Let. . .," she tried to speak, but she was struggling. It hurt to breathe, and every breath she could hear the rattling in her lungs. "Let . . . Lano . . . go . . . please. He is the . . . innocent one here."

Legion laughed. "Aren't they all? Tori, they are all innocent until they are no longer innocent."

"Let him be, and I will surrender myself to you. You can do whatever it is you wish to do to me."

He leaned down to where his lips were near her ear. "As tempting as that sounds, what would I use you for now—a loser, a throwaway, one whom no one wants? Even the great Alliance leader, Leah, wanted to discard you. She wanted nothing to do with you. To her, you were the trash, another human that wasn't worth her time. Now, you lay here, broken. Even your body is no longer a vessel worth my inhabiting."

"This is not who I am. I am asleep in Eden."

"You know nothing, do you? Do you not remember being told that what takes place here is very real, Tori? Do you really think that you can experience all of this and that your heap of flesh that you call your body not suffer?"

Legion looked up. "Bring me the boy."

Several segments of him left the room; but in one breath, they came hurling back through the doorway, smashing against the wall. The room became like a disturbed anthill. It was filled with high-pitched screams, swearing, and an ancient language that Tori could not understand. She could not move to see what was going on, but she sure did recognize the voices.

Through her pain, she laughed, "So, tell me what you are going to do to my small group of friends?" Her words were drowned out by the booming voice of Zarius.

"Greetings . . . I guess, technically, you would be my nephew . . . well, at least one part of you, anyway . . . but since I don't know which part, it won't bother me too much if I take out all of you!"

He could feel gore covering him as he began to fight, punch, kick, and slash his way into the room. He caught sight of Tori's mangled body, and it caused an animalistic rage to swell within him.

There were several segments of Legion that had gotten behind him, and he turned to make sure that Lada was safe. He was encouraged when he saw that Leah had moved the little girl behind her as she also sliced her way through the segments of Legion. He tried with all he had to get to Tori; but with each segment he and Leah disposed of, more would break away.

"That blue, glowing thingy you had earlier would be great right now!" he yelled back to Leah.

"I can't. It would take Tori out, also; and if we are close enough, it would take us out!"

"Well, a lot of good that does us!"

"Is Tori ok?"

"I can't tell. She looks in bad shape, but I can't get to her!"

He was pushed back into the hall. He felt pain on his right side, and he looked down and saw a huge gash across his midsection that was opened up pretty well. As he looked up, his eyes went toward the other doorway. He saw Lano inside the other room. "I found the boy!"

"Get him, and I will get to Tori!"

He was surrounded and couldn't move. He felt pain in every part of his body. There were creatures biting and clawing at his feet, legs, arms . . . well, everywhere! He felt himself being dragged down, so he allowed his body weight to fall into the room where Lano was being held. The boy still could not move.

"Legion has him paralyzed with fear, Leah!"

He reached up to try to touch the boy to reassure him. "If we can cause a big enough distraction, we may be able to release Legion's hold on him!"

Leah was trying to make her way into where Tori was; but she was also concerned that Lada would get caught up in the fray of things and become part of the battle or maybe worse: a victim of it.

"Didn't you have a plan to get the twins out of here if need be?" Zarius yelled out.

"Yes, but it is either both or neither; and if we take Lano out of here right now, he could permanently be affected by Legion!"

"Ah . . . the great and mighty Leah!" Legion's voice rang out. "You are also wise."

Shadows and darkness rushed inward through the doorframe of the room in which Tori was as Legion took form in front of her. "You still have an option that will allow you to live, Alliance Leader!"

She stood trying to catch her breath. As he spoke, she noticed that the other segments of him were not fighting. They were standing still, and all were looking at her. "He can't hold his form and fight at the same time!" she thought to herself. "He has to concentrate to pull himself into his manifestation because he is not all here." She hoped that Zarius would realize this, also. This could give him a chance to rescue Lano. She had to make sure she kept Legion focused on her.

"I am no longer an Alliance leader, Legion."

He cocked his head to the side. "Oh? Now, why is that? Too many losses for the precious Arch Council to look past?"

"No, it was by choice. I no longer had faith that they could find the best in humanity, and I could no longer stand by and watch your kind destroy that which I have sworn to protect!"

"To protect? Is that what you call it? Did you protect Joan? Have you protected Tori?" He nodded in the direction where Tori's body lay. "It seems to me that it is *you* who can no longer do what is best for humanity."

"Taunt me all you want," she quipped. "I had to learn what Tori had to learn: I had to forgive myself. I have done that."

Zarius was standing inside the room, holding Lano. The little boy was zombie-like. His eyes refused to blink, and there was no response to anything Zarius said to him. "For the sake of Jah and all that is good, please, please, come back to us!" he begged.

He felt a small body press up against him, and he looked to see Lada. She had crawled on her hands and knees past Leah and behind the other segments of Legion and came into the room very quietly. Zarius held his finger to his lips. "Shh . . . be quiet."

"Is my brother ok?" She reached out and began to pet his head.

"I don't know, Lada."

"He will be ok. I know it."

She bent down and gently kissed her brother on his forehead. "Lano, wake up."

Zarius could not hold back the tears. They flowed like faucets that had been under a lot of pressure. His body shook silently as he held the young boy.

"Lano, I want to go home. Please, can we go home?" Her voice was quiet, soft, and loving. Her hand continued to caress her twin's head.

"I'm afraid he isn't coming back, Lada."

"He is. We are going to go home together. I know, because I listened to Momma and never left Ms. Leah. I obeyed."

Zarius leaned his head against Lada's, his tears wetting her hair. "Yes, Little Girl, you did."

Lada quietly and gently kissed Zarius' cheek and then turned to her brother. She placed one hand on each side of his head. Words began to flow from her lips. They didn't even sound as if they were coming from a little girl. They were words of ancient origin, words of power. *"Teacht ar ais chugam, Dearthair. Teacht abhaile liomsa,* Lano."

Zarius sat back, unable to move or speak. Her words wove deeply into the fabric of Zarius' being, and he sat in awe as Lano's eyes began to blink. Even in the darkness, he could see color coming back into the boy's skin. Lano sat up and rubbed his eyes.

"Is the monster gone?"

There was only one response Zarius could think of at that moment. "Leah! *NOW!*"

Legion's head snapped to the direction of Zarius' voice. Leah grabbed her blade and, with a swift motion, cut a gash into the palm of her hand. Legion screamed out; and just as quickly as she was able to cut her palm, he vanished. Every segment around them rushed in on Zarius and the twins. The room was black as Lucifer's soul!

*****

"Look at Leah's hand!" Serenity yelled out.

The room where the group was sedated was chaos. There were bloody bandages on the floor and fresh ones that were being applied as quickly as the team could administer them to Zarius, Leah, and Tori. Serenity had been administering different medications to Tori as they watched her body convulse in agony. Her heart rate had spiked numerous times, and now Serenity had been doing everything she could to keep her from flatlining.

She had begged Gene to wake all of them up, and he had refused. He reminded her that everyone was aware of the risks of what was taking place and even the bigger risk if it was not successful. He had made it very clear that the only ones to be awakened were the twins, but only if he or Ann gave the order.

Gene looked over and saw that a cut had opened on the palm of Leah's hand. "Wake the twins *NOW!*" he yelled.

Serenity threw a vial of medication to Ann who already was grabbing two syringes to inject the medication into the I.V. bags. Gene moved quickly over to where she was standing between her sleeping children. "Give me one! We have to get them awake!"

"What is going on?" Serenity was so confused. "Can someone help me with Leah, also? We need to bandage that cut."

"It can wait!" Gene yelled back at her. "It was an agreement."

"An agreement?"

Ann looked over at her as she finished injecting the bag of fluid for Lada. "We had agreed with Leah that if things became too much for the twins that she would give us a sign that would let us know to wake them up immediately."

"The sign was to cut her hand?"

"Yes . . . more specifically her palm because, if she was fighting, that would be one area most unlikely for her to get cut."

Both Lana and Lado's bodies were ridged; and as the effects of the sedation wore off, both of them awoke suddenly, screaming, their eyes wide in terror. Ann put an arm around each of them as they hung on to her as if their life depended on it.

"The monster is not gone!" Lado was screaming.

"Help!" Lana screamed.

Coming out of such sedation was hard enough most times for an adult, but the young kids were very confused. They both focused on their mother and clung to her like baby cubs.

Gene grabbed some gauze and moved over to wrap Leah's hand. "How is Tori doing, Serenity?"

There was no answer. He looked up and saw a look of deep concern and almost fear on Serenity's face. "Serenity!"

She snapped back. "I'm sorry. I was responding in my head. I didn't realize I wasn't talking out loud." She looked down at Tori and at all the bruising that had formed. There was blood that had crusted around her lips. Large gashes covered different portions of her body, and Serenity was doing everything she could to control the bleeding. Her breathing was very shallow, and Serenity had to keep looking at the monitors to see if the young woman was still alive.

"I am not sure what is going on, but she is not doing well at all. Should we wake her? I can't do proper medical care if I don't know what I am treating."

"*NO!*" Gene stated emphatically. "They had to have made contact with Legion, and we could lose all of them if we wake them up at the wrong time!"

"Come on, Tori, stay with us!"

Chapter Thirty-Two

Ann checked over her children and could find no injuries, at least physically. They both started rattling off stories about weirdly-colored grass, creepy toys, a dark building with rooms and walls that would appear, and dark monsters that wanted to kill them.

"Lano left Ms. Leah, Momma," Lada tattled on her brother.

"Nuh-uh, I did not."

"You did! You left her, and the monster took you away!"

Ann's eyes widened in horror. "Lano! You made me a promise!"

"The lady was friendly, Mom. She then became a really mean man. He told me he would kill me."

She kept the tears inside as she gave her son a huge, protective hug. "Thank you, Eden, for bringing my children back to me," she whispered under her breath. Looking at Lano, she directed her instructions, "Momma has to help Mr. Gene and Ms. Serenity get everyone back, ok? You both stay in your chairs. You understand?"

They both affirmed that they understood, and then Lada spoke up. "Momma, Tori isn't coming back, is she?"

Gene and Serenity looked up from what they were doing. They looked at each other, to Tori, and then to Lada. "She is, Sweetheart. Serenity is going to wake her up in a little bit."

Lano shook his head. "No, I heard her screaming, Momma.

She also told the monster that if he would let me go, she would let the monster take her."

Ann looked over at the other two as she gave her children another hug. "We will see, Kids. Let me help Gene and Serenity."

They each watched as their mother moved over to Tori. She bent down and kissed the teenager. "Thank you."

"Lada?"

The little girl looked at her brother. "Yeah?"

"You didn't have to tell Mom."

"I know."

Her brother flopped back in his seat and rolled his eyes. "Also, thank you for loving me."

His sister smiled and looked down at her palms. "It can be a hard thing, sometimes."

*****

He saw Tanisha in front of him, but he knew she was not there. She was calling out to him, pleading with him to return to her. He was trying to reach her, but he couldn't. "Zarius, I am not ready to let you go. We still have so many dreams to chase together."

"I know, My Love. I have no more strength. I am worn out. I am weary. I hurt."

"I know you do but let me help carry you. Eternity is not yet for you or me. My Warrior, my Soulmate, the desert is calling us both back. Remember our home. Remember the love that has built it."

"This is my time. I have done what has been asked of me. I am sorry that I have let you down, Sweetheart."

She reached out to him. "You have let no one down, Love. You are braver beyond anyone I have ever known. You chose to live, and living takes courage. You chose to love me, even with all my flaws and my aging."

Her voice was fading away . . . or was it that *he* was fading? "You have no flaws, Beautiful, and you never seem to age."

There was nothing left to give. For ages, he had secretly longed for this moment . . . the moment where the end would come and everything would be complete. "Tanisha?

Through the darkness, he could hear her. "Zarius, I love you. Come home."

*****

Leah took advantage of Legion's rush towards Zarius and the twins. She shoved her way through the mass of darkness, allowing her blades to find anything soft they could rip through as she reached the room where Tori was lying. She fought her way to her side. "Tori! I'm going to grab you; and if you have any strength at all, I need you to use it to hold onto me. I'm getting you out of here!"

Tori could hear Leah's voice but could not see the Vapor. It was hard to see from the swelling around her eyes. She was struggling to speak and acknowledge that she had heard Leah's instructions.

Leah grabbed Tori's arm and tried to pull her up in a way that would allow her to get underneath the teenager. "Tori! I need you to help me. I can't fight these damn things off and pick up your dead weight!"

There was no reaction or response to that statement. Leah slammed her boot into the demonic and twisted face of a segment of Legion. She was able to prop Tori up to where she could squat down and put her arm around Tori's waist.

She looked at Tori and realized that she was a lot worse than what she had expected. The girl had taken a beating beyond anything that most could have handled. Blood was coming from everywhere and causing everything to be slippery and hard to hold onto. Her left arm was hanging limp and useless by her side.

Leah pulled out the metallic blue disk that she had checked before and firmly placed it in Tori's right hand. She wrapped her fingers around it and placed her index finger through a small ring. "If we can't make it, then I want you to pull your finger back. I don't care how painful it is and I don't care how much strength you don't have. Trust me! It will be the last thing you will need to do."

Leah grabbed a big handful of the young women's waistband and got underneath Tori's arm. She tried to carry and drag her toward the door, at the same time feeling blows, bites, and cuts from a force determined to not let them get out.

"She is ours! You are ours!"

"Yeah, go to hell!"

They reached the hallway, and Leah couldn't see Zarius from the onslaught he was going through. "Zarius!"

Tori barely could lift her head; but through her swollen eyes, she could see the fight that Zarius had on his hands. She tried to speak above the noise of the chaos, "He isn't going to make it, Leah."

Leah could not hear her. Tori felt a laceration across her lower back. Leah turned and with one swing they were splattered with the liquid of battle.

"Leah," she was able to get it out a little louder, "I am sorry!"

"What did you say, Tori?"

Tori mustered every bit of energy that she had left within her shattered and broken body. She stood on her own and shoved Leah toward the doorway of the room where Zarius was being swarmed and attacked.

This caught the Vapor off guard, and she tripped over the creatures at her feet. As Tori shoved Leah, she herself fell backwards into the room that she had been pulled from. "Come get me, Legion!"

The dark figures all turned in unison and saw her lying inside. There was the sound of rushing wind as Legion once again manifested himself. This time, though, there was no other creature left. He had pulled every segment together and towered over Tori's body.

He grabbed her right leg, pulling her further into the room. He stood over her, leering and drooling. "You have no idea how much more pain I can make you suffer, the madness I will bring to your existence."

He knelt over her and grabbed her by a fist full of hair. He picked her head up and then slammed it down. Blood splattered as the back of her skull split open. He pulled her head back up and held her face-to-face with himself. "I will say, Tori, you took more than I ever thought you could take. You not only have taken everything I have thrown at you, but you managed to forgive. Too bad, it took you so long to figure it all out. You are stronger than you know; and if you had figured that out before, I would have never been able to take you over."

She tried to open her eyes but could not. She could imagine him, though. She felt his body weight, and his breath was hot against her cheek. "Maybe I should have figured it out before . . .," she fought to say, speaking every word with immense struggle and pain. "The truth is, Legion, it is never too late to change and never too late to forgive yourself. So, all you have done to me, I actually give back to you; and with that . . . I win!"

As she pulled her index finger straight, she felt the ring become free from the device that Leah had placed in her hand. She had nothing more.

She didn't need anything more. She was free. She was free from bitterness, from self-loathing, from the feelings of being abandoned. She had freed herself from being a victim. There was no sound; just a bright light that overtook everything within the room. She felt her soul separate from the broken and torn shell in which she had resided.

*****

"NO! Come on, Tori! Come on!" Serenity kept her chest compressions going on the girl as she watched the monitor. "Gene, she is still flatlined!"

Gene rushed over while yelling for Ann to take the children out of the room. "Get Chad in here now!"

"1, 2, 3, 4, . . ." She could feel the crunching of the ribcage as she compressed down, but there was no response.

"Get the defibrillator. We need to shock her."

Chad had heard Serenity's orders as he ran in. He grabbed the crash cart and prepped it. "What is she doing on the floor?"

"We had to move her when her vitals crashed so I could do CPR."

They made several attempts, but with each jolt of electricity,

Tori's body remained lifeless. Even in the bloody and bruised state her body was in, there was a peaceful expression on her face.

Serenity started screaming and rocking back and forth. "No! She was supposed to *win!* She was supposed to win!"

Chad wrapped his arms around her, holding her. She continued to rock back and forth, unable to control any of her emotions.

*****

Leah fell back against the wall. She couldn't move; she couldn't speak. She had heard the screams of Legion as the device had gone off in the other room. Her chest quickly rose and fell as she attempted to catch her breath. Her left hand rested on Zarius' bleeding chest just to make sure he was still breathing.

"Zarius, I need to check on Tori."

He turned his head slowly. "Look above you, and you will have no need to check on her. We are going home."

The Vapor turned her head upward, and she watched as the roof began to wisp into nothingness. Where they were was the thread of Tori's existence, and now it was fading. They had come to the end of the thread. She leaned her head back. "She is gone."

*****

It was snowing again. It had stopped for about 30 minutes but then started right back up. The beauty of the snow was a stark contrast to the way she felt inside.

"She would be sitting here just like you and watching the snow fall."

Serenity moved over as Leah sat down beside her. They both kept looking out the large and expansive window that faced the back property of Eden.

"Maybe . . . who knows? What I do know is she isn't here."

"She isn't, but she is. She is here with all our memories. She is here in the voices of Lano and Lada. She is here with each of those snowflakes that fall out there."

Serenity tucked one of her legs under her and the other she brought up to her chest, wrapped her arms around it, and then placed her chin on her knee.

"Can I ask you a personal question?"

"Sure."

"Leah, is all of this worth it . . . the years, the pain, the loss . . . and all for what? I know you have struggled with the loss of Joan for longer than anyone on earth has been alive . . . then the struggles you had with Eve. Why? Why do we keep doing this?"

The Vapor shook her head and let out a long breath. "I have asked myself those questions so many times . . . over and over. Honestly, if you had asked me that just a few days ago I would not have been able to give you a clear answer. Now, I know."

"And?"

"Serenity, it is about the cycle of life. It is about each individual and their journey, and it all weaves together. Overall, it is about the ability to look in the mirror and appreciate your own uniqueness, your flaws, your special qualities, your mistakes, and your success. If, at any time, your focus gets off balance with any of those, then life takes you for a ride in an attempt to rebalance it all.

"You ask if it is worth it. It is if, in the end, we can forgive ourselves, love ourselves, and in doing so, love others."

"How do you forgive? How can you look in the mirror and say, 'I forgive you'? I just don't know. There is no way I can tell you. It is something you must come to on your own. It isn't easy, but when I stood before the Arch Council and chose to step away from everything, I was left with just myself. When I began to realize that we were going to lose Tori but that, even with all her physical pain, she had shed her emotional pain, then I understood. To not forgive ourselves or, for that matter, forgive others, we willingly accept a life sentence to the different elements that have caused us that pain and feelings of failure.

"I know now with Eve and Joan that I did everything that I could within my power and with my flaws. Sure, I made mistakes; but in the end, what I could control, I dealt with."

Serenity just pondered the words. "If I had listened to you, if I had not disobeyed your orders and left her at the hospital, . . ."

"She would have never been set free," Leah finished the sentence. "She would have been destroyed and never understood that, in forgiving herself and others, she could live the life she had been looking for, even if for a split second . . . even if for a moment . . . here now . . . and gone."

"Like a Vapor."

Leah nodded her head, "Yes, just like a Vapor."

Epilogue

"Lada?"

"Yeah."

"Do you dream a lot?"

"I don't know."

Lano thought for a moment and then looked at his sister. "I do."

"What do you dream?"

"I dream about the monster."

"The one that tried to eat you?"

"Yeah."

"Do you dream about him eating you?"

"No."

She looked up from her coloring book. "What do you dream, then?"

"That *I* swallowed *him*."

"That is weird!"

"I think I did, though."

"You swallowed the monster?"

"Yeah, I think so."

"How?"

"I don't know . . . but he is *inside*."

Glossary

Alliance, The —

The Alliance originally was a group of Eternals known as the Host. The Host consisted of Eternals ranked as Guardians, Warriors, Intercessors, Messengers, or Healers.

It was the Host who fought against the rebels in the War of the Serpents. Once the rebellion was cast down, the Host took a vow to protect mortals. They began to make themselves known to select mortals and revealed to these individuals the supernatural war that was being fought to dominate and subdue their kind.

The joining together of the Host, the Watchers, the Jerusalem Breed, and humans brought about the need for a new name: The Alliance.

Arch Council —

The governing body of the Eternals. Originally, the Arch Council consisted of Lucifer, Gabriel, Michael, and Metatron. After the War of the Serpents led by Lucifer (the Morning Star), Nemamiah was chosen to replace Lucifer. The Arch Council reside upon Scintillantes.

Azrael —

Known as the Angel of Death. It is also the name given to Michael the Archangel by the Fallen.

Cerberus —

The two-headed Demon Dog of Hecate. Legend states that Cerberus actually had three heads, but this is based on myth and legend only. The twin brothers Steirbeubar and Stidoch both swore allegiance to Hecate and joined together with their possessors to form Cerberus, Hecate's protection. *(See Steirbeubar and Stidoch.)*

Clan Wars —

Shortly after the account told in *The Nephelium*, the Clans began to war against each other, each House not trusting the other. This became the bloodiest and violent war recorded amongst the Fallen. Many Clans were left in disarray with very few members. During this time, the Arch Council took a hands-off approach with the idea that the Clans would destroy each other. Some Clan members even branched out during the war and created their own Houses, although never recognized as true Clans.

Deltas —

The Deltas were formed to harness the energy of life. One delta was stolen by the Fallen during the War of the Serpents. One remained in Scintillantes. The third was made of a clear stone and was given to the Grigori. *(See Grigori.)* When the two ancient Deltas were placed on top of each other, point facing point, they balanced perfectly and took on the appearance of a triangular hourglass. The one given to humans was larger and intended to encase the other two, symbolizing the joining of all three.

Demon Dogs —

A type of Halfling that is also known as Lycanthrope or Werewolf. They typically take on the form of a malicious canine form but can manipulate themselves to appear as a human. They are the foundation of the mythology of vampires.

Dracon —

The Order of the Dracon would give birth to the rise of one Dracul or Drăculea. Probably the most highly recognized Fallen or, at least, Vampire (the manifestation of the human mythology dealing with the Fallen), Drăculea embodied the largest collection of segments of Legion at one time since his banishment into Malebolge. It was at that time the Fallen believed they were the closest to Legion's return; in fact, they were not far off on their assumptions.

Dumah —

The Brother of Mantus and guardian of the gates of Malebolge. He followed his brother's leadership during the War of the Serpents and was exiled for his role. He then followed his brother to Malebolge when Mantus was given the realm to control. He is loyal to a fault to his brother. He has never been in control of any Clan but, instead, has chosen to exist as Mantus' right-hand man.

Eden —

The physical representation of life energy and source. It is wherever *Etz Chaim* is *(See* Etz Chaim *and Tree of Life.)* and where the planter is. The life energy of Eden has been also known to take the form of a lady who guides those in need in their time of turmoil and trouble.

Enoch —

Enoch was a mortal man who was offered the opportunity by Jah to become immortal. He was taken into the realm of Scintillantes and given a new name. There, he would be known as Metatron *(See Metatron.)* and would take up a seat in the Arch Council, replacing the banished Morning Star.

Eternals, The —

Original beings brought forth from the thoughts of Jah; those whom humans have called immortals. Their existence is beyond the comprehension of the human mind, for the minds of mortals are limited in their design compared to an Eternal. The Eternals originally existed on Scintillantes.

Etz Chaim —

Also known as the Tree of Life. Its trunk was thick and was the deepest, darkest, and richest wood that one could imagine. The wood seemed polished with natural oils, glistening almost like glass. The branches reached out in the regal glory of natural perfection: lush with leaves that had no sign of insects or disease or lacking natural nutrients and radiant in vibrant greens. It is the source of creation and source of pure life and energy.

Familiar —

A mortal who has chosen to pledge their loyalty to and follow a particular Clan.

Grigori —

The original name of the Brotherhood of the Watchers and is still used by some in reference to the Brotherhood. *(See Watchers, The Brotherhood of.)*

Guardian —

An Eternal whose purpose of existence is to guard and protect individuals to whom they have been assigned by the Arch Council. They were originally members of the Host, now known as the Alliance.

Halfling —

A unique classification that came about only after the exile, due to the requirement of a mortal. This classification is found within the House (Clan) of Hecate. A Halfling is many times confused with a Possessor, Undead, or sometimes a Nephelium.

A Halfling comes about when a Possessor not only takes over the living body of a Familiar but when that Familiar allows a Soul Slayer to imprison or even destroy that Familiar's soul. Within this submission, the Possessor taps into the spinal cord and brain cortex of the Familiar and takes full control of the Familiar; in essence, the Familiar becomes a Fallen but not immortal. The body will live longer, giving the impression of immortality; but being a true Eternal is not able to be achieved by a mortal.

The classification of Halfling is from where many legends of Vrykolakas (humans who were changed into Vampires) came.

Hall of Heroes —

A hall in Scintillantes, full of statues that immortalize Heroes of the Alliance and Watchers throughout the ages.

Jerusalem Breed —

During the fall of Babylon, Rephaim, one of the original Nephelium, was rescued by Leah, a Guardian. He was delivered to a Jewish family who took him to Jerusalem; thus, the descendants of Rephaim are called the Jerusalem Breed.

In Jerusalem, Rephaim was raised and taught in the ways of Jah. He was given a choice to nurture his Fallen heritage or to embrace the way of Jah. He chose the latter; and in so doing, he set up within the Alliance a faction of Nephelium who would work beside the will of Jah throughout mortal history. Many heroes throughout mortal history, who were able to do that which seemed impossible and, thereby, change the tide of evil in favor of innocence, were Nephelium. *(See Joan of Arc in the Appendix of The Nephelium, Book One.)*

Because of their importance and because they were half mortal, each of the Jerusalem Breed was given a Guardian. As time marched on, many of them chose to blend into mortal roles and requested not to have Guardians. These individuals lived as humans; and as the ages rolled on, many did not even pass on to their children the understanding of their supernatural heritage. Many mortals today possess powers that they do not understand.

Malebolge —

Also known as Hell by mortals, it is a place where those who are damned or imprisoned; a place to where the Fallen are banished; the place of exile for a major portion of Legion; a place of eternal damnation, pain and suffering, and eternal flame and heat. It is ruled by General Mantus *(See Mantus.)*, and the gates into the Abyss are guarded by his brother, Dumah *(See Dumah.)*, and the legions that Dumah leads.

Mantus —

Once a powerful Eternal, he served as a General of the Warriors of Scintillantes. He chose to rise up with Azrael *(See Azrael.)*, Hecate, and the other Overlords in attempt to overthrow Scintillantes during the War of the Serpents. For his role in the rebellion, he was banished and exiled. At that time, he discovered he had been a pawn of Hecate, his wife, for a larger purpose and plan that she formed in order to rise to the top of the power of all Eternals. He was sent to control Malebolge *(See Malebolge.)* with his brother, Dumah. *(See Dumah.)* He also believed Legion to be his son but later discovered that he was one of many who helped father Legion.

Metatron —

The name Enoch *(See Enoch.)* was known by while in Scintillantes and serving on the Arch Council.

Michael —

One of the original Arch Council members. The Archangel became the leader of the Arch Council. He is also the Angel of Death for humanity and is known to the Fallen as Azrael. *(See Azrael.)* It was unknown to most other than the Clan Leaders that he had played a very large role in the War of the Serpents. He is also one of many who helped father Legion.

Overlord —

An Eternal who held a position of power and leadership within Scintillantes before the War of the Serpents.

Possessors —

A Fallen found within the House (Clan) of Hecate who, upon agreement/submission of a Familiar, possesses the living body of a mortal. A Possessor is many times confused with an Undead or a Halfling. These three classifications are very similar. A Possessor embodies and controls that which the Familiar allows but does not fully take over, as in the case of a Halfling. *(See Halfling.)*

Raphael —

The Eternal name of Zarius *(See Zarius.)* before the War of the Serpents.

Scintillantes –

The immortal existence of the Eternals. To explain Scintillantes to mortals is very difficult. Mortal man's mind and thought process works within set boundaries, and Scintillantes is outside of those boundaries. It is like attempting to describe a color to one born blind or harmonic unity to one born deaf. To the mortal man, it is best described as the planet or realm where the Eternals live. This does not describe it fully but must suffice for now.

Steirbeubar —

One of the twin brothers who swore allegiance to Hecate and took on the form of Cerberus. *(See Cerberus.)*

Stidoch —

One of the twin brothers who swore allegiance to Hecate and took on the form of Cerberus. *(See Cerberus.)*

Tree of Life -

The mortal manifestation of the energy of Life. *(See* Etz Chaim.)*

Vapor —

An Eternal who has chosen the way of mortal man; one who has accepted the weight of the mortal realm and the blanket of mortality. They no longer live to be eternal, even though their lifespan is one that will last longer than any mortal.

Vortex, The —

The gateway, nest, and Clan House where Arioch attempted to establish his own Clan; a nightclub established by the Fallen. It was destroyed in a fight between the Alliance and the Clans. It is also considered by many to be ground zero for the Clan Wars.

Warehouse, The —

A newly-built nightclub established for a breeding ground for a new Clan that would follow Legion once he became complete again.

Watchers, The Brotherhood of —

Before the sect of Watchers was organized into a Brotherhood, individuals carried out what would become the duty of the Brotherhood later. No one is truly sure when the Brotherhood started. It is known that the true organization of what it is today came from a group of 12 men who, after the death of the mortal embodiment of Jah, realized the importance of not only recording what happened with the Eternals but also to ensure certain artifacts were hidden away.

The Oath of the Brotherhood holds each Watcher to secrecy; even members of the Alliance are not fully aware of what is known or written down by the Brotherhood. The Watchers have not only recorded happenings, but many also have been given prophetic visions and have recorded these. A struggle with which the Watchers deal is bringing all the information together to see if they can decipher a bigger picture to it all. It is not the job of a Watcher to change the course of history but simply to record and annotate what they discover and watch it take place.

The Fallen have manipulated many Watchers over the ages in an attempt to find many supernatural artifacts that are guarded by the Watchers. Watchers, who have turned and betrayed the Brotherhood and survived, become Watchmen, who are kept within the circles of the Abyss in order to record its occupants and that which is done there.

Zarius —

Once a high-ranking member within the Eternals, he followed his brother, Michael, along with Hecate, Mantus, and other Overlords in kicking off the War of the Serpents. He realized shortly after that he had been deceived. Unable to return home and not willing to be part of the Fallen, he chose the life of a nomad, neither human nor immortal. He would become the first of what would be known as a Vapor.

About the Author

Nathan and his family reside at the base of the beautiful Rocky Mountain Range. His first book in the series, *The Nephelium*, has been read and downloaded by fans around the globe. He has been praised for his ability to draw the reader into a world of fantasy while making way for the reader to feel it is happening within his own daily life.

When not writing novels, working on his blog, or encouraging people through his motivational podcast and videos, he spends quality time with his family. His passion for his family is evident in everything that he does, including watching his kids as they play sports and act on stage or joining in the excitement at their success in college.

He is currently working on the third and final novel within the original *The Eternals* trilogy. Nathan has plans to expand the universe and storyline of the original trilogy and has several other novels intended through which he will take his readers into the supernatural.